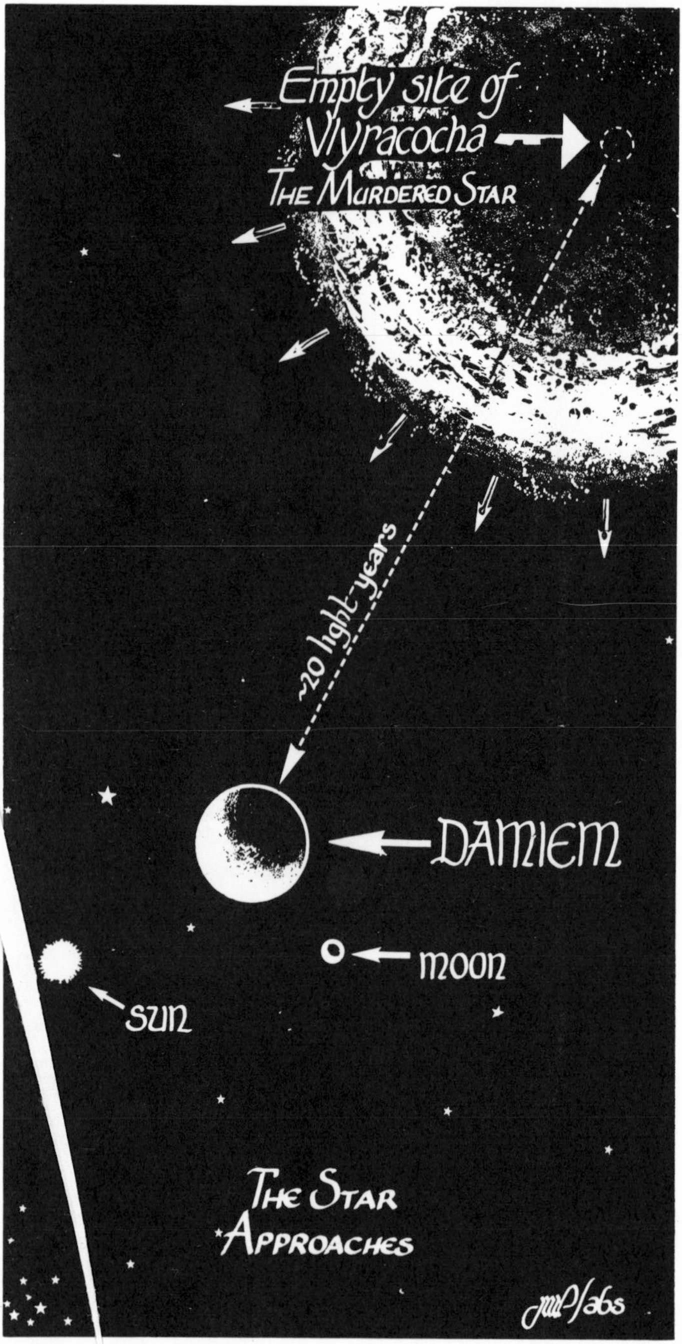

Empty site of
Vlyracocha
The Murdered Star
~20 light-years
DAMIEM
moon
sun
The Star
Approaches
jmp/abs

JAMES TIPTREE, JR.

BRIGHTNESS FALLS FROM THE AIR

TOR

A TOM DOHERTY ASSOCIATES BOOK

BRIGHTNESS FALLS FROM THE AIR

Copyright © 1985 by James Tiptree, Jr.

A TOR Book

Published by Tom Doherty Associates
8-10 West 36 Street
New York, N.Y. 10018

Printed in the United States of America

Dedication

To Steven Lipsius, MD, former ace battle surgeon in fact as well as in fiction; a humane healer among the throng of androids with MDs—and a friend without whom there would have been little brightness and less air.

AUTHOR'S NOTE

Some readers will be interested to know that at time of writing (1983), the vastly attenuated nova-front of an exploded star, like the one in our story, was reported to be passing through the Solar system and our Earth.

Acknowledgment

The events narrated here took place in the First Star Age of Man, when Galactic was the virtually universal tongue. All credit for back-translation into what is believed to be an antique idiom of Earth, circa 1985 Local, must go to my esteemed colleague in the Department of Defunct Languages, Rigel University, Dr. Raccoona Sheldon, along with my profound personal gratitude.

CONTENTS

Coldly they went about to raise
To life and make more dread
Abominations of old days,
    That men believed were dead.
                —*The Outlaws,* R. Kipling, 1914

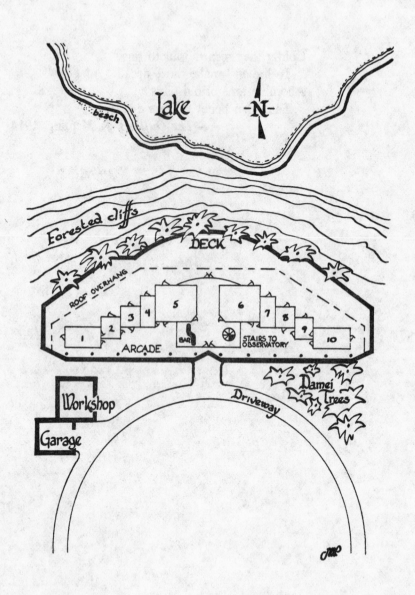

DAMIEM
Station and HOSTEL

Map Key

1. Hannibal & Snake
2. Bridey & Stareem
3. Zannez
4. The Marquises
5. Dr. Baram / Infirmary
6. The Korsos / Administration
7. Linnix
8. Ser Xe Vovoka
9. Dr. Ochter
10. Yule & Hiner

I

NOVA MINUS 20 HOURS:
All Out at Damiem

Dawn is tenderly brightening to daylight over the beautiful small world called Damiem. The sun, called here *Yrrei,* is not yet up, and the pearl-colored zenith shows starless; Damiem is very far out on the Galactic Rim. Only two lights inhabit the sky. One is a great, complex, emerald splendor setting toward the west; that is the Murdered Star. The other is a fiery point, hurtling down from overhead.

The landing field in the foreground is lush with wildflowers and clearly not much used.

Waiting at the edge of the field, under the streamer-tree withes, is an open electric ground-jitney, hitched to a flat freight trailer. Three Humans, a woman and two men, are in the jitney's front seat.

Their eyes are fixed on the descending ship; they do not notice the small animal quietly approaching the freight trailer. It is a handsome, velvety-purple arachnoid about a half meter in diameter; the Dameii call it *Avray,* meaning doom or horror. It is very rare and shy. In another instant it has disappeared into or under the trailer, as the Humans begin to speak.

"They seem to be sending down the big shuttle," says Cory Estreèl. "I wonder how many extra we'll get?"

She stretches—an elegantly formed, happy-looking woman in the bloom of midlife, with a great smile and glossy brown hair. Cory is Federation

Administrator and Guardian of the Dameii and also, when necessary, keeper of the small guest hostel. Public access to Damiem is severely restricted, for grave reason.

In the driver's seat beside her, Kipruget Korso—known to all as Kip—squints up at the descending fires. He is Deputy Administrator and Dameii Guardian-Liaison, as well as Cory's mate.

Cory's brown eyes slide sideways to him, and she smiles. Kip is the handsomest man she's ever seen, a fact of which he seems quite unaware. He's a few years younger than she, with all the ingredients of the ideal Space Force recruiting ad—big, lean frame, a tanned, aquiline face with merry gray eyes of transparent sincerity, a warm, flashing grin, and a mop of black curls. She had mistaken him for some kind of showperson when they'd first met. That was over a decade back, during the last Demob. She'd been looking for Federation service on some unpeopled planet, and so, it turned out, was Kip. She was a bit disconcerted when this glorious specimen was assigned as her deputy, until other Spacers told her of his real war record.

And then it had turned out that they'd also both been looking for somebody like each other; they'd declared a Mateship in their first year on Damiem. The end of their second Mateship had come and gone a couple of years back, but out here, a hundred light-minim from the nearest FedBase, they'd simply gone on being mated.

Looking at Kip now, Cory's smile broadens. The prospect of visitors has inspired him to dig up fresh clothes; faded explorer's whites and a vermilion neckerchief. It'll be pure murder if there're any susceptible people coming, she thinks. But she can't comment, not while wearing the shorts that show off her own well-turned legs; she'd forbidden herself to wear them before, because of poor Bram.

Waiting there in Damiem's balmy, scented air, Cory's hand steals toward her mate's. But she pulls it back, remembering the man sitting miserably on her other side, who is holding himself so rigid that the jitney-bus trembles.

Doctor Balthasar Baramji ap Bye—Baram or Bram to friends—is Senior Xenopathologist and Medical Guardian of the Dameii. He's a lithe, bronzed man some years Cory's senior, with prematurely white hair and brilliant turquoise eyes. Now he is staring up at the descending shuttle with ferocious intensity.

"You sure it's the big one, Cor?" he inquires.

"Absolutely," she assures him warmly.

Kip grunts agreement. "They retrofired about a half minim early. And that reddish tinge in the exhaust is oversize ablation shielding. We only get old rocket drives out here. Burn everything. I just hope our Dameii don't decide to move away."

"Here, take the glasses, Bram." Cory thinks it will help if he can end the uncertainty fast.

Baramji isn't suffering from any illness but only from the needs that can bedevil any vigorous male living celibate with a happily mated pair. His own mate had been killed in space years back, and for a time Damiem had helped him. But he has mended his heart again, and the enforced austerity of his life really torments him now.

She'd seen the full measure of his misery one night when Kip was on a trip to the Far Dameii. Baram approached her, red-faced and sweating with shame.

"I'm breaking the Code, Cor, I know. *I know.* Can you forgive me? I'm pretty sure you've never meant—but sometimes I think, or I dream—I had to be sure. Oh Cor, Cory, lovely lady—if you only knew . . ."

And he'd fallen silent with his heart in his glorious eyes and his fists in his armpits like a child reminding itself not to touch.

Every friendly feeling urged her to ease him; she loved Baram as dearly as a sister could. But she could foresee the complications what would follow, the inevitable repetitions, the falseness in their group.

And worse: In a man like Baram, relief could turn to real love with frightening speed and hurt them all. In fact, she and Kip both suspect that Bram's basic trouble is not in his loins but in his heart, which he's trying to fill with friendship and the Dameii.

So she refused him, almost weeping, too. Afterward he tried to thank her.

And now they're waiting for what promises to be quite a crowd of tourists. A free woman for Baram must be up there behind those growing fires! The last time a tour came to see the Star pass, Bram hadn't been so desperate. This time, Cory guesses, a female reptile would have charm.

Gazing upward, Cory's eyes go involuntarily to the enormous green swirl of the Murdered Star, at which she always tries not to look. It isn't really a star, but the last explosion-shell around the void where the Star had been. It's still called the Star, because for decades it had showed as a starlike point of green fire, blazing almost alone in the emptiest quadrant of Damiem's Rim sky.

But it is in fact a nova-front approaching Damiem at enormous speed, enlarging as it comes. Over the past years it has swelled from a point to a jewel to this great complex of light whose fringes touch half the sky. Two other, outer nova-shells have already expanded and passed over Damiem, generating awesome auroral displays but little danger. This is the last, the

innermost shell. When it rises tonight, the peak zone will be upon them—
and in another night the last remnants will be past them and forever gone.

Only from Damiem can this sight be seen. By the time the shells have
expanded to pass other worlds, they will be too attenuated to be detected
by eye.

"Hey," says Kip, following Cor's gaze, "it's really growing fast. And it's
different from last time, too. We may have a real show yet."

"I hope so," Cory says abstractedly. "So embarrassing, all those people
coming so far to see a nova-shell pass—and then nothing but pretty
lights."

"And a time-flurry," says Baram unexpectedly, "which I never got to
experience."

"Right, you were under cover."

"With fifteen pregnant Dameii."

"Yes." She chuckles. "But they're nothing really, Bram. I told you—one
merely feels sort of gluey for like a minim or two. But it's not in real time."

"What's coming now is the heart. The core," says Kip hopefully.
"There has to be *something.*"

As Cory looks up her lips tighten. That cursed illusion again. It consists
of four hairline cracks racing up from the four quarters of the horizon,
converging on the Star to make a very thin black cross against the sky. She
is the only one who ever sees this; it does not make her happy. She blinks
hard, and the illusion goes. Tomorrow it will be gone for good.

Sound is coming from the shuttle now—a growing wail punctuated by
far sonic booms. It will be down in minim.

Just as Kip is about to start the motors, they see above them a small,
pale, finely shaped face peering down from the high withes of the tree.
Behind the head can be glimpsed enormous, half-transparent wings.

"Hello, Quiyst," Cory says gently in the liquid Damei tongue. The head
nods and looks at Kip, with whom the Dameii have more rapport.

"Tell your people not to be afraid," Kip says. "These visitors are only
coming for a few days to look at the Star. Like the last ones. And did you
warn everyone to get under cover when it grows very bright? This is the
last time it will pass, and it may drop bad stuff on us all."

"Ye-es." The exquisite child-man continues to stare dubiously from Kip
to the oncoming shuttle, which is starting to suck up a roil of dust. Quiyst
is old; his clear, nacreous skin is faintly lined, and the mane that merges
into his wings is white. But his form and motion still breathe beauty.

"Don't worry, Quiyst," Kip tells him through the uproar. "Nobody will
ever harm you again. When we go, others will come to guard you, and
others after them. You know there is a big ship out there to make sure.
When these new people leave, would you like to visit it?"

Quiyst looks at him enigmatically. Kip isn't sure how much Quiyst has heard or believed. The Damei withdraws his head and turns to get away from the horror of the oncoming fires and the noise that must be hurting his ears. Quiyst is brave, staying so close to a landing. *Burning wings* is the worst terror-symbol of the Dameii.

"Don't forget, hide your people from the sky-light!" Kip calls after him. "And tell Feanya!" But Quiyst is gone, invisibly as he'd come.

Kip kicks up the motors and they start for the field. The Moom, the huge, taciturn, pachydermatous race who run most Federation lines, are famous for arriving and departing precisely on schedule, regardless of who or what is under them. It isn't clear that they distinguish passengers from freight, save that freight doesn't need cold-sleep. Their ground operations go very fast.

With a great splash of flame and dust the shuttle settles and a ring of fire crackles out through the flowery brush. Kip drives the jitney in as fast as he dares. The flames have barely sunk to coals when the freight chute comes down, followed by the passenger-way, which ends on soil almost too hot to touch.

"Someday they're going to fry some passengers," Kip says. "I just hope our tires stand up for one more cooking."

"The Moom don't care," says Cory. "Give them that Life-Game thing and let them run the ships."

"There's more live coals. I've got to stop here or the tires will blow for sure."

Doctor Baramji's glasses have stayed on the ship through every lurch and jolt. As they stop, the passenger port swings open above the gangway, propelled by a giant gray arm. The arm withdraws, and out bounces a totally bald, red-suited man loaded with holocam gear, who races down the ramp and turns to face it. The heat of the ground disconcerts him; he backs away, making quick, complex adjustments to his cameras, while mooing hoots come from within.

"All right, kids!" he calls. "Watch it—the ground's hot."

Baramji gasps audibly. Out through the port steps a silver-blonde dream of a young girl, revealingly clad in some designer's idea of what explorers wear. One hand goes to her throat and her huge eyes widen more as she hesitantly descends the ramp.

A minim later Baramji lets out an involuntary croak. A male figure follows the girl—a handsome blue-black youngster, clad in the same idiotic suiting. He solicitously escorts her to cooler ground.

Next instant the scenario repeats itself, led this time by a slim, tan-blond boy. He moves with a curious slope-shouldered undulation and turns back to beckon imperiously. A beautiful black-haired girl, with eyes that glow violet even at this distance, hurries to him and submissively allows him to guide her rather roughly down to where the others stand. Seen closer, the boy's face has a look of sleepy, slant-eyed malevolence. The new couple is clad like the first.

"Those shoes will scorch through," Kip mutters. He raises his voice. "Here! Bring your bags over here! Come and get in!"

Baramji is sighing mournfully. "How many did you say there are, Cory?"

"Ten—Oh, wait, my audio's picking something up . . . There may be more. Well, hello!"

On the gangway appears a quite young Human boy, impeccably dressed in a miniversion of a man's business tunic. His head is topped by an oddly folded garrison cap sporting three gold plumes. Hearing Kip's calls, he hops off the ramp—his boots, they see, are serviceable, if ornate—and, lugging his bag, he trots over and climbs nimbly into the jitney, giving them a nod and a smile. He has an attractive smile and a manner remarkably composed for one who can't be over twelve. As soon as he settles, his head turns and he begins watching the four who disembarked before him with a look of worried concern.

Two older men are coming down now. The first is tall, heavily built, with ruddy-gray skin. Behind him limps a small tufty gray-haired gnome, clad in old-fashioned cloak and panters. They seem not to know each other. Both stare about until they locate first the Star and second the baggage chute, before they heed Kip's call.

More hootings from the port—and then another gasp from Doctor Baramji.

A heavily gilded, curtained rollbed, complete with suspended flasks, batteries, bottles, pumps, and other life-support equipment, appears on the ramp, reluctantly guided by a young Moom ship boy. Pacing beside it comes a cloud of tawny gold-sparked veiling, which reveals rather than hides a woman.

And such a woman! Small, with flawless, creamy skin, glowing black eyes that speak of antique harems, luxuriant dark curls teased into what Cory suspects is the style beyond the style, a bursting bosom above a hand-span waist, and ripe oval haunches. Her hands are tiny and heavily jeweled, and her equally tiny toes are velvet-clad. Cory judges her to be just beyond first youth. One of her small hands keeps possessive hold on the rollbed, though she is in obvious distress on the gangplank. Her sweet voice can be heard thanking the Moom; there is, of course, no reply.

Baramji's binoculars fall to the jitney floor with a thud. "There's a patient in there!" he exclaims hoarsely, vaulting out, and heads for the vision's side at a dead run.

"Woo-ee," says Kip. "I'd like to know which gods Bram prayed to."

Baram's arrival on the gangplank is greeted by a brilliant smile so compounded of relief, admiration, and seduction that they can see him all but melting into the rollbed for support. Both Korsos chuckle benignly.

"I gather the patient is no threat," Kip says. "Listen, okay with you if I risk the tires one more time to get the freight trailer closer to that rollbed? The Moom will never help us, we can't roll it through this stuff, and I have a hunch it weighs a ton."

"Green, go. Oh, look. Something's still going on," Cory says as they plow through the ring of half-live ashes. The port stays open above them, emitting sounds of Moom and Human discord.

Just as they draw up by the rollbed, a disheveled and angry-looking young blond fellow emerges onto the gangway. Behind him comes a tall, dark, narrow-shouldered man who looks to be in his thirties and is wearing a long, severe dark cloak.

Halfway down, the blond wheels around and shakes his fist at the port. "I'll sue you!" he yells. "I'll sue the line! You've *ruined* my life work— putting me off on some pissass planet I never heard of, when all my vouchers say Grunions Rising!" He brandishes a fistful of travel slips and jerks at his modish sports tabard, which is on crooked. "The University will sue you for this!"

There is no response from inside.

Meanwhile the cloaked man steps around the vociferator and continues on down the ramp. Though he makes no outcry, his thin lips are very compressed, and there's a glare in his close-set dark eyes. The high collar of his cloak is ornamented with parallel silver zigzags, and his boots have the same emblem on their cuffs, giving his outfit the look of an unknown uniform.

Ignoring Kip, he heads straight to the freight chute. The blond, after a confused look around, shouts, "Make sure my luggage comes off!" and goes to the chute, too.

"Oh, hey," says Kip. "I just remembered. Do you know what that is, in the cloak? An Aquaman!"

"A what?" says Cory. "Aqua—water—you mean those people with gills? I've never seen one close up."

"You'd think he'd be going to Grunions."

"Yes . . . well, it does look as though there's been some kind of a mix-up."

"On a Moom ship? Not likely."

Meanwhile a white-clad figure with flaming red hair has appeared at the top of the ramp—a slim girl with ship officer's insigne on her shirt. She's carrying a small bag. It can only be the ship's Logistics Officer. Apparently there are no more Human passengers left on board, so she can stop over at Damiem until the ship comes back from Grunions Rising to pick them all up again.

What can have gone wrong with the passengers for Grunions?

As soon as the girl's feet touch the ground, the gangway snaps up and the port slams. Only the freight chute is still open.

"And that makes thirteen," Cory says. "She must have decided to get off here to see the Star and rejoin the ship when it comes back."

"Nice-looking kid, and some hair," says Kip. "Look, I'm going to have to help Bram push that thing aboard. The Moom freight crew will do the bags but they won't touch this. All right?" He gets out, shouting, "All you folks, grab your bags and get aboard this jitney as fast as you can! That Moom shuttle will take off on *their* schedule even if you're standing right under the tubes. Formalities later—right now it's all aboard!"

The two senior men have found their luggage and are docilely carrying it to the jitney; the small pixielike old man has one of the new and very expensive floaters on his bag so he can manage despite his limp. But the bald red-clad cameraman bustles up to Kip.

"I am Zannez!"

"Congratulations. Get in."

"I see you don't understand, Myr . . . ah, Korso is it? These four young people are Galactically famous hologrid stars. You must have heard of the *Absolutely Perfect Commune?*"

"No, nor you, either."

"Hey, kids! We've finally hit the frontier! Nobody here knows us."

"I know you're going to have four Galactically fried show stars if you don't let me get you away from this ship."

"But we need a car for ourselves, of course."

"Sorry, no go. We have a small electric work-car, but even if there was someone to bring it, there's no possible time before that ship takes off and flames the lot of you."

"Yes, I gather there's need for haste. But surely there's time for one brief shot of the planet chief greeting the kids?"

"Well, if it's *really* brief. Cory, can you come over a minim?"

"Oh, no, not you," Zannez snaps at her. "Get back."

Kip comes very close to him.

"Listen, whoever you are. That lady you just yelled at *is* the Planetary Administrator. And incidentally my mate. Either you change your tone or she'll have you pulled out of here by Patrol ship and kept in the brig until the Moom come back. She can also impound all your gear; so can I."

"Uh-oh," said Zannez, not sounding too abashed. He stares intently at Cory for an instant, taking in the long tanned legs, the well-filled shorts below the trim waist, the queenly shoulders and throat exposed by her sunshirt. "Look, she's fantastic, it isn't that. But having a lady chief makes it seem . . . well, not so wild. And a double host figure will get the audience confused. My apologies, ma'am, I certainly do want a shot of you—but couldn't your mate just greet the kids beside the ship—in your name, say?"

"Oh, for—great Apherion!—here: Hello, hello, hello, hello, hello," Kip says. "Now, do you want to get cooked alive or get in the jitney? I'm not risking the others for you."

But Zannez wasn't through. "I want them up beside you in the front."

"No way. We have instruments to run. You get places like everybody else."

"Well, can I at least group them in back? That way I can frame them like they were alone."

"All right, go on in back."

Zannez, pushing into the jitney with his load of gear, suddenly sees the young boy.

"Oh, no! I don't *believe* it."

"Oh, yes." The boy smiles. "Why not? Others wish to see the Star, too, you know."

Groaning and shaking his head, Zannez turns to focus on his charges getting in. As she passes, the blonde girl murmurs, "Funny. I dreamed I saw him."

Zannez grunts and then demands of Kip, "Is that trailer with that bed thing going to stay in our view? Couldn't you leave it along the way and come back for it?"

"If anybody gets left, it'll be you," Kip says levelly and turns away to help Baramji secure the bed.

Zannez moves to the back of the jitney behind his four stars, yelling at Baramji. "Hey, Myr whatever, keep out of sight, you'll ruin the shots. Myr Korso, *please* tell him to scrooch down if he has to be there."

"Scrooch down yourself," Baram yells back. "And point your stuff up. Don't you know that if you see any Dameii, which isn't likely with the noise you're making, they'll be *up*? Up in the trees, like most life here. Now, Kip, go slow. What's in here is delicate."

As Zannez subsides, Cory sings out, "Thirteen aboard. All set? Anybody missing any luggage?"

No one speaks.

"Green, then, go. Kip, take us out."

The jitney motors howl up, and it begins to move, faster and faster. "Gods help those tires now," says Kip. "We run on the rims if we have to."

A Moom voice speaks from the radio. The jitney picks up even more speed, rocking from side to side.

"Take it easy, take it easy, Kip!" Baramji shouts from the trailer.

"Can't!" Kip yells back.

They are barely at the edge of the burn when a rumble starts in the tubes of the shuttle behind them.

"Hang on!" The jitney, lurching and leaping, rockets toward the rise and finally plunges down into shelter among the streamer-trees beyond. The passengers can see flame and steam rolling over the ground they were on.

With a head-splitting boom, the old shuttle stands up on its pillar of flame and accelerates ever faster away from Damiem. Kip drops speed, and the jitney runs relatively smoothly over the rock ruts. The spaceport road has never been graded.

"Another nice peaceful disembarcation party," Cory remarks. "Moom style."

"Do you see what I mean now, Zannez?" Kip calls. He has checked the rearview a couple of times. Each time he looks, Zannez is holding some perilous position, shooting, panning, changing lenses; he has managed to get out another camera.

"You know, Cor, despite the fellow's horrible personality, I think we have to give him marks for dedication."

"I guess the pushiness goes with the profession." She can't resist adding, "Did you notice, beautiful as those young people are, there's a kind of unnatural quality? Everything exaggerated. And so thin!"

"Yes, I've seen it before. I don't need any hologrid stars when I have you, Coryo."

"Ahh, Kip. . . . I wonder how Bram's doing?"

"Well, at least his dream-houri managed to hang on. Just for your information, that stuff she's wearing is real, or I never had a course in mineralogy. That's one ferocious lot of Galactic credits we're towing. But what do you suppose is in that rollbed? I couldn't get a peep."

"We'll find out at the hostel."

"We'll find out a lot of things. I hope we like them."

II

NOVA MINUS 19 HOURS:
Meetings

The road improves. Damiem's yellow sun is rising through a pink fleece of fine-weather cloudlets and igniting little rainbows in all the dewy foliage. The streamer-trees give way to flowering shrubs and light green bird-trees. Many of the mobile bird-leaves take off and flap curiously after the jitney. As usual, the tourists love this; even the dour Aquaman brightens as some leaves settle for a brief rest on the edge of the jitney near him.

"They'll get bored and go back to their trees when we've gone inside," Cory explains. "Well, here we are. Damiem Station Hostel. The Star will rise over the lake in back. We'll watch from the deck on the lakeside."

They have drawn up in a circular driveway, lavishly edged with flowers, in the arc of a crescent-shaped, one-story building. Beyond it the ground falls away abruptly to a forest-edged lake. The hostel consists of a large, high-roofed center hall, with two short wings of rooms extending from each side. Running along the whole front is a simple open arcade. Atop the central hall is an array of antennae beside a small cupola, clearly an observatory. On the left of the main building is a neat garage and workshop, and on the right is a grove of fern-leafed trees, up among whose branches can be glimpsed a woven treehouse. All roofs are of thatch.

The main double doors of the center lounge stand open, or rather, their lower halves do; as the tourists approach they can see that the doors have a second upper section, which can be opened to at least twice Human height, and the front arcade rises accordingly there.

"How perfectly charming," the gnomelike little man exclaims.

Zannez is panning his camera. "Natives build this?" he inquires.

"No," says Cory. "You're looking at the builders of most of it. The previous man, the first Guardian, just put up two main rooms. And we do not, repeat not, call people natives. The people of this world are the Dameii. As you may have noticed, a Damei family lives in those trees beside us, but it's for mutual instruction only. They do no menial work. Those of you who are able will unload and carry your own bags. We'll help you all we can, but the addition of three unexpected people means we have to scurry about making some end rooms habitable. Kippo, why don't you take them in and sort them out while I do some of the preliminary scurrying?"

"All right, honey," says Kip, "but don't overdo it. I'm here for that. . . . Very well, Myrrin, welcome to Damei Hostel. The lounge awaits you with edible refreshments and light drink—and I do mean light; alcohol so soon after cold-sleep drugs will flatten you. You might even miss the Star. We've developed a Damei soft drink I think you'll like."

He's ushering them in as he speaks, to the large central hall or lounge. It is walled chiefly with translucent vitrex. On the left side is a long, beautifully grained and polished wooden bar, plus other housekeeping facilities; on the right is a small circular staircase obviously leading to the observatory on the roof. Directly opposite are vitrex double doors opening onto the deck over the lake. They are flanked by two rooms which seem to be the staff's permanent quarters. The one on the left has a red cross on the door, an old symbol still recognizable as meaning a place of medical aid. The room on the right has "Admin." on the doorplate.

As they move to the chairs around the bar their footsteps echo oddly. Looking up, they see why: the underside of the thatch is lined with heavy antirad shielding.

Kip has unfolded a computer readout and laid it on the bar, glancing at it as he passes around trays of snacks and tidbits, and pours a golden drink into exquisite shell-form glasses.

"These glasses are Damei work," he tells them. "They've been into glass for hundred of generations before . . . uh . . . contact. Now let's introduce ourselves formally, and I'll play a guessing game—the Moom finally passed over a rudimentary passenger list. Your hostess, and the boss here, is Corrisón Estreèl-Korso, Federation Administrator. I'm Kipruget Korso-Estreèl, Deputy Administrator and Damei Liaison. The Medical Officer over there is Senior Xenopathologist Balthasar Baramji ap Bye, known as Doctor Baram. Don't let the white hair fool you. We're all three officially charged with guarding the Dameii, after the atrocities inflicted on them by Humans were discovered and forcibly stopped, and we have Patrol backup on call."

"Now"—he bows to the vision in beige veils—"would I be correct in assuming I address the Marquise Lady Parda—uh, sorry: Parda-lee-anches, that's Lady Pardalianches, of Rainbow's End?"

She graciously acknowledges it.

"And . . . ah, sister? No name is given."

"Yes. My sister here is the Lady Paralomena, my poor twin. She suffered a terrible riding accident some years back. It's left her helpless but conscious—you *must* believe that, Myr Korso, some people won't. Luckily I have the resources to keep her healthy and stimulated, against the day, which will come—I *know* it will—when she wakens fully. I've brought her here in the hopes that some of this extraordinary radiation from your Star will help her where doctors can't."

Kip approaches the curtained bed.

"May I see her, Lady Pardalianches? It's not just idle curiosity—though I am curious—but you could be concealing an armed man or a dangerous animal in there."

"Oh, what an idea! My poor darling. Very well, if you must." Delicately she opens the curtains before him an inch or two. Kip looks in, and his eyes widen before he draws back.

"One—one would swear she was sleeping. And very beautiful."

"Oh, yes, Myr Korso. I see you are sympathetic. She *is* just sleeping. But there's more to it than that. Did you notice her gold mesh cap?"

"Ah, only dimly."

"I wear one just like it, under my coiffure." She touches her thick curls. "We experience everything together. It is the product of the highest science. I will *not* let her become a vegetable."

Kip gulps. "Of course not."

"And now," says the Lady, "since we are both very tired after this demanding trip, might I ask to go to whatever room is ready? Anything will do. I have my own bed linen, of course."

"We've assigned you Suite A." Kip points left, beyond the bar. "The name's a joke; there isn't any Suite B. Doctor Baram sleeps there normally. Perhaps he'll help make you comfortable."

Baramji, sitting proprietarily beside the rollbed, all but drops his plate as he leaps up.

"I'll help you, of course, my lady. Any time."

The rest of the group watch them exit, in somewhat stunned silence, and all eyes go to Kip.

"She really was beautiful—like a healthy, sleeping fifteen-year-old. But if they're *twins*—this thing must have been going on twenty years. It gives me cold shudders. And that's absolutely all I'm going to say about that. Now, taking the easiest one next—Zannez Beorne and four actors, sexes mixed."

The strange-looking blond boy lets out a nasal chuckle. The grid-show people have grouped themselves at the far end of the bar.

"That's right," says Zannez. "Now this may sound freaky to you, but it's been so long since I've been among people who didn't know the *Absolutely Perfect Commune*—I mean, billions of viewers all over the Grid tune in every night, sometimes I think they know the *Commune* better than their own families. So I've sort of lost the art of introduction. I'm Zannez Beorne—nobody uses the last name—cameraman and production manager for these four. Girls first, I guess." He places a finger on top of the silver-blonde's head, as though he were going to twirl her. "May I present Stareem Fada? Our Star—one of them."

"Hi." Charmingly modest smile from the blonde.

Kip notices that the small boy is smiling, too, leaning back from his plate and looking around with a calmly challenging air. What's with him?

"And this young lady"—Zannez tips back so they can see the black-haired beauty—"is Eleganza."

The brunette smiles obediently but suddenly bursts out, "I'm not Eleganza! I'm Bridey McBannion."

Zannez grunts. "And you'll end up cooking slosh for two hundred kids in a welfare kitchen, *Bridey.* If you can do better than Eleganza, which I admit is not sublime, there's just time to go ahead. But Bridey McBannion —if I hear that again—"

The very black youth cuts in. "Myr Zannez, take it easy. You have me."

"And may the gods bless you. Myrrin, may I present Hannibal Ek, who was born to Caesar and Jocelyn Ek and christened Hannibal in the tenth diocese of Orange World. Hannibal Ek; E-k. . . . And this is Snake Smith."

"We're together," Hannibal says. "I like to make things clear."

"He's not really Snake Smith, either," Zannez says. "But he was born to carny folk who changed his name so often I don't think anybody knows what it really is. I don't."

"I do," Snake Smith says. "And if anybody ever finds out and uses it, I'll *kill* them." Suddenly the malevolent, sleepily lethal look drops over his features like a mask. Kip sees with surprise that it *is* a mask. Unless the boy deliberately assumes that look, which seems to be his grid-show persona, he is a perfectly normal, rather cheerful and friendly-looking young Human, wherever he got those picturesque slant eyes. Catching Kip's eye on him, he laughs pleasantly and then switches it to his nasty snicker.

"Well, that wraps us up," Zannez says. "Somehow I don't think the Lady Pardalianches will mind having missed us. But I'm going to mind not hearing the rest of you firsthand, because, Kippo, I want your permission to take the kids around and do some shooting now. This may be the last day things look normal. But if our rooms aren't ready, can we help?"

"No," says Kip. "Yours are three that are ready. Just go down the arcade past Suite A and you'll find numbers one, two, and three—that's all there are on that side. Or better, come out on the deck here and go in from there—all the rooms open onto the deck as well as the arcade." He waves them toward the far doors opening on the lake view.

As they rise, Zannez remembers something. "Oh, by the by, what was that spectacular, big purple tarantula that jumped off the trailer just as we got here? About ye huge . . ." He spreads his hands a chair's width apart. "If it's a pet, I'd love a shot of it—but not when I'm in the dark."

"Pet *spiders?*" says the brunette on a high note.

Kip is frowning.

"No, that's no pet," he says slowly and smiles at the girl. "But if we had pets, they'd almost have to be arachnoid—spiderlike—'cause all the ground beasties here of any size are. You sure it was purple, Myr Zannez?"

"Honor bright. I was lucky, I picked it up in the viewfinder. Why, did we catch something special?"

"In a way, yes. They're very rare. But perfectly harmless—Cor actually managed to pat another one we ran into. But the Dameii are scared out of their wits by them, they believe them to be an omen of death, only worse. . . . I can't think what it was doing with the trailer, unless it has a nest in the garage. Oh, bother; that means I'll have to root it out and carry it to some safe place, before our Dameii see it and leave. Cory'll have fits, she'd love to see the young. . . . You really did get a lucky shot."

"What's worse than death?" asks the slant-eyed lad lightly.

"This is serious, to them," Kip replies in an odd tone. "Not like our thing about white *gattos.* I must ask officially, all, keep this to yourselves. And now, Myr Zannez"—Kip had ushered them out to the deck—"you're welcome to shoot anything you like so long as you stay away from the Damei grove and house—hear me? And don't get too involved because we plan a visit to the Damei village just before noon. The days are thirty Standard hours long here, see. You'll have plenty of time for a rest before we start Star-watching— No, wait, please," he says to the boy, who has been watching alertly and is following Zannez' group. "You haven't been introduced."

"Of course." The lad smiles, goes back, and applies himself anew to the refreshments.

The plump blond young man who had threatened to sue speaks up. "It must be our rooms that aren't ready."

"And mine," adds the red-haired ship's officer.

"Well, yes," Kip says to her. "Although you're no problem, Myr . . . Linnix, is it? You go in my study next door here, after I get some biological specimens off the bed. . . . But wait, this list doesn't give you any other name."

"I haven't an agreed-on one," Linnix says. She shakes her flaming head, as though a fly were bothering her. "So everyone just uses Linnix. Even the payroll." She grins. "Back in the world of computers I get Linnix MFN NCN or even NN Linnix. Which confuses everybody. I *am* rather tired, though, and we've been through quite a mess, as Myr Yule and Doctor Hiner will tell you. If you'd let me move your materials, I would appreciate a quiet lie-down."

"By all means—here, I'll give you a hand," Kip says, and escorts Linnix out the other wing to the small bedroom he's been using as a lab. They find Cory has already cleared living space.

"I'll call you in time for the trip." He draws the curtains to darken the room. "Nighty night."

"Thank you," comes her sleepy voice.

A good kid, he thinks. But what was this foul-up?

When he returns, the blond youth, who turns out to be named Mordecai Yule, is bursting to enlighten him. "Grunions Rising! See, everyone!" He fans his handful of vouchers.

Kip knows Grunions Rising only as the next and last world in the line, out here at the Rim. A water world. "What, you're a student of aquatic worlds? Are you and, ah, Doctor Hiner together?"

"I never saw him in my life before this happened," the thin, dark Aquaman says scornfully. "I am a member of an official survey team compiling a Galaxywide report on worlds suitable for colonization. Our mandate is to make the first—and, I may say, sorely needed—truly comprehensive update of the *Aquatica Galactica*. I appear here alone because, when we had completed our joint work on the A and B candidate planets, it was voted to disperse and individually cover the C class, which includes very distant, or dubiously reported, or otherwise questionable candidates. I selected Grunions Rising as the last stop in the list, which I have already compiled.

"And now to my inexpressible dismay I find myself disembarked on your planet here, which is of absolutely no interest, and am told that I cannot reenter cold-sleep in time to continue to Grunions. And if I wait over here for the next Rim ship, I shall not only upset the schedules of the whole team, but shall fail to make my contribution to a newly found candidate in the Hyades complex for which we have high hopes.

"A complete, disgusting disaster. Damage to my work, and doubtless to my reputation—damage to the work of the team, waste of project funds—and all of it quite irreparable. It can only be due to sloppiness—inexcusable sloppiness on the part of that young woman who calls herself an officer. Oh, she brandished two empty Grunions syrettes—but it would have been the work of a minim to empty their contents down the waster, and get rid of two incriminating used Damiem syrettes. There's no explanation other than blaming a company which has never, I repeat, never—have you ever known a case?—been known to foul up. And I shall certainly see that the A. A. initiates a strong request for disciplinary action against her. We Aquamen are not to be so treated with impunity, I assure you!"

He folds his arms.

"Well, I admit it looks bad," says Kip. "But let's not be too hasty in judging the kid. After all, people in chemical companies sometimes slip up just like individual people. . . . I take it this is more or less your case, Myr Yule?"

"Oh, it's worse—much worse—for me. Hiner has his doctorate and his rep, and if he has to, he can wait for the next ship. But I'm on a predoctoral research grant with a time limit—and I just don't know what I'm going to do, Myr Korso."

From rage he has turned nearly to tears.

"The Grunions Rising bit was the centerpiece of my whole dissertation —I chose it partly because no one'd been near it since the old *A.G.,* and now you're going to cover it, Hiner. You'll probably be in print before I even get there—if I get there at all—and in short I'm ruined. Just *ruined.* Oh, that intolerable smug girl and her syrettes—"

He breaks off to heave sigh after sigh.

Kip thinks he should at least feel sympathetic, but somehow he finds himself disliking both of them. The prospect of housing one or both until the next ship dismays him.

"We'll see what we can do with messages, for both of you," he makes himself say heartily. "And it's conceivable the Patrol might help. Meanwhile, you've at least been dropped off here just as a celestial event of very great interest is about to occur, and you're on a planet many people would give an arm and a leg to visit."

So they are, he says to himself. And with no security check.

"And I'm puzzled, too," he concludes. "I've simply never heard of a destination failure before, and I don't know anyone who has. Have you Myrrin"—he turns to the two older men—"ever heard of such a thing?"

"No," says the tall, heavyset man expressionlessly.

"Never," declares the gnome. "Never, never, never! And I don't think the girl did it, either. Practically speaking, people who are liable to make mistakes of that order don't make just one. And she'd never have risen to Senior Logistics Officer if she'd made any such mistakes—not to mention a trail of them. . . . By the way, you must be puzzled as to which of us is which—I'm Doctor Aristrides Ochter, a very amateur student of novas in my old age. My former work, from which I retired five Standard years ago, was in neocybernetic theory. But novas have always fascinated me, so I thought to spend what time I have left"—he glances at his thigh—"in going actually to see some. I have no family to save for, you see. And I can't tell you how much I'm looking forward to tonight!"

"And then you are Myr . . . ?" Kip addresses the taciturn man.

"*Ser* Xe Vovoka," the stranger corrects him. Apparently feeling that something more is really called for, Vovoka adds slowly, "I am an artist . . . a light-sculptor." He smiles briefly, which changes his whole face.

Kip recalls that "Ser" is a technical honorific, somewhere beyond "Doctor." Not to call him "Myr."

He turns to the boy, who has been listening carefully, his plumed cap on his knees, while he finishes his fourth helping of snacks.

"Then you must be Prince Pao?"

The lad—he looks nearer eleven, even ten, than twelve—nods.

"May we know your first name, Prince?"

"That's it." The boy swallows and grins. "Prince-Prince Pao, if you wish to be technical. Simplifies things. I'm a student of everything, before I must return home to my duties." His smile vanishes momentarily. "I'm praying for long life to the present ruler. Pavo's only a small world principality, but it's sort of a diplomatic, financial, and arbitration center. . . . Problems!" He flings back his hair and slaps on his ornate cap so the gold feathers dance. "Right now I long to watch stars!"

"Stars . . . I see," echoes Kip. But he's not sure that he does. "Well, then perhaps you won't mind the quarters we prepared for you, up in the observatory? It's only a cot."

"Fantastic!" The little prince points. "Up there?"

"Right."

The lad picks up his small, costly looking kit-bag and commences hauling it up the circular stairs. "No help needed, thanks. I had it packed light."

He vanishes above as Cory comes striding in, rolling down her sleeves.

"Well, I have things just about livable for you two young men, assuming Kip helps me move a bed, and that you two can room together. You're . . . ?"

"Doctor Nathaniel Hiner and Myr Mordecai Yule," Kip tells her.

They nod glum assent to sharing space.

"It's the very end room on the east wing." Cory gestures toward the wing where Linnix sleeps. "You'll find sawdogs and vitrex make very nice tables."

"You shouldn't have done all that, honey. Do I assume that Ser Vovoka here and Doctor Ochter have their separate rooms now?"

"Absolutely. The two between your lab and the end one. That's where the bed gets moved out. Come right along with me, one and all."

"I hear and obey," little Ochter says gaily. The others, silent and unmerry, hoist their bags and follow her along the arcade to their respective rooms. Vovoka is next to Linnix, Ochter beyond, and Yule with Hiner at the end. The extra bed is in Vovoka's small room. It's of a native wood, and very heavy; Kip and Cory strain to jockey it out.

No one offers to help, until Vovoka abruptly drops his bag and seizes the bed by its middle. Amazed, the two find themselves all but towed with it out into the arcade.

"Thank you," Cory gasps. "My heavens, Ser Vovoka, you *are* strong!"

But she's speaking to a closed door. The artist has dropped the bed in the arcade and retired into his room.

"Well!" says Kip. "Myr Yule, Doctor Hiner, since this bed is for one of you, perhaps you might give us a hand?"

"If only *I* could," says lame old Doctor Ochter, staring meaningfully at Yule.

Thus encouraged, the pair put down their bags and the bed is soon in the unfinished room, which now looks pleasantly habitable.

"A minim, Myrrin," Kip says as Ochter leaves. "Most regrettably, the regs say we must inspect your luggage. No choice. Everyone else went through it back at Central. It'd be actionable if we don't."

"Oh for—! This is *the* last straw," Yule cries. "Of all the damned insults —on top of everything—"

"And search us, too, perhaps?" Hiner inquires viciously.

"Not at all." Kip steps behind him. "Sorry." With deftness acquired in wartime days, he runs his hands down Hiner's flinching body, pats his pouches.

"We hate it a lot more than you do." Cory has hoisted their bags onto the new vitrex table. "If only they'd give me a scanner. We do appreciate your cooperation."

Yule's and Hiner's faces are making it plain that their "cooperation" relates chiefly to Kip's commanding height and both Korsos' notably superior condition.

Their persons reveal nothing, and their bags hold only the normal travel items plus a mass of multimodal recording equipment and water-planet gear. It disconcerts the Korsos for a minim when they realize that no oxy tanks, pumps, or scuba gear are in Hiner's bags. Of course! All Hiner has to do is to uncover his gills and dive in. Spooky.

Kip recalls illustrations; Aquafolk's gill-covers ride on two large, fleshy masses running down from under the ears past the collarbones. The covers are hard and horny and open along one side, like clamshells, to flood water in over the oxygenating tissues. That's why Aquapeople wear big high collars, like Hiner's cloak, on land.

The Aquaform is a long-ago Human genetic engineering triumph, which breeds true. They're interfertile with ordinary Humans but, both by circumstance and desire, seldom mingle socially. Briefly, Kip wonders what the women are like. . . .

Meanwhile Cory has been rooting among Hiner's coldsuits and runs onto some gas propellant cans that could shoot anything.

"What are these, Doctor Hiner?"

"Pure oxygen—in case I get into dead water, swamp and so on. . . . Really, are you going to mess up everything I packed?"

Kip sees Cory frown and knows she's wishing hard for that scanner. Anything could be in those assorted containers—not to mention the linings, pads, handles, and the unfamiliar electronic equipment.

"That's lovely music, I envy you," Cory says pleasantly, reading a title.

"Don't paw that. Be careful," Hiner snaps.

Kip clears his throat.

On the last bag, Cory pulls out a bronze-and-glass object and sniffs. "Myr Yule, what *is* this?"

"An antique hookah," Yule answers sullenly. "My water-pipe."

"It burns plant leaves?"

"Plant? Oh, yes."

"I'm sorry, but we must hold this for you while you're here. You didn't know, of course, but the Dameii are violently sensitive to any form of carbohydrate smoke. Do you have any other smoking materials?"

"No. Oh—a few cheroots."

"I'll take them if I may, please. And perhaps you'll check your pockets. Combustion lighters are just as dangerous."

"But I won't smoke near them! I enjoy a pipe at bedtime, and they won't be coming in here."

Kip takes over. "Look, we wouldn't do this if it wasn't necessary. When Myr Cory says 'violently sensitive' she means it. Adult Dameii can be knocked over merely by being in a room where people smoked some days ago. Actual smoke is like a blow on the head—it might kill a child. Why do you think we use an electric car? We can't even lubricate it with hydrocarbons. Fire is their worst nightmare-symbol." He decides not to add the part about burning wings.

"We've finally persuaded one Damei family to live near Humans, and we're not about to permit them to be driven off. I can sympathize with you, I smoked before I came here. But you will please hand over all burnable or combustible materials *right now.* You'll get them safely back when you leave."

Docilely enough, Yule collects a handful of foil-wrapped objects Cory had taken for CO_2-indicator cartridges.

"And you, Myr—Doctor Hiner?"

"Don't smoke . . . but if they're so sensitive, how do you get your electricity? Assuming you have hydrogen generators like everyone, how do you heat the hydride?"

Hiner isn't stupid.

"There's a Federation power-cell buried three hundred meters under the hostel. They had to run the shaft in from the cliffside, under water."

Hiner whistles.

"Yes. But nothing was too costly to repair the situation here. You'll hear about that."

Hiner nods ungraciously, and Cory and Kip depart after delivering one more severe warning to Yule.

"That baby has held out a few," Kip tells her as the door clashes to. "I know smokers. Lucky the *V'yrre* wind is on; it's blowing away from them to us."

"That's why Wyrra built there." Cory smiles worriedly. "I wish I hadn't put those two on the Damei end. Maybe I—"

"Maybe you can sit down." Kip lays firm hold of his mate's arm to prevent her doing more and fairly hauls her back to the lounge, singing out, "Visit to the Damei village just before solar noon. You'll be called."

Looking out on the drive, they glimpse Zannez and his troupe, en route to their rooms in the other wing.

"And what do we call *them?*" Cory murmurs, only half-facetiously, as they reach their own private chamber behind the "Admin." door.

"One fairly strange kettle of fish," Kip says reflectively. "Still, remember that lot of Sleeping-God worshippers we got first time?"

"Whew!" Cory shakes out her rich brown hair.

"I wonder if we'll ever see Bram again?" Kip's tone changes. "Speaking of which, if the Planet Administrator has a moment, I have a problem requiring her undivided attention. . . ."

A wordless time later, Cory pulls back.

"A minim, darling—I have to go up and call the Patrol."

"Huh? What for?"

"To get that uncleared pair off-planet."

"What?" Kip recaptures her. "Wait, honey. Think. Aren't you over-reacting? What makes you think their story's not straight? I saw no signs they were together, or that they didn't loathe being here. Did you? Hmm?"

"No. But cold-sleep just doesn't fail by itself, Kip. I asked the Log Officer, she'd never heard of a mislabeling case. And two at once, right here, on the one planet where Central clearances are essential."

"Two is just as likely as one, when you think of it. And it's made by Human hands. Everything Human slips a bit, sooner or later."

"Granted. But the fact remains that I'd be letting two unauthorized strangers stay on Damiem."

"Well, go ahead. But Dayan won't thank you, he's taking the cruiser over by that new Grid-relay asteroid so his men can catch the games. And the Moom ship will be back almost as soon . . . Oh, honey, come on."

Cory sighs deeply, looking into her lover's eyes. She knows she's overfond, but what he says is true.

"You really, really think it's all right, Kip?"

"I really, really do, Cory my love."

"Well . . . okay, then. Oh, Kip—"

Later, she contents herself with putting the facts on the routine-channel landing report, attention Captain Dayan of *Rimshot*.

III

NOVA MINUS 12 HOURS:
First View

The musical summons that rings through the hostel comes from an
extraordinary crystal gong and hammer hanging by the main doors. Kip's
cheery parade-call follows: "All aboard to visit the Dameii! Departure as
soon as loaded."

He is standing by the jitney-bus, now freed of its trailer. His normally
carefree grin is somewhat tense. As usual when visitors come, he's torn; he
loves seeing others enthralled by "his" Dameii—but will these strangers
appreciate their beauty and delicacy? Will they understand it is a privilege?
Or will they do some crude thing to upset the Dameii and undo the trust
he's spent years building? This is a perfectly rational fear, he tells himself;
Damiem is his first big solo assignment as a xenologist, and he's not about
to have it messed up.

Linnix, looking much refreshed, is first to join him, followed by Zannez
and his four young ones. Little Prince Pao comes trotting from the observatory, and Hiner comes along the arcade.

"This gong is another piece of Damei work," Kip tells them. "Spectacular, isn't it?"

Hiner is frowning at the gong. "How do they work glass if they're so
spooked by fire?"

"Good question," says Kip. "Might take a while to guess the answer, too: burning lenses! What they can do with a set of lenses on a sunny day is hard to believe. And then there are big deposits of high-grade natural volcanic glass about; their ancestors worked it like obsidian, by flaking and grinding. They still do hack out the rough forms before they pick up a lens, unless it's a melt for casting or blowing. They place a lot of importance on the sound, too. They have whole orchestras of crystal percussion instruments. We have some nice recordings I'll play for you. I wish you could hear it live, but they don't play with strangers around."

"Just exactly why are they so shy?" Zannez asks.

Kip stares hard at him. "Don't you know, really? Do the words 'Star Tears' mean *anything* to you? Stars Tears? *Stars Tears?*"

"Uh . . . no. Except I seem to have heard of some exotic mythical drink."

"Just so. Well, I'll tell you the story after we've seen the village. We won't be able to get close, you realize. We view it across a ravine. You better have your longest-range equipment. We're going there now because it's when the youngsters fly home from school; you'll get the best chance to see people. But I warn you, the story is rough. Even I hate to tell it. It might be hard on your kids, especially Stareem and, uh, Eleganza."

He glances at Prince Pao, confirming his impression that that young man could cope.

"After Gridworld?" Stareem's chuckle is a strange sound from her tender face. "Not likely."

"All right, but I don't want to add to your nightmares. Now, Zannez, don't fret about seats in the bus. We get out and do the last part on foot. Their ears can't take motors; we'd find a deserted village if we drove up to the ridge."

Cory ambles up carrying containers of juice, which she stows in the jitney.

"What's all this about nightmares?" little Doctor Ochter asks genially as he hobbles toward them.

"The Stars Tears story. Zannez wanted to know why the Dameii are shy. I'll tell it for anyone who cares to listen, after we've seen the village."

"Oh." The little man sobers quickly. "Of course. This is where it took place, isn't it? And these are the people. Oh, my. . . . Well, I'll be grateful to get a straight account after all the bits and whispers."

"By the way, Doc, there'll be some walking uphill, about half a kilom. You'll be all right with that leg?"

"I can make it all right." Ochter smiles wryly, patting his vest pocket. "I've a shot for special occasions, and this is certainly one. But what about the Lady Marquise and her sister?"

"They aren't coming," Cory says. "She's interested only in the effects of the Star on her sister tonight." Grinning, she adds privately to Kip, "Bram told me. Through the door. It seems the Lady believes she should keep her sister stimulated."

They both laugh unmaliciously, happy for their old friend's good luck. Ser Vovoka has now appeared and is eyeing the jitney.

"Now we may be able to show you some beauty worthy of your artistic interest," Kip tells him. "The Dameii are acknowledged to be among the very loveliest humanoid races, although they are in fact evolved from pseudoinsectile forms."

Vovoka gives one of his politer grunts.

"Superinsects, eh?" Zannez exclaims. "You mean like those spiders? Giant praying mantises?"

"Nothing of the sort; don't get up hopes of some new alien monsters. Their only insectoid features, outside of the wings and arms that indicate three pairs of functional limbs, are some peculiarities of the mandibular substructure, and a few traces of exoskeleton. It's one of the Damiem mysteries I'm studying."

"Myr Korso," says Hiner suddenly. "Regretfully, I fear I shall have to miss the tour. I feel much more unwell than I thought."

In fact, Kip sees, Hiner's face has taken on a greenish pallor.

"Oh, dear, what a shame," says Cory. "Is there something we can do for you?"

"Not at all, not at all. . . ." The Aquaman's eyes turn toward the cool blue of the lake below. "It may be that I've been on land rather long. I assume it won't cause any difficulties if I go for a swim while you're gone?"

"Heavens, no—and I'll bring you some extra towels just as soon as we return. How thoughtless of me!"

"And by the way," Kip puts in, "the spot we normally go in is at that little beach down to the left. You'll find the path passing your end of the arcade. There's a good deal of fallen timber in a lake like this, and we've cleared out from there. . . . And the area right in front of the hostel cliff is believed to be the deepest part—but you'll soon know more about our lake than we've ever guessed. The original survey had a waterman—sorry, I mean an Aquaman on it; he reported no dangerous snakes or fish, and we've never found any. So, pleasant swimming to you."

Hiner moves off without reply, his narrow shoulders raised as if huddled against cold, though the day is warm.

"Maybe you kind of leaned too hard on the bugs, boss," says Hanno Ek.

"Huh? Oh . . ." says Zannez. "I forgot."

"What? Forgot what?" Kip asks.

"The bugs. Insects," replies Hanno. "He's a waterman—I mean, an Aquaman."

"So? You've lost me, help."

"I thought everybody knew that," says Hanno.

"Knew *what?*"

"Hanno, somebody's going to kill you one day if you don't straighten up." Zannez grinned. " 'Scuse my son here, Kippo. What he means is that all Aquapeople—*all* of them—loathe, hate, and fear insects. Men, women, babies, grandmothers—everyone. It's so widely known it's become a saying: 'I love her like a waterman loves bugs.' Outsiders don't know what started it—some horrible predator on one of their first worlds, maybe. Of course, it isn't born in them. They let it go on as a tradition. But it's real enough. With some special effects. I've seen 'em get sick, go berserk, and I don't mean joking. I forgot Hiner for a minim or I'd never have said all that. Now I've ruined his sight-seeing trip."

"Whew!" said Kip. "Well, live and learn. . . . Did you know all that, Cor?"

"Umh . . . yes, I knew there was something. . . . Oh, dear, Myr Zannez, what a shame. Maybe your inventive mind can think up some way to repair it. Meanwhile we'll just have to hope he really wanted a swim, too."

"Right," says Kip. "And now, where's that other blessing, Yule? I'm not about to let you all miss the flight for him."

"I'll go raise him," the boy Snake offers. "Uh-oh, there he is."

Yule is sauntering across the drive from the direction of the Damei grove.

"Didn't I warn you to stay away from that area?" Kip snaps as Yule comes in range. "No, I guess you were inside when I told Zannez. My fault. But in the future, everyone will stay strictly away from that grove of trees."

"Oh?" says Yule. "What's so special about them?"

"That's the home of the Damei family who have volunteered to interact with us. If anyone bothers them, they'll leave."

"So?" asks Yule rudely.

Little Doctor Ochter lays his hand on Kip's arm to check the oncoming explosion. "Young man, I assume that for some reason you don't mind spending time in a Patrol ship's brig. But allow me to exercise my academic status and point out that you are not in a research situation here. Moreover, there are still those who listen to Ari Ochter, and you could find future grant credits very, very hard to come by. In case you didn't know, you are on the planet where the Stars Tears tragedy took place, and you will behave precisely as the Federation representatives suggest, or the results will be most unpleasant in career terms."

Yule takes this in silence and seems subdued until they hear him muttering, "Stars Tears, eh? Lot of money in that. Lots and lots."

"There will be no further comment from you." Ochter's voice cracks like a whip. "Especially along those lines."

Kip's stomach has been giving him cold jolts. He sees that Cory hasn't heard the interchange, and he's struck by regret for the advice he gave her earlier on. Still . . . what could such a shallow idiot do, even assuming Hiner helps him? And Hiner seems to have too much regard for his own well-being to get mixed up with Yule in some wild scheme that would only bring disaster. As these thoughts run through his head, Kip is swinging into the jitney's drive seat, waving them all in.

"Thanks for the help, Doc," he says as the small man limps by. "How much lead time you want for that shot?"

"None." Ochter smiles. "The words *'Here we are'* will give my chemical angel all the time it needs to work."

Zannez and his troupe are in the row of seats just behind Kip and Cory. Kip takes pity on the hardworking man.

"We have an empty seat in front, Zannez, if that'll help you."

"That's what I call heart," Zannez exclaims. "Ek, you've had the least exposure—scramble over by the Korsos. Star, sit right behind him where you can put your arms around his neck."

Little Prince Pao, watching critically, nods to himself.

The other young couple sit beside Stareem, while Zannez climbs into the row behind, between Vovoka and Ochter, with his gear. "Beautiful setup, Kippo. I'll try not to get my stuff in you Myrrin's way."

"Put some back here with me," offers Linnix from behind him, where she sits alone. Kip had noticed her pausing to see where Yule settled before choosing her place.

The ground-jitney starts off. Instead of turning toward the spaceport, they continue to run straight along a broad, smooth, meadowy avenue, climbing toward a range of low, tree-covered hills.

"Lovely and peaceful, isn't it?" Kip remarks sardonically. "This was the main route for the Stars Tears gangs in their horrible heyday. It got widened in the fighting with the Federation troops; you'll hear all about that. . . . In early days Cory and I were still rooting the odd live shell out of the flowers." He raises his voice. "Next ridge is our point, Myrrin. We stop and get out about halfway up, where that line of trees ends."

From the corner of his eye he sees little Ochter's hypo case appear as if by magic. With the deftness of long practice the doctor's hand disappears under the corner of his bushcoat, aiming for his hip. A flicker of pain crosses his face, and then the empty syrette is being pocketed as the jitney draws to a stop. What? Cancer of the pelvis or femur, Kip guesses. No fun. But the little man seems to enjoy life thoroughly, and his is not a bad way to end, chasing novas.

"You'll find those trails to the top quite easy going. I suggest you scatter onto different paths going up. You'll come to an old cross-trench just under the summit. Get into it, and do not—repeat, *do not*—stand up. Anybody who stands up, or talks, or tries to even crawl beyond it, or makes noise, will spoil it for everyone else, and I'll personally see that he regrets it.

"Of course the Dameii know we're here. That trench is the agreed-on limit of approach, and we'll get a few nice clear looks from it before they start disappearing."

He hands out binoculars to those without their own.

"Now remember to look closely at people's bare backs, from the wing-line to where the buttocks would begin on us. You'll see the glands work, if you're lucky. The kids will be coming home right over our heads, and the parents are out on their porches, waiting. The females are the slightly larger ones. The homes are *high* up, you realize, mostly built around the main trunk and forks, just where the heavy leafage begins.

"As I said, we've notified the elders of our visit and obtained their consent, provided we cause no commotion. But the other Dameii don't like it. As they get tired of being stared at by us, they'll start to slip out of sight. Most of them won't actively leave or hide in the central hut, but a Damei in a tree can vanish right in front of your nose. Moreover, they've bred and trained some of those flying leaves you noticed by the spaceport to cloud around us.

"If anyone is wondering how these paths and the trench got here, it's hard to believe with everything so peaceful now, but this was the final assault jump-off for the Federation. You can see the extent—it took a Fed battalion.

"Now up you go—remember, no talking! And look for those backs."

He waves them on, finger to lips.

Then he and Cory scramble up a side path until they come to the trench, at a bend that was an old sector point. The trench is shallow here; they lie down in it and Kip motions to Cory to start watching the Dameii; she's had less chance to view them than he. She wriggles forward and parts the grass, while he turns to check on the tourists.

Doctor Ochter, freed from pain, is climbing well. Zannez is frantically trying to catch his troupe coming up and simultaneously get first look at the Dameii. Suddenly he bursts into muffled swearing and gesticulates savagely at something in the brush. Kip peers and sees little Prince Pao solicitously attempting to assist the larger and athletic Stareem up a gulch. Comical.

Cory glances back, grins at the sight. Zannez' face is turning as red as his suit; the prince ignores him until Stareem is on smooth ground. Then he swerves aside and becomes a normal boy again.

Meanwhile Yule has been climbing steadily, looking at everything, even back toward the hostel. Such attentiveness rather surprises Kip. Tall Vovoka, bringing up the rear, surprises him, too, by his inattention. He seems interested only in his frequent scans of the eastern sky. Well, light-sculpture is probably purely abstract.

Cory beckons urgently to him, glowing-eyed and nodding yes. He knows she's seeing what they hoped for—the Dameii out in plain view on the circular porches that surround each sleeping-hut. Damiem has no winters, so construction is tropical.

It's almost time for the children's noon flight home.

This village—his special village—comprises thirty-one families with a total of about forty school-age young. The school is about a fifteen-minim flight away, in a stand of old-forest trees near another of the numerous lakes, where it serves several villages. Schooling is far more serious business now that the Galaxy has come to Damiem; in fact, one of the Korsos' main jobs is the composition of texts to go in the beautiful tissue-leaved Damei books.

Kip takes a final look around; all his charges are in place and behaving themselves. Even Yule has shed his sneer and looks like what he probably is, a decent young scientist. Zannez is aiming everything he has at the village, while his four young actors stare transfixed. Good; Kip crawls up to the viewhole Cory has made him and looks.

The scene is as he'd envisioned it: Dameii perched on every porch, a few with wings relaxed, the rest with their great vanes overhead, gently fanning the air in anticipation.

The first impression is always of those wings and their beauty, as though enormous flowers have opened petals in the trees. It's only after absorbing these that the eye can take in the even greater beauty of the Damei form and motion. Alone of all the alien races Kip knows, the Dameii are exquisite, by Human standards, in every aspect.

In early days Kip had tried to describe them to friends but soon despaired. His words wouldn't convey their surreal elegance of limb and wing, the way they flowed naturally from pose to pose, surprising and caressing the eye in a series of delicious visual shocks. And it was more than beauty for the eye; the heart was caught by their fragility, paradoxically combined with the gift of soaring flight. Could they have some unnatural power to bewitch?

He'd ended by simply listing their features.

Color: This village is large enough to show almost the full range of Damei coloration. Most have ivory skins and masses of green-glinted, feathery bronze hair. Their head hair merges into lustrous bronze manes or mantles growing over the joining of wings and body and running out to form the upper margins of the wings. The wings themselves—both the enormous upper wings and the shorter, stronger underwings—are clear greenish paned, but iridescent, so that they flash a rainbow of hues. The panes are edged with dark furred ribs that carry the oxygen-rich Damei blood.

Among the bronze-haired Dameii are a few of spectacularly deviant coloring. Two families have brilliant red manes, one fiery vermilion, the other pure dark ruby. Their skins are cool white, and all their wing-panes are in various lucent pinks edged red, a startling effect.

But loveliest of all, to Kip's eyes, is a turquoise-green mutation. These Dameii have hair and manes like rivers of emerald, verdigris-tinted skin, and pale wing-panes of electric green blue. They like to dress in a deep black gauze that sets off their exotic beauty to perfection.

The Damei bodies are humanoid, and look child-size between those wings, though they're actually over man height. The torsos and limbs are preternaturally slender and elegant in line. Their backs are long; close inspection reveals the long mothlike wing-bases that serve the wing-muscles in lieu of the breast "keel" that other winged races bear. The Dameii walk so little that their hipjoints are no fleshier than elbows.

The gauzy garments they wear reveal this; they may be cut long or short according to fancy and often are wrapped high at the throat; but always they dip low behind to join across the buttock area, leaving backs bare below the wings. Their dress is marvelously embroidered in the rich hues of natural dyes and set with foliage patterns and gleaming native jewels.

No sex differences are apparent at this distance, save for the slightly larger female size—another possibly insectoid remnant. Their faces also are too far to be distinctly seen, giving only the impression of pale ovals dominated by huge slanted eyes, shadowed by feathery brows and lashes of the same color as the flowing hair. Kip knows their features to be slight and smooth, inhuman but as appealingly modeled as a human child's. It is still hard to remember that the Dameii convey expression not by facial changes, but by wing-posture; and nuances of emotion by hands in continual graceful movement.

So much for plain description, Kip thinks. The magic, the essential beauty of these winged people, escapes all words. He pulls back to look rather savagely along the line of tourists, willing them to grasp the vision. They all are quiet and seem intent. So far so good. He sighs explosively and returns to his view.

For a minim more the scene stays. Then the Dameii seem simultaneously to tire of being spied on and begin to melt away. There is no concerted flight—only a simple sidestep to the far side of the tree trunk, or a downsweep of wings that lifts the owner to an invisible perch in the leafage above, or a wing-folding that allows the waiting parent to shelter behind a slight upturn in a porch wall. Before the watchers' eyes, the village empties.

In a few breaths, not an adult is in plain sight save for two elders, who are the Korsos' main contacts and spokesmen for their people. One of these is Quiyst, who was at the spaceport, and the other is an equally aged Damei named Feanya. These two sit in apparent calm, sharing a basket of dried *quiyna* fruit and watching the Humans. Only their nervously raised wings betray their tension. Kip waves to them and receives a minimal headbow in acknowledgment.

Seeing only deserted porches, several of Kip's guests begin to murmur and stir, but Kip glares and hisses at them to be still. The "trained" leaves he'd spoken of are now coming into evidence, flapping about distractingly.

And then comes the moment he awaits—above and around them, the trees are suddenly alive with a rush and tumult of wings and musical voices almost too high for Human hearing. The Damei children are coming home.

The young Dameii's wings and hair are bright yellow to silvery gold; their coming is like a sunlit cloud.

All ages and sexes fly together; here and there older children are helping young ones keep up by allowing them to ride their legs. Almost all carry homework. Seeing that, Kip flinches; he is late with his share of a text on Human and other off-world physiology.

Seeing the line of Humans, a few pause to look, or rise higher. One older child laughingly dives at them, ending in a swift aerobatic stunt. But most of the young are too eager to reach their homes to bother with the strangers.

As the children reach their home porches, many of the parents draw them into seclusion; but there are couples whose joy overpowers their dislike of Human eyes, and who stay hugging and petting their youngsters in plain sight. To Kip's satisfaction, one of the nearest families has turned their bare backs to the watchers, and all can plainly see the faintly colored exudates of emotion springing from the lower back skin-glands—those terrible, priceless, scented juices that have cost the Dameii so much agony and nearly ended their race.

"They're really fond of those kids," says a too-loud whisper near him. The insufferable Mordecai Yule again. Kip shoots him a bloodcurdling glare, joined by Ochter. But it's too late. The near family hurriedly slips from sight, and others, taking the cue, do likewise. In no time the village is visually empty again.

But the general movement has shown one thing more: Beautiful as the adults are, they are surpassed in sheer exquisiteness by their children.

"Well, that tears it." Kip stands up and speaks normally. "Now you go." He walks along the trench to get them started down. When they are all below ear and eye range, he gestures for a halt.

"We were about at the end of the allotted time, anyway—they want their midday meal now. Most of them eat communally, in that big house the elders are sitting by. . . . I think you've had one of the best viewings of any group. How did you like it?"

There are murmurs of almost wordless appreciation. The girl Linnix, still gazing back toward the village with longing eyes, demands softly, "What can you say? What can you say when you see real live actual angels? I never . . . I never expected, I never knew what they meant. . . ." She falls silent.

"Do we get the story now?" Zannez asks with unaccustomed gentleness.

Kip sighs. "Yes. If I must. Funny thing, after all those years and tellings I still hate to. Worse each time. But we have to move farther down—take that grassy space under the trees, below the jitney."

"Why not in the bus?" Zannez asks, struggling to collect his stuff.

"Because," says Cory, "I'm going to be in there out of earshot. Any of you who find you don't want to hear more can join me. I'll take some of your gear, Zannez, if that's a problem."

"Thank you very much, Myr Cory." He hands over his used canisters and she strides determinedly away.

IV

NOVA MINUS 11 HOURS:
Abominations of Old Days

When the tourists are assembled around him under the trees, Kip fetches another long sigh.

"Well. This all began, you understand, long before the Federation, but it ended only in recent times. I've spoken with a couple of old Spacers who were in the final action. One still has bad dreams. . . .

"The start came sometime in dim antiquity when it was discovered that those secretions you saw on the Dameii's backs have a most delicious taste to Humans. There was only a little Human space travel then, and a party or two of explorers passed by. But someone must have been up to something, because that's a strange thing to find out.

"Later it was discovered—gods know how—that if you fermented and distilled the stuff, you got a liqueur that wasn't just a nice drink; it was superlative, literally out of the worlds. It had psychoactive properties, you see, it produced a real happiness—with no side effects or hangovers. It's been described as being better than heaven because you didn't have to die. Heaven for a shilling, as some old writer said—call it our quarter credit. But this cost no quarter credit, it cost a cool thousand Gal. Or more.

"Naturally I've never tasted any, but those old Spacers I mentioned told me of people trading their life savings and mortgaging their homes for the stuff. One man literally sold another his wife and daughters, just for one of those tiny amethyst flagons it was sold in. That was the last, you see. Even before that, people would pay anything for what was called a good 'vintage.' It was only for the ultrarich. . . . The quantities, of course, were minute. You saw their backs shine—a cc or two of raw material at most.

"Unfortunately, this happened at the time of the great rare-asteroid rush, some of which came out here beyond Grunions. You may have read about that in history. So space traffic through here for a time was heavy. It must have been Spacers from the rush, stopping or wrecked here, who discovered how to make the liqueur and started the subsequent horror.

"At first they would just capture a Damei or two—they caught them at night, with stick-tight nets over the central huts—and scrape the prisoners' backs with a special long curved open tube. Sometimes they'd scrape the whole skin away and distill that. . . . Then, when they had enough distilled—a dozen or so tiny flasks—they'd seal them and send them back to their agent on some rich world.

"They soon had to start counterfeit-proofing them magnetically; the stuff became a sensation among the rich everywhere. Nobody knew where it came from—they kept that secret till the end—or how it was made. But there was an aura of something strange about it, and it picked up the name 'Stars Tears.'

"Then began the worst part. These men weren't dummies, see, or at least the dummies got eliminated early. As the credits piled in, there were gang wars for control of the trade. Anyway, someone started testing correlations between the quality and all kinds of factors, like food and other conditions, among them, between the mood of the victim and the eventual quality of the liqueur.

"I mentioned 'vintages.' Well, this had nothing to do with years, as people thought. It had to do with what the prisoner was feeling when they took the exudates. They found that happiness—gods know how they managed *that*—gave almost no flavor. Physical pain, plus fear, which they'd started with, gave what was called the 'standard vintage,' which was terrific. And then they found that *psychic* pain alone, or mixed with just a trace of joy, gave the most extraordinary quality of all.

"How do you produce purely psychic pain? . . . The bastards would capture a young couple, and after discussing before them which one's wings they would saw off first—imagine the poor lovely things, tied up helpless, with these monsters scraping like mad—" Kip was having trouble with his voice. "They would decide, say, on the girl, and get set to carve her up before his eyes. Dameii don't faint, or pass out—there was no relief. Then they'd pretend that something was wrong, that her juices were no good, and finally start to release her, until the two really believed they were setting her free. That gave the brief joy trick. And then they'd laugh and tie her up again; and simply torture her until she died before his eyes. They even had the timing worked out to keep the glands working as long as possible. . . . That gave the super vintage, from him. And the 'standard' from her. And when she was dead . . . they just tortured him to death, too, for more 'standard.' They had evolved methods I can't think about; someone showed me shots of one of their torture rooms before they burned them. . . . And all that for only a few cc's of raw material. When distilled, worth millions, of course.

"And then—oh, Apherion, you've seen them; the beauty, the vulnerability—they have no more defenses than a butterfly. They can't even scream. To call the devils that exploited them beasts is an insult to the animal world.

"Just to give you an idea—over time the raiders left quite a load of writings, recordings, notes. Some are so atrocious you can't read them; at least, I couldn't. But I've talked with people who had to. Not only for tracing down people, but for tracking money—all credits derived from that trade were forfeit to the Fed, you see—and here's the strange thing: Nowhere, but nowhere, in no place and no way is there any mention whatever that the race they were exterminating is of the greatest humanoid beauty. You'd think someone, somewhere, even out of sadism, maybe, would note it. No; they might as well have been dealing with a race of hairy bowling balls. Of course, the ethical horrors would be the same if the Dameii *were* hairy bowling balls, don't misunderstand me. It's merely an indication of a human type so blind that of the hundreds—or more—engaged in the destruction, not one would remark on what it was that they destroyed. Especially when they—and here's where I simply can't go on.

"They discovered their love for their children. . . . You've seen that, too; these people love their youngsters as much or maybe even more than their mates. Plus, you have two parents and maybe several kids and aunts and uncles—so the quantity problem—"

He breaks off and sits with lowered head, staring unseeing at the horizon where the Star would rise. Then he goes on more calmly.

"Those of you who don't have imagination enough to see what followed, I pity. You'll have to work it out. Those who do I pity more. . . . And this went on, you see, no one knows how long, until in the Last War a small Federation cruiser followed up certain rumors and found Damiem.

"Give them all credit. They didn't wait for reinforcements—they just went on in with everything they had, down to the galley boys, and started cleaning the whole mess out. They didn't take any prisoners, either—at first they hanged or bayonetted the gangsters right on the line, until they found it was upsetting the Dameii worse. So then they just threw them in some old tunnels and sealed and gassed them.

"But they needed reinforcements and more reinforcements before the end—the gangs had quite an organization by then, and money can buy you a lot of mercenaries and weapons. Too many good Spacers died here; I'll show you the cemetery tomorrow, including the two fifteen-year-old galley lads. But the end came fast—right near here, as I've mentioned. Then they leveled everything the gangs had built and got the hell off the planet fast. They figured the Dameii's best chance for recovery—they'd stopped having kids, see—was to be left in utter peace. So they stationed one small, very quiet human observer who spoke Dameii—they left him a tent, in a new place—and parked a blockade squadron in orbit.

"It took five years, but finally the observer spotted one baby, and the next year, two more. And after about a decade he was replaced by another acceptable observer, who stayed thirty years and built the nub of a station. That's the man Cory and I took over from, and now things are as you see them.

"Ah, but wait—I was forgetting. Of course there was a network distributing this stuff back in the Galaxy, and that's where the big, big money was. Enough money to bribe a planet, in ordinary terms. But this wasn't ordinary. To their credit, the Feds cleaned that out, too, although I don't know any details because, of course, it was the Special Branch. I do know that a couple of planetary governments got turned inside out and there weren't any arguments about compassion or Rehab. Those criminals ended up just plain dead.

"And even now you can't get a permit to use anything like the name, or market anything drinkable in little purple bottles, even cough syrup. Some of you may have run into the purple-bottle ban and wondered. Now you know.

"Well, that's the period at the end of the last sentence of the blackest and probably the most loathsome chapter of Human history in space. . . . And you should know, too, that there's a permanent reward out for information leading to any activities about Damiem, or even too much talk.

"I hope you understand now, Yule, why your remarks about money were out of line? And why no similar manifestations of ignorance—not to say crassness—will be tolerated."

There is a silence, broken only by sighs and a few noseblows from the Zannez group. The two girls have drawn very close together, and Snake has an arm around Hanny Ek's shoulders.

Kip throws down the handful of grass he'd been braiding as he talked and gets up. "And now it's back to the car."

As the party approaches the jitney, they're surprised to see Cory standing beside it, talking with old Quiyst, Feanya, and three other senior

Dameii. Their tall wings go involuntarily aloft from nervousness at so many oncoming Humans.

Kip gestures the others to stop and goes forward alone to greet them courteously. In a moment he turns and calls to the group. "I'm going to introduce you. When you hear me say your name, just step a pace forward and sort of bow. And then stay put where you are. This is very unusual, and we don't want to foul it up."

In a moment they hear him call. "Doctor Ari Ochter!" Ochter limps a pace forward and bows. The elders bow back, staring intently.

"Myr Stareem Fada!" And the ceremony repeats. As he finishes the list, they notice that the visitors' wings have definitely relaxed.

"And now, what may we do for you?" Kip inquires in Damei. As they speak together, Cory comes over to the Humans to explain.

"They say that since we come to look at them, they, too, wish to look at us. The learning shouldn't be all so one-sided, they say. This is a point which has come up before, by the way. I try to tell them that we have no objection in principle, but the sticker is that they want to inspect us individually *without clothes.*" Her normally glowing face shows a high flush. The others suddenly realize that this is the world of the Spacers' Code.

"I've tried to explain that we have, uh, tribal taboos there, but it doesn't go down well. Also, they want to see infants."

There is a pause.

"Well!" says Stareem explosively. "I can't do anything about the babies, but I've stripped for clowns all over the Galaxy. So have you, Bride, and Snake and Hanny, stripped and a lot more. If it'd really help . . . here, Zanny, hold my junk."

"Really? You mean you wouldn't mind?" Kip notices that the little prince is nodding and smiling encouragingly at the girl.

"Any time!" Stareem's voice is muffled as she pulls her turtleneck over her head. Hannibal Ek, not to be outdone, begins unzipping his suit.

"Oy, Kippo!" Cory calls. "Tell them to look here! Oh—meanwhile, I strongly suggest, in fact I insist, that all other Humans step back under those trees with me. Yes, you too, Myr Yule."

The two beautiful stark-bare youngsters, one white, one black, start toward Kip and the five old Dameii. Bridey and Snake are getting undressed to join them. The seven other Humans stand in an awkward group beside the tree trunks, trying not to stare, as the elders gravely begin to circle around and around the show-kids. Zannez has unlimbered all his gear.

Cory goes over to the inspection group, her eyes carefully averted from Hanno and Snake.

"I must say you four are terrific good sports," she says. "You've no idea

how much this means. Kip and I were going to have to nerve ourselves
. . ." Her voice trails off embarrassedly.

"Absolutely," Kip agrees. "You deserve medals for Galactic unity."

"I guess this is the only worthwhile stripping I've ever done," says
Stareem. "Look, what's he trying to say?"

One of the new elders is twittering incomprehensible Galactic and ges-
turing to her.

"This is Elder Zhymel." The old Damei bows. "He wants to know if he
may touch your upper back, you know, where the wings should be."

"Feel away," says Stareem. Her eyes open wide as the old Damei very
lightly lays his long fingers on her shoulder blades. "Hey—it's like being
brushed with electric feathers. It tickles! You better warn him to press
harder or I may sneeze."

They get the matter adjusted, and other Damei take their turns. Cory
says to Kip, "I have an idea, subject to your xenological approval. What if
you tell them they're seeing exceptionally perfect specimens, very young,
whom Humans consider superbeautiful?

"Then tell him the rest of us are unwilling to strip because we are far
less beautiful? We deteriorate very fast with age or we've other defects
considered ugly, and we don't wish to offend others' eyes. Be sure they get
the whole thing. I think it'll clear the air, don't you? And I suppose it's
essentially true."

"Righto. Good idea, Cor. Elders Quiyst and Feanya, et al., listen." He
delivers a long melodious speech in Damei. The elders nod as if greatly
enlightened but still look a trifle puzzledly at himself and Cory.

"Yes, yes," she says vigorously and, looking about, as if ashamed, pulls
up her shorts' legs briefly. They get a glimpse of a nasty scar she'd picked
up in her first tree-climbing days.

Kip thinks a moment, then opens his jerkin to show two wrinkles across
his belly and hastily zips up again. This seems to satisfy and please the
elders, who recommence their grave circuits of the four young people. Two
go down on all fours to view the kids' toes and ankles; another takes out a
small glass to inspect their nails and eyebrows, handing it around in turn.
The scene would be hilarious, Kip thinks, if it hadn't been so serious for
the Damei-Human future. As it is, Cory has to blow her nose twice to hide
her giggles. Zannez is shooting like mad.

Just as it looks as if this may go on forever, little Ochter calls from the
group by the trees.

"Myr Kip, I hate to be a bother, but this analgesic is wearing off fast,
and it has some unpleasant side effects. Could you possibly take me—"

"Right. Sorry Doc. Can you hold out two minims more?"

"Oh, yes."

"Look, you great kids—is it possible you can repeat this act in the village tomorrow? I meant what I said about the value of what you've done here. Just say no if the village is too much."

"I'm perfectly game for the village," Bridey says. "How about you?"

"Count us in," they all say.

"You'll never know," Kip says, "or maybe you can guess. Look, a medal is probably beyond us, but I can personally guarantee you each a superofficial document attesting to your services to the Federation—all differently worded and signed and dripping with gold seals and special stamps."

"That's beautiful," Snake says.

"But you don't need to," Hanny Ek tells him. "After hearing what happened here I'd hang by my tail if it'd help. Funny thing, isn't it? That just the sort of people you needed wandered by? We all started as kid-porn stars, you know, to be blunt about it. I can just see Ser Vovoka—!"

Laughing, they bow farewell to the elders and run over to dress and rejoin the others, while Kip explains the offer to Quiyst. The elders seem extremely pleased; their now relaxed plumes make an odd curling, furling gesture he's never seen before.

With a final warning to keep their people under cover when the Star brightens, Kip joins the others in the jitney, and they start down. Zannez hands over the last of the clothes and gets in heavily, for once neglecting his cameras.

"You must be exhausted, Myr Zannez," Linnix says sympathetically. "Lucky this planet has long days, you've worked yourself half to death before the Star you came for has even showed up."

"You'll all probably be glad to know that the next thing on the agenda is a nice long nap," Cory tells them. "There's food on call in the lounge when you want it, and I thought we could start a buffet supper about sunset. The Star doesn't rise till an hour after sundown, but it might be earlier tonight, being closer. And the sunsets alone are worth seeing. So we can have our appetizers and drinks at the bar, and then take our dinner plates out on the deck for the Star's rise."

"Excellent, excellent," says Ochter.

"Just so long as we do not miss any of the Star," Vovoka surprises them all by saying in his curiously accented tones. "I think that is a very good plan."

The jitney speeds hostelward down the calm grassy avenues, once the scene of so much blood and pain. Kip notices that the visitors are unusually silent. Good. Maybe they've been caught as he is by the beauty of what they've been allowed to see of Damiem; maybe their hearts are shadowed, like his, by the dreadful story of the Tears. But no stranger can really grasp it in an hour or two, he thinks. Even Cor doesn't totally get it; to her it's just one more job.

His handsome brow furrows; he tries to brush aside his perennial worry: Who will come after them to safeguard his precious, vulnerable winged people? How long will the Federation guard Damiem?

V

NOVA MINUS 10 HOURS:
Linnix of Beneborn

The girl Linnix has been increasingly impatient to get back to the hostel. Despite the overpowering interest of the Dameii, she has an interest of her own more compelling still, and she feels no need of another nap. As the others make for their rooms, she goes through the lounge and out to the deck, near the infirmary's semitransparent vitrex walls. The infirmary and Doctor Baramji's cubicle appear to be, as she feared, empty.

To distract herself she watches the gyrations of the mobile tree leaves, which flew up in a cloud on their arrival, now settling back on their stems. Some look dusty and weak. Linnix wonders if they followed the tour. And must they return to their parent tree, or will a strange tree give them harbor? Mysterious.

There is as yet no movement behind the vitrex; the doctor is still with his sex-queen. To Linnix, the Lady Pardalianches, like other planetary nobility she has tended on shipboard, seems somewhat more pathetic than impressive—and more than somewhat irritating in her self-centeredness.

To a man, she supposes the ultrafeminine body, the seductive promise of fleshy delights, reverses matters entirely. Especially a lonely man like Doctor Baramji, driven by those needs she doesn't really share. Doubtless he'll be with the Lady a long while yet.

But no! There's a figure moving behind the pale green vitrex.

With a silent prayer to the gods of chance—is it now the thousandth such prayer?—and knowing her own foolishness, she knocks.

"Come in, come in . . . Oh, it's you, Myr Linnis, is it? I fear I didn't catch your full name."

He is brewing an appetizing-smelling drink on the lab burner, having clearly just waked from a nap on the rumpled cot she can glimpse in his personal cubicle. His snow-white hair is wildly rumpled too, and he's barefoot.

"Linnix, actually," she tells him. "And I really have no family name. Just Linnix will do."

"Linnix it is." He rummages out a clean cup, spoon, and saucer. "And I'm Bram." He grins, pushing the white hair out of those brilliant blue-green eyes. "You'll share some of my kaffy? A very old drink made of dried beans, but cheering. My new lot just came in on your ship."

"I don't want to rob you." Linnix is thinking what a fine-looking older man he is. Not handsome, but well knit and wiry, no fat on him, and a rugged face that radiates both warmth and toughness, lit by those spectacular eyes. She redoubles her silent prayer, knowing it's hopeless but unable to still the longing.

"Let's sit here." He sweeps a chair clear for her. "Not as elegant as the deck, but I am not fit for public view. And now, what may I do for you, Myr Linnix?"

Sampling the intriguing kaffy, to which he's added a sweetener, Linnix lets herself study him a moment more, postponing the death of hope. She notices what she hadn't seen before: several scar-lines in the tan of one elbow, and others running into the hair from his right shoulder. The war? Well, time to find out later. As if idly, she asks, "Might I know what color your hair used to be, before it . . . before?"

"Firetop. Rooster red. Just like yours only not so pretty. . . . And of course, our eyes are both the same odd shade of blue."

Hearing her involuntary gasp, he looks at her sharply, his doctor persona showing through. "Is the kaffy that strong? Give me your wrist a minim, it affects some people."

"Oh, no, no." She babbles, scarcely knowing what she's saying while his fingers seek her pulse. "I like it, I really do—"

"Sssh."

He rises and goes behind her, and she feels his fingers on pulse points, touching her delicately with the strong hands. An odd warmth has somehow sprung up between them. And the objective indicators are excruciating. "Firetop—like yours . . . and our eyes . . ." The disappointment when it comes, as come it must, will be more painful than in many years.

And such a *good* man—she knows that without evidence. Let me have a few minim more, she bargains with fate. I'll take it fine if I can pretend for just a little while more.

"How did you lose your firetop?" she asks as he releases her and sits back down. He pushes the kaffy away from her and pours her a glass of the golden drink before answering.

"Oh, I picked up parts of a microscope in the wrong places when our ship took a hit. That was in the so-called Last War—may it be so. My unit was up against those Terran supremacy addleheads in the far side of the Orion Arm. The war came a year or so after I made my certification. I'd been interning in various lines of work on various planets. As far as my souvenirs go"—he indicates the scars, the white hair—"it was the treatments rather than the original wounds that did those. The first paramed who operated on me had found a tape on orthopedic surgery beforehand—he said. I had quite a bit of plastite in me, too. We simply didn't know some of the repair lines that are routine today. . . . You were being born just about then."

She sips the kaffy and asks, as if it had been puzzling her, "Tell me, Doctor—Bram, I mean—there was one thing Myr Kip didn't go into, and I was embarrassed to ask. The Dameii—he spoke of males and females, but how do they, uh, reproduce? Do they . . . lay eggs? Are they mammals?"

"Well, that's a very legitimate interest, but it's a shade complex. No, they're not mammalian in the strict sense, but they're not oviparous, either. Do you know what 'haploid' and 'diploid' mean?"

"It's about cells and chromosomes; I think haploid means having half the usual number. I remember it by h-a—half. Is that right?"

"Absolutely. I see you do read. Well, the forms we call 'males' are all haploid. That may account for their slightly smaller size and the greater number of defects among them. And the true, complete females are diploid —except for a group of haploid structures just below their breastbones, the egg-receiver, or oviceptor, we call it. It's folded back V-shaped, that's what gives the impression of breasts. When a female is in season—they show definite changes, and it's a slow, you might say unusual, event—it stimulates her mate to produce a kind of quasiembryo—all haploid—under *his* breastbone. And at a given time, when she's ready, this egglike object is passed over to the female's oviceptor. Then, if she's really receptive—or really a complete female, we don't have too much data here—she contributes a kind of shadow embryo, also haploid, which has the ability to merge with, you might say invade, the male's contribution and transform it into a diploid fetus which will be a complete female. . . . Have I lost you?"

"Oh, no! Please go on." She smiles. "Now I can see why Myr Kip didn't—"

"Yes." Baram chuckles. "But wait, so far we've only made a daughter. Now, if conditions aren't just right, the process doesn't work perfectly and you get an incompletely diploid fetus, which goes on to become, socially, either a sterile male or sterile female, depending on which parental aspect predominates. I don't think the Dameii themselves can tell for sure until the young grow up and try to mate."

"But true males, sons . . ." Linnix frowns. "How . . ."

"Our best guess is that something we don't understand at all yet happens in the female oviceptor, so that the fetus is only peripherally influenced and grows up completely haploid, as a normal, fertile male. But one thing certain is that in all the families with fertile male children we've been able to examine, the mother always contributes *something*, as judged by gross features of resemblance. That is, she's a true mother, not just an incubator. . . . As you can see, the whole process is still full of mystery. And it's slow, and it occurs only rarely. The Dameii pass most of their lives in the asexual phase.

"So we suppose their evolution is slow and chancy, too. Does that answer your question, Myr Linnie?"

"Um-hmm. . . ." She nods solemnly. "Thank you very much. . . ." She's thoughtful, gripped, despite her preoccupation, by the strangeness of alien lives. But her fingers have been twisting on the mug's handle, trueing and retrueing the odds and ends on the table. And behind her interest in the Dameii, the inner voice keeps whispering, *Wouldn't it be wonderful if . . . Is it possible, possible at last?*

Baram's eyes have never left her for an instant as he recounts the Damei cycle. Now he captures one of her restless hands and says quizzically, "Myr Linnix, it's simply no use pretending you came here to hear war stories and learn about the Dameii. What is it, my dear?"

All right, she tells herself. Happy time is over.

She can't know that Baram is telling himself much the same thing. During their talk his intuition has come up with a horrible surmise: Suppose that there had indeed been an error in the faulty cold-sleep syrettes, an error for which she was responsible. And she has chosen him to confess it to. Oh, no. No. Just as he is beginning to like her so much. But what else can be on her mind to cause such indirection, such intense trouble? He dreads her next words.

When they come, he is so astonished and relieved that he has to suppress an inane grin.

"Well, in a way, I did come to hear about your life. Back then, before you went on the ships, were you ever on a planet called Beneborn? That is —was—my homeworld."

"Beneborn . . . Beneborn . . . Doesn't seem I ever heard of it. I'm

from Broken Moon, in the Diadem. Beneborn isn't near the Diadem cluster, by any chance?"

It's hurting worse than she ever imagined it could, after all the years.
"No," she says drearily, "nowhere near. But I meant, during your intern
work. Between leaving Medworld and whenever you shipped out to the
war." But she knows the answer; her words come out dull and flat, not real
questions at all. This penetrates Baram's relief.

"Beneborn . . . Beneborn . . ." he mutters. "Look, details aren't too
clear to me from before the smash, but I can still list the planets I worked
on. No Beneborn among them. . . . Linnix, my dear, I seem to have hurt
or failed you in some way." His voice is very gentle. "Please, won't you tell
me what it is? What have I done?"

"Oh, you haven't done anything, Doctor Baramji, except be nice. It's
just the facts. I was a fool to h-hope." The beautiful turquoise eyes
threaten to overflow. "But the hair, the eyes, the timing, everything looked
so *right*. And I *wanted* it to be you. Oh, what a fool—a fool—a f-fool—"

He opens his arms, and she's crying on his breast.

"Let it out, my dear. I'd guess you've been very alone."

The sudden shaking violence of her weeping almost frightens him. He
holds her tight, stroking her lovely hair, and finally the storm passes. For a
moment she lies back in his arm exhausted, then swallows hard, uses his
proffered handkerchief vigorously, and sits up, moving back to her own
chair.

"Oh, Doctor Baramji—"

"Just Bram, my dear."

"But I never, I'm not the crying type."

"Everyone is the crying type, my love, if it hurts bad enough. And I
gather this does. And now you tell me about it."

She half sighs, half laughs. "Oh, it's nothing, really, unless . . . well,
you see, Beneborn people, it's like a sickness. It started with some things in
our history, but nobody really remembers that. What it is now, they want
to improve our race. They have a hugeous big biologic storage facility. I
know other planets do that, too, but not on the same scale by half. Ours—
theirs—is almost a religion. They keep records you wouldn't believe. And
people, couples, save up to buy the finest available. Or what they think is
the finest for them. Usually just an ovum or sperm; sometimes both, so the
child isn't even related to one of them. People even start savings accounts
at the Spermovarium in a newborn child's name, so when it's old enough it
has the price. And they reserve special strains far in advance.

"My—my parents saved to buy some of the last Lintz-Holstead sperm.
He was a multifacet genius, both math and biology, and very healthy—he
died in an accident at ninety-six. That was supposed to be me. . . ."

"Well, great," says Baramji. "But I gather something happened?"

"Oh, yes. Lintz-Holstead was dark, see. Also blood type A-pos. Dark skin, black hair and eyes—and so were all his forebears and relations to four generations. And my mother and every one of her family were dark, too. And all but one were type A-plus. That's partly what I mean by 'records.' But me—well, you can see." She runs her hand roughly through the glorious hair that has ruined her life, and tears well again in the blazing blue eyes. "And I'm B—B-neg. . . .

"And I wasn't multitalented—they test you practically from birth—in fact I wasn't talented at all, except at . . . uh . . . *speed skating.*"

"But . . ." Baramji gropes wildly. "I don't want to hurt your feelings, but even mothers have been known to have affairs—"

"No way. And especially after spending all those credits—it was her money. She wasn't crazy, she and my, quotes, father, were dying for this high-status kid."

"Well, then it could only be that some technician in the storage works got to playing smart, and augmented Linx-whoever with himself."

"That's exactly what we think. The trouble is that in the last prewar days we had young doctors interning there from off-planet, and their records aren't complete. And nobody knows where they went afterward, with the war and all. There's not even a name for some. The Beneborn authorities contacted several hospitals who had sent us people in the past, and ran a few ads, but nothing turned up."

"So you started out to hunt through the whole Galaxy yourself? My poor little idiot."

"In a way I had to, B-Bram. You see, there was a terrible stink, and my family literally hated the sight of me. So when I was thirteen the Spermovarium settled a small life annuity on me, and threw me off the planet on condition I never come back. I mean, they signed me up as cabin girl with the next Moom ship. And that's what I've been doing ever since. It's nice safe work and all the education I can read. After the sleepers are down I read—I mean, I really read books—for a couple of days before I go down, too. And I have seniority now, so I can pick runs to far planets that should have Senior Medical Officers on them. Somehow I figure *my* father would like frontiers, that he wouldn't be a big-city society specialist or whatever. So then, when your hair . . . and—N-no!" She sits up straight, jaw clenched. "I positively will not cry all over you again, dear, dear Bram."

He takes both her hands in his.

"Don't you think you might call this off one day, and have some babies of your own, if you want? There's an old saying: It is better to be an ancestor than a descendant."

She smiles politely.

"My advice, if you want it, is, to the devil with this Limp-Holstein. What did he know about Moom ships, or far planets? You're a beautiful girl. There's any number of fine, handsome, dedicated men on lonely planets who would give an arm and a leg for the chance, well, in the Universe's oldest cliché, a chance to make you happy."

She's staring into space, only half listening.

He gets up and firmly turns her face up to him. "Linnie, darling, give it up! Let some other man—" He goes down on one knee beside her, holding her tight. Too tight; an instant later she feels his grasp relax. He combs her mussed hair off her face with his fingers.

"I tell you what." He grins. "Let me be your adopted father while you're here. No reason a child can't temporarily adopt a father, is there? And my first fatherly admonition to you is, go on back behind that screen and wash your pretty face and then we'll chat a moment."

She laughs shakily and goes to find the washstand.

"How did you like the visit to the Dameii? Aren't they lovely?"

"Oh, my," she says through sounds of splashing. "But the story Myr Kip told us—"

"Yes. Best not to think about that. After all, the Dameii you're seeing today are three generations or more from the ones it happened to."

She emerges, toweling vigorously. "Are they long-lived? Do they have sickness, I mean—"

"You mean, do I have much work here? Am I earning my keep? Well, here again Kip left something out. . . . You recall I said that the haploid forms we call the males are prone to various defects? Yes . . . well, there's another village, or settlement, that isn't such a happy sight. We call them Exiles. It's low down, built partly on the ground, you see, for Dameii with defective wings. The normal Dameii are pretty rough on winglessness; flight is a very big thing with them. We suspect, but don't know, that there may be infanticide where a newborn is really wingless. At any event, a child who isn't perfect is soon taken, or finds its way, to the village of the Exiles. I've been working there, and I've had some success. In fact, one of the Dameii who live near us is a patient to whom I restored flight. . . . One problem is that they heal with amazing speed; too much speed, if an injury isn't promptly set properly. And the normals aren't too interested in medicine. So I'm building a nucleus of future doctors among the Exiles, who have a natural self-interest in the topic."

"I'd like to see that, Bram—my dear adopted father—if you have time before we go. Look—you need some clean towels. I'll tell Cory, green?"

"Green, daughter dear."

With a burst of returning spirits, she asks, "And did *you* have a nice time with the Lady Pardalianches?"

He actually blushes, a startling sight under the shock of white hair.

"Smartass daughter—you have to remember I've been alone on this damned planet for years. But yes—I had a nice time, even if I'll smell of musk and patchouli for weeks. I needed that."

"We'll be here several days."

"Yes. One problem, though. She wants to sample every willing body in the place, male or female. . . . You in line?"

"No."

"It *is* a little heavy, to be frank. After I got over thinking I was in heaven I started to get too conscious of that twin sister in the bed. You know about that? Of course you do—you took care of them."

"Yes. Poor thing, she's just a vegetable, isn't she?"

"I fear so. But her sister won't give up. They both wear those gold-mesh skull caps with electrode implants, you know. The Lady claims hers transmits everything she experiences, including speech, to her sister, and moreover, she thinks she picks up responses, back transmissions. Not verbal, but as feelings."

"Oh, how weird."

"Yes. The poor twin is leading a hectic brain-life, if true. I doubt it, though the Lady seems to be rich enough to buy any amount of respectable science."

Linnix is combing out her hair, making faces at the condition of Baram's brush.

"Well my dear man, dear almost-father—I guess I better get back and get my own place organized. I just dropped my bag in a tangle of lizard skeletons when we arrived."

"Get along with you, then." He grips her arms; their eyes meet in wordless tenderness, and he kisses her forehead. She smiles back, straightening her shoulders, raising her chin.

"That's my girl."

"I . . . I wish I were." She can say it without undue agony now.

"Kip'll be ringing the dinner chimes in—let's see . . . about four hours."

"Right." She smiles and suddenly grabs his hand and kisses it hard before she goes out into the mellow afternoon light of Damiem.

He follows her to the doorway in time to see her wheel and march straight back to him. She halts by the door.

"Sorry." Her voice is low, but direct.

"Whatever in the stars for?"

"That last bit." She looks down, embarrassed. "I've been seeing too many grid-shows. Oh, I made a big thing about reading and I do read—but I look at shows, too. Sometimes . . . I just wanted you to know. I thought that"—she makes a brief hand-kissing gesture—"was a little . . . sickie. I am, I'm very grateful to you, Doctor Bra—Bram." Her head's up now, the blue eyes straight. "But I'm not sick. I think. You don't think I am, do you?"

"If I grasp what you mean, my dear, no. I don't. You're . . . intense. But given your culture, no. You're not sick."

"Whew."

She blows at a lock of hair, genuinely relieved. "Thank you. Well, good-bye again."

"Good-bye."

Their eyes meet, and the same hearts' longing jumps across. Or is it the same? "I'll try what you said," she mutters and gives a broad smile, only a little twisted. "Good-bye, *Dad*. . . . Hmm!"

Then she turns and is really walking away down the deck.

Baram stares after her, jolted to the core. It had hit him when he'd held her the second time, kneeling beside her; hit him so hard he'd had to force his arms to relax their grip on her. Among other and complex things, she's a Spacer, of a sort. Like himself . . . but doctors are different.

The fact is he *wants* her, this girl, this Linnix No-name. Not as a father surrogate—though her story touches his heart. Thrown off her home planet at thirteen for having the wrong father! . . . But he can't be her father. He wants her, herself. If love could bloom so quickly, he'd say he loves her, passionately and completely. Maybe it can; he feels the grand old cliché he joked about, the same thing he felt for his first mate. (He catches himself—is this the first time he's called Jimi his "first" mate? Yes. Oh.) The point is, he wants her to be happy, to make her so.

And he wants *her,* this long-legged, boyish, sensitive, funny, flame-headed kid—wants her so hard it's pain to conceal it.

He scratches his white thatch in wonder at himself. Two hours ago he could have sworn that his poor old body wouldn't respond to any woman for weeks—or at least a few days, realistically. The Lady Marquise had been everything a man could ask for as sex object and sophisticated bodily playmate. And sympathetic, pleased at his need, attentive to his every signal. . . . At least he can be sure his desire for Linnix is no deprivation effect.

But what in the worlds can he do? Be he Linnie's lover, mate, friend, whatever, in a few days' time she's going up that ship ramp and off forever, on her hopeless quest. The idea makes his heart ache. And it would always be that way, unless . . .

Unless he takes her on her own terms. And all the Human planets he knows have a strong incest taboo. To have her on her terms means making a mockery of his desire by day, by night, forever.

But still it would be *something;* he could be sure she would return again and again, arrange her life to join his. He could be sure of her love.

Sighing grimly, he starts to paw through the laundry that has somehow enveloped his library and drags out *Brazilier's Encyclopedia of Worlds.* Pouring himself another cup of cold kaffy, he sits down to prepare his doom.

Maybe, just maybe, somehow, he won't have to use it. But all he knows of Human emotions tells him that he will.

VI

NOVA MINUS 6 HOURS:
Zannez Worries

Zannez, indefatigable and worried, also feels no great desire for sleep. He lies fretting while the kids are dozing off—they've opened the connecting doors to turn the room into one big suite—and chews on a thought that just came to him: Could it be that any or all takes of Damiem are classified? How bitter, if their big trip, with the best semidoc work he and the kids've ever done, should end up in some Federation safe. . . .

Travel Admin should have cleared it, of course, but on Gridworld—who knows? Just plain stupidity, or an enemy in the works, could ruin it all. He was the stupid, not to have thought of it and asked. Maybe the Korsos can tell him; but it's always been Zannez' experience that people in the field have no idea how picky their headquarters are.

From the boys' room are coming murmurs about the excitements of the day. They seem deeply affected—and not least by the promised letters of commendation. He hears the words "gold seals" repeated from the bed where Snake and Hanno lie asprawl.

This starts Zannez on a happier track. Imagine that—Federation commends for his kids! He's proud of them, the team he's built almost literally out of dirt. And here they are, mixing it like veterans with marquises and princes and Planetary Administrators—and now this! Those speech lessons he starved them all for have really paid off.

His thoughts run back over the ways they came to him.

Bridey—Eleganza, dammit—was the first. She'd been half of a brother-sister roller stunt act. When her brother broke his neck, the studio'd torn up the contract and thrown her out on her twelve-year-old ass. She had some money saved, but a brat pack got it, and nearly got her, too. He'd come around a corner and found her trying to stone them off her. She was such a feisty little thing, and she threw like a boy; he'd taken her home with him and later drawn up her contract himself.

Snake and Hanno had been apprents in a third-rate acrobat show; they were already into kiddie porn. Zannez caught a sample, liked their control, and was able to pick up their contracts cheap when the show broke up.

And Star—he'd been looking unsuccessfully for a natural blonde to go with Hanny. One night he was sitting in a port bar, dismally considering bleaching Bridey, when a tramp shipper came up to him with something gray and hairy on a rope as thick as his wrist. The animal was so dirty he thought it was an alien or a small ape, but they went in the can and the tramper wet its head to show a white-haired, bewildered, Human girl-child. He decided she showed promise. Oh, be honest, he tells himself, you decided to buy it as soon as you saw that rope. Anyway, he took it home, and he and the gang washed and fed it, and after it finished wolfing, it sang a little tune and said its name was Sharon Woba.

And that became Star.

In the years that followed he'd groomed and sweated and trained them in any work he could scrounge, until they got this big break with the *APC*. But now it looks like this is failing. The kids sense it, he thinks.

Only last month Hanny had startled him by asking to enlist for space. They were on Beverly—Gridworld had no recruiting office—so Zannez said go ahead. He'd been pretty sure of what would happen. Sure enough, the space officer threw him out, because of the porn. "The Space Patrol doesn't take animals." Hanny's never discussed it, but Zannez has a hunch the hurt goes deep. The boy has a real itch for space.

The girls in the bed nearby are still whispering sleepily. Zannez hears one of them say, ". . . just for a little stripping. They didn't even care about crotch shots. I wonder what . . ." And the other, almost asleep, repeating softly, "Respectful . . . they were so *respectful.* . . ."

This sends Zannez' thoughts down another track that he positively will not pursue. Porn. Yeah—it's shameful, it's criminal. *It's a living.* Children selling something like soul's blood to make Human sharks richer—and he, Zannez, can't change the system. All he can do is take care of the people he's directly responsible for and keep them out of the really rough stuff as long as he can. And if he's going to start worrying about basics, he better get up and get some work done for tonight.

The girls are hard asleep now; Zannez quietly gets himself into a fresh red jumpsuit and finds his chalk. Outside, in the afternoon blue and gold and greens of lake and forest, he feels a lot better.

The deck is a long narrow crescent around the lake side of the hostel, with its center bulging toward the lake, and a low parapet edge. Beyond the parapet are treetops—the land falls off really steep here in a series of forested cliffs right down to the lake. The whole shore is wooded, with a little beach way off to the left. Really pretty.

As he glances down at the beach he sees some quiet splashing—it's the Aquaman, Hiner, coming out. He's been exploring the bottom of the lake. Weird. Zannez pauses for a minim, wondering if there's an angle there for his documentary; decides no. Too confusing—and Hiner didn't look very cooperative. . . .

Back to his business: The Star, they tell him, will rise to the right and sail overhead across the lake, getting bigger and bigger and emitting whatever it emits. The sky is almost cloudless and expected to stay so; perfect conditions.

But what will the Star look like as it actually surrounds them?

Well, there probably won't be a center at all, but a whole skyful of Star-stuff, maybe fantastic auroras and other wild manifestations. It's really a nova-front sweeping past. And it may change fast. He'd better set his sky cameras on one-second lapse to start with. And, say, a full sky-and-lake sweep every twenty secs or so. And an extra cam on a light-sensor gimbal.

A peculiar chilly sensation is troubling his insides. Zannez finally identifies it as the realization that all this isn't just some full-screen effect concocted by Visuals; it's reality itself. This is an honest-to-the-gods real great Star, or the exploding core of one—explosions in which billions of people died—*that's* what's coming onto them tonight.

There's nobody he can call to stop the run, or get a retake, or even turn it down if it starts frying them all and the hostel, too. It's *real.*

Well, if the others can take it, he can, too. He just isn't quite used to reality yet. . . . And that terrible business about the poor wing-people, that happened right around here—His mind shies from it. Better to think about the superb takes he already has in the can, enough to make a doc in itself—before they've even started!

Now, where to base his people?

The forward center of the crescent is his natural spot, but the main party of guests is bound to congregate there; and they may have some official instruments to go there, too. He doesn't intend to get anyone peed off with him again, he's just being his natural working self now. That "I am Zannez!" line was Gridworld garbage that doesn't play here, in reality.

Reality has another aspect, too—one Zannez has postponed thinking about. But now he's placing his people, he can't dither any longer. Face facts: we're working in a world that plays strictly by the Code.

The Code is very strong among space people. They're reared in it, it's second nature. It's simple: *No uninvited sexuality,* in word, deed, or intent. Whew!

No Spacer would violate it, because everyone knows that universal adherence to the Code is all that makes workable the free, close contact of the Human sexes in the cramped quarters and isolation of space. "The Code has given us the Stars." Violations are unthinkable; if one occurs, it grounds the guilty for life; they could be out of the Service in a snap.

Even the kids have sensed it. Zannez sees that. They haven't needed his repeated warnings. He himself is impressed, feeling his way through the odd combination of liberty and automatic self-discipline the Code produces. He recalls an old saying: "To the pure all things are pure." Not to laugh—these people, he guesses, can sleep in the same bed untouching, if a job demands it . . . a far cry from the obligatory couplings and the ever-emptier—and bloodier—search for sensation of Gridworld.

But how in the name of the gods is he going to shoot porn here without getting lynched?

Well, technically he's in the clear, they'd told him back home, because he isn't addressing his stuff *at* anybody and has no "intent." But pragmatically, it stinks.

He'll have to screen off the kids somehow. A curtain would be best, but there's no way to hang it, the parapet is too low. It'll have to be screens. And the sound track to be slapped in later; that's sheer drudgery, but there's no other way. Thank the fates the deck is long and narrow, easy to screen across.

So, where to set up?

Well, there's a slight bay in the deck just outside the boys' room; that'd be about ideal, given screens. They can get at any of their stuff, they have room to spread farther, and it's right for the angle the main lounge doors open at. He begins visualizing holographic frames and distances, wondering idly if the trees around the lake might catch fire. Whew! again.

They've given him a script for the Star-scenes; he takes it out and flips through it. The idea is that the exotic energies released by the Star are hypersexual, and the kids are to do an increasingly bizarre erotic act as the Star brightens. Zannez himself is supposed to be a doctor. And he's directed to do the whole thing so it can be cut as a normal segment for a regular *APC* episode, with a second hard-porn version for appropriate distribution.

Zannez looks it through with growing disgust. Back on Gridworld this sort of thing is standard. But here, above this magically calm, remote lake, under the flawless sky—he suddenly tears it into shreds. There don't seem to be any automatic trashers about, but a tub by the parapet wall that ends their bay has some papers in it. He pitches the whole script in. The kids can do some interesting sex, with a commentary dubbed in later about whatever cosmic wonders appear—but the cheap porn dialogue they were supposed to mouth he will positively not impose on this scene.

He is now positively going to get fired, too; he can just see himself explaining his actions to the knife-eyed money boys who own *APC.*

His mind starts back around its usual worry track. The disastrously slipping ratings of his group within the *APC* cast of thirty-five; his own folly in sticking with them when he's had this perfectly good offer to make docs. He's good at documentaries—loves them, in fact. And offers like that stay open about three hours on Gridworld. . . . When they get back, nobody will recall his name.

Why does he stick? Some obscure loyalty to the inept four, especially Snake and Bridey—ahh, Eleganza. If he quits they'll be on the surplus list in a month and from there to Endsville. Selling, if they're lucky, welfare soup; if they aren't lucky, themselves. That scenario has a quick ending; Gridworld is full of them, the beautiful almost-made-its, the tried-and-couldn'ts. The planet is infamous for having the largest obituary listings and the youngest corpses among the Human worlds.

No. Himself and this crazy trip he's dreamed up to see the third shell of the Murdered Star go by is about their last chance. The pitiful part is that he isn't even the director they need. The right man for them would make more of that weird sinister quality Snake can project, and the sheer dumb-ass lusciousness of Stareem when she's in the mood, and half a dozen other things he can't do. The gods know he tries, but it isn't in him. So they're having their last chance with the wrong man, a bungler.

Ah, he thinks, trash it all. We're gods know how many light-years from the studio now. Anything can happen. Maybe the ship will fall apart on the way home.

Meantime, let him do what he's good at. That deck bay looks bare, it needs something. Native—oops, excuse me—*Damei* artifacts. Rugs, pillows, statuary—maybe they have a big idol. He'll have to ask Kip or the boss lady when she shows. . . . Too bad about Myr Administrator, he thinks. A great lady in person, but she'd screen like a balloon.

He settles himself to wait. A few minutes back he's noticed vaguely that another figure has come onto the far end of the deck and is looking over the lake. It's that red-haired, white-clad girl from the ship, the Logistics Officer. And now another of Zannez' talents comes into play, one he rarely tells anyone about anymore.

The girl is standing straight-shouldered and neutral, apparently enjoying the beautiful scene. But Zannez knows: *She's just had one tough kick in the udder.* . . . He wonders, as always, how he picks these things up.

People talk about "body language," but his perceptions are subtler than that. Some things—not necessarily the most important—he just *knows.* In the same way he knows that that young crud Yule, and the Aquaman, who are supposedly enraged at being dumped off here, aren't really angry at all. And that silent so-called artist Vovoka stinks of death. And the Kip-Cory love thing is real love. And dear little old jolly Doctor Ochter would cut your throat for a half credit.

Zannez can never understand why things like that aren't as plain as soap to everybody. But after a long string of blackened eyes and split lips in his early youth, he's learned to keep his mouth shut.

Ah, but wait a minute, go back. If that pair, Yule and Hiner, aren't furious at being here, it must mean either that they really don't want to go to Grunions whatsis, or—they wanted to come here. And it's hard to get clearance to come here, Zannez knows that. Yet here those two are, no security checks or nothing. Very slick. And his instincts tell him they're together or linked up somehow.

Why? What's here for them?

He's been staring unseeingly over the beautiful, now uncannily calm lake. A ruffle of motion by the far shore draws his eye. A pair of great pale wings fan out and rise among the treetops, followed by another. They're carrying containers. Up through the topmost branches they flit inconspicuously and are gone.

Zannez' insides give a cold lurch.

What's here are the Dameii—and the golden credits they represent. And that baby goon Yule and the unpleasant waterman, with their faint Black Worlds stink, have pulled off getting here very neatly indeed.

Zannez rubs his knuckles on his bald head, feeling colder and a trifle scared. For decades he's lived in unreality—fake characters, fake plots, fake everything except ratings figures on computers, and signed—or unsigned—contracts. Now he's in reality.

The beautiful, totally vulnerable wing-people are real, not just exquisite makeup jobs. The dreadful story he heard that afternoon really happened; it isn't just a storyline that can be changed, it's real. The real tortured and dead do not get up again. And the wealth that was gained from bloody atrocity was real—riches that some men would dream of, and work for, take ultimate risks for. Lay elaborate criminal plans for. All real.

Evil, if it comes here, will be real evil involving not only the Dameii, but the deaths of any who stand in the way. To lay hands on a Damei is death; another murder—indeed, a massacre—wouldn't increase the jeopardy.

And now he, Zannez, has the hunch of trouble from these two, Yule and

Hiner, who certainly arrived here without checkout, in what could be, given resources, a preplanned job. Does his hunch point to anything more? Nothing—except that this script calls for more smarts than those two have between them. Well, what about the deathly Vovoka? What about that little cutie, Ochter? Either could be the planner, the main man. . . .

Is he crazy? Probably. . . .

But who knows what else could be waiting in the wings? Space is *big;* Zannez really understands that now. Waking up on shipboard, it had impressed him mightily to see the great light-swirls of the Galaxy behind them. And then that Linnix officer-girl had led them to another port and pointed out Damiem's sun ahead, blazing so utterly alone, with only a few stars hanging in utter blackness on beyond.

The Rim. . . .

Anything could be lurking out here. Who would know?

And now he has this hunch, this Black Worlds whiff about these two. If it were only a matter of himself, he'd be glad to ignore it. But this could concern others. Not only the Dameii, but innocent others like the Korsos and the other visitors, who would certainly not be left unmolested if anyone were actually planning a Stars Tears thing. . . . In short, for the first time in his life, he maybe has a *duty?* Crazy.

Well, crazy or not, it's oppressive, distracting from his work. He longs to get it off him.

But is there anyone here who wouldn't laugh him down? . . . The boss lady, Cory, she seems his best bet—and the proper person, too. Yes, Zannez decides. I'll tell her and let her decide how seriously to take a stranger's sixth sense.

Yet even as he decides this, doubt strikes him. That unreality he's so trained to: what if his very hunch is unreal—is a hunch, not about reality, but about what should be in some standard story plot? He knuckles his head again in confusion, cursing Gridworld. . . . Well, he'll tell Myr Cory *that,* too.

She can make up her own mind as to what's reality.

As though on cue, Cory herself comes out backward through the main doors, followed by Kip. Between them they're pushing out a large, old-fashioned multi-channel terminal cum transceiver, which they station just where Zannez guessed something official might go.

Kip trots back into the lounge while Cory waits, panting a bit.

"Oh, hello, Myr Zannez. Everything going well for you, I trust?"

"Yes, indeed. I'm setting up in this bay. Is that all right? . . . But there's a serious word I need to have with you before too long. Would that be possible?"

"Certainly," she says warmly. "This isn't quite the time, though. Is there anything more immediate you need?"

"Well, the thing we would very much appreciate is a few Damei artifacts —say, a rug or throw for the parapet, a cushion or three, or a big mask or some unique large piece of sculpture. Is that too much? Needless to say, we would treat them with extreme care."

"No reason why not." Cory smiles and shouts up. "Oy, Kip!"

Kip appears above them on the roof, with the connector ends of a fat cable sprouting from his hand. Prince Pao's plumed cap bobs behind.

"This is all ready for you to wire in, Cor."

"Listen, while I'm hitching this monster up, could you go in our rooms and select a Damei rug and some other artifacts for Myr Zannez here? He needs local color for his scene. And the big Damei figure by the pool."

"Can do, Cor. If you'll just take this—"

"In a minim. . . . Just how serious was that other matter, Myr Zannez?"

Zannez hesitates, takes a deep breath. "Myr Cory, this may sound crazy, but I have hunches sometimes. Hunches of trouble. And they usually pan out. And right now I have one so strong I can't live with myself if I don't pass it on to a person in authority."

"Cor!" Kip shouts. "For pity's sake, let's get started—we can't keep the main input dead much longer."

"Righto," Cory shouts back. "Look, Myr Zannez, I do want to hear what you have to say, and I promise you I take such things seriously. I'll make time to listen fully. But right now, as you can see, isn't it."

"Cor!!"

She turns away and goes to the roof edge below Kip.

Well, Zannez thinks to himself, what more can I ask?

"Thank you, Myr Cory, thank you very much. But please—don't wait too long."

He has no idea whether she's heard him or not. She catches the connectors and becomes absorbed in wiring them into the old console. To occupy himself while he waits for Kip and the artifacts, Zannez starts chalking off the positions and distances and permanent camera sites he's visualized. The light is changing around him as the sun drops. There will probably be quite a sunset.

Little Doctor Ochter has come out and is watching him. As he finishes, Zannez recalls another question that's been bothering him.

"Look, Doc, if this front is coming on at the speed of light, how can we get messages about it? Wouldn't any messages simply trail behind? They can't stake c-skip transmitters out there—or do they? My boy Ek studies these things a little and told me to ask."

"Yes, it is quite a trick, isn't it?" the little man says. "Of course you realize I'm no astrophysicist, but the way it was explained to me is that they use what we used to call tachyon effects for a sort of leapfrog between ships or stations along the route. Maybe starting with the original ship that did the damage—Kip tells me you'll get the whole story of that when we're assembled in the bar. I do know it's very expensive and used only for special nova-fronts and the like."

"Tachyons," Zannez repeats. "That satisfies me—I wouldn't be able to follow a really scientific explanation anyhow. Our audience will be perfectly satisfied with the tachyons. Just give 'em one sciency-sounding word they've heard before and they're happy."

At this moment the main lounge doors open and Kip comes out. Over his shoulder is a load of elegantly colored leafy fabrics and other mysterious objects, while held in both hands before him is a two-meter-tall figure of a Damei, in pale carved wood.

"Oh, lords—gorgeous!" Zannez breathes. "I never expected—"

"Cor said local color, local color you get," said Kip. "Just no spilling or breaking, on pain of murder."

"Suicide," Zannez corrects him. "Look, one of my boys—Snake—has real artistic talent. May we lay this stuff down carefully while I go rout him out? It's time I raised the kids, anyway."

He takes a deep breath. "But listen, Myr Kip—I've got trouble. Our camera work, see—it's well, in the nude, and more—*much* more. To be blunt, one take may be used for a porn show. Pornography. Those are my orders. But I most sincerely do not want to offend. You all and this place are a long, long way from Gridworld and I appreciate every light-minim of it. So, I'm squeezed. The only thing I can think of is screens. Screens and more screens to go right here, between the kids and the rest of you. It doesn't matter if people see me and the cameras, does it? What do you say?"

"Cor and I are ahead of you," Kip tells him, momentarily sober. "We got the picture fast. She decided that since you're taking all the measures you can for privacy, no one should get spooked. I agree. After all, it's your work, it's not as if it's personally directed in any way."

"And the screens?" Zannez is vastly relieved.

"Can do. We built some when the Dameii were in here."

They pile the beauty gently by the parapet, and Zannez goes off to their rooms, leaving the Korsos immersed in the innards of the console.

He finds the four awake and in an odd mood.

Not sullen or snappish or sick: simply . . . odd; a mood Zannez hasn't seen before. Can it be the same reality trauma that affects him?

"By any chance is the realie-realie of all this getting to you kids?" he asks. "It's different from anything we've met, you know. I've been fighting off strange feelings all afternoon. A real Star is heading for us, all these people and events are real and never heard of us and show world. It makes me feel a bit shivvo."

"We know what you mean, Zannez," Stareem tells him in her sweet nonacting tones. "Thanks for trying to help."

"There's another reality, too." Snake's chuckle is not quite lighthearted. "An even simpler one."

"What is it?"

"Later, later," Snake says calmly. "We have days here, you know. And I bet you've got some work for us right now."

"And isn't it suppertime *yet?*" Hanny Ek demands. "These thirty-hour days are killers."

"As a matter of fact," Zannez tells them, "I have our stations all marked right outside here and Myr Kip brought us a load of the most gorgeous Damei artifacts you ever saw when I asked for local color. I want you and Snake to arrange them as background in our bay. Of course they're much too delicate to sit or lie on. If you girls could select and bring out a batch of ordinary neutral-colored blankets and pillows, I'd be very grateful. They say the night temperatures don't change much, if at all."

"And food!" says Hannibal. "You're forgetting food!"

"Well, the way I understand it, shortly we all go in the bar and have hot snacks and drinks while Kip tells us the story of the Star. Then we take our main course out to the deck and watch the Star rise. So if you can hold out long enough to get that stuff arranged, we ought not to lose you to starvation. Green? . . . Green! So, on with the clothes we planned, and let's go! . . . I'm supposed to be your doctor, by the way, watching to see you don't get cooked. And I'm going to wear a monocle, cursitall. I always wanted to."

That gets a nice natural laugh and they all start piling into costumes and the special body makeup jobs required by night lights.

As he dresses, Zannez berates his brain, trying to decipher Snake's "Later, later," and "a simpler reality." *Sixth sense, where are you when I really need you?* Nowhere, it seems.

Miraculously, the monocle stays in place above his absurd fake-doctor whites, and they all issue, laughing, to arrange their bay. Snake and Ek are fascinated when they see the Damei things, which have already attracted bystanders.

"Priceless. Don't even breathe on them."

"We'll arrange it as background and then put Star's and Bridey's stuff down to use." Ek even forgets his famine as he delicately handles the bronze-and-turquoise tissues, the two great pinion fans.

"It's made with their own plumage!" Bridey exclaims over a superb green-blue mat.

"Yes. Maybe it has some religious significance. Kip didn't tell us anything about that. For the worlds' sake, Snake take care. . . . Funny, I sense something sad, about them. Does anybody else?"

"Unh'm?" Brows knit in perplexity. "Maybe it's because we know the story," says Stareem.

"Better we not know more," says Bridey practically.

"Kippo brought the screens I asked for." Zannez points. "We have to rig 'em to hold. You all recollect what I told you about the Code here?"

A chorus of assent, quite different from the knowing grins that greeted his first warning, back at the staging-in.

They're feeling plenty uneasy about the whole thing, Zannez sees.

Looking for something to cheer them, he sees that the red-haired officer-girl is among those who've come to watch. The onlookers all seem impressed by the artifacts; even Vovoka inspects them thoughtfully. Yule visibly restrains himself from remarking on their potential price.

Zannez addresses Linnix.

"Look at this lady's hair, Snako," he exclaims. "Now *that's* the color you should have! Myr . . . ah, Linnix, if young Smith here asked you very nicely, do you think you could tell him your numbers? After all, you're literally worlds apart, you couldn't conflict."

"Numbers?" Linnix asks blankly.

"Numbers—brand grades. Yours'd be just perfect for Snake here. You can see he has a problem, with that dead-mouse-nothing color."

"Oh, if you only could, Myr Linnix. . . ." Snake has approached her—but it's a different Snake, all slouch and slyness gone, his face alight with half-humorous boyish appeal and frank admiration of her as a woman. "I'd never tell one soul, depend on it."

Linnix is torn between suppressing laughter and fascination with Snake's new persona. This is what actors know how to do, she thinks. A pro. If she knew what "numbers" were, she'd give them to him instantly.

"I haven't any idea what you're talking about, Myr Zannez—I've never heard of numbers."

The appeal in the boy's face increases a couple of watts, trembles between disbelief and disappointment. Linnix feels as if she's kicked a puppy.

"I *am* so sorry, if it would have helped you. But this is just what I was born with."

"Natural!" Zannez almost spits the word. "It would be. And the funny thing is, Myr Linnix, I believe you. Well, take a good look anyway, Snako, notice that blue-bronze glow in the shadows, and no brass anywhere. That's one of the greatest hair effects we'll ever see."

"I guess I'm supposed to say thank you"—Linnix laughs—"but the way you put it I feel I should apologize."

"Not to worry," Zannez tells her. "I wonder where Myr Cory has got to? Her electronics work looks to be all set up." He strolls over to the aged console. The Federation appears to be conserving credits on this aspect of Damiem.

"She's up here in my observatory," comes Prince Pao's voice from overhead.

Startled, they all look up to see the boy's face grinning down at them from the overhang. "And Myr Kip is behind the bar, preparing to serve food."

"Hear, hear!" says Hanny Ek.

"Prince!" It's Cory's voice. "Do please come back in!"

The head withdraws, after saying severely to Stareem, "Myr Star, your vest is fastened crooked."

Star refastens the vest, laughing. "My little guardian. Zannie, you have to admit it was dear of him to come all this way."

Zannez is still frowning over the computer.

"Shameful." He shakes his head. "Do you children realize how many takes we've made of the wise old scientist or the merry brain-boys, routinely punching out messages or calling for help on machines like this? All very convincing. And yet could any of us actually do the simplest thing with a real one? Could you send an alarm, say, or an SOS? Ek, you studied something along these lines. Could you message the Patrol with this thing? Or read radiation danger signals?"

Hanny Ek looks it over dubiously. "Well, given time—a lot of time—I think I might convey that something had gone wrong. At least that the regular operator was missing."

Laughter.

"You might as well know the truth," says Zannez. "As to Herr Doktor Zannezky—if you come to me saying the place is invaded and everybody's dying of plague, all you'll get is sympathy. *I can't even turn the cursed thing on.*"

Amid the laughter, a thin yellowish hand slides out onto the console board, clicks a tumbler, and at once several dials and a small readout screen flickers to life.

"Those are the status reports from several distances before and behind the front," Hiner, the Aquaman, informs them in a nasal voice. A high-collared vest covers his gill area.

"But they're compressed from the main readouts upstairs, you have to analyze—"

"Who did that?"

Kip is at the doorway, his hair literally on end with rage and a great boning knife in his hand. His glare lights on Hiner.

"Turn that off, you godlost fool, before I gut you! *My mate is working on those relays.* Do you know how close you just came to murder? What are you, some kind of defective? Don't you know that one never—*never*—"

"It's all right, darling." A cool voice from the roof above cuts through Kip's fury. Cory is standing on the thatch. "Luckily no damage is done. Myr Hiner was seen approaching the panel, and I suspected he might not understand the potential of in-air wiring. What Myr Korso was saying to you, young man, is that on land it is taken for granted that you never, never touch—let alone turn on—other people's electrical or mechanical equipment, without their explicit instructions. Perhaps this is a useful thing for you to learn here and now—for example, Myr Zannez' valuable cameras with their irreplaceable recordings are left unattended because of the force of this unwritten law. And of course it applies doubly to the infirmary, and even in the kitchen. And if you are ever in a home with an open fire, remember the old joke: It is safer to poke a man's mate than to poke his fire. Now do you understand?"

The little speech has its effect; Kip has gone back in the lounge, and everyone has moved away from the console. To Cory's question Hiner says quite civilly, "Yes, ma'am, I do. My apologies."

Cory vanishes from view as she scrambles back up the thatch to the cupola window she popped out of.

Hanno Ek restores normalcy, closing menacingly on Zannez. "Food, Zannez," he growls. "Food!"

"Hold it, Hanno, we want to make our entrance."

Stareem, watching by the open lounge doors, reports that the Lady Pardalianches is coming in, followed by Doctor Baramji from his infirmary.

Ochter, Hiner, and Yule take a final glance at the sky, which is showing the start of a normal, if very beautiful, sunset, and saunter into the lounge. Far down the deck a lone figure stands by the parapet, face turned up to the sky, apparently oblivious of all else.

"Oh, stars," Linnix says, "it's Ser Vovoka. I better go get him."

Kip calls from within. "I've saved the door end of the bar for you and your group, Myr Zannez. Just beyond where the Lady's rollbed can park. Then I tell the story from here, as if I were talking to you alone."

"Wait one minim," says Doctor Ochter. "Admirable as Myr Zannez' work is, he is not the sole guest. We all wish to hear and see."

"And you will," Kip assures him. "See, I stand here and talk sort of to the middle, including you all. I thought Zannez can get the privacy effect with a camera down here. They have their backs to the open doors, sunset,

Star-rise, et cetera. They don't see it, but you're looking directly out and see everything. How's that, Myr Zannez? Frankly, I'm rather proud of it."

"Done like a pro," says Zannez. "Well, I see Myr Linnix has lured Vovoka toward the food. Snake, Hanno, your effect here couldn't be finer. Time for us to form up and go in."

For the millionth time he triggers the magic whereby a formless group coalesces into two so-natural looking couples, pointing out to each other the attractiveness of the lounge, the heavy radiation shielding overhead, the beautiful local wood of the bar and the delicious food odors coming from behind it, plus Kip's forthcoming story of the Star, while "Doctor" Zannez puts in a word about the necessity of food after long cold-sleep— all so plausible, yet so far from actuality.

Zannez muses often on the paradox: Skillful falsehood is what it takes to make a true-seeming documentary. Just as the kids' almost grotesque thinness is what it takes to make a beautiful body on the screen.

As they gain their places, he notices that Ser Vovoka, at the far end of the bar, is still gazing eastward through the vitrex. That's where the Star will rise. When they end the sequence, Zannez looks back outside and sees the light has changed slightly; a cold pink luminescence is now coming from the east.

That thing really is coming, he tells himself. Well, the crowd here is attending expectantly only to Kip's doings with the food. It has to be all right.

Just as Kip starts lifting servers off the heat-shelf, everyone is again startled by little Prince Pao, who comes rocketing down into the lounge astride the helical stair rail. He alights with an only slightly wobbly bow and addresses Kip.

"Myr Cory will join you shortly. She is still with her machines. She asks that you hold the story till she comes."

"Righto," says Kip. "We'll hold."

"Story, yes; food, no," Hanny Ek tells him.

"Here you are, Myrrin." Kip begins producing the hot servers. "Puffs of local lake life, cheese from a Damei herbivore we're domesticating, good old Galactic iron sausage. This is appetizers, main course to follow. . . . Myr Ek"—he grins as Hanny starts wolfing—"there really is a main course coming."

"Don't worry," Snake assures him. "He's unfillable."

"I hope it's all as good as this!" Young Pao has a snack in each hand.

General murmurs of assent from all but Vovoka and the Lady Pardalianches, who is looking restlessly about. She is now clad in a glittering mist of lavender. Doctor Baramji has courteously taken a place beside her, but the Lady's attention strays. Suddenly she leans across Baramji to place jeweled fingers on Vovoka's arm.

"Oh, Ser Vovoka, my poor sister—she's all alone, and that bed is so heavy! Could you possibly help me bring her here? It will only take a tiny moment."

The tall artist merely glances down at the hand and silently resumes his gaze eastward. His plate is untouched.

"Well!" says the Lady helplessly. Linnix has automatically risen at her plea and is moving to the door, but the marquise's imploring gaze passes over her.

"Oh, Myr Zannez—"

But Zannez is shaking his head. "I'd be glad to help you, Lady P., but I never leave the cameras. The first rule of documentaries."

"Oh, but surely just for a minim—and there's a reward, too." The Lady's voice drips myrrh. "Wouldn't you like to see my sister? She's very beautiful. We are—were—identical twins, you know."

"Dear lady, I do appreciate the honor . . ." Zannez bethinks himself of an old Gridworld ploy. "But if I may be candid, it's no good wasting beauty on me." He pauses theatrically. "I was one of the damn-fool cameramen who went to the planet Thumnor in mating season. Three mortal weeks. Someone else—perhaps Officer Linnix there—can tell you what *that* means."

His tone is final, his gaze tragic.

"I'll help you," says Linnix from the door, "if it really is only a few minim."

"Thank you so much." The Lady's coo has gone. "But whatever did he mean about Thumnor?" she asks Linnix as they pass from sight.

"Is it really true about Thumnor?" the girl Bridey, or Eleganza, asks Kip. "Or is our Zannie just faking out Lady P.?"

"We can't believe a word he says." Stareem giggles. "*You* tell us, Myr Kip."

But before Kip can answer, Zannez has an idea.

"Speaking of cameras, Kippo, d'you think Myr Cory would mind if I snuck up and caught a nice take of her in this glorious light, surrounded with all her high-tech doodads and backed by the views up there?"

And I can lay this cursed Yule-Hiner hunch on her in privacy, he says to himself. "I don't want to anger her for the worlds," he adds aloud.

"I don't see why not," Kip's saying. "Sounds great. The worst that can happen is that she throws you out—but it wouldn't anger her, no."

He goes to the foot of the stairs.

"Honey, can Zannez come up and take a shot or two?"

"Come ahead!" The voice sounds lighthearted.

Zannez has snatched up a double-range hand camera and is leaping up the circular flights. As he passes from hearing, he hears Ser Vovoka saying in apparent approval, "The light of Damiem makes all things beautiful beyond their counterparts on other worlds. Do not feel too secure."

VII

NOVA MINUS 5 HOURS:
Cory's Wiring

Cory Korso, alone again in the rooftop cupola, after Zannez has come and gone, allows her deep happiness to rise.

She has put it aside to listen to Zannez, she has postponed it to get her relay wiring done—the task was to lay in readout and communication links down to the old computer console on the deck—and now Cory wants a few minim simply to enjoy.

She sits cleaning solder paste from her abused fingernails, listening with pleasure to the rising conviviality from the bar below and looking with critical satisfaction at her newly made relays. The cupola, which had started as a mere observatory and transceiver housing, is now their main computer facility as well. With its array of antennae outside, including the vacuum-cased c-skip sender, it is a compact, sophisticated little center, rivaling that on many FedBases.

Inconvenient, of course—she's had to run a panel of alarms to their bed —but with the eight great windows circling sky and world, a tour of duty up here is pure pleasure. There aren't many such tours—watching for a lost ship, tracking a bit of space debris, mapping the Damiem borders of a meteor swarm, taking the periodic all-modes record of her allotted segment of space—simple outpost routine; but always spiced by the threat that someday some mythical evildoers may have Damiem in their sights.

Just now the sunset is flooding the cupola and the world with golden light, along with which she can feel a little tension. The tension, she believes, is caused by the rapidly fluctuating ion count, one of the normal precursors of the oncoming Star.

Or it may be personal to her, because this sunset is special. It marks the last night that the Star will dominate Damiem's sky. The Star has always oppressed Cory, though she can't imagine why something so beautiful should cast a shadow on her happiness here with Kip. Yet it has, though she's never spoken of it. Perhaps the shadow is because it's always *there*, she thinks; always coming at us. When one shell finally passed, there was always another behind, ready to loom up at them.

But this is the very end. Every instrument, including the drone that FedBase sent through the Star-front for her, tells the same thing. Beyond this last shell is nothing. No core, only empty space. By this time tomorrow the last of the Star will have forever gone by, to expand, attenuate, and dissipate away among the lights of the Galaxy.

I hope so, some superstitious imp of her mind whispers. Jeering at the imp, she straightens up, takes a couple of deep breaths of Damiem's sweet air, and puts the nail file away. Stop dreaming, and final-check those connections!

But what about that premonition, or whatever it was, that the funny bald cameraman—Zannez—told her about so solemnly? Trouble, he said, from those unlisted, uncleared two, Yule and Hiner, who might be in league with Vovoka, or, of all people, little Doctor Ochter. And that *she* should decide how seriously to take him. . . . Lords, she thinks, how can I? For all she knows, Gridworld is full of mad psychics.

As to Hiner and Yule, she certainly agrees—she expects nothing but nuisance from them the whole time. But real trouble—like a Stars Tears attack—is hard even to consider seriously. In the first place, if they want to take us by surprise, why be so outstandingly obnoxious that we're watching them every minim?

And that absentminded Vovoka and poor little lame Ochter do seem very unlikely confederates.

But Zannez was so earnest. He meant Trouble, capital T. . . . Could it be that he's very sensitive to the ion fluctuation? In any event, she thinks, for Trouble, capital T, we always have Mayday. Or, wait, no we don't, at the moment. I let Kip lend the main circuit chip to Captain Dayan for *Rimshot* until his refit next month. Bother.

Well, she has something almost as good. She looks with approval at the Deadman's Alarm she's constructed and wired down to the deck console. If it isn't reset periodically, it will blast off a pretaped SOS to *Rimshot* and Base. Of course it doesn't have its own subsurface 360-degree antenna or remote multitriggering like Mayday, but the chance of anybody bothering to knock out the regular antennae when no one is near the console seems slight. Pace Norbert, the previous Guardian, had said the Korsos weren't paranoid enough. She hopes this will satisfy him; it was a lot of work.

As she reflects, the possibility of scrambling a battle cruiser to a false alarm makes her wince. And what if it needs to be reset just when something major's going on? Isn't this just a mite *too* paranoid?

She ponders while she double-checks her other relays. . . . All green. Then, back at the Deadman's Alarm, she inspects the solder with a stress-scope. Imagine Dayan's reaction to being summoned to a faulty solder job! Then, on impulse, she doubles the safety wait lapse so she couldn't possibly miss if it came at an awkward time. Good.

She casts a final look at the battery of readouts from the drone. Still no indications of any danger ahead. All green, go.

Her last job is fun. She picks up a bag of sweetener and swings featly out of the big window where the cable exits, into the full sunset blaze. It's getting rosy, she should hurry. But she allows herself a minim just to look.

Beautiful, beautiful . . . the far shore's like fire, against it the near point is velvet black. And down in the bar below Kip has put on some Damei music. Oh, my. . . . The guests are getting their trip's worth of sunset.

But that isn't what they came for. Cory cranes her neck to stare straight up. Yes; against a few high wisps of cirrus she can just make out a faint quiver, a not-quite-imaginary shimmer of bluish light. That's from the Star; it's really coming.

Dropping to her knees on the thatch, she scrambles down to where the cable runs over the eaves and backs up along it, scattering sweetener. Sure enough, she passes some rinds of tree spores; Damiem's wildlife has already been investigating her cable. They hate sweet, which is why she's dusting it, to keep their sharp little pincers from the cable.

As she dusts, she sighs—she'd love to make a pet of one of the big, playful green arachnoids. She's sure it would tame well. But that's against policy—what would happen to it if she and Kip left? The Dameii view them all as vermin.

She sits on the sill to swing back in, bare legs gleaming, and catches a look at the laundry line across the deck that Zannez and Kip have erected. From here she can see the far side, with an arrangement of mattresses and pillows that sends her eyebrows up as she tries not to picture what will go on there. Unbeknown to her, the tip of her pink tongue steals out and delicately wets her lip. Gridworld! She suddenly recalls the marvelous flask of perfume little Prince Pao gave her; she pivots inside and finds it on the computer printout. It proves hard to open, but she persists.

While she's at it, Kip's baritone rises from below, promising to tell them all the story of the Murdered Star. A shadow crosses Cory's face. *This time, just this one time, let him tell it straight,* she prays to fate.

But she isn't hopeful.

It's Kip's weakness, known to all their friends, that he can rarely tell a story without implying that he's been there or was in some way part of it. He never actually lies, only hints and makes artful "slips" that are all too convincing.

Their friends try to tell her it's funny.

"Look, Myr Cory," an ex-gunner said one night at a reunion party, "Kip's the genuine beast. Don't take his yarning to heart. Does he ever talk about his own space days?"

"No! I caught him throwing out a box of medals. I saved them, I could see they're his. But when I ask him what they're for, he won't say. 'Oh, just the sort of thing that happens,' " she mimicked.

"That's Kipper," an ex-navigator said with a grin.

"Well," said the ex-gunner slowly, "I can tell you about the VS. That's the big green one—Valorous Service. . . . We were out in an antique REB, no armor retrofit to mention, and we got rocked up by a booger in a fake satellite.

"Everybody got it, and the boat was leaking air enough to move her. I remember Kip was sluicing blood down both legs. And he was better off than most—we all looked bloody dead. See my homemade ear?" He ducked his head. "I always thought the hair they put on that side came from a hamster."

Even in the party lights Cory could see the scars of massive reconstruction. He must have been a boy then, lying in a puddle of blood with a smashed head and who knew what else. "Gods, Myr Kenter."

The gunner grinned wryly. "The gods were out to lunch that year. Or maybe they weren't. Anyhoo, Kip should have used his escape pod, express to Base. No one else had a chance. And the water unit was smashed. . . . He flew that stinking REB home using the belts as tourniquets. Six days, no water and less air. Which is why I'm here, plus two others." He was looking past Cory.

"Janny and Pete died on the way, with him giving them the last water. Saro went in Base Hospice. . . . Kip was about seventeen then, I found out later. Looked older. He didn't give a—*that,* for the VS. . . . See now why we don't take his tales too serious?"

Cory was pale. "Oh, my. . . . But why, Mr. Kenter?" she persisted. "Why *does* he?"

The navigator spoke up reflectively.

"I guess the thing is, aliens, Myr Cory. You'll notice it mostly concerns aliens. Kip never had much but Human stuff. But if somebody mixes it with other races, that strikes him as really worthwhile. Alien adventure! He craves it. That's why he went for xenology. Strange karma; the real thing is always somewhere else, for Kipper."

But all their efforts to make her take it lightly failed. Kip's habit shames and alarms her, as if it might draw some evil on him.

Now, as she pries at the gold-sealed flask and frets by habit, the light of the Star's passing shines suddenly through her mind. Kenter's image of Kip comes to her—a wounded seventeen-year-old, parched and poisoned, getting his comrades home, all that agonizing time—when at any moment he could have gotten in his pod and with no blame at all gone home free. . . . That was reality; it happened. By what right does she judge Kip now?

What had she done in the wartime, anyway? Mostly sat in Rehab, checking quartermasters' supply lists and having her brain washed. Presumably because something horrible happened to her family, she'd always thought. The Mem/E people never tell you what they erase, but most people were there because of atrocities happening to someone. While Kip was having a pretty fair atrocity happen to *him.*

Only Kenter and his friends had the right to judge Kip. And they'd told her what to think. And by the gods, she *will,* now.

She may not love his habit, but she loves and respects Kip, and she won't be such a rigid rat's ass—and look out, you're cutting through this lovely bottle.

Cory heaves a long, relieved breath, dusts herself off energetically, and opens the perfume. The scent of *mugets* fills the cupola. Oh, just right! Kip'll love it. So long since I had any, she thinks, dabbing it lavishly on her hairline and inside her shirt. She glances in the small utility mirror and sees a glowing Cory—with her hair full of thatch. Hastily she roots out a comb and wields it.

The artist-man, Vovoka, had told her this morning that Damiem had a particularly flattering light. No, *peculiarly.* Good for me, she thinks, peculiar or what, we can't let those Gridworld kids take it all. And remember to thank Prince Pao.

Time to go down. Close up shop.

As she passes Pao's cot she sees his personal things neatly laid out on a chair alongside. Cologne, comb, toothcare, sponge bag, hankie, book— *Rim Stars.* Tidy as a little Spacer, even if the implements look like solid gold. She clicks on a night-light for him and starts down the small spiral stairs.

The colorful group around the bar comes in sight, and Cory's own glow intensifies. It's really pleasant to have company again, despite that wretched student, Yule, and the unpleasant Aquaman, Hiner.

A large draped and gilded object is just swaying through the arcade door opposite—the rollbed, escorted by the marquise and propelled by Officer Linnix. Cory pauses to watch.

"Oh, please!" The Lady sounds excited. "Please place her here where the Star-light will shine on her! That wonderful pink light *is* from your Star, is it not, Myr Kip?"

"Yes indeedio! Looks brighter than last time, too." Cory silently agrees. "And that's only the forerunner."

The rollbed placed to her satisfaction, the Lady tenderly—and not un-dramatically—draws open its drapes.

All heads turn to see. Involuntary exclamations; Cory herself gasps.

Lying on embroidered pillows is a very lovely dark-haired young girl—or what appears to be a young girl, smiling faintly in her sleep. A great, loose, lustrous braid of dark hair reaches to her knees. She's clad in a lacy, long-sleeved nightdress with gold ribbons, a golden lace cap on her curls and little velvet slippers on her feet. No hint of tubes or wiring, all the intricate machinery that must be sustaining her life, can be seen. Only—the slipper soles are creamy, pristine. *Twenty years? . . .* Cory shudders.

She bats the thought away from her and comes on down, favoring every-one with her jolly all-purpose smile. As she passes Zannez to go behind the bar, the cameraman repeats his thanks for their session in the cupola. "But I still want a more formal sequence of you, ma'am, at your administrative duties."

"My administrative duties?" She laughs. "Turn your cameras away for a minim, here goes one of them."

Next instant only her shapely rear is visible as she burrows deep under the bar. She comes up with two big dusty guest bottles. "Excellent whis-key, I'm told. A Spacer brought it from Highlands. I better get out some *laangua* and gin, too." Another dive into the bar storage. "Here you are, Kippo," she calls. "We have one more whiskey and two *laangua*, but that's all the gin."

"Can you pour, honey?" Kip is scraping ferociously. "I'm cleaning up; those puffs blogged all over the heat-shelf. . . . We have to fix a bigger one."

"Right." She takes the bottles down to Ochter's end of the bar where the ice and glasses live. "Gin, whiskey, or *laangua*, Myrrin? I fear water is our only mix. And you've all had at least five appetizers, I trust. Doctor Hiner? Myr Yule? Ser Vovoka?"

Yule is leaning toward her with an earnest, open expression he hasn't shown before.

"Myr Cory, ma'am, I'm really sorry I blew my shoes like that this morning. On top of putting you folks to a lot of trouble. Doc here—"

Cory intercepts an approving look from Ochter. Aha, so there'd been a lecture.

"Doc says I'm lucky I don't remember half all I said. My sincere regrets, all, and special to Officer Linnix, ma'am. I sure remember the Dameii, though. Wouldn't have missed that for the worlds. This place is marvelous."

He gives himself a mock blow on his yellow head, a very changed young man. "Beastly embarrassing."

"Handsomely said!" Kip bows acceptance, flourishing his scourer, as Hiner leans forward, obviously with the same intent. "Pour 'em a toast, Cor."

Cory beams as this last blot on the evening's happiness removes itself. The ghost of her former reasoning brushes her mind but has no power; more pressing is a threatened shortage of ice.

"Mordecai spoke for me, too," says the Aquaman.

His narrow face now looks appealingly aquiline, almost poetic above the immaculate flowing white collar. Only the tips of white lines under his ears show where his once angry gills lie. "And I believe my profound personal apologies are due Officer Linnix. Doctor Ochter has told me that ships sometimes exchange whole sets of destination shots when they switch to an unusual run like this, and it's easy to see how a mix of labels—or expiration dates—could eventually occur. I must say I felt quite ill for a time, and I know Mordy did, too. Most deeply, deeply sorry, all. And most sincere thanks for any help you care to give in getting us where we belong."

"Goodness—the things we don't know about ships!" Cory chuckles warmly. "It must have been absolutely wretched for you. Do have a cheering drink. Whiskey, both? I'm afraid we're a little skimpy on ice. . . . Now, Ser Vovoka, won't you take something? Ser Vovoka! Ser Vovoka, *please.* That Star can't rise for two hours, honor bright."

The sculptor finally turns his gaze from the vitrex long enough to select the popular alien *laangua.* As Cory is pouring, Prince Pao bobs up on the seat alongside Ochter.

"Myr Cory, Doctor Baramji advises me to ask you about the time-flurries. I've never heard of them! What are they, please? Shall we get one tonight? Do all nova-fronts have them? How long do they last? How far do they extend in space and time?" His cap is under his arm, its gold feathers bouncing with excitement.

Cory grins at him. "Prince, if you'll just let me finish serving the Lady and Zannez' group while I compose my thoughts, I'll tell you all I know—but don't be disappointed, because that isn't much."

"Oh, forgive me. Certainly . . . I await you back there." He goes off to his place by Zannez, cheese puff in hand.

Cory gets them all poured. The Lady turns out to have her own gold-chased flask, from which comes a fragrant light liqueur utterly unknown to Cory; she takes only ice.

Zannez is keen to record Cory's time-flurry explanation, and the problem of keeping the prince out of his frames is acute. When they're finally settled, Cory begins.

"As to what time-flurries are, no one really knows. There're a number of theories; the one I like best is that a local concentration of positrons is so dense it gives a brief ambient regress. Nor does anyone know whether they form and dissolve on the spot, or appear that way because they're passing you. Subjectively—here you are, Myr Ek—what you feel, if you're in the open—shielding stops them—is a kind of murkiness; and you see a running backward of things that have just happened. But it's all very confused. In the one Kip and I experienced, there was one clear minim where the Dameii repeated what they'd recently said, like replaying a scene. But we felt all stiff. *Gluey* is the best word I can find. And alone. And then things start forward again, but all mixed up and shadowy, very fast—and you're suddenly in real time again. The whole thing only lasted a few breaths, and we don't think it took up actual time."

"But could you move?" Pao demands. "Could you *change the past?*"

Cory laughs. "We never tried. It's so short, and so confused—and as I said, one feels odd. Static."

"But if you'd intended to, you *could* have moved?" the lad persists. "Oh, how I'd love to experience one! *I'd* try to move something!"

"If you get a chance, I'd appreciate it if you'd move these cursed cheese puffs." Kip laughs, shaking off the scraper. "All right, honey, you sit down. I'll take over."

Cory takes her drink around to sit by Vovoka. She's followed by Pao.

"Do you think we'll get one tonight?" the boy asks.

"No way to tell. But if you're really interested, make sure you stay out from under the antirad roofing, otherwise you won't even know one's been by. Doctor Baram was looking straight at us and never noticed a thing."

"Oh, I shall, indeed. . . . But tell me, there must be more, elsewhere, aren't there?"

Cory, tired, looks around for help, and Doctor Ochter catches her appeal. "There are said to be some in the remains of antique Earth's moon," he tells Pao. "And there's a large one, or a succession of them, in the Crab

Nebula; they're considered a danger to shipping. And I believe some have been reported near Orionis M–forty-two. But—"

"You have left out the most important feature." Vovoka's deep voice suddenly startles everyone. "Concentration of positrons, indeed. . . . But what could cause such an anomaly? Young man, you will find, in every case, that an astral-scale body has been suddenly—instantaneously—destroyed, vaporized, by some *totally unforeseeable outside event*—as in the acts of war that annihilated so many planets and suns. It is perhaps not too biomorphic to say that the formerly organized matter does not yet 'believe' in its disorganization; that the shadowy persistence of its former state—its memory, if you like—is so strong it can distort the local time-flow. It generates turbulence in a backward direction, as though the debris strove to reassemble, to reexist in that last instant before the catastrophe, when perhaps it could have been averted. As to whether some form of life is also necessary . . ."

His voice has softened and roughened, his gaze is on some space beyond them all. As suddenly as he spoke, he sighs and falls silent.

There is a brief general silence. Cory, who was helping Kip cut the hard sausage, has paused, knife lifted. Just as she resumes, a small scream from the Lady Pardalianches almost makes her hand slip.

"She moved! My sister moved! And she's trying to tell me something—"

The Lady's at the rollbed. Cory sees Zannez swing his hand camera to follow, but no motion is visible in the still form.

Doctor Baramji is with them at once, inspecting the patient, soothing her sister. He produces two large blue pills. "Water, please, Kip. Hurry."

"Take these right now, dear lady. We don't want the feedback from your cap to injure your sister—or vice versa."

"But she moved! It's so *tense* here, she feels it. Something bad's bothering her. . . . What's this?"

"Swallow them quickly, lady dear. It's a cortical calmant cum buffer I prepared this evening, in case. I apologize for their size. My guess is that the transceivers in your electrode caps may be overloading. I want you to turn them down a bit, lest you or sister be harmed."

"Oh-h-h. . . ." She takes the pills.

"I'd also guess that we're receiving some unusual energies from the Star. Cor, what do your instruments say?"

Cory replies carefully, wanting to confirm him without alarming the others. "Unusual, yes, very. Dangerous, no. As of ten minim ago, prediction is we won't even need UV glasses. But the ion count is running wild; that's known to affect some electronics as well as people."

Baram nods. "And those electrode caps are extremely sensitive. My dear lady, I want you to let me turn both yours and hers as near to zero as they'll possibly go. The danger is that they might climb into a mutual condition of runaway forward feedback, oscillation, which would severely damage you both. May I?"

"Oh, my goodness." The Lady's chewing on her thumb but she's calming. "Yes, turn them way down, please. You can, can't you?"

"Yes." His hands move among her sable curls.

"The tension . . ." The Lady sighs. As Baramji turns to disconnect the silent child-woman in the bed, her sister cries out, "I don't want her to feel alone!"

"I doubt she will, my dear," Baram soothes. "To make sure, why don't you hold her hands tight for a while, or massage her neck and limbs, as you must have done so many times? That will tell her you're near. Now remember—you hoped the radiance of the Star might help her. Here we're in the realm of the totally unknown. No one can say. What if this tension is a sign of beneficial effect?"

"Oh, yes. . . ." The Lady takes up her sister's limp hand and begins tenderly to massage it. "Sometimes"—she sighs—"sometimes . . . I don't know. I've done this against advice. *Expert* advice." She laughs bitterly. "Was this such a good idea for her? What do you really truly think, Doctor Bram?"

Baramji has never shed the boyish habit of crossing his fingers when he tells a "white" lie. Now both Cory and Linnix see him cross them behind his back. Cory chuckles to herself; an endearing man.

"I really truly think it *might* affect her," he says. "Provided we can control it."

"Oh, thank you . . . thank you so very much, dear doctor."

Meanwhile Zannez has been glancing from the pink-lit vitrex to Kip and back.

"How about that story now, Kippo?" he demands. "We'll be needing to get outside pretty soon."

"You finished there, Doc?" Kip calls.

"Tell away." Baramji returns to the bar. "And do remember, all, those drinks of Myr Cory's will hit you twice as hard as usual."

Cory, scraping ice, asks Baram, "What was all that with m'lady in aid of?"

"Taking steps to pry her loose from that living corpse. But it would take more steps than I have to do the job, and gods know what you'd have at the end."

"Umm. She's going to miss the story, too. She mustn't. Go get her, Bram."

"I'll try. I'll tell her her sister should know it."

"Quick, before Zannez goes crit."

Baramji returns with the reluctant marquise, while Kip begins the tale.

"Of course it was long before your time, just after the Last War," Kip tells the young actors. "I was younger than you then, I'd lied about my age to get into uniform and on a ship. There was real A-one chaos going for a while as news of the end of the war spread. People getting in last shots, blowing up pacification teams, what have you. You had this old Class X cruiser, the *Deneb,* Captain Tom Jeager commanding, 'way out here on the Rim. We—I mean, they—never did get word of the peace."

At that "we," Cory Korso stares at her man through narrowed eyes—but her lips quirk in a smile.

"Well, *Deneb*'s recon had spotted a star system where someone seemed to be building a superweapon. The builders' planet was named Vlyracocha in the ephemeris, that was all they know. Captain Jeager and his science team worked up the data. The thing was loaded with ultrahigh-energy stuff, it could knock out a star system if it blew. Of course they weren't building it on the planet; they had it in a Trojan orbit behind a big asteroid they were using as a construction base. The thing was enormous. Here," he interrupts himself, "I'm forgetting your suppers. I figured a one-dish spread'd be best." He begins transferring filled and covered plates from storage to the heat-shelf.

"Six minim. Anybody wants more puffs meanwhile, they're over here, drinks on your right. . . . Well, this Captain Jeager we had—" Here Cory bumps his arm. He glances at her puzzledly.

"Jeager was an unreconstructed old Human Supremacist. He wasn't about to allow some group of aliens to complete a superweapon that could dominate a sector or maybe even, as Jeager said afterward, be sent right into the heart of the Federation. So he took *Deneb* out there and used his last planet-buster blowing up the so-called weapon. Lords of the worlds, what an explosion!

"And just for good measure, he sent a salvo of T-missiles at the planet Vlyracocha, and another one into their sun. Which shortly destabilized and blew, too. All that was dreadful enough, but it wasn't really the point. The worst thing—Here, Ser Vovoka, you've let your ice melt. Fix him up, Cor. And let me fresh you up too, Doctor Ochter. Zannez, are you trying to make abstainers out of those kids?"

He pours everyone's glass full before going on.

"The appalling thing came out later. A Federation Pacification squadron caught up with *Deneb* and took him and the whole crew into Rehab, and tried to salvage anything they could of Vlyracocha. D'you know they now have techniques for capturing energy patterns from a dead planet? But here—nothing.

"It turned out, incidentally, that the captain really was crazy; he'd been notified that the war was over and hadn't told anybody. All those poor little swabbies still thought they were fighting the good fight, dreaming of green *horropoi* coming down their bunks all night. Oh, gods! You'd have had to go through it to know." He exhales noisily, half laughing; definitely one who has been there.

Cory is staring past the pink-lit vitrex, smile gone. Tomorrow . . . She holds the thought.

"The point—the horrible point—was learned from the Federation," Kip goes on somberly. "Because there were a few Vlyracochans—diplomats, students, technicians—who had been off-planet when we—the Humans—*Deneb*, I mean—attacked.

"The Vlyracochans, you see, hadn't been building a weapon at all. Their race was very old, and they were dying. Some condition of cell fatigue no one anywhere could cure. So they'd decided, many lifetimes back, to leave a memorial—the most beautiful work of art they could conceive. And they built into it all their finest literature and music and their history and everything about their race. That was what all the energy was for, to keep it going to eternity. . . ." Kip shakes his head and looks down, unable to face the thought.

"And that was what we destroyed."

"Ohhh . . . oh *no!*" An indrawn breath from his audience as the full tragedy is realized. "Couldn't they . . ."

Kip shakes his head again, no. "Nothing the Federation had could bring more than a shred of it back. . . . I tell you, sometimes when I look up at the Star I literally can't take the thought of what I—I mean, my race—did. People call it the Shameful Star, you know."

There was a pause, and then Cory says, "You've left out the very end of the story, Kip."

He looks up, runs a hand through his hair, and blows out a breath. "Oh. Well, yes. . . . The story of Vlyracocha—that's one Humans never talk much about, any more than necessary. It wasn't just the shame, the Human crime. You can hear worse, maybe, on a smaller scale—take Damiem here. But Vlyracocha wasn't quite over, see.

"At first we called it coincidence. Some still do. The fact is, of all the crew on *Deneb*, not one was alive five years later. Jeager went first—an oxygen fire in his hospital room. There were fatal accidents in Rehab. Then the Federation used some as the crew of a survey boat, and it disappeared on its second trip. Others went in other ways. The Fed medicos said it was subconscious guilt and death-wish. A friend of ours—remember Marta Dubaun, Cor?—started looking into it. Marta died next year in a local *favana* epidemic, by the way. There's even been considerable mortality among the shell handlers who had originally loaded *Deneb*, before she left base. . . . There really were Vlyracochan survivors, see.

"No more, of course. Their sickness made them short-lived. But people still have the idea it's not a healthy thing to know about. *Deneb* herself was towed out and sent into a Lyra ninety sun."

Kip breaks off and opens the heat-shelf to peek in, releasing a delicious smell. Cory begins distributing forks and water glasses.

"One minim." Kip leans back, lifter in hand. "So you had three separate radiation shells from those terrific explosions, expanding out into space. The first one passed here—Vlyracocha was over thirty lights away—just when Cory and I came. That was partly what we came for, in fact. It had been determined that the nova-front contained a lot of nasty hard stuff, and it was our first job to help protect the Dameii. The previous Federation observer had been here for the simple purpose of keeping them safe from Stars Tears sadists—you've had *that*—and there were Patrol ships on call. This observer's tour of duty was about up, and he needed help getting them all to go under adequate cover when the Vlyracochan radiation came through.

"It was quite a job, I tell you—I mean, you pointed to this star that just looked a trifle fuzzy, and tried to convince them it was about to swell up and rain death all over them. They just laughed. But Cory was a marvel—believe me, being an Administrator is a lot more than brain work. I can still see you chasing that kid through the treetops, honey!"

Cory's smile at last comes back.

"Then came the night the first shell of radiation started to pass through us. By incredible luck the first layer was long wave lengths in the visible spectrum, harmless but spectacular. They showed the thing ten times its size and going mad. And we had such auroras—there wasn't any night. So the Dameii at last began to believe us.

"By the time the really hard radiation peaked we had shelters finished and the Dameii would go in them.

"That passed fast, and it shrank back to being just a big star. And all was calm for about five years. Then the second energy shell came through. We got ready—and scads of tourists came—but as someone said, it was mostly pretty lights.

"Now tonight sees the third and last act of the tragedy of Vlyracocha. The Base scientists haven't bothered getting such a detailed prediction. We've been told that anti-UV glasses will be enough. Probably they're right and we'll get no more than spectacular pretty lights. But some of us wonder; this front is from the core of the great work of art itself, which contained all the really exotic artificial energies, and just perhaps we may get some strange phenomena.

"Cory has stationed warning sensors out, and she got the Patrol to lay a monitor drone headed into the front. They're all rigged to readouts in the deck console. So if she says 'Take cover,' don't argue. Just scoot under the nearest roof. This lounge and the overhang out there have antirad shielding, they were built for the first wave. We had over two hundred Dameii in here alone, I was breathing feathers for a week. . . .

"And now—supper!"

He starts lifting out servers, uncovering each with a flourish as he sets them before the guests. Polite smiles answer him. But Cory sees his story has been all too daunting for many.

"Is this the only planet the Star can be seen from?" Linnix asks.

"Yes," says Cory. "By the time the fronts reach the next worlds they'll be too dissipated even to be seen as clear events."

"So Damiem is witness to two shames of mankind," Linnix says reflectively. "The Stars Tears horror and now this dreadful murder of Vlyracocha and all its people and works."

"Double Shame Star," Zannez says. "Almost a title."

"Oh, you showpeople!" Linnix is angry. "You see everything as titles or plots, or takes—"

"He didn't mean it that way," the girl Bridey, or Eleganza, speaks up. "That was just an automatic aside, it's stamped in us so. He feels the badness just as much as you do. If he has the technique to make a bigger public share it—isn't that worthwhile?"

"Hey, my little defender." Zannez grins. "I didn't know you cared." But his eyes don't smile.

Surprising them all, a few chords of music come from the girl Stareem's side. They see she has brought an odd little skeletal zither. "Lament for a Star," she says shyly, and plucks a brief minor theme.

"Bravo!" exclaims little Prince Pao, clapping his hands and looking around so peremptorily that Cory and others find themselves clapping, too. The small melody was really quite lovely. But the child—surely he *is* a child?—behaves like a grown man in love. Could the boy fancy it so? And what about Stareem's, ah, profession?

Abruptly the silent Vovoka stands up. "The light is changing," he announces in his stiff accent. "I go to the outside."

"I've been noticing that, too," Cory says. "Perhaps it's time." She leaves the bar and goes to throw the main doors wide before him. As she does so a feeling of finality comes to her—this will be the last, last time to open on the Star! . . . Radiance floods in.

"Ah!"

"Oh!"

"Ooh, Zannie, look!" The others come thronging through the doors in Vovoka's wake.

"Thank all the gods I had those sky cameras set up and running," says Zannez as they go out into the glory.

Only the Lady Pardalianches lingers, looking from the door to her sister to Kip.

"I'll wheel her out," Kip promises. "Just as soon as I fetch out the suppers you've all forgotten."

"Oh, thank you." The Lady bends to draw up a satin coverlet, to kiss the still brow and smooth the hair. "Doctor Baram turned our caps almost off, you know. I *never* do that. Oh, I hope I'm not abandoning her; it's the first time in ages she's been so alone."

"Won't be a minim. Scoot out and enjoy."

The Lady goes. Kip sets the servers onto a tray. "Cor, help me mark what's whose. Where are those marker thingies?"

"Coming."

As Cory leaves her view of the spectacular scene outside, she passes the giant crib where Lady—what is it, Paralomena?—lies. *Has lain, will lie,* Cory thinks, glancing in. The sleeper shows no sign of distress at being left alone. Alone? Cory wonders. Alone—or free? Can she really be suffering the lack of her sister's strange companionship?

As Cory gazes a very faint flicker stirs the quiet face, so fleeting that Cory isn't sure what she's seen. She looks hard. Isn't that hint of smile a bit stronger now? For the first time it comes to her that this still body might be more than a giant organic doll, might be truly alive. . . . What can it be like, reverberating hour by hour to the Lady Pardalianches's brain?

She hunts out the plastite markers, grimacing at the thought of what it would be, for her, to lie in thrall to that Lady's perceptions.

"Kippo." She sticks a "V" on Vovoka's untouched plate.

"M'love?"

"Just on a crazy hunch. . . . Don't hurry too fast bringing that poor thing out."

VIII

HOLDING:
Lady Loma's Ride

Reality is coming back at last, coming out of the strange star-studded mists, cutting through the bizarre and often embarrassingly sexual hazes that have gripped 'Lomena for so long. Real silences are breaking into the endless flow of Pardie's voice, which has gone on and on and on so incomprehensibly. An almost forgotten freedom is returning, severing the intimate hold of Pardie's limbs and body that have felt ever stronger and more vivid than her own. The reality of self is coming between her and Pardie's will and actions, which have been playing themselves out through Loma as instrument, while her own voice and body and mind receded to nowhere and nothing, as if her very hold on life were slipping, thinning away.

And all this Pardie-life has been so dreamlike. Like a true dream, she supposed in the beginning that only a minim or so might have passed in the real world. Yet as it has gone on becoming ever more complex, she has come to suspect that its real time was much longer. Hours, perhaps, or—she hasn't dared think more.

But now, sudden and exhilarating, she's waking! Coming back to life, feeling reality solidify, within and around her.

Reality is an immense vista of dark, blue-green, gently rolling moorland, stretching from horizon to horizon, a world kept smooth and parklike by her father's innumerable flecks of small herbivores. At the moment every leaf is shining from a recent shower. Over the shoulder arches one of the planet's perpetual rainbows, which have given it its name: Rainbow's End. This had been meant quite simply in early days, until the finding of the fantastic veins of diamond, zeranaveth, emerald, and gold put a double meaning to it.

And this real world is only background for a realer reality, which occupies a level stretch just before her: a high-fenced, oval extravaganza of eight-foot brick walls, white-and-scarlet pole structures, potted shrubs marking wide water ditches, great hedges behind gaudy panels—a mad construction which any fifteen-year-old horse-lover would instantly recognize as a replica of the official course for the Interplanetary Jump-Offs coming up a month hence.

The Lady Paralomena gazes upon this surreal object with love and fierceness, sniffing the fragrance of the moist tanbark that floors it. Then she turns, shading her eyes to see where the central reality of all approaches: her old groom Davey, on his old brown gelding, leading a gleaming silver creature who dances on a short lunge and cavesson.

He—it's very visibly a male—his full name is Silver Emperor Comet the Eighth. Eyes of another age might have been slow to recognize him as horseflesh. Some centuries earlier, jumpers had finally been freed from the tyranny of the running form, with its big barrel body and four all-purpose legs at the corners—"porkchops on the hoof," they had scornfully been called.

The ensuing effort to breed a perfect jumping machine has produced a creature that might be taken for a giant springbok with overtones of kangaroo; short-coupled, with flowing mane and tail and heavily muscled quarters. To the eyes of Davey and Paralomena, he is an animal needing only wings to go permanently airborne. Among the new strains is a half-expressed albino gene; the Comets have always been silver-coated, with dark eyes and points.

His full silver tail—a functional feature in jumpers—swirls around her as they came alongside.

"I don't know, Lady 'Loma." Davey sighs, reluctantly handing over the lunge. She's afoot, having walked out to meet them, and Comet's saddle is above her head. "A young lass like you, if you'll pardon me, m'lady, riding an entire. And them's some awful tall fences there."

"Oh, entires like lasses, don't you, Mischief?"

Two velvety pink noses caress each other.

"You aren't seriously suggesting that I have the best Comet of the crop gelded, are you, Davey?"

"Oh, no, ma'am!" Davey blushes to his ears. "That'd be a crime! It's just that, begging your pardon—"

"Begging my pardon for the thousandth time, what you mean is that I should have some boy—say, Gemmy—show him, eh? To which I say for the thousandth-and-first time, begging *your* pardon, No! This is my horse, I've trained him and jumped him every show of his life, and the subject is now closed."

"Yes, ma'am—Ah, look out!"

The huge stallion, neglected while they argued, is rearing and threatening to come down on her with all-too-obvious intent.

Paralomena dodges and fearlessly pulls him down, laughing. "No, no, no, boy! You have your species mixed. What you need is some exercise—and then we'll show you something you'll like better than Human girls! Now hold still."

Shaking his head mournfully, Davey dismounts to help her up. But with a nimble twist of the climbing stirrup, the girl leaps up into the white fur saddle and expertly unfastens and discards the climbers and the cavesson.

"But ma'am! Suppose you took a fall—you'd need these!"

"And if we fall in the waterhole, I'll need a bathing suit, too, I suppose."

Davey laughs helplessly and undoes one of his saddlebags, which are generally used for luncheon and canteens.

"What's that, a pudding-bird? . . . Oh, no!" He pulls out her black velvet hard hat.

"Just for an old man's sake," Davey says. "Just so's I won't get heart failure on top of a tongue-lashing from your father. Please, ma'am."

"It gets in my eyes—oh, all right." She half braids her long dark hair and slaps the helmet on with a rap on its top, secretly conscious that it's exceedingly becoming.

"Anything more? An air bag?"

"Here they come, ma'am."

A huge old open hydrocar is appearing and disappearing in the dips and twists in the moorland road. In back sits Lord Perdrix, her father, and her twin sister, the young Marquise Pardalianches.

"Is the bugler with them?" Comet is taking all her attention, whirling about so she can scarcely see.

"Yup."

"Good. Tell them to hurry up."

Davey swings a red bandanna in the universal sign language.

Comet does not like cars. He gives an experimental buck, for which he is ill suited, and then stands stock-still, snorting his disdain.

"Hi, Daddy! All right, Davey, gates! Bugle us in, you."

The gates swing wide, the bugle neighs, and the two beautiful creatures melded to one charge in. Once around the piste, then straight at a towering brick wall.

Up and flying over, his delicate forelegs folded to his chin, goes Comet. And then down and away at a stand of head-high bush. Both are simple jumps to allow riders to gait and calm their mounts. But Comet is hard to gait today, Davey sees. The girl is frowning as they round a corner on the wrong lead.

She has barely time to throw her weight on the inside foreleg; Comet stumbles and comes up on the proper lead. But the space to the next jump —a tough in-and-out—isn't quite enough. He sails over the outside wall off-balance, takes one stride in the center, and gamely tries to jump the outer wall, a structure of heavy poles.

The audience gasps as one—in the rough landing the girl's hard hat slipped down over her eyes, and she's knocked it off. Now Comet rises like a rocket, but he can't clear. He crashes up through the top, and two great poles come rolling down his neck. As the heavy poles come at her, Loma sinks her bare head in Comet's mane. No use: they hit her exposed head first on one side, then, as her neck droops, on the other, as though she's being battered by a giant wielding trees.

"Why don't she drop the reins 'n' cover her head?" Davey moans, running into the ring.

"No daughter of mine would." Lord Perdrix is getting out of the hydro-car, looking worried. The Lady Pardalianches, in the height of her fifteen-year-old beauty, only holds her perfumed hands to her mouth, gasping and watching intently.

Comet cavorts on down the piste for a few strides. Then, feeling the change in his limp rider's balance, he slows sedately and halts; he is a gentleman.

The girl still clings on by reflex, her bleeding head staining Comet's immaculate neck. Davey gets to her first, reaches up, and gently pulls her leg. She rolls down unconscious into the arms of her father and the bugler boy. Lord Perdrix has to open his daughter's fingers to release her death-grip on Comet's reins.

"Cooee, cooee," Davey soothes the great beast, who stands like a statue, rolling his eyes and snorting at the smell of blood. But Davey's voice fails him as he sees the girl's eyes are wide open, almost smiling.

He knows then that she really is dead.

And so she would be had not little Lady Pardalianches made the chauffeur get on the car's special transceiver to airports, flight doctors, hospitals, brain surgeons. As Perdrix carries his daughter toward them, a 'copter bearing a great red cross whirls precipitately down alongside. Three medics jump out and take over.

Lady Pardie, who cares nothing for holding on to horses' reins, cares greatly about holding on to her twin sister's life. She is not about to release that life to Death. Hour after hour, while the surgeons work, she sits by; from hours to days and nights, to weeks and months. And when those surgeons give up, she finds others, and others yet, who give up in their turn.

But still the young Lady Pardie will not let go; with her sister on total life support she stays by, talking to Loma, massaging her, arranging every possible intricate stimulation so that no part of her should atrophy. She teaches herself to read the medical literature, she threatens to squander her patrimony offering rewards on a dozen scientifically famous worlds. And she achieves finally the neural transfer mechanism of the golden electrode caps, with their marvels of circuitry hidden beneath the gold rollbed where Loma spends her life.

The rollbed, which now, twenty-two years later, stands momentarily unattended in the rosy Star-light in the lounge of a hostel on far Damiem, while the Lady Pardalianches joins the other guests in exclamations at the sky.

IX

NOVA MINUS 3 HOURS:
Kip in the Dark

Kip Korso carries his tray of servers out into a world on fire. The dark deck he stands on seems a narrow bridge of solid matter thrust into a sea of light.

Dazzled, he backs under the overhang to get his bearings. His eyes have always been slow to adapt to darkness. But his ears are sharp; he can hear people breathing, stirring, and an occasional peremptory mutter far to his left.

As he stands blinking, comes a fast patter of footsteps, and a small body bumps him so hard he barely saves the tray.

"Oh, sorry!" says Prince Pao excitedly. "Myr Cory says I may use the scope! She showed me how this afternoon."

"Righto. But remember, Prince, this stuff is all in-atmosphere. A scope won't do much."

"Of course." The lad's voice sinks to a tone suitable for imparting secrets of state. "Frankly, I have a selfish desire for the splendid view up there."

"Good seeing!" Kip grins in the darkness. Behind him the lounge doors bang.

By now, Kip has made out that the rosy light they saw through the vitrex shines up from the mirroring lake. Flame reds mingle with a cold gas-blue flicker—that would be the Star's auroras seen through shoals of sunset cloud. The sky overhead must be glorious, but he dares not look up and blind himself anew, or his guests will never get their suppers. Luckily the stay-hot servers really work.

At the east horizon of the lake an eerie lime-green glow is brightening—a close precursor of the oncoming Star. That's the source of the change Vovoka noticed from inside. As Kip looks down, the reflected radiance sends out an unearthly green ray that touches the central fires and dies back, to be replaced by two others. . . . Indrawn breaths and murmurs from the dark deck.

"Last time this stage lasted nearly an hour." Cory's voice comes from straight ahead of him, across the deck. Kip locates the dark line of the parapet and a shadowy blur against it that has to be Cory at the console. A taller darkness looms nearby. Vovoka?

"I think it's developing faster tonight." Cory gives her soft, warm, contagious chuckle, a sound Kip loves. "We called it by the disgracefully unaesthetic name of Green Fingers."

Just as he starts toward her, an earthly light abruptly glares out to his left.

Gods! He's forgotten Zannez and his act. And the screens—oh, murder, the screens aren't opaque! Weird shadows of the actors writhe on them, evoking uneasy stirrings on the deck.

Kip stares paralyzed while a shadow on the brightest screen turns into an unmistakable crotch shot, a girl kneeling spread-legged, while between her thighs the distorted shadow of a head in profile rises to her, tongue out—

"MYR ZANNEZ!!" Kip and Cory shout together.

The shadows leap and the lighted figure of Zannez, camera in hand, steps back into view, multicolored lights gleaming from his bald head and monocle.

"You'll have to hang blankets over those screens, too!"

The lights go off as the problem is explained. Pale forms race for their rooms, return laden with bedding and drapes. Zannez hangs the stuff himself.

"A thousand apologies, Myr Cory, and Kip—Myr Linnix, do forgive. . . . It was just my logo, we do that black on red. . . . *There,* those should do it! . . . All right, now, kids! Back to your places, got to get some work done." To Kip he adds, "We're starting a live imitation of those terrific color effects up there. Could be an art winner—after I'm fired."

"What am I supposed to be, those trees?" plaintively inquires Hanny Ek's voice.

"You're the surprise factor. Now dammit, get on down." Zannez vanishes. A glow of light springs out on the hostel side of the now opaque screens, too mild to interfere with the view.

Kip is dazzled again, and more than a little bemused by Zannez' definition of "work." But the light has shown him Baramji sitting with Linnix in the loungers outside the infirmary, not three meters to his left. He gropes his way to them.

"Bram, you can read here, check me. I think these are your two." He hands them down. "Who's where? You know my night eyes."

Baramji checks the markers in the soft light from the infirmary vitrex. "Right. Linnie, this is yours. Eat. You'll find you need it, my dear." He turns back to Kip. "Well, Zannez' lot you know. Lady P. is right behind you, where the screens meet the parapet. I have a hunch she's peeking. Vovoka's standing along from her, near Cory. And Doctor Ochter and our two nuisances are back here on the far side of the lounge doors, toward their rooms. They're fretting about something—"

"Oh, Myr Korso!" the Lady's voice cuts in. "My sister—*please* don't forget!"

"Just one minim more, truly." As he says it Kip recalls Cory's admonition to delay. Well, the twin's had the benefit of the Zannez commotion.

He off-loads five servers. "Myr Zannez! Here are your suppers. If you're, ah, busy, they'll stay hot. I'm putting them on this ledge back here."

Sounds of upheaval behind the screens. Ek's voice rises.

"Zanny, you slave driver! Time out for chow, or I strike."

Kip turns toward the Lady and finds he can follow his nose to a reclining shadow that glitters.

"Charming perfume, Lady Pardalianches. I believe this to be your supper. Let me put this napkin around it, it's hot."

"Thank you. But *please* hurry."

"Hurrying. . . . Cor! Supper coming!" He edges along the parapet.

Cory knows his problem and is already by him.

"Could you take Ser Vovoka's, too?"

"Done. . . . The Star-front seems to be developing just the same pattern as last time, Kip, only faster. You'll see, it's fantastic when you can look. . . . Wasn't that awful, with Zannez?"

"Dire. My fault, I should have checked."

"No harm done, I think. . . . What's a 'logo'?"

"Best not ask, it might be his grandmother. . . . Hey, I have eyes, I can see you." Forgetting that others can see better, he bends and kisses her warm, scented neck.

"Wush, love! Watch it—Ser Vovoka's plate—"

He leaves her urging supper on the star-gazing man and finds Doctor Ochter seated to the right of the lounge doors.

Beyond him under the overhang Kip can just make out a pair of empty chairs.

"Your supper, Doctor O. But where are our unwilling guests?"

"Definitely not unwilling now," says Ochter genially. "They're fascinated. But they also seem somewhat alarmed. I noticed them huddling back under your antiradiation eaves and Yule told me he'd managed to get a heavy dose near some defective equipment, just before he left. His doctor warned him not to add to it until he could get his course of shots. And Hiner is just naturally goosey about in-air radiation.

"I tried to tell them their apprehensions are groundless. But they've slipped back to their room for goggles and helmets—and cameras, too, I'm glad to say. I'll put their suppers on the ledge here."

"Absolutely unnecessary." Kip frowns. "Damn. I should have told everyone that UV glasses and shield hats are piled under the stairs, in case you want them. Feel free."

"Oh, goodness, as long as Myr Cory is satisfied I am, too. . . . Ah, this is welcome. I failed to eat much, earlier."

"Goodo."

Impatient tappings are coming from the marquise. Kip decides he's delayed as long as he decently can and takes the empty tray in, holding one eye closed to keep its adaptation.

The Lady is before him.

"She's *moved!* Oh! Myr Kip, look—her arm."

Squinting, Kip can see that the still figure really has moved—or been moved, if the Lady's unconscious is playing tricks. The right arm is now across the body, fingers tightly clenched. He recalls Baramji's line.

"Well, perhaps the Star really is helping her a bit."

"Oh, yes! Quickly, please, do bring her out. She *must* have the full Starlight!" In her eagerness the Lady actually tugs at the heavy bed.

Kip takes over and wheels the giant crib out.

"I'll put her right beside you here. See, Doc Baramji isn't a jump away." And the big rollbed will help block off Zannez' "work," Kip adds to himself.

"Oh, thank you. . . . Doctor Baramji! Myr Kip saw it, too—"

He leaves the Lady distractedly telling Bram about the arm and takes his place opposite Cory at the console. There he can finally raise his eyes to the spectacular light-show of the sky.

Overhead, the fiery vermilion of sunset is still lighting up a filigree of high cirrus. Above this hang arches of cold blue auroral light, shaped into great curtains rippling silently across the sky.

Over the hostel roof, the western horizon has paled to lemon, where float a few last flame-edged violet clouds like celestial fish.

But the east! Its bank of green witch-fire has brightened to a dazzling astral arc-light beyond the black lace of the horizon trees. Above this green lies another bank of black, unlit by stars, that's hard to recognize as normal night sky. Crossing it are now many of the gaseous green light-spokes, growing from the fire below. They blaze out, fade, and are reborn; seem to wheel like stately searchlights before being lost in the zenith splendor.

And all, all is mirrored in the still lake below, an almost bewildering double beauty.

Across the console Kip can see Cory's face lift briefly between bites of her supper and careful studies of the dials; he wishes she could for once relax.

Meanwhile he's listening hard between his own bites; there's an old myth that very bright, moving auroras make faint sounds. . . . But he can hear nothing unusual—until suddenly he's startled by a familiar whispery beat overhead.

He grabs Cory's wrist. "Wyrra!"

"Oh, no!"

"Shshsh."

They strain their ears while Kip's raised hand follows something inaudible to Cory. Then he makes a down-slashing gesture. "He's landing!"

"I can't believe it!" Cory's eyes shine.

"Damn, he's going to walk right by Hiner and Yule." Kip rises. "Cor, can you warn the others while I go meet him? And turn on the deck lights, too. They're almost as blind as me."

"On your way." She sets his board on standby.

Kip starts cautiously along the deck, steering by the parapet. Shortly a soft glow springs up behind him. Ahead lie pools of dense black shadow cast by overhanging trees. He stops by the first.

"Myr Yule? Doctor Hiner?" he calls as loud as he dares.

On his third try an unintelligible response comes from the end room. Kip gropes closer.

"Would you mind staying put for a few minims? Our local Damei may be passing, and we don't want to scare him. He's used to your room being empty."

"With pleasure," says Hiner's voice.

"And when you rejoin us, please come as slow and quiet as you can."

"Certainly."

"Will do," Yule chimes in.

Kip waits. The Dameii always make a reconnaissance pass before landing. It was the beat of Wyrra's defective wing as he looked them over that Kip had heard. Wyrra is sensitive about it; he always lands out of sight on the front side of the hostel and walks around the end, where Yule and Hiner are now.

Shortly a moving spot of light appears at the bend of the deck. Human flashlights are one gift the Dameii really appreciate; they depend only on natural phosphors, since they cannot bear the by-products of flame.

Wyrra's light is high; as usual, he's walking on the parapet caping. Kip gropes his way forward to meet him.

"Welcome, Myr Wyrra!" he calls softly in Damei. "Your visit brings much pleasure. We feared you would not care to be near so many Humans."

"Nyil wished to experience a group of your people."

"She is here, too? What a delightful surprise!"

A burst of high-pitched laughter from overhead answers him.

At that moment the tall form of the Damei steps into the light between two trees. His great blue-white wings meet above his head, quivering with nervous resolution so that they send out prismatic reflections of the sky. He is of deviant coloration, the only truly blue mutation Kip has ever seen. His hair, which he wears half-coiled on his head in imitation—or mockery —of Human style and half-cascading to his wings, is a stunning blue bronze, as are his brows and lashes. And the huge glittering eyes he fixes on Kip are a celestial blue.

He's clad from throat to toes in floating white gauze richly blue-embroidered, and Kip knows that when he's near Humans, his back around the wing-bases where the glands are is completely covered, too—a great annoyance to him. On his child-slim feet are white-and-blue-ornamented slippers; he's one of the few Dameii Kip has met who wears footgear.

Seen close, the Damei is both more and less Human-like. His hands are three-fingered and have no true nails, and the thumbs are very high-set, like dew claws. His hidden feet are three-toed, too, and carry his most alien feature—stiltlike, backward-tending heels, the evolutionary remains of heels and toes adapted for perching.

But his masklike smile is very Human, though his "teeth" are a white line of cartilage. His nostrils are much like a Human's, and the eyes are bigger homologues of Kip's own.

Just before he passes again into shadow, there comes a flash of small pale gold wings, and a tiny Damei child lands on the parapet in front of her father. She begins walking, almost dancing, toward Kip—seeming not at all afraid.

"Nyil, my dear, many welcomes to you. So you wish to meet a group of Humans?"

"Oh, yes!" Her voice is a very high, pure soprano. "But what is the word for—for people who come?"

"Well, there are two useful words. *Visitors* are people who come to see a friend, or the friend of a friend. You and Myr Wyrra are now *visitors* to me and Cory, for example."

The two reach Kip and he walks along beside them as he explains.

"And then there are people who travel to see a place or an event of great interest or beauty, without knowing any of the people there. This is called *sight-seeing* or *touring,* and people who do it are *tourists.* The Federation often provides places to stay, like our hostel here. Tourists may pay the Federation for their rooms and food, and being shown around, as we do. Tourists who wish to visit sensitive worlds like Damiem must also be carefully examined first. These tourists have come here now to see the last beauty of the Star, which is known of on other worlds. They're not here to see Cory or me. You yourself, Myr Wyrra, and certainly Nyil and her friends, might one day make a *tour* to see interesting sights on other worlds. Then you would be tourists. The Federation would be happy to pay for your way."

Both Dameii listen attentively, slowing almost to a stop. When Kip finishes, Wyrra exclaims, "Ah, this *pay,* this *money* thing again! I fear I don't truly understand."

"Would you like a talk on money at our next session, Myr Wyrra?"

"Yes, very much."

"Me too—I mean, I also," says Nyil in Galactic. "And also more on when I use formal. Why are you calling Father 'Myr' tonight?" Her accent's excellent.

"To show respect in the presence of strangers," Kip says slowly. "Also, this warns the other Humans to address him respectfully." He switches back to Damei. "I don't explain this well—you see, it is taught to us when we're very small children, so I don't remember the rules. I just know when it feels correct. For example, I know I should call your father Myr Wyrra when we have lessons, and I think it is because he has placed himself in the childlike position of student, so it is polite for me to emphasize that he is a superior, an adult. You see how complicated it is? I can't even explain clearly."

"I think I understand that," says Wyrra in his careful Galactic. His long lips curl in a rare smile. "Like flying. When I finally had need, we could find nobody able to explain. All had learned so young."

"Exactly!" Kip smiles, too; Wyrra is referring to the joyful day when they knew that Baramji had really succeeded in repairing his bad wing.

They've now reached the edge of the pool of light around the Human group. Wyrra halts, Kip and Nyil follow suit. From the console, Cory waves a greeting. Only Nyil waves back.

Kip sees that Zannez is out and has his camera trained on them. The faces of the four young actors are peering from joins in the screens.

"What is that man pointing at me?" demands Wyrra. "And what are all those heads?"

"He is a *cameraman*—a record-maker. Now he is making a record of you and Nyil. We will show it to you before he leaves. I believe you will enjoy it. The heads belong to his four young *actors*—something like your story-dancers. They act out stories for him to record. They can't come out before Humans because they aren't fully clad. We consider them very beautiful, by the way. They're the Humans who are going to show themselves in the village tomorrow. Will you and Juiyn be there?"

Wyrra frowns.

"Oh, Father, *please!*" Nyil begs.

"If not, perhaps we can arrange a private showing," Kip says tactfully. He knows there is some unexplained tension between this family and the village.

At this moment the lounge doors open quietly and Prince Pao comes out.

"Oh, look, Father!" Nyil points. "That must be a Human young! Isn't it? Oh, how interesting! What kind is it, Myr Kip? And how old?"

"Kind? . . . Oh. He is a male, a *boy,* of about seven of your long years."

Hearing the word, the prince glances at Kip with raised eyebrows, then doffs his plumed cap and bows formally to the two Dameii.

"I have only five years." Nyil frowns. "Is he the child of some of these tourists?"

"No. He has come alone. This is very unusual, but he's an unusual child. In a few years he will be the ruler of a small but important world."

"Oh," says Nyil, staring hard at Pao. Then she looks around and points again. "What's the matter with that female?"

"She was injured in an accident. Her sister there hopes the Star's light will help her."

"*Kiflayn,*" comments Wyrra—an untranslatable term meaning a bizarre and hopeless enterprise.

"Probably," says Kip. "And now do you wish me to escort you to meet others, or is this as close as you care to come?"

"I wish at least to greet your mate," says Nyil firmly. "And Doctor Bram, too. Is that not correct?"

"That would be polite, customary—unless you have come specially to speak with me alone. Or unless you wish to show displeasure with one of them."

"Oh, *no!*" says Nyil. "Father, you *must* greet Myr Cory! You just must!"

"It would give her great pleasure," Kip tells him. "But she will understand perfectly if you don't wish to go among so many strangers."

"Certainly. I will be happy to greet your mate," says Wyrra. But the nervous lofting of his wings belies his words.

As Wyrra begins walking toward her, Cory looks meaningfully at the other Humans, finger to lips. Kip sees with relief that the parapet side of the deck between her and the Dameii is clear of people; only little Ochter and Pao are on the hostel side. Everyone is still, save for a faint whirring from Zannez' cameras.

Halfway to Cory, Wyrra levels his great wings and floats down off the parapet, to continue his march along the deck. But Nyil stays up, reluctant to lose her view.

As they near Cory, Kip hears quiet footfalls by the hostel wall and turns to see Hiner and Yule take positions near their chairs. They're wearing goggles and elaborate shield hats. Even through the lenses Kip can see their eyes rounded in fascination. It's considerate of them not to risk making a clatter by sitting down. Good.

Wyrra turns to follow Kip's gaze.

Next instant, Kip is all but bowled over by air blast and deafened by the clap of Wyrra's bad wing. The Damei whirls, snatches up his child, and leaps or flies up to the parapet, where he balances with tensely upheld wings, poised for flight.

"What are—*those?*"

Kip realizes what a bizarre sight the goggled, helmeted students present.

"It's all right, Myr Wyrra—truly! They are only ordinary Humans wearing antiradiation protectors. Myr Yule, Doctor Hiner! Would you mind taking off your glasses and hats just a minim? Wyrra hasn't seen any before, and got spooked."

"Certainly. Here, show him." They remove the offending gear, revealing smiling faces, although Kip notices that Hiner's smile seems oddly strained, and he retreats behind Yule. Gods, is it possible that he senses Wyrra and Nyil as *insects?*

Prince Pao has already trotted over; he seizes a helmet and goggles and carries them to Kip. Nyil squirms around in her father's grip to inspect Pao. He smiles and twiddles his fingers at her, while Kip explains.

"Your people wore those when they had to leave shelter during the bad first passage of the Star. There's also a heavy suit to cover the whole body, and a cape to protect the wings, but one can't fly in it. You must have been too young then to recall this, Myr Wyrra."

"Umm . . . yes." Wyrra's wings relax as he handles the hat. Nyil gets the goggles and holds them to her eyes, making horrible faces and giggling as she stares around. Wyrra lets her slip down to stand on the coping beside him, one hand still grasping her shoulder.

"Why are the Humans wearing them now? We were told the Star isn't dangerous."

"It isn't. Do you think I would expose Myr Cory? But . . ." Kip simply isn't up to discoursing on Aquapeople tonight; perhaps the gods of truth will forgive him if he packs Hiner in with Yule. "These two accidentally received a dangerous dose just before coming here, and their doctor told them to wear these against the chance of any more radiation at all, no matter how weak, until they could have their corrective injections. In fact, we should pass these back at once, if you're satisfied. It was courteous of them to risk damage to reassure you."

"Many thanks indeed, from us both." The Dameii hurriedly pass the gear to Pao, who runs back to the overhang. Wyrra bows formally to Hiner and Yule, an action of pure beauty, his long wings crossing over his back. Nyil copies him as best she can under her father's hand.

"Do let go, Father," she complains in Damei. "You're a worse menace than a hundred goggles and hats."

Wyrra smiles at last and lets her go. She runs along the coping to Cory, her stubby gold wings standing straight out with excitement. Cory is in the console seat, her head not much below Nyil's. Nyil holds out a tiny hand.

"Good evening, Myr Cory," she says in her very good Galactic accent. "I trust you are feeling well?"

Cory takes the hand as though it's a flower petal.

"Yes, thank you, Myr Nyil, and I do hope that you and your family are all in good health, too? It was so kind of your father to visit us tonight. And what a delight to see you here! Do your friends tell you that you're growing taller every day? Soon we shall have to call you Myr Nyil in earnest."

The child sighs ruefully. "It seems very slow to me."

Cory chuckles. "Yes. I remember it seemed slow to me, too. . . . And did you have an interesting time in school today, Myr Nyil?"

"Pleasing, thank you—we had digitals." And with that, Nyil's careful dignity breaks up entirely. Peals of irrepressible, contagious giggles, musical as a flock of songbirds, spill over the dark deck and are joined by others who don't know what they're laughing at but find it impossible to resist. In the midst of it, Nyil manages to ask her father something in Damei.

Wyrra's lips quirk as he turns to Cory. "My daughter wishes to be told honestly if her conversation was correctly done."

"Absolutely perfect," Cory tells him. "You're going to have trouble to keep up—*avrew loren mori na peer*—with your bright child."

"Her accent is remarkable for a person of any age," adds Kip.

"Thank you, Myr Cory and Myr Kip. This will make her very happy. She works much at it, you know."

Meanwhile Nyil sobers herself by studying the console lights and switches. "When I am bigger I intend to learn all about such things," she announces. *"Everything.* . . . what's that light that just came on? The big red one, there—is it telling you something?"

"It's telling me to reset it." Cory wishes the child had picked on anything else. She lowers her voice. "If I fail to reset it, that means there is real trouble here—suppose we were all struck by lightning, or something very bad—so, if it's not reset, the Patrol will automatically send a ship at once, with a party of fighting men, doctors and so on, to fix whatever may have happened. It's called a Deadman's Alarm; see if you can guess why. Almost every faraway place has one."

"Dead-man?" She loves puzzles. "Oh, I will think!"

"And *I* think," says Doctor Baramji, who now stands beside them, "that I will never get a handshake or even a smile from this young lady unless I come and ask."

"Oh, Doctor Bram, I was coming to greet you, truly I was on the way." Nyil extends the delicate hand, while her small wings rise. "Good evening, dear Doctor. I am so very happy to see you."

He takes the hand, barely closing his fingers on it, and switches to his rudimentary Damei.

"And I am very, very happy to see you, Myr Nyil, and to see you looking so well. Tell me, how is your father?"

Baram's grammar is fair, but his accent is lamentable. In medical work he relies mainly on his superb bodily empathy.

"Father is well, I think. It is good that you came away from the others, because now he can tell you himself. He doesn't like to experience new Humans, as I do. Go to him, please."

She skips down from the parapet and over to where Kip is making space for Wyrra and Baram to approach each other. Wyrra's wings shoot up, trembling so they flash rainbow lights, as he forces himself to step toward Baramji. They exchange a sketchy handclasp.

"Myr Wyrra," says Baram, in his stumbling Damei. "A question of your health. . . . We go over there"—he gestures at a space between the console and the parapet—"so we may speak alone?"

"Certainly."

When they had gained the privacy by the coping, Kip sees Wyrra relax.

Baramji and Wyrra inspect the rebuilt wing. Then Baram steps behind the Damei and climbs up on a planter box, where he begins to manipulate the wing carefully from base to tip.

Glancing up, Kip sees that the beauty of the sky is still there, beyond the deck lights. It's changed to sumptuous, hypnotic violets, blues, greens. But it can't compete with the interest of their visitors, on whom all eyes are fixed.

Just then he feels a light tug on his arm. Little Nyil is fearlessly pulling him toward the hostel wall.

Amused and delighted, he lets himself be guided, first past the Lady and the rollbed, then toward Linnix. To the Lady, Nyil gives a poised bow and a murmured "Good evening," then leaves her starting a flowery barrage of talk. To what she can see of the bed's occupant, and the medical arrangements beneath, Nyil gives a long, serious look. Linnix she passes with another brief bow and greeting—and then Kip sees where he's being taken. Straight past the screens to Zannez!

He holds back for a moment, but an urgent tug convinces him that his duty as a Damei's escort transcends the proprieties of the Code.

As they pass the screens, bare bodies seem to be flashing everywhere. He tries not to look, but a ravishing nude clutching a wholly inadequate scrap of lace—Bridey?—imprints itself on his brain.

"Tell names, please."

Kip comes back to himself to find Nyil's wings standing straight up with the excitement of her adventure. As she gets a close look at Zannez' shiny bald head, monocle, and big dark camera eye whirring straight at her, Kip can feel the hand on his arm begin to tremble. Luckily, at that moment Zannez drops to one knee for a level shot, where he appears less formidable. The four young actors, suddenly all clothed in black short robes red-blazoned "APC," have the tact not to come too close.

"Zannez! Quick, stop shooting, take that monocle out, and stay down. You're scaring her."

The cameraman obeys with all speed; the trembling quiets.

"Myr Nyil, may I present Myr Zannez? He is an expert recorder who has come a very long way to record your world and the Star."

"It is a pleasure and an honor to meet you, Myr Nyil. We were not told that your people and your world were so beautiful. You see, we are really *very* far away."

But Nyil seems to have tired of small talk and things Human. She glances at the four actors, who are sitting cross-legged some meters away, but doesn't seem to care for a closer view. Instead she says, "I wish to see your records of Father and me."

"You shall," Zannez assures her. "Kippo, explain that it takes time to process, and different equipment to show. We thought we'd give a viewing here tomorrow night, Star radiation permitting. And tell her they're life-size, in color and sound."

Kip ripples off a Damei speech, adding that there will be a private show for her and her family if they wish. "The last sound you'll hear will be me telling Zannez to stop recording. . . . Would you like now to have him record you saying hello to your father and mother? It would be a nice surprise to end your private show."

"It records in Damei?"

"Oh, yes. Just stand as you are and say, 'Hello, Mother,' or whatever you wish."

"Um-m. Yes. I find I'm tired but I will do this."

Kip explains to Zannez what's wanted, and in a minim or two the recording is made.

"Tell her that tomorrow I'll show her how to make a recording herself if she likes."

But Nyil breaks into Kip's speech by asking Zannez in Galactic, "Why do you not have hair?"

Zannez laughs. "On my world we all want to look different from each other. So I cut my hair off close. Feel." He bows his head for her feathery touch.

She's not too tired to giggle at the prickly scalp.

"Thank you. Now I go."

"Thank you for coming, Myr Nyil." A murmur of agreement from the ring of watchers. Nyil nods politely to them as she and Kip emerge from the screens.

Everyone seems to be looking at them, even Ser Vovoka, who stands silent and alone beyond Cory. Wyrra has a wild, staring look in his great eyes. Kip guesses he's torn between pursuing his daughter and dread of going among Humans—and if he takes off to overfly, he'll be humiliated by his defective wing. Probably they've emerged just in time to head off a scene.

Nyil releases his arm and runs to her father, disregarding the Humans en route. Wyrra snatches her up in his arms and gives her a squeeze and a hard shake.

"Father! I made a surprise for Mother and you!"

He says something fast and low in Damei, then lets her wriggle down to the parapet.

From behind him Kip hears the renewed whirring of Zannez' cameras. He evades the marquise by going past Linnix and Ochter; both are beaming. But the chairs beyond Ochter are empty again.

"What have those two gone for now? Chain mail?" he asks Ochter.

"Camera reloads." The little professor sighs comically. "And they missed the best shot of all. Wasn't that perfectly *charming?* Is she his only child?"

"Yes, so far. They don't have big families."

He rejoins the group at the console in time to hear Cory sending their greetings to Juiyn, Wyrra's mate.

"Is she well? Or has she gone to a Damei society meeting, leaving her husband and child alone to face the monsters?"

She's cut short by a startling thunderclap of huge, dark-furred wings. A female Damei fetches up on the parapet behind Wyrra, silhouetted against brilliant green sky. Her hair and dress are darker, plainer versions of her husband's. Under her gauzy gown are what appear startlingly like two high, virginal breasts, which Kip knows to be the folded lips of her oviceptor.

"He-ere is Juiyn," she announces, laughing, though her wings stay upright, forming a magnificent arc. The Humans realize they haven't appreciated the size of a fully wingspread female Damei.

"Greetings, Myr Juiyn!" say Kip and Cory together. "It gives much pleasure that you came." Kip adds a formal welcome in Damei.

"Gre-etin," Juiyn replies. Her Galactic is obviously elementary compared to her family's. She shoots some rapid-fire Damei phrases at Wyrra. Then her long arm stretches down, extending a hand at Cory.

"Go-od even-in, Myr Corree."

Cory gives the hand a brief, delicate clasp.

Juiyn repeats the routine with Kip and adds firmly, "Also I thi-ink now go-odbye. Pleasantness."

Wyrra bows to all, and the two adults set off, walking, for their home. Juiyn paces the deck beside Wyrra on his coping path. Little Nyil lingers for a formal handshake with the Korsos and Baramji, despite her mother's abrupt calls. When she finally takes off to sail over her parents' heads, Kip and the others see Wyrra catch her foot and unceremoniously haul her down out of the air. He plonks her on the coping to walk before him.

"I'm afraid Nyil's in disgrace. Did you see her kidnap me?"

"She is a handful." Cory chuckles. "Let's see, I better leave the deck lights on awhile. I hope you folks don't mind."

A dozen voices assure her they didn't.

"I hope Hiner and Yule remember not to bang around," Kip says worriedly. "Maybe I'll just ramble down after them and check."

He sets off as he had before and again is stopped by the deep black shadows of the trees. Here he waits until he sees Wyrra's light come on far ahead, cursing himself for forgetting his own. He'd left it recharging in the workshop, along with their three hand weapons, whose sights he'd checked. . . . He should recharge Wyrra's light, too. Better yet, teach him how.

All stays silent in the end room, aside from some mutters and the bump of a travel bag on vitrex. Finally Wyrra's yellow light turns the corner at the far end and disappears behind the hostel.

Kip walks back, enjoying the glorious green radiance of the sky and the luminous violet-blue auroral curtains which seem to ripple just above their images in the lake.

"All clear!" he calls as he approaches the group. "Douse the deck lights."

When the man-made glow goes out, the celestial splendor brightens tenfold; Kip is sure he will soon be able to see by it. He can hear Zannez' excited voice; the cameraman seems to be relieving pent-up feelings.

". . . absolutely marvelous, Myr Cory! Tremendous, unbelievable! This afternoon was so great I thought that was *it*, but then this Star-scene—whew!—and then actually having two of the wing-people here and one of them a little girl! Alien or Human, *the* most exquisite little girl ever in front of a lens. She makes Leila Carlea, the divine nymphette, look like a gods-forgotten lump. And the action she showed, the voice—oh, kids, wasn't that one glorious eyeful? What'll you bet the Feds are besieged by Gridworld idiots wanting to come out here and sign her up?"

Amid the laughter Stareem asks anxiously, "They wouldn't let them, would they, Myr Cory? I mean, they have so much money—"

"No way," says Cory firmly. Kip, arriving by the console, backs her up.

"Don't forget, they've had planetfuls of money waved under their noses for Damiem before. Plus some fairly wicked personal threats. That doesn't play, either. A few tragedies happened, but they rolled up the biggest crime ring in the inner planets from Damiem leads. I trust your Gridworld friends will understand 'No.' "

"I guess we've been privileged," Zannez says soberly.

"Yes." Cory shakes her head in wonder. "I *never* expected them to come. Did you, Kip?"

"Nh-unh. It was Nyil's idea, Wyrra said. I guess she holds a lot of clout with her father. . . . Well! Can I bring anybody anything? More chow, a drink?"

"Just marvelous . . ." Linnix says dreamily, still dwelling on the Dameii. "That little Nyil . . . I keep thinking of your story, Kip. It was children like Nyil they tortured. . . . How could humans be so—be so bestial, so—" Her voice breaks.

Baramji leans over her, lifts her chin. "Linnie, don't—that's all in the far past. Think how marvelous they are now, enjoy it."

She looks up at him gratefully, manages a smile. "Yes. . . . But it mustn't *ever* happen again. Never, never."

"It won't," Kip assures her cheerfully. "That's what we're here for. . . . And now what can I bring who?"

X

NOVA MINUS 2 HOURS:
Doctor Ochter Reports

"Oh, my goodness!" Doctor Ochter struggles up from his chair. "It was all so marvelous I almost forgot! I brought along a little hostess gift, Myr Kip, in case the Guardians of Damiem turned out to be as gracious as reputed. You've been quite widely heard of, you know." Beaming, he makes a little bow to the Korsos and to Baram. "If Myr Cory agrees, I thought it might make a suitable toast to our good fortune while we await the Star."

"How perfectly lovely," exclaims Cory. "Whatever can it be? As to time, the probe is predicting at least ninety minim—"

"Shshsh!" Kip holds up a hand, pointing to the dark far end of the deck where the Dameii vanished. Everyone listens hard.

"Did you hear it, Cor?"

She nods slowly. "I thought it was Wyrra taking off around on the front side. But—twice?"

"I thought I heard a very faint voice," Stareem puts in shyly from the end of the screen where the four have been watching. "Like a call, or cry. Not words. Is it true they can't make loud sounds?"

"Oh, gods. D'you suppose Wyrra took a fall?"

"Go look," says Cory.

But Kip hesitates. "If he did fall and it wasn't too serious, the last thing they'd want is a Human poking in. If it's serious, Juiyn or Nyil will come for Bram."

Ochter speaks up. "Look, I'm going to my room anyway, and I have pretty fair night vision. Why don't I just take a good peek out, on the arcade side, before turning on any light? They'll never know I'm there. If I see anything that looks unusual, I'll report straight back here."

"Oh, thank you so much!"

"Good plan, if we're not overworking that leg," says Kip. "I'll come with you as far as those shadows."

"No need, no need." Ochter bows his head at them and hobbles, with surprising speed, down the dark deck toward his room.

As his uneven footsteps die away, Prince Pao comes over to the console.

"You know that Patrol ship you said was in orbit? I saw it! Through the scope, just as it got really dark. That's what I was coming down to tell you."

"You—what?" asks Kip.

"I saw your ship!" Pao repeats impatiently. "The Patrol ship you said was in orbit. I wasn't looking for it, the scope just picked it up."

"But—" Cory broke off, looking at Kip; he recalls telling her that Dayan was taking *Rimshot* nearer to the new relay satellite. "What part of the sky did you see it in?" he asks the boy.

Pao gestures toward the southeast. "There was a strip of clear sky there, down low."

"What made you think it was a Patrol cruiser?" Cory asks him.

"Well, naturally—" Pao begins rather loftily. Then the Korsos' seriousness gets through to him, and his manner changes at once. "Inference only," he says carefully. "Knowing there was a Patrol ship, when I saw what appeared to be a ship I jumped to the conclusion—may I ask, why the concern?"

"That isn't the Patrol's normal orbit," Cory tells him. "And out here on the Rim things aren't like your Fed-Central traffic. Ships are very, very rare. Could what you have seen have been a stray rock or a satellite?"

Pao considers. "Unlikely. When I found I couldn't pick it up again, I fed my estimates of apparent brightness and velocity into your scope computer. I assumed it was moving normal to my line of sight, plus or minus fifteen degrees. Oh, I also assumed it was shining by reflected light. The parameters intersected at a ship-sized body at two hundred thousand km, plus or minus fifty. The, uh, albedo is awfully high for a rock, and the size is huge for a man-made satellite. And a closer distance puts you terribly slow. So I took it for a ship. Going toward the north, by the way; I estimated an angle of forty degrees from the horizon."

"Well done, Prince."

Kip and Cory look at each other for an instant while she unhooks the microphone and starts the old transmitter up. He sees her face taking on what he calls her *"c*-skip look." She's debating whether this information is hot enough to justify powering-up for the huge energy expense of transmitting it to Base via *c*-skip. The instantaneous transfer of information involves, among other things, supercooling the antenna, necessary to perturb the local gravity-field configuration. They've been around this before.

"Listen, Cor. The power-up will lose you half the time you gain, working through this rig." He waves at the old console. "And you don't want to do it upstairs—by the time that antenna is cooled down you'll be right into Star-rise time. You don't want to be sending then, do you? And that ship can't get itself lost out here, not for days. Unless it has 'skip, in which case it's an official vessel. Chances are a hundred to zip it's some joker who misjumped out here and is looking for a FedBase anyway. . . . Remember the *Golan?*"

Cory grunts; years back she *c*-skipped a warning of an unknown ship—which turned out to be an official visitor Base hadn't warned her about.

"Send a regular transmission with an override on it. It'll be there in a hundred minim—and let Base decide whether to pull Dayan in."

She nods, reluctantly convinced.

"Thank fortune I ran the voice relay down here."

Federation Base Number Ninety-six is in a huge, slow-orbit rock about a hundred light-minim away, made lavishly comfortable, by space standards, to compensate for the bleak Rim duty. The "override" signal will put her message in the Exec's hands as soon as received—if Commo isn't playing paddleball. She trips in the automatic recorder, which will loop the receiving wire, and jacks the transmission power to max, to punch through the Star's static. When the Ready light finally goes green she begins speaking quietly.

Only Bram and Officer Linnix are in earshot. Vovoka is clearly preoccupied, and the Lady Pardalianches's attention is divided between her sister and Zannez' screen.

Little Prince Pao watches the transmission with excited eyes. Once Cory breaks off to ask the time of his sighting, and when she resumes Kip catches the words "intelligent amateur." Pao nods to himself with a satisfied air.

Recalling his intention to get his hand light, Kip beckons the boy.

"Would you do us a favor, Prince? Another favor, I should say."

"Pleasure."

"You know where my workshop is. My hand light is in the recharger on the back bench, and I shouldn't leave here. Could you get it?"

"Two minim."

"Hey, wait. Our three Tocharis are on the bench, too. I meant to start one on the charger this afternoon. By any chance do you know how to put a standard Tochari hand weapon on to charge?"

"Oh, yes. But they aren't there, you know."

"They aren't . . . there?"

"No. I thought you'd taken them. I saw them this morning, but when I went to sharpen my pocketknife before supper—you have a really neat old stone, you know—I noticed the weapons were gone."

Kip's stomach is doing a slow cold slide toward his boots.

"You're sure?"

"Of course. Naturally I assumed you—"

"No, not me." Kip manages a grin. "Must be Doc or Cor, assuming they were charged. Things have been a shade uncoordinated around here. But I do need that light before I step on somebody, if you'd really be so kind."

Pao has been watching him sharply. Now he nods and heads for the lounge doors.

Cory signs off and turns to Kip. "Poor Dayan, he'll never forgive me if his men miss those games."

Kip takes a deep breath and leans across the console.

"Cory, listen. Due to my carelessness and stupidity, someone has taken all our three Tocharis. I left them in the open workshop to be charged. Pao saw them there earlier and this evening he went there again and they were gone. Any forlorn hope Bram has 'em—you can assess that. There's only one lucky point, if you can call anything about this lucky: I also forgot to put them in the charger and they're all dead dry. So whoever took 'em has only hunks of plastite. Unless he has some magic charger of his own."

Kip pulls back and drops his head in his hands.

"Oh, my gods, Cor, what can I say? Careless, criminally careless. Stupid —lazy—*sloppy* . . . Guardian of the Dameii!!" he says bitterly. "You have to report this, you know, Cor. Or I will."

Cory is silent for a few breaths, taking it in.

"Oh, my dear," she says brokenly. "Oh, my poor dear man." She straightens up. "We can discuss all that later. Right now the question is, who—"

"Halloo, halloo!" Doctor Ochter's limping footsteps sound behind them. "I return bearing large information and a small gift."

Kip pulls himself together and sees that despite Ochter's cheery tone, his face is drawn with fatigue and pain; he looks ghastly in the emerald light. Clasped in his arms are a large, thickly wrapped parcel and a travel pouch. Kip quickly pulls a chair toward him. "Here, Doc, let me give you a hand."

Ochter all but collapses into the lounger. "Thank you, thank you. . . . I also have . . . a confession to make, when . . . I get my breath." He gasps a moment, gratefully accepts Kip's water glass.

While he's recuperating, Prince Pao arrives with the hand-flash.

"Is there anything else I can do for you and Myr Cory?" the boy asks quietly.

"Just go on keeping your eyes open, as you've done damn well so far, Prince. Oh, there is one thing. If Cory is talking or listening on the transceiver, and you see someone apparently trying to overhear, we'd be eternally grateful if you could break it up. You can do things I can't." Kip forces a grin.

"I know." Pao grins back and goes along the hostel wall to take a seat behind Zannez, where he can watch both sides of the screen. Kip sees him lean forward and smile approvingly, doubtless at Stareem.

Kip wants to tell Baramji of the strange ship and the theft of the weapons, but Doctor Ochter has revived and is starting to speak.

"Well—first things first," the small man says briskly. "On arrival in my room I left the lights off and was able to inspect much of the arcade and the area in front. No Dameii, no Humans, nothing. There's quite a breeze on the entry side of the hostel, you know; one doesn't feel it here. But apart from the wind all seemed still and silent. I trust my eyes more than my ears these years," he adds wryly.

"So I ventured to open my door and slip along the arcade toward Yule and Hiner's room, staying in the shadow, until I passed their side door and could see up into the treehouse area. The branches were tossing, but I caught glimpses of a greenish phosphor light. I also thought I saw some movement up there, and I watched for several minim, but it may well have been merely the effects of wind.

"From where I was one can see only the start of the parapet—you know how the rooms are offset. So I continued around the next corner until the whole curve of the parapet was visible, well past the point where Myr Kip lost the Damei family's light. Still nothing. I could also check that the deck was empty, except of course for the small angle directly beyond the hostel's end. There seemed to be nothing to suggest that your visitors had not reached their home in safety. But the sounds you heard; what could account for them?

"Listening hard, I had become aware of the muffled echoes of some activity in the two men's room behind me. Your walls are admirably thick; even in the lulls of the wind I could make out nothing. But just as I turned back toward their door, the most extraordinary uproar broke out. Loud imprecations, thumps, bangings, and what seemed to be one of them groaning or sobbing aloud.

"A minim later their door flew open in my face and Myr Yule rushed out, followed by Myr—ah, Doctor—Hiner, who was forcefully remonstrating with him.

"I could catch only 'You must!' or perhaps 'I must,' or 'We must,' and 'I can't,' or 'You can't'—all quite incoherent and emotional. Through the open door I could see their room in great disorder, open duffels and gear strewn about, a case jammed shut with garments protruding.

"Hiner saw me as he came out; I must say that I have never seen a man's eyes actually roll before. Next moment he'd left Yule and clutched hold of my shoulder quite painfully, pulling me about and in a loud whisper alternately demanding and pleading that I 'help Yule.'

"At first all I gathered was that they were *afraid.*"

Ochter pauses to drink more water, sighing.

"Good glory—what *of?*" asks Cory. "Is it more of the insect-thing? I should go to them. Bram—"

Ochter shakes his head vigorously, swallowing water.

"No, wait please. . . . What they feared? Everything! Radiation of course, and the Star; but also those charming flights of tree leaves, and Myr Zannez' cameras, and Ser Vovoka here, and the poor paralyzed Lady. Virtually everything and everyone, even to the Dameii. Especially the Dameii! Yule kept muttering about 'eyes flying over' and dashing back inside to make certain their end door to the deck was locked. By this time I had observed two open liquor bottles, and their breaths were noticeable despite the wind.

"But the serious part of this idiocy was that Yule wanted to smoke. 'To keep them off,' he said. I surmise that he is also simply an habitual smoker craving his smokes.

"Hiner said he'd put a stop to that, although not, I think, in time. As soon as he mentioned it I recognized a faint smoky odor between the gusts of wind and alcohol. . . . It also occurred to me that this episode might have been the origin of the sounds you heard."

"I'll buy that," says Kip. Cory nods.

Ochter sighs again, sipping his water, and adds reflectively, "By the by, although Hiner was superficially more coherent, I did sense it as that type of pseudocontrol—you've doubtless met it—which can go quite far into unreality before overtly breaking down. . . .

"In the midst of it all, he muttered something about the power-cell shaft, which, if true, could be very serious. But that can wait till later." The little man paused for breath before resuming.

"A curious point which has baffled me all evening: From being slightly hostile strangers, these two have progressed to a degree of intimacy—if not exactly comradeship—with amazing speed. You'll see as I go on—it's as though they've discovered some overwhelmingly important need or bond in common that overrides their personal differences.

"Well. To make a messy matter brief, they'd seen me inject myself this afternoon and taken me for a medical doctor. First Hiner wanted me to give them something—he called it, oddly, a *special shot*—to calm Yule. Then he wanted it for himself, too. When I demurred, they became threatening. They were coming out here and, well, bother Myr Cory, and tear up the infirmary, if I didn't help them."

Baramji, who has come over to listen, grunts ominously.

Kip sees that. Ochter is really disturbed; he misunderstands Baram's grunt and hastens on apologetically. "Yes—of course I should have come for you, Doctor Baramji, and for Myr Kip. But I feared to leave those two alone in that state, and frankly, I wasn't sure I could. You see, at this point they were hanging on me at the door of my room.

"And here is where I must confess, Myr Cory. I recalled that our clinic had given me several syrettes for use in case of insomnia. So I offered Hiner two, quote, special shots, unquote, on condition they hand over Yule's smokes. D'you know, I was quite relieved when they accepted?"

He smiles shyly.

Kip gives an indignant snort, imagining the little old fellow in the clutches of those two young clots. He sees Cory's face has taken on her Administratrix frown: such things should not occur in her hostel.

"To, ah, add verisimilitude," Ochter goes on, "I managed to make an inconspicuous cryptic mark on certain syrettes as I took them out." His twinkle has come back, with a tinge of mischief that tells Kip he had secretly enjoyed his little adventure.

"Which I duly showed to Hiner, as evidence that they were 'specials.' He seemed satisfied. . . . Of course I checked the true labels," Ochter concluded seriously. "Three milliliters of twenty percent ambezine hydrate solution each. Doctor Baramji can define it for you better than I. I've always understood it was harmless, apart from its soporific effect, but I worried about the interaction with alcohol.

"Did I do wrong, Doctor?"

Baram stirs. All nearby—except Vovoka—have been fascinated by Ochter's account, despite the growing marvel of the sky.

"No problem there, Ochter. Though personally I'd have been more inclined to give them a good strong emetic and a kick in the tail. But no, you did no harm."

"Your verdict is more than welcome." Ochter sighs again, relieved, and begins fishing in his pockets around his lapful of bundles. "Especially since the effects came unusually fast. Yule threw himself down on his bed as soon as they were back in their room, and had difficulty telling Hiner to lock the door after me. Which Hiner didn't bother to do. So—dear me, I nearly forgot to give you these."

He holds out two slim packets of cheroots to Kip. As Kip takes them he recognizes his old Federation brand and feels a momentary pang. For a moment he doesn't see that Ochter is holding up the travel pouch for him to take, too.

"In the confusion I seized the occasion to secure those," Ochter tells them in a lower tone. "Perhaps you will make out a receipt in the morning? The pouch, by the way, is mine. I glanced in an open bag and decided they belonged in your hands as soon as possible. It is, after all, a serious matter even to bring such things here. Though in their case it was inadvertent, I'm sure."

Puzzled, Kip peers into the bag. His eyes widen and he reaches inside for an instant and then passes the pouch to Cory as fast as his shaking hands will work.

She doesn't look inside but only feels it appraisingly, watching Kip. He alone hears her faint gasp. He nods.

"Three Tocharis," he confirms quietly.

XI

30 MINIM TO CONTACT:
The Royal Eglantine

Cory hands the unopened pouch back to Kip. "Put these in a safe place, Kippo." To Ochter she says soberly, "I think we have much to thank you for, Doctor. . . . As for Yule and Hiner, while I'm normally opposed to doing things to people without their full consent, in this case they literally insisted on it, didn't they? It's not as if they'd demanded some substance by name. They wished to feel better, and I'm sure they do. . . . But will they be ill in the morning, Bram?"

"Only from the alcohol," Baram replies. "But by the way, Cor, does it strike you as odd to hear two presumably healthy young men asking for injections? The young Human male is usually my most needle-shy patient."

Ochter speaks up. "If I take your meaning, Doctor, a number of other small matters brought that thought to my mind, too. First, the peculiar sudden intimacy I mentioned. And then Hiner insisted on injecting himself and Yule, too, and he had quite a little ritual. He also turned so that I couldn't see their arms. But all that is strictly in the realm of invidious conjecture. I'd prefer to leave it there."

"Unless it translates to action," says Cory thoughtfully. She's thinking that Zannez' "hunch" may have been based on solid indicators—if these two turn out to be druggers, and stealers of guns to boot. What did they want the guns for? Invading Baram's infirmary supply seemed more likely than some Stars Tears plot. "Bram, dear, I think you'd best lay on some security. Remember that plan we worked up when Dayan put us through the drill?"

"Ah, seven devils take it," Baramji grumbles. "You're right, Cor, of course. . . . Oof . . . but there's no hurry, the doses those lads gave themselves should keep them out of trouble quite a while. I can do it in the morning. . . . And maybe they have some supplies of their own they couldn't find in the confusion, perhaps that's what Hiner was rooting for. Meanwhile I say let's forget it and enjoy the Star." He turns back to Linnix, who's been courteously ignoring the conversation. "Oh, my, look how it's changed while we talked!"

"So I'm forgiven?" Ochter asks Cory.

"Indeed you are, Doctor Ochter, and our thanks with it."

He beams. "But I shall never forgive myself if I fail to present you with this small gift before the Star is up." He hoists himself to his feet and formally presents Cory with the large wrapped parcel. "I do hope it proves enjoyable."

"Oh, thank you! But Doctor Ochter, you shouldn't—" She sits smiling like a girl, rather helplessly holding the cumbrous thing. "Kip dear! Could you . . . ? Is it all right if he unwraps it, Doctor?"

"Most certainly. How thoughtless of me!"

Kip starts from his private thoughts to find himself gripping the miraculous travel pouch so hard his hand aches. It takes him an instant to recapture what Cory is asking him to do.

"No problem. Here, let me lay this on the console where you can keep an eye on it, honey. Now, let's see. . . ."

At that moment the lights behind Zannez' screens go off, and the cameraman comes out, for once without a camera. He's sopping his shiny head, the monocle's dangling, his medic's whites are stained and rumpled: he looks dead beat.

"Whew! May we rejoin civilization, Myr Cory? I've got all we need in the cans and then some, and the automatics will take care of the sky. I told the kids to get decent and come on out. Green?"

"Green indeed, Myr Zannez. Do make yourselves comfortable. Would you or your actors care for some refreshments?" Her long smile twitches a trifle at the contrast between her formal words and the "acting" that must have tired them.

Zannez waves his hand exhaustedly and flops into the nearest lounger. "Ah, thank you, just tell Hanno where the food box is—no, on second thought, Bridey'd be safer. . . . I'd love some *laangua*, but what I *really* crave is a look at that sky without lenses in the way. . . . Oh! Hey kiddies," he calls, "for the gods' sake watch those artifacts! Don't try to move 'em; we leave the screens up to protect them. Hear?"

A chorus of assent comes from behind the barrier.

Kip sees Prince Pao unfolding two glittering, fragile robes, one silver, one gold, that he'd secreted somewhere. The boy gives them a last critical look and vanishes with them behind the screens.

Beside the parapet, the Lady Pardalianches is still looking through her peephole. Suddenly she gives a start and a faint squeak, and her eyes open wide. Zannez has spotted her and winks broadly at Kip. Now he abruptly shouts, "Snake!"

"Yes, boss," comes Snake's voice.

"Cool it—or I'll edit you out."

"Yes, *sir!*"

The Lady has turned away and begun energetically working on her unconscious twin's arms and hands. Her face is perceptibly flushed.

Aside to Baramji, Zannez says, "Tomorrow remind me to get Snake to show you how he got his name. It's one for the books." He chuckles, sopping his neck and head; then he glances absently at the mop—a scarlet lace garter belt—and stuffs it in his pouch.

Meanwhile Kip had undone the outer wrapping of Ochter's gift. It is now visibly a large, long-necked bottle, with a small package attached to its neck. Kip carefully detaches this and lays it aside before proceeding to slit open the costly constant-heat and blow-resistant inner layer. He's working with more and more caution, occasionally glancing quizzically at Ochter.

"Lords of the suns!"

The last layers fall apart, revealing a large, squared-off bottle elaborately scripted and sealed in gold. Its contents gleam deep purple in the mingled emerald and turquoise from the sky. Zannez, Baram, and Linnix stare hard at it; Cory and the four young actors, just coming out to join the group, look questioningly from the regal bottle to the others.

"If this is what I—" Kip begins, then breaks off to address the Lady. "Lady Pardalianches, you're from Rainbow's End—by any chance does this look familiar? I believe it's made there."

The Lady glances up. "Why, yes, it's just Eglantine, isn't it? Or perhaps an illegal copy, there're so many about. . . . Oh, Doctor Bram, her muscles *do* feel so, well, so different tonight."

Prince Pao has come up behind Kip to inspect the bottle. "It's no copy," he says. "We use a lot of it. See the numbering in that special FWA seal? Anyway, the smell will tell, as they say. You can't copy that."

"I smelled some once," Stareem says proudly. She looks almost luminous, an exquisite moon-child in Pao's silver lace gown and her own natural platinum hair. Bridey, sitting on the parapet with one fine leg swinging, is a child of the sun in glorious golden lace. But Ser Vovoka, beyond them, is attending only to the sky.

"I've barely heard of Eglantine." Bridey grins affectionately at Stareem. "That shows you *my* class of friends."

"But Doctor Ochter—" Cory begins, and is drowned out by Zannez, who's been glaring at the Lady.

" 'Just Eglantine,' eh? Just Royal Eglantine—just its weight in zer-anaveths, right? Cameramen's pay doesn't run to 'just Eglantine.' But I've tasted it a couple of times at the feed troughs of the rich—and my, oh my."

"Neither does Federation pay," says Kip. "But I can confirm. Just Eglantine—oh, my, my."

From the shadows, Linnix and Baramji murmur agreement.

"Nor do academic salaries." Ochter beams. "I've neither tasted nor smelled it; in fact, I'd never heard of it until my students gave me this as a retirement present. I didn't know what to do with it, till a friend volunteered to store it in his wine cellar. When I decided on this trip and heard of you, I inquired and was told that it was universally enjoyed. It seemed to be a suitable hostess gift for Myr Cory."

"Very good," says Pao.

"But Doctor Ochter!" Cory finally breaks in. "This seems a fearfully extravagant gift. A sip would be just lovely. But I am beginning to believe this passes the limits of what we may properly accept. Please don't think I'm being rude. I wouldn't for the worlds want to cast a shadow on your wonderful gift, but—"

"No problem, as the good doctor would say." Ochter holds up a lecturing finger: "You'll find that the regulations do not apply to—I quote— 'potables and comestibles to be shared by all present, especially upon a special occasion; and/or the remainder thereof.' Note that 'remainder.' That's straight from a Federation legal body. Frankly, he objected to a trinket I'd first thought of, from my home planet. And that reminds me! Everyone I spoke with told me I must warn you of the salted peanuts effect."

"You mean it's salty?" Cory asks.

"Oh, goodness, no, Myr Cory. That's merely an old phenomenological term from antiquity, for something you cannot easily stop eating or drinking if you take one. Today we'd say spice-berries, or those little biscuit-bites, I forget the name. It seems Eglantine has this property."

"Of course!" says Cory. "Morpleases. But how amusing!"

"Not all that amusing if you want to keep any, Cor," Kip says. "Also, it's powerful stuff."

"Everyone knows you don't drink Eglantine by yourself," Pao says severely. "I had a great-uncle who set the trophy room on fire that way."

"Right," says Zannez. "You must not, repeat not, leave that bottle open near. anybody you're not watching every minim. And that includes you and me and the most devout abstainer you know. The compulsion fades in five to ten minim, faster if you're talking. I'm not joking—I got briefed by the Gridworld wine board for a documentary. But we used—phew!—cold colored tea."

"My goodness! Perhaps we shouldn't open it," says Cory.

Zannez groans.

"Of course we will," Ochter reassures her. "I've been told exactly how, too. We all pour one drink apiece—I have the glasses in the little box. But before anyone drinks, two or three people escort the bottle to the next room, say, or any well-lighted place where no one could go unremarked for the next few minim. Then we all start at the same time, as one does a toast. And when it's properly time for another we just fetch it back and repeat. Isn't that what you do, Prince?"

The boy starts to speak—then shuts his mouth abruptly. It comes to Kip that the prince's style of home dining doubtless includes a wine steward and other liveried assistance. Next instant the lad finds the tactful words. "That is the proper principle. And you see, storage is no problem; it's like any other liquor unless you've just had some."

"Well, this *is* a new experience!" Cory laughs. "We have to thank you very much, Doctor Ochter— Oh! Look up, everybody, it's really starting at last!"

Kip looks up with the others, anticipating what they'll see.

The Green Fingers stage has passed during the Damei visit, giving place to an immense and ever-changing upper-atmosphere auroral display. The eastern sky, behind the black horizon trees, is a radiant green striped with a few horizontal black bands, which are out-of-season clouds; Kip has been privately fretting about these. But now, between the black treetops, a sparkle of scattered diamonds is erupting all along the east. As the watchers gaze, the diamonds float upward, joining, until the whole eastern horizon is one long blaze. The brilliance clears the treetops, passes behind a cloud or two, and emerges upward as a great arc of white light, in which facets of vivid spectral hues appear, change, and vanish, like flights of astral birds.

For an instant this fiery apparition could be a limb of the Star itself, and many watchers gasp; but Kip knows otherwise. Sure enough, just as the arc's edge approaches the zenith, down at the horizon its central area darkens. The darkness spreads fast, becoming an inner edge, and the vast curve of brilliance becomes an arc, a segment of a ring or halo whose center is below the horizon.

The arc spreads upward and outward, diffusing, changing, always with its internal play of color—and as it diffuses, the diamonds of a following arc break out among the eastern trees. It is as if the oncoming Star were shedding off great haloes.

On the hostel deck, people can be heard sighing out held breaths. As the second arc rises, pursuing its stately, ghostly course, only to give way to another—and another—Kip explains. "They're actually shells," he tells the watchers, "thin outer shells partly in the lower frequencies that we can see. The apparently empty space between them has quite a hash of the shorter wave lengths, but nothing dangerous. Last time we had a dozen or two of these before we got to the maximum, the peak density of the nova that we call the Star. . . . I regret to say that some poetic soul christened 'em the Smoke Rings."

A groan from somebody.

"Oh, look—it's all jiggling! Or is that me?" It was Bridey's young voice.

"No, it's not you." Kip chuckles. "Actually, that shimmering, quivery effect has been going on since, oh, before dinner—but you don't notice it until the rings come up. They stay steady, see? . . . Later on, that perpetual flicker can get a little maddening; you feel as if you can't think straight. We don't know what causes it, either."

In fact, he thinks, that skywide pulsing and strobing is already a little disturbing. It makes everything feel unreal. The eyes seek relief in the brilliant arcs, which seem to be immune.

"Perhaps we should make haste," little Ochter suggests, looking at the unopened bottle in Kip's hands.

"Righto." Kip returns to his struggle to clip the heavy wiring of the Eglantine's cork. Ochter picks up the little packet Kip has laid aside and opens it to reveal twenty elfin goblets, fragile as bubbles. . . .

"That's correct," Pao approves.

"They're so small," says Ochter, "I was amazed. But everyone assured me . . ."

"Not to worry. You'll see."

"How many?" Ochter counts heads. "Two and five and one and two, and you and I—I assume you'll take some, Prince?"

"Half a glass only at my weight . . . that's twelve so far."

"And the Ladies will share one glass?"

Lady Pardalianches nods sadly. "I'll moisten her lips from mine."

"So, thirteen, my young computer."

"I'll set them out on the ledge," Pao offers, "and stand guard while you stash the bottle, if you like."

"Excellent, excellent." Ochter counts out thirteen delicate glasses.

"You mean we all get some?" asks Snake Smith.

"Why, of course!" Cory is shocked.

"Oh ma'am, that's beautiful. Thank you very much." The others echo him. "It'll be a memory for always," adds Stareem.

"Ah-h-h!" Kip's labors are rewarded by a gentle pop. As he withdraws the cork, a vinous fragrance of a richness and delicacy beyond compare spreads across the deck. Prince Pao nods with satisfaction.

"Oh, my!" The little doctor sniffs appreciatively. "I do believe my advisers were correct. Myr Kip, would you pour it? These old paws are a trifle shaky for that freight."

"Righto." Kip carefully carries the Royal Eglantine back to where Pao is lining up the tiny glasses, with his own placed apart.

"I believe I'll take the bottle into your infirmary, if you don't mind, Doctor," Ochter says reflectively. "It's just a mite safer, if all this is fact."

"No problem," says Baram. "I'll go with you."

"No. With all due respect to you, Doctor, I have already chosen my guardians for the task." Ochter raises his voice. "Myr Stareem, Myr Eleganza, would you both be so kind as to accompany me into Doctor Baramji's domain, when our host finishes pouring? You see, there *is* a plan," the old man adds archly, to general chuckles.

The two beautiful girls rise and from long habit regally pace the few meters down the deck—Bridey the queen of golden fire, Stareem the queen of silver snow. Kip sees they can't resist the extra swirl of skirt and smoothing of waist that betrays their pleasure in the beautiful new robes. Ochter struggles up to meet them, bowing creakily.

Kip feels his throat choke up a trifle. They're such kids—Stareem is what? Fifteen, maybe less? And Bridey-Eleganza not much more. What a life for them. Don't think of it: maybe their alternatives are worse. The Federation has a few dark Human worlds, too. Maybe these two are fortunate. He finishes with Pao's half glass and recorks the Eglantine. It now displays a superb warm ruby glow beneath the whitening light.

"Let me carry it, Doctor Ochter," Bridey says. "You lead the way. If I trip you can have the Dameii fly me up and drop me. Here. . . ." She scoops up the flowing skirt and tucks it in her sash, so high that Kip sees where the scarlet item Zannez pouched belong. Stareem hastily readjusts the skirt while Ochter tactfully looks away.

Baramji rises to open the infirmary door and turn on a light, Kip hands over the Eglantine, and the little procession sets off. As Stareem closes the infirmary door behind them, Prince Pao, grinning, takes up an extravagantly bellicose sentinel station before the line of little ruby lights.

"This becomes more serious later," he says. "We'll have to persuade the Lady Paralomena to take my place—sorry, ma'am."

The Lady Pardalianches wheels on him, her face a mask of fury. "You—you cruel boy! Oh—"

"I humbly beg your pardon, Lady. I meant no disrespect." He bows to her, his plumed cap held across his breast. But Kip, who can see his face, reads trouble brewing and hopes to the heavens the Lady will shut up. Inspiration comes:

"Oh, look!" He points. "Your sister, Lady Pardalianches—I believe I saw your sister move!"

She's at the bed in a flash, Pao forgotten. And to Kip's amazement he and the others can see real movement there. The gleaming coverlet over the unconscious woman's legs rises once, twice, as though Paralomena is trying to bend both her knees. Her sister gasps out, "Doctor!"

Doctor Baramji is already at the other side of the rollbed, his ear pressed to the invalid's chest. The bent-up legs subside as he listens. Kip's stomach lurches. Have they seen the poor creature's death throes? His mind begins to work on the grim practicalities of storage, transport—the Moom are notoriously averse to carrying the dead.

But Baramji raises his head, nodding reassurance to the marquise. Then he bends beneath the bed and adjusts something invisible to Kip. "A little more oxygen and blood sugar," Baram says, "if she's going to be so active."

"Oh, *Doctor*—oh, Doctor, my darling *lives,* she'll live again, I always knew—"

"We can only let time do what work it will, my dear." Baramji produces two more of the large blue capsules. "These will help you to be patient. Ah, thank you, Linnie." He takes the glass Linnix offers and presses it on the marquise. "I must insist you take these quickly, my dear. Much might depend upon your steady nerves."

"Oh—"

Kip can see her hand shake as she seizes the capsules. Linnix is at her side, steadying the glass as she drinks.

"There. Now I suggest a light—very light—massage of those legs, if you have the strength." Baram pats the Lady's shoulder. "I'm right here, you know." He and Linnix retire to their loungers by the infirmary wall. The marquise is already at work on her sister, murmuring and cooing fondly to her.

Kip catches Baram's eye and looks a question. The doctor shrugs, letting both hands fall wide in total bafflement.

At that moment the main infirmary light goes out, and Ochter, with his attendant nymphs, emerges.

"We placed it by your night-light, Doctor," the little man says. He looks fatigued and limps straight to his chair.

"It took us hours to find it in these weird shadows." Bridey laughs, shaking her beautiful head. "We sure could tell a bachelor lives there, too. Do you always keep your soap in your shoes, Doctor Baram?"

"Ah, so that's where it went," Baramji says absently, watching the rollbed.

"Myr Kip," calls Stareem, "I thought you told us that you don't have any Damei servants."

"We don't," Kip tells her. "Why?"

"Well, when we were in there I heard somebody giving the arcade a good sweep-out. Are there any other Humans here?"

"No—at least, I hope not."

"I, too, noticed those sounds," Ochter puts in. "I concluded that one of those large featherlike trees must be brushing the outer wall. As I mentioned, there's a pronounced breeze on the entry side, though one doesn't feel it here."

"That's the *V'yrre,* the dry-season wind." Kip chuckles. "For sure we don't have any visible little helpers—wish we did, eh, Cor?"

"And I'll take a medical orderly while you're at it," says Baramji as he wrestles to let down the back of Linnix' lounger.

Kip quietly beckons him over to the console.

"Bram," he says low-voiced, looking at Cory. "I want you to put this in your infirmary safe, soonest." Cory nods agreement. "It's our three Tocharis. Ochter found them in Yule's and Hiner's bags. They're dry. They must have been taken from the open workshop, where I stupidly left them for recharging."

He can feel Bram's whole attention abruptly focus on him, but he continues to look away. After an instant Baram murmurs, "Yule *and* Hiner?"

"One or both, we don't know. In one of the open duffels, Ochter says."

"Hm'm. . . . Right." Baram tucks the bag under his arm and heads for the infirmary. At the door he checks and turns to the others. "I have to go to my quarters for a minim. Anyone who fears I may be after the liquor bottle is welcome to observe."

"Oh, we trust you, Doc," Zannez says piously and adds, as Baram vanishes into the infirmary, " 'cause you haven't touched your drink yet."

Amid the general laugh Kip begins rechecking the console displays he'd been supposed to watch. On the eastern horizon, two arcs of white fire are now expanding quite close together; the invisible center of the rings—the Star itself—is now obviously very close to the horizon. They'd better get that Eglantine toast ready.

"I wonder if somebody would be good enough to pass out these drinks?"

he says over his shoulder. "Then we can start as soon as Bram comes back and the Star actually shows."

"Hear, hear!" Zannez jumps up. "How about me and the kids deal it around? And seeing this is in your honor, Myr Cory, isn't there some way we can pry you off that computer for half a minim, so you can enjoy?"

Linnix pulls herself up from the comfortable recliner. "Myr Kip, you're monitoring overall inputs, aren't you? I believe I can do that for you, if you want to relieve Myr Cory."

"Sold to the first bidder," says Kip over Cory's protests, "with thanks from both. Cor's had quite a day. All right, Madame Administrator honey. Do you go quietly, or must I carry you? Frankly, I'm a little out of condition."

Cory rises and stretches, smiling gratefully at Linnix. By the lounge doors, Ek is handing Ochter a tiny ruby goblet. Cory says, "Doctor Ochter, why don't you go right ahead and have some? It's yours, you know, and—forgive me—you do look as if you could use it."

"No, no, I thank you, Myr Cory. That would not be right." The old man carefully accepts the tiny glass. "But I confess I'm very curious to learn whether all this is true, or is some great joke."

"You will, Doc, you will," says Zannez. He's presenting a glass to the marquise. She leaves off massaging her sister's legs to clutch it with both jewel-lit hands.

"Oh, thank you! I'm *so* tired." She sighs sweetly.

The deck is steadily darkening, despite the blaze in the east. Kip can just see Bram come quietly out of the infirmary. The doctor peers about till he locates Linnix at the console and then sits down beside her empty lounger. Bridey sees him, too, and brings him his drink.

"All here and ready when the Star is," she announces.

Heads turn eastward, and Kip hears exclamations of dismay. He looks up to see that what had seemed to be the dark-forested horizon is in fact a solid black bank of low cloud, its edges glittering with silver light. The great halo of diamond light swelling above it shows where the Star will rise —and moving toward that spot, on the wings of the *V'yrre*, is a huge black-and-silver cloud promontory.

"You godlost cloud!" Kip explodes. "By the nine purple devils, with the whole sky to flap around in, why? . . . Well, we'll just have to wait till the Star rises past it. It does look to be moving pretty fast."

The current ring of light swells in majestic silence toward the zenith; beneath it is an unusually wide band of black, and from behind the cloud layer come rays of a somewhat different quality—the outermost fringes of the hidden Star itself. A feeling of something huge and alien and unnameable coming onto them grips the watchers on the deck.

Cory is lounging on the parapet behind her mate. He looks around and catches her smiling fondly at him. As usual, a warm, complex tenderness sparks. He smiles back, thinking, not quite experimentally, My Cory.

Permanent mateships are quite rare, and it's never occurred to Kip—or to his friends—that he might be capable of one. But he and Cor have been together far longer than either has been mated before, and it's getting harder and harder for Kip to imagine life without her, or with someone else. They've never discussed it. But he's pretty sure their mateships here on Damiem have been as happy for her as for him. . . . He grins, remembering Kenter's old joke: "All this and money, too?"

Right now, Cory's smile is untypically relaxed, almost dreamy. She's enjoying her unexpected freedom to watch the Star. In their life together she's so seldom without some background occupation or concern. Seeing her now so peaceful, he wishes for the thousandth time that he could give her some of his own easygoing nature. I'm good for her, he thinks.

Beyond her, along the parapet, Kip hears little Stareem urging a glass of Eglantine on Vovoka. Surprisingly, the sky-obsessed man takes it. Kip shifts to look past Cory and sees Vovoka lift and drain the glass in one draught, quite oblivious to the general plan.

"We-ell!" The Lady Pardalianches sounds scandalized.

Kip peers into the shadow beyond Vovoka and makes out the golden rollbed. That glimmering female blur beside it is the marquise. As he looks, a white elbow upraises itself from her veiling. Despite her disapproval, the Lady seems to be indulging herself in a generous sip. Kip grins.

Meanwhile, Vovoka hasn't turned back to the sky, as Kip expected. Instead he's lingering over his glass, eyeing it sharply, tipping it up to roll a last drop on his tongue, and rudely spitting into the treetops below. Then, as if satisfied, the tall man sets the glass bubble on the parapet and looks deliberately around the group until he finds Ochter.

"It will not work, you know," he says directly to Ochter, with a cold sound that might have been meant as a chuckle.

Everyone falls silent. Vovoka continues to examine Ochter for several long breaths, during which the small man gazes up at him like one helplessly hypnotized.

The odd scene holds long enough for Kip to puzzle over it. Vovoka's strange remark sounds as matter-of-fact as if he's referring to some well-known project of Ochter's. And Ochter's peculiar, almost cringing reaction seems to acknowledge it. Yet so far as Kip knows, the two men have barely exchanged a word. How could Vovoka be privy to anything Ochter plans?

Or—can Ochter and Vovoka be already acquainted, but for some reason not admitting it? And what "will not work" about the Eglantine? Could

Vovoka have some strange notion that Ochter is trying to ingratiate himself with his handsome gift? Why? Or is this Vovoka's idea of a joke? If so, it doesn't look it. The tension between the two men looks real.

What the scene reminds Kip of, in fact, is one of the old grid-shows he'd seen as a back-planet youngster, where the villain reads people's thoughts against their will. That was kids' nonsense, of course; for centuries everybody's known that Human-Human telepathy doesn't exist.

Nonsense aside, Kip decides that this must have to do with some earlier conversation he's missed. Probably it's plain to everybody but himself.

But when he looks around he sees only expressions as mystified as his own. Cory's questioning gaze is moving from Ochter to Vovoka, from himself to Bram. And Bram is taking careful sniffs at his untasted Eglantine. Even in the strange light Kip's sure he can see Bram's eyebrows rising as he sniffs.

Kips raises his own glass to sniff, but at that instant Vovoka breaks the stasis.

"I haven't time. Pity," he says shortly, still in the same conversational tone, and turns his back on the group to resume his watch on the sky. Complete enigma, Kip thinks. He can hear Ochter exhaling as though he'd been holding his breath.

"Well! My goodness!" the little man says shakenly. He takes out his old-style cloth handkerchief and dabs at his face. "My!"

Kip's trying to frame a tactful question as to what Vovoka meant. But before he can speak, Ochter essays a smile and says in his normal genial tones:

"Well, if everyone is served, shall we ask Myr Cory to lead us in a toast to the Star? And we shall drink to our hosts as well."

No explanation of the scene with Vovoka appears to be forthcoming. Ah, well, Kip tells himself, with the perfume of the Eglantine tantalizing his nose, probably the sculptor just frightened poor old Ochter into temporary paralysis with weird personal remarks of which only he knows the meaning, if any. Kip glances up at the artist's powerful figure. Anyone who'd seen Vovoka's tremendous strength and totally self-centered behavior might well be disconcerted if Vovoka suddenly singled him out.

"All set?" Ochter lifts his glass to the chaotic lights above. "Myr Cory, will you bring the Star out of hiding?"

Everyone raises their tiny drinks, looking at Cory. Kip swivels around to face her, glass high.

There is a tiny pause.

Cory lifts her wine to the dazzling sky: "To the passing of the Star!"

And just as she brings her glass back to her lips, a light, authoritative voice says clearly, "Hold a minim, all!"

It's little Prince Pao, who has his glass raised, not to drink but to examine. Everyone stares.

"You know," says Pao, still studying the glass, "he may have a point, that light-sculptor chap. The fragrance is there—in the Eglantine, I mean —but I've been here smelling it quite a while now. One becomes aware of a funny chemical undersmell that doesn't belong—"

He's interrupted by a sound from the vicinity of the golden rollbed beside which the marquise luxuriantly reclines. Her Eglantine glass is in the lounger's holder, and Kip can just make out that it appears to be nearly empty.

The sound comes again, now unmistakable. In the most refined, gentle manner, the Lady Pardalianches is snoring.

XII

CONTACT:
Kip Remembers

It takes Kip a minim to make the connection between the state of the Lady and the state of her glass.

Meanwhile Baram has gone to her and is attempting to rouse her. In vain; the light is now so bright that Kip can see Bram turn the Lady's eyelids and check the position of her tongue, while she sleeps on. She is not, in fact, asleep, but unconscious.

Something *is* off with the Eglantine, all right. Murmurs are rising around the deck.

"I suggest that no one should drink any more of this lovely wine till we find out what's wrong," says Cory pleasantly. "Don't you agree, Doctor Baram?"

"I do." Baram has produced his pocket kit and is listening to the Lady's heart.

Little Doctor Ochter has made his limping way to them, his face a picture of dismay. When Baram looks up, Ochter says anxiously, in tones loud enough for all to hear, "How is she, Doctor? Apart from my natural concern, a most disturbing thought has come to me. Is there any possibility that she has taken a fatal poison?"

"*Fatal?*" Baram eyes Ochter in puzzlement. "There's a strong odour of ambezine hydrate on her breath—that's the same drug you say you gave

Yule and Hiner, a simple soporific. We didn't catch it in the wine because ambezine has the unique property of being virtually odorless until ingested. And all her signs are consistent with a moderate dose of it. But fatal? No. Why?"

"Oh, that *is* a relief!" The little man again mops his brow. "Of course I offer my inexpressibly abject apologies to Myr Cory and her guests for having presented such a questionable gift. But my first reaction, aside from wonderment at how some drug got into the sealed bottle—" He breaks off and looks around at Pao. "I suppose there is no question of Eglantine's going bad, or developing, say, a toxic mold, from improper storage?"

"Absolutely not," Pao replies. "It's easier to store than most wines, but if you do manage to spoil it, you just get some fancy vinegar."

"So it must be an introduced substance." Ochter sighs. "As I was saying, my first thought was simply to curse my own naïveté. Why had I not suspected that some of those so-surprisingly generous students might have thought to play a trick on their old professor? Such episodes aren't unknown. I should have been on my guard.

"But then I recalled that the bottle had spent five years in the custody of my friend, who is an active jurist in the Criminal Division. I know of two occasions on which his life has been threatened by vengeful convicts or their confederates, and only last year the Special Branch kept a protective watch on him for some months. Suppose some malefactor had got at his cellar and seen that bottle, believing it to be his?"

He shakes his head worriedly. "My students may have found me boring, or even obnoxious. But certainly they would not carry a joke so far as actually to kill me. On the other hand, the death of my friend is exactly what an enraged, vengeful criminal—or his allies—would desire. Supposing *two* sets of persons, or two substances, were involved. Are you sure, Doctor, that the Lady's condition may not mask a far more serious agent, while giving it time to work?"

Baram is frowning. "I see your concern. . . . Well, I'm no toxicologist, but medical xenology pokes its nose into many places. . . . No," he says thoughtfully, "I'm not aware that there is any Human poison so tasteless that a lethal dose could be unwittingly drunk in wine. . . . Nor do I know of any which in lethal concentration would show no symptoms—pain, convulsion, gastric bleeding, nausea, heart arrhythmias, tremor, et cetera —over so long a time, with the patient apparently in normal stage D sleep. . . . There is a rare amanitoxin, an alkaloid which slowly dissolves the liver, but the process isn't symptomless and a very large amount is required.

"So I would say no. Even if we hypothesize that two separate operators had tampered with the wine, I conclude that the Lady has taken only a simple soporific, perhaps reinforced by this." He picks up the marquise's gold-chased flask and opens it to release the pleasant dry-wine odor.

"And as to how Soporin got into the Eglantine bottle," Baram goes on in his ordinary informal manner, "Kip here is the custodian of the cork." This is news to Kip, who looks about hastily and recalls that it's back in the bottle. It'll be wanted for examination; he'll dig up a replacement next time he goes in.

"And when we examine it," Bram finishes, "I'll wager we find puncture traces. There are sophisticated techniques for injecting through glass, but the cork is far more likely where the victim isn't suspicious."

Ochter chuckles bitterly. "That aptly describes me. . . . What a pity, though. If only I could bring it home to those young rascals how many people's pleasure they've spoiled. . . . If they thought at all, they probably envisioned me opening it in my study with a couple of similar old fuddy-duds. . . ."

Two or three people laugh halfheartedly.

"Listen, all," says Cory's warm voice. "I've just remembered a most interesting bottle of Ice Flowers liqueur someone gave us. It's made by the hermits on Glacier. Of course it isn't Eglantine, but if you've never tasted Ice Flowers, you really should. When things quiet down here"—she gestures at the console—"I'll go root it out and we'll at least have something pleasant to celebrate with."

"Oh, ma'am, you shouldn't—" "No need to do that." "Oh, how beautiful—" "Coloss!" The voices sound cheerier. The deck darkens suddenly as the Star's light submerges wholly in cloud, but there are glorious fringes escaping toward the zenith which promise a grand spectacle to come.

Meanwhile, Cory's gesture has recalled Kip's attention to the dials he's supposed to be monitoring. Linnix' hand is pointing to three—no, four—readings, which are showing very high averages of Star-radiation un-stopped by the cloud. Kip must run them over in detail to make sure the component maxima are within safety limits. He sets to work just as Ochter goes past on his painful way back to his chair. The little man's face looks wretched, Kip thinks. Poor little chap, to have his splendid gift turn out that way. Those students . . .

But as Kip's hands and eyes work almost automatically, an odd thought comes to him: How strongly Ochter has injected himself into the evening's events! In fact, their whole version of what's gone on seems to have come from him. First there are these students, mythical or otherwise, who doped Ochter's gift-wine. And then—Kip thinks back—the whole story of Yule and Hiner, and their sleep shots—and the Tocharis in their bags—

—and even, gods! the safe departure of Wyrra and his family. Only Ochter vouched for that.

Kip's fingers slow to a stop on the knobs as a voice replays itself in his head. It's the voice of Pace Norbert, the Guardian from whom they took over. Kip had accused _him_ of being a trifle paranoid. And Norbert had lectured him.

"All over this Galaxy," Norbert had said, "for as long as you live, there will be big crooks and little crooks and lonesome weirdos, Human and otherwise, dreaming up ways to get their hands on Stars Tears stuff. Too abhorrent? Don't you believe it. On the Black Worlds there are Human beasts who salivate over the prospect of torturing children. And passing in any crowd are secret people whose hidden response to beauty is the desire to tear it into bleeding meat."

Kip had flinched away. He'd fought a war, that was over now. This stuff he didn't want to know.

"And everywhere," Norbert had gone on inexorably, "there are beings who'd do anything for riches, for money, wealth, credits— Get it through your heads what the Tears you're guarding represent: pure treasure. Mountains of credits. Better than their weight in zeranaveths, those can be traced. Riches, worth taking any sort of pains for, worth scheming complex plans, worth killing off a dozen people for. One big haul can make a criminal rich for life. And the whole Galaxy knows it. Do you fancy nobody is dreaming about that?

"With the Federation guard, an ordinary armed raid wouldn't work. Entry must be achieved by cunning and stealth and the guard taken out from behind. And every quiet year that passes leaves us less alert. No, one of these years when you've forgotten all about him, the devil will show up. Say, maybe a lost Spacer girl—a genuinely nice girl. And some kind friends come looking for her. . . . Who's going to check them out before you're all dead, or poisoned, or your communications are cut?

"Don't go to sleep, Kip."

Dear gods of the universe, thinks Kip now, slowly resuming his task, have I been asleep? A harmless little old lame man, who's so helpful and sympathetic. . . . Of course he could do nothing alone, but by coincidence two odd young men have landed, uncleared, and so obviously angry at being here that it never occurs to me to wonder—and just in case it _does_ occur to someone, the dear little old man can vouch for their being drugged asleep—and he even returns the guns they've stolen—after they proved dry, by the way. And he kindly gives us all some luxury wine that comes within a hair of laying us all out senseless!

As it should have, Kip sees. If it hadn't been for Pao—and who could expect a person really familiar with Eglantine among the handful of tourists to a minor astronomical event on a Rim planet? Not to mention a greedy, almost equally familiar marquise?

As he thinks this, Kip is distracted by the memory of the Vovoka and Ochter incident. Why isn't Vovoka flat too? He must have spat out more than they'd realized. . . . But—wait—there's a possible explanation for the strange dialogue—suppose *Vovoka* was Ochter's confederate and had decided to back out? "It will not work"—that would account for Ochter's dismayed reaction, too.

On the other hand, if Yule and Hiner are Ochter's confederates, there's no proof that they're out of commission in any way. They could be just waiting until everyone was unconscious from the wine. . . . And as for the coincidence of their being here—it's hard to think it, glancing at Linnix' starlit eyes, but she could easily have switched syrettes. A *genuinely nice girl* like that. Or they could have been switched on her; Kip's noticed that Ochter has very deft fingers. . . .

Kip's head is whirling; only a minim or two have passed since Cory spoke, but he feels as if his world has been turning over like a kaleidoscope, with each turn displaying a new, nastier set of possibilities. But—are they possibilities? They seem only barely so; what's truly impossible is for him to think that this is real, is the actual leading edge of a Stars Tears attack.

What he needs is proof. And the only available proof he sees is the status of Yule and Hiner. If Ochter lied about that, if they're in fact up and active, then any or all of the rest follows. But if—gods, may it be so!— they're deep in drugged sleep as the little man said, then all the rest recedes into fantasy.

Half rising, he spins the console seat to face Cory, his mouth opening to announce his plan to step down to the end of the deck and check out those two.

He finds her in low-voiced conversation with Baram. Before he can speak, Cory smiles and says firmly, "No.

"Kip, dear, I think I know what you were going to say." She straightens his scarlet neckerchief. "The answer is, you must not. If the improbable is true, you would be walking into a trap, and also leaving us in serious danger, together with these innocent, unwarned, unarmed people for whom we have responsibility. . . . Was I right?" She smiles mischievously for the benefit of the watchers, and Baram gives a surprisingly lifelike chuckle.

"Yes," Kip admits, "I guess I've been a little slow."

"Oh, no, darling. Three heads are better than two. But we can't talk long, if any of this is true—and we must act as if it is until we're sure. . . . Baram was just saying, this is the classic dilemma: if the danger is real, there *is* no safe way to confirm it. . . . My plan is simply to let the next Deadman's Alarm cycle go through. I explained to Baram that we don't have Mayday just now."

"I hope you explained that was my doing," Kip says morosely.

"My responsibility," she says shortly, grinning her good grin. "Do smile for our public, dear. . . . If Dayan's sore at having his boys miss that game, too bad. We aren't calling him on guesses alone; the three facts we know add up to Mayday by themselves." She holds up three slim, tanned fingers.

"First, two unlisted, uncleared landers—Coincidence A. And, parenthetically, when I think of what we could have missed in those duffels— and how much of that so-called underwater gear could be used for climbing, I'm sick. . . . Coincidence B, a strange ship is accidentally sighted nearby. And finally, a drugged wine is offered to us under conditions that —by Coincidence C—would have rendered us all unconscious at once. What's the old saying? Once is coincidence, two is something or other, but *three times is enemy action.*

"And our question has to be, the wine trick having apparently failed, what do they do now? What's next? Is there a fallback plan?"

"By the gods, I'd missed that ship," Kip says. "Suppose it's full of bastards waiting for a signal to land and start work on the Dameii?" A pang strikes him; he has an instant of acute, almost physical longing to be sure that Wyrra and Nyil are safe.

"Or that ship could simply be their getaway," Baram says. "Yule and Hiner could work alone; more people means more splits, not to mention more risk."

He rises to stand with his hands on the console, apparently studying a readout. "I've got to get back to my seat before this looks too much like a council of war. But I want to impress this thought—we mustn't scare anybody into cutting our communications. That cable and those little webs up there are a very vulnerable lifeline, if any of this is true. Green?"

"Green as you go."

As Baram passes Linnix, who has been politely intent on the console, he pats her hand. To his surprise her other hand snaps around to cover his, holding him in place.

"Doctor Bram," Linnix breathes very softly, "and Myr Kip, too, if you can hear me. I couldn't help overhearing your general subject, and there's something you should know. . . . No, don't look at me, please, look at this readout here."

She removes her hand to point. They bend over it.

"That man Ochter," she whispers, "he's well acquainted with Hiner and Yule. On shipboard they were last to go down, they all three spent, oh, four hours, chatting in the view-room. They seemed very friendly, they laughed a lot. And then when they came in, Hiner was making a little fuss, and Ochter said something like, 'Don't make me sorry I chose you'—in a very sharp tone, that's why I heard. At the time I thought he meant he'd chosen Hiner to take the berth above him—we load from the top down, so he couldn't turn in until after Hiner. . . . And, wait, he added, 'Look at Mordy here.'

"I began to realize they never expected to see me again, you know. So I thought Myr Cory should know. I may have gotten it all wrong, probably it's nothing. And they said good-bye when they went down, not like they expected to all wake up together . . . or, wait, was there just a little something funny? . . . Oh, I could be imagining anything. But about the other, would you tell her, please?"

"Great Apherion, I should hope to say so," says Kip. "Look, we can't flank march this minim, Baram; I'll have to grab an inconspicuous chance."

"Good gods." Baram straightens up. "And good girl, Linnie."

"Wait. . . ." she says, remembering hard. "One other thing. After I left you, B-Bram . . . I looked at the lake. Hiner was swimming. The point is, I don't think he's a true Aquaman—he's, what do they call it, a spoiled Aqua? His gills must not work right. He came up and gasped and gasped and gasped. Poor man . . . I don't think he saw me. When people came out, he left the lake. There! That *is* all."

She starts running an analysis on the twenty-minim readout.

"Lords of space," mutters Kip as Baram departs. "What an earful." Now to find a likely minim to tell Cor that the probabilities have changed.

Thinking of Cor he smiles a little: his girl—and a real Spacer. It for sure hasn't escaped her that if any of this *is* true, it wouldn't be in the plan to leave any witnesses alive. But he won't get a word, a nuance, to admit *that.* No, it's "responsibility for other tourists." Well, let's hope that Deadman's Alarm works. Let's hope this is all one big false alarm. He'd give a lot to hear old Dayan cursing them out for a pack of spooky fools! . . . But Dayan would be first to admit that those three "coincidences" justify a Mayday, even without Linnix' news.

When he turns back to the console, he finds that Linnix has run out two of the worst-looking inputs for him.

"Hey, thanks. . . . That microwave is still plenty high, isn't it?"

"Yes. . . . Would it do damage?"

"Not unless it's intense enough to generate heat—we're a long way from that."

"Good. I don't want to be a smoked oyster."

Kip, chuckling, gets a look over her shoulder at Ochter, sitting by the main doors—and the contrast between his imagined enemy Ochter and the bewildered-looking, little lame old man there, with his anxious old-pixie face, shakes him. Is he insane?

As he starts to turn around again to Cory, every surface on the deck suddenly lights to glittering silver, and bizarrely colored shadows pool beneath their feet.

All eyes look up.

In the fringes of the cloud bank, a huge, sky-filling diamond is separating itself from the darkness and the green auroras, and welling upward, reflected in the lake. As it moves higher, it seems to loom closer and its facets shed flakes of ever-stranger and more violently colored light, which blend to spectral white. A last moment of tattered cloud edges—and then the great apparition comes totally free and floods the world with brilliance.

The Star has risen at last.

And with it, the whole Human situation changes.

XIII

NOVA ONSET:
Alien Eruption

Ser Xe Vovoka, who has ignored the others' doings, suddenly turns full east and flings both arms up toward the risen Star.

"O Beautiful!" he cries in a deep, rough voice. "Enslaver! Radiant enchanter! Killer of worlds from none knows where—at last you are avenged. *Avridar!*"

With that he puts a hand to his forehead and with the speed of long practice rips off what seems to be the skin of his whole ruddy face and head—eyelids, lips, ears, jowls, hair, and all. It's a stiff gauze mask. The revealed skin is a dusty-looking, pebbled, drab purple.

"He's—he's not a Human!" cries Stareem.

With two swift gestures, Vovoka peels his hands and forearms, crumples all together, and throws it down by the screens.

This all happens so swiftly that Kip, wheeling around from the console, has time for only a bewildered impression of prune-dark skin and a long, vertical nose. Now he begins to take in the true Vovoka: The head is narrower than Human, but the features aren't too different, save for a prowlike forehead that runs with no break into the straight, nostrilless nose; long, thin-lipped mouth; downstretched eyes under heavy frontal bones that extend back, without temples, to circular ears; and pale stubbled crown that must have been recently shaved, showing an odd pattern.

All trace of jocularity has vanished from Vovoka's expression, leaving a strong-jawed face of great gravity and sadness, and some menace. Without the Human head, it can be seen that his shoulders are disproportionately wide and powerful, even for his height.

The alien takes two quiet paces along the parapet to Cory's chair. She sits unmoving, gazing at him with an unreadable expression. As he nears her, a small object gleams in his right hand—a hand, Kip sees, that is abnormally large and five-fingered.

Vovoka has been moving deliberately. Now, so suddenly Kip's eye can't follow, he's holding the object against Cory's temple.

She still doesn't move or flinch away but only continues to look up at him watchfully.

Kip, beyond them at the console, has twisted out of his seat and started for Cory, too. Now he freezes in midstride, seeing the object at Cory's head.

"Get away from my mate, Vovoka."

Vovoka addresses him in level, curiously weary tones. "This is a weapon. It will do any degree of damage I choose, but she will never be the same. You will return to that console and set incoming communications on standby. If you do exactly as I say, your mate will not be harmed. But try no tricks. I know those boards well."

Unexpectedly, Cory speaks. "Do as he says, Kip. It's all right." To Vovoka she adds, "Most of those left-hand keys aren't functional, Ser Vovoka. I only laid in a channel to Base frequency, and one broad-band sweep. The rest are data on the nova-front."

"I know that," the alien replies, and tells Kip, "Deenergize the modular antenna, and that's all."

Kip reluctantly goes back to the console, where he flicks two toggle switches and runs a slide switch to zero.

Watching him carefully, Vovoka says to the others, still in the same expressionless tone, "Please be calm and have no fear. I assure you that one person only, who is guilty of great crime, need be afraid. This weapon is intended solely for that person. The rest of you are entirely safe so long as you remain still and attempt no furtive action. If you insist on moving, I cannot guarantee your safety; and my reactions are very, very much faster than yours."

To Kip he adds, "Reset that alarm, Myr Korso."

The Deadman's Alarm has come on so recently that Kip himself hasn't seen it. Vovoka's claim about his reaction time appears to be true. Grimly, Kip resets it, thinking, A whole alarm cycle lost.

"May I go back to my chair, Ser Vovoka?" Linnix asks. "I should be near in case help is needed with the paralyzed girl."

"Very well."

Linnix carefully makes her way back to her place beside Doctor Baram. When she's seated again, Vovoka looks over at Stareem, while his weapon remains at Cory's head.

"Yes, small female," he says, his voice subtly more alien now and dark with sadness, "I am not Human. I am Vlyracochan, the last of my race. Others have given their lives, their vital essences, that I alone may live to complete our task. For—"

As he speaks Kip is wondering how in the name of the seven devils Vovoka brought that weapon on a Moom ship undetected and through the Federation check to Damiem. The first is virtually impossible, the second incredible. The weapon itself seems to be a relative of the X5 Daguerre, uncommon but not unknown in military Spacer circles. Its merits are good accuracy for such a small piece and an easy adjustment from stun to kill. But is it really a Daguerre, or is it only a toy, a harmless piece of plastite for children playing Spacer? That would explain its presence here. . . . Possible.

And now Vovoka begins to talk. It's axiomatic that when a man with a weapon begins to explain himself, his attention is as distracted as it's ever going to be. Right now is Kip's best chance to act—if he can bethink himself of anything to do.

But he can't—knowing nothing of Vovoka's intentions—and in any event, the danger to Cory is too great. That Daguerre could be real.

At that moment he sees a twitch or jerk of Vovoka's weapon hand, and something happens by the lounge doors, where Ochter sat. Kip looks around and sees Ochter against the doors, bent over and gasping, nursing one hand in the other.

"I warned you," Vovoka says tonelessly.

"But my *finger,*" Ochter protests. He holds the wounded hand up for an instant; Kip sees that the first finger is completely gone. The site is scarcely bleeding, it appears cauterized. "My error," the little man says gamely, "I was only going to my room to take some analgesic and lie down. Or to the infirmary, if you prefer. I didn't want to interrupt your talk."

Ochter must have figured along the same lines he himself had, Kip thinks. Thank the gods he didn't gamble with Cory's life.

He notices a tiny plume of steam or smoke rising from one of the door's lock handles, catching the multicolored radiance of the Star. Ochter must have placed his hand there when Vovoka picked off the finger. And Kip hadn't even seen the weapon swing away from Cory and back, so fast had been Vovoka's act! Whew.

"May I now go to my room? Obviously I am no possible threat to you, and I know I am not the one you seek."

"Go."

Ochter goes, this time hobbling down the Star-silvered deck toward his room.

This act of Vovoka's jolts Kip. "The one you seek"—subconsciously, he realizes, he'd been assuming it was Ochter. Now it's clearly not. Oh, gods, then—*who*? Zannez seems improbable. But Baram's a xenological doctor, he's treated all sorts of aliens. Could this be some crazed ex-patient? Or a relative? Oh, Lords of the Sky, please not Bram.

"Perhaps we may have an end to nonsense?" Vovoka sighs. "As I said, our investigations revealed that, contrary to the tale you heard tonight, there is one last crewman of the killer ship unaccounted for. A very young person. The regular gunnery crew seem to have refused to obey their mad captain's orders. Only this young one, little more than a child, would actually aim and fire the so-called planet-killer missile." He sighs again. "It has taken years and deaths, but our informants finally located the one who had been that child—here on Damiem."

All this while Cory has shown the strange peacefulness with which she submitted from the start. But the alien's next words galvanize her.

Vovoka looks at Kip. "And tonight I have heard it confirmed from your own boasting mouth. Kipruget Korso, perpetrator of abomination, prepare to die."

"No! No! No! No!" Cory screams. And to everyone's amazement she seizes Vovoka's gun hand with both her own and holds it tight to her own head.

"No!" Kip is shouting, too. "Don't harm her—she's crazy! Go ahead, shoot me if you have to shoot somebody."

"I do not intend to harm this female unless she forces me to it," Vovoka tells Kip. "I am giving you these minim to compose yourself, to die like a Vlyran."

Cory gets control of herself.

"Ser Vovoka, hear me! Doesn't the prospect of killing the wrong, innocent person, and letting the guilty go free—doesn't this bother you at all?" she demands. "Especially since I gather this is your last chance?"

"It would, very much," Vovoka replies slowly.

"Then forget Kip. He is the wrong person. I know, because—because—" The words are halting and ragged and Cory's eyes stare up unseeing, as though ghosts are breaking through deep burial in her mind.

"Because—*I did it!*" she cries. "Yes"—her voice is raw—"I was *Deneb*'s cabin girl. In those last days . . . Jeager only had me. I did it f-for him—" The words are wrenched out savagely. "*I did it.* I aimed and fired. I am the right person, the one you seek. You must kill me."

Kip's heart thuds, crashes. He simply will not accept or think of what

Cory's saying, refuses also to recall what she'd let slip in their first days, when she mentioned that she'd been in Rehab after the Last War. So what? Many had. But he's bewildered. He needs a minim to counter this mad, dangerous notion of Cor's.

Suddenly Zannez speaks. "Ser Vovoka, may my girls get up and get their robes? They're cold in that metal lace. See, one's shivering."

Stareem and Bridey, clad in their new finery, are sitting up in the loungers with their arms wrapped around themselves.

"Let them do that," Vovoka replies gravely. "I have no wish to commit unnecessary cruelty."

The girls rise and go quickly behind the screens. Kip shoots a grateful glance at Zannez and tries furiously to plan. Bridey and Stareem return wearing the APC short robes.

Kip gives a bark of jeering laughter. "Unnecessary cruelty," he mimics, "Oh, dear, no!" Can he infuriate Vovoka past reason? No good: the alien doesn't even look at him.

Cory is remaining calm, but still she clamps Vovoka's weapon to her forehead. Futile—he can break her hold any instant he chooses.

"Your spies were quite right, Ser Vovoka," she says gravely. "The criminal is here. But you are in danger of wasting your whole great effort by mistaking Kip for me—as happened once before, didn't it? You see, I know about the two Dav Caltos. But in those days there were others of your race to correct it. Now you say you are the last one left. You *must* be right. And I can prove to you that I did it. That I am the criminal you seek, not Kip. It is I you must punish."

"Be silent, woman. Your effort to save your mate is, I suppose, admirable. But futile. Any doubts I might have had died when I heard the boastful tone and joking manner in which he told the story—while *preparing food.* Now let the brute compose himself and die with that dignity he can muster."

"Oh, no, no—that tone is his one stupid weakness—when those who know him hear it, we know he is telling false tales of what he has *not* done. Let me make him tell you of things he *has* done, you'll hear his true voice."

"Ah, she's only trying to confuse you, Vovoka. Believe your spies, shoot me and have done with it."

"Ser Vovoka! Did your informants ever specifically tell you the sex of the criminal? Or was it just taken for granted as male? Look—we need facts. I can give you facts and prove them! Allow me ten sentences—with all my heart I beg you. If you refuse to hear so very little, your life's great mission will end in shame and mockery."

Anger burns now in his alien eyes, but she's taken the right risk.

"Go on."

"First, Kip was never on or near *Deneb*. He knows nothing of the whole dreadful business beyond what I was fool enough to try to remember in our first years. Old—*Deneb* was *old,* she had major differences from other Class X cruisers. A question or two about her structural peculiarities would prove that Kip never was aboard her. But we don't have *Deneb* here, or even a diagram. By any chance did you go aboard before they took her out to her end?"

"No."

"Pity. What you'd have seen might resolve this in a moment. You might even have seen me—I was part of the last skeleton crew. Before that, of course, I was *Deneb*'s cabin girl. *I* was the young fool who still thought that Captain Jeager was the last great hero, a god. So when the gunnery crew refused to use our Class L planet-breaker missile on this world-sized 'weapon,' I called them cowards and mutineers. I convinced Jeager I'd memorized every manual—I had—and I could do it myself, for him. If we had time, you could ask me anything—mass-thrust ratios, gee-loadings, markings, missile-ready procedure, settings, point of impact—but we don't. Wait—here's a crucial one: Kip, when you say you fired, what was your last full view of the, the target, before the automatics cut in, and what did you see?"

"Well, the computers got the last good look"—Kip's a cool gambler—"and since their sun was behind the target I merely saw a huge unfinished-looking spherical body, with construction activity moving on one dazzling limb. And—"

"You hear, Ser Vovoka? Computers—*Deneb* had *no* computer capable of initiating an L-missile! *I* laid in the conversion factors and sighted that master launcher myself, eye-hand. We'd mounted an old AW-Four firing scope with primitive cross hairs. Jeager's hands shook too much and we were alone, so it was *I* who aimed visually, and fired. Unbelievable as it sounds. But the terrible thing—" She's losing control of her voice; it's as if the words are torn out of her throat. "Oh, Ser Vovoka, that head and face. *That face* . . . it slowly formed as I aimed—it wasn't there at first. . . . Beauty. Transcendence—no words. And I aimed and fired . . . right between the eyes. I had to watch it swell, and distort horribly, and break apart. . . . Child as I was, I knew then I had done something abominable. The appalling radiance—no one who ever—could ever—"

She draws a long shuddering breath. The watchers hang on the scene; Stareem is weeping silently.

"I still see it—very f-frequently. The days are worst, I see the cross hairs converge against the sky. I'll never be free. Ser Vovoka, will you believe I was not unhappy when I thought you had found me? Couldn't you *feel* it?

"But then, when you changed to Kip— Oh, I can only beg you, beg you, beg you—do not make an error and kill poor blameless Kip—and leave me alone with . . . that. . . ."

Quite disregarding the weapon, she covers her own face briefly with her hands, then looks at her mate.

"Beloved—beloved, let me go. It is just. And now I know. It's kinder."

Kip's face twists with love, but he's no fool and he is fighting for that love.

"This is a ploy!" he exclaims to Vovoka. "She should have been an actress; she's trying to rush you. I, too, have seen the face she speaks of—of course, I first described it to her. It haunted me, too, for a time. But our races are so different, Ser Vovoka. What was almost a god to you, was to me a piece of very fine sculpture wrapped around a sun-smasher bomb. And what you heard as 'boasting' is simply that for many males of our race it is considered improper to appear very deeply moved, and the more moving the subject, the more taboo to appear touched by it. Sorry? Of course I'm sorry—sorry beyond words. For a time I considered ending my life."

During this speech Cory sits in exhausted silence, her eyes pleading with Vovoka, both trembling hands still clasping his weapon to her forehead. The others watch mesmerized. Above them the enormous Star-diamond is growing, changing, convoluting, while all around, the auroral backlight pulses, strobes so that rational speech and thought are becoming difficult. The glory is passing beyond mere splendor into a realm of strangeness.

Vovoka studies them both in silence. Kip, returning his gaze, suddenly becomes conscious of a vague disorientation and remembers Vovoka's stare at Ochter. Oh, gods, no—is the alien reading their minds? Quick, break it up—talk, say something!

Snatching at a memory of Spacer gossip years back, hoping against hope that it refers to Jeager, and that his voice conceals near panic, Kip says, "Moreover, although Cor claims she was a little cabin girl, she was still a *female*, right?

"It so happens—and your informants could confirm this by message— that Tom Jeager hated having women on his ship. He was truly crazy, you see—although he may have had a semirational aversion to the kind of emotional display you've just seen—forgive me, Cor. But the idea of a cabin *girl* allowed to fire their—our—biggest weapon by hand is pure fantasy. I can't recall a single woman on *Deneb*. He'd have found some excuse to get most of 'em off at the first stops."

"Nonsense," Cory says weakly. "N-nonsense!"

Vovoka makes an ambiguous sound. Gently, he releases one hand from Cory's clutch and takes from the inner pocket of his tunic a small sheaf of diagonally cut papers. Possibly an alien computer readout, Kip thinks. His heart begins to sink as Vovoka glances down the pages with lightning speed.

"Is Irien a male or female Human name?"

"Female," says Cory determinedly.

"Male," says Kip.

"And Glynnis?"

"No telling."

"Either," Cory says faintly. Her hands are shaking badly; she lets Vovoka carefully free his gun hand, too. He stands with the weapon pointing straight up as he reads on.

"Lee?"

"Male," says Kip.

"Not if it's s-spelled with, with an 'i,' Li," Cory manages to say.

Kip's own hands are trembling, his heart races. Has he really won? Was it really Jeager that Kenter had made that offhand remark about, twenty years ago? It seems so. For a moment he exults, quite oblivious to the fact that "winning" may mean his own death.

But then Vovoka speaks. "You do not recall any Human females aboard *Deneb*. And yet, without such ambiguous cases, the crew list shows thirty-two first names which I recognize as female."

Kip has lost, after all. His world collapsing around him, he forces his voice steady and belligerent.

"Such as?" he demands.

The alien sighs and consults his damned printout. Kip's gaze strays up to the glorious Star, then moves deliberately, meaningfully, from face to face of Zannez and his crew. Surprise, mass force, is the only hope left. ". . . four; Kara, two," Vovoka's saying; "Marye, three; Rhealune or Realune, five; Aytha, two."

"Oh, well," says Kip with the calm of desperation, "these are, if you'll forgive me, typical unskilled-worker names. Women from planets like Shoofly where they get no education. There could well have been some galley girls, or storekeepers, maintenance people who worked nights or in special areas one never saw. Forced on Jeager by the old equal-rights law."

From the corner of his eye Kip sees Snake untie his robe, while Zannez tightens his.

Vovoka consults his list again and says with finality, "Lieutenant-Commander Tali Temarovna, Chief Communications Officer."

Without visible warning, Kip leaps bodily onto the tall alien, both his arms locking around Vovoka's weapon arm, while his legs wrap Vovoka's free arm to his torso. The alien's body feels like stone.

"Take the gun, Cor! The gun, the gun!"

But she makes no move.

"Cory! *Get—the—gun!*"

His words are almost drowned in a stampede—Zannez and Snake are charging at them along the parapet, Ek and Bridey rounding the rollbed to get at Vovoka from the other side; even little Stareem, naked, is sprinting at him. A pileup capable of throwing a robot is coming at the alien.

Doctor Baram catches Linnix by her belt as she takes off to help and yanks her back down into the seat beside him. He himself continues watchfully sitting by the rollbed. Little Prince Pao makes one leap toward Vovoka, then checks and, frowning thoughtfully, returns to stand by Baram.

Only milliseconds to go—but they're enough here. Kip finds his arms holding nothing—Vovoka has lifted his weapon arm free as easily as a man would lift his hand from water. Even as Kip grabs for a hold he hears the weapon's fast click—setting change—and Vovoka sweeps the oncomers with a whispering beam.

Four people become unguided missiles in midstride—slumping, falling, skidding, piling up around the console. Only Snake is untouched, still coming on the coping. The alien holds his fire and shifts place with a jolt—if he shot now the boy would certainly fall off onto the treetops below.

"They're merely stunned," Vovoka says at Cory. His words come out so fast they're high-pitched, barely comprehensible, like a speeded-up recorder. Kip, grappling the alien's stony neck, understands that Vovoka has some sort of ultra-high gear he can throw himself into.

Abandoning all standards, Kip goes like a madman for the alien's eyes. The eyes are protected by a hard, transparent shell. Vovoka merely blinks in annoyance. Kip whips out his pocketknife to stab or cut around the eyeball if the knife won't penetrate.

But the alien forestalls him before dealing with Snake. Kip feels one incredibly fast and powerful surge of muscles, feels himself seized by arm and leg—torn free—and flung whirling through the air.

He lands hard, a leg twisted under him across the edge of a heavy deck chair, his head ringing from blows. Consciousness gutters. He's scrambling to his feet by reflex, confusedly aware of bodies in motion around the console, as the leg gives way under him and sends him crashing again to ground.

He drags himself up by a chair, trying to force his good leg to push his body upright. The deck is a dark silver chaos of agonies into which he essays to step—only to go down once more, striking his forehead on the chair.

An instant of bewilderment, in which he calls, or tries to call out, "Cor, I love you!"—and then the world flickers away and does not return.

As Kip falls, Doctor Baramji comes quietly to his feet.

He looks from Kip to Cory—who during all this has moved only her head, to follow Kip—and from her to the alien. Vovoka is standing by the console, where he's just caught Snake's lightning karate double-kick, pulled him safely out of the air, and stunned him.

Behind his composed face, Baramji is in torment. His muscles ache from the effort to restrain himself from a suicidal attack on this alien who has injured Kip and threatens—incredibly—to doom Cory. Incredibly—yet all too convincingly to Baram, who has long sensed the shadow under Cory's cheer. Her first words of guilt instantly rang true to him; appalled, he understood that *this* was the trauma all Rehab couldn't erase from her young mind.

Yet that this should have happened to Cor! Cory, whom he loves so deeply, Cory who was a lifeline to him when his own mate went—only one implacable fact can prevent him trying to go to her aid.

His duty. Duty is there, chaining him: he is the sworn Guardian of the Dameii, in the name of Humankind; most probably the only one left. *And the Dameii may well be in danger right now.*

The events of the past hours have added up for Baramji—even faster than for Kip—to a growing conviction of menace from Ochter, Hiner, and Yule. Unproven but not rationally to be dismissed. Until the Dameii are known to be safe, the lone Guardian may not waste himself for friendship or any personal concern. And now he is compelled to still other actions by his deepest duty as a doctor—an agonizing triple bind.

He addresses the alien, seeking frantically for some way, anything he can try.

"Ser Vovoka, may I, as a doctor, go to Kip? He has clearly broken a leg and seems to have other injuries. I will also need Myr Linnix to visit the surgery with me for splints and medical supplies."

"Do that." Vovoka's speeded-up voice slows and deepens as he goes on. "I regret . . . Was this why you did not join the others in attacking me?"

"No. I thought there would be needs, other than those you generate, I mean. And it seemed unlikely they would succeed."

"Wise."

"Tell me, are these unconscious people brain-injured or harmed in any way other than the obvious? Will they need my help?"

Vovoka has already turned away: he turns back impatiently.

"No. They will awaken in about an hour, just as they were before, apart from a few bruises. Now, doctor, go to your duty."

Suddenly a possibility comes to Baram.

"But *your* duty, Ser Vovoka—will you ignore the high duty so plainly before you?"

The alien eyes flash scorn at him—but Vovoka pauses.

"You have already disabled one Guardian of the Dameii. In the name of Star-justice, you must not disable the other until relief arrives. The innocent Dameii have suffered at least as gravely as Vlyracocha—yes," Baram says sternly as Vovoka's eyes blaze, "there are worse ways to die. I call on you to delay your revenge on Myr Cory. As you see, she will wait."

Vovoka glances around at Cory, who doesn't seem to hear them; her eyes never leave Kip.

Vovoka turns back to Baramji. He appears to be growing more alien, to have difficulty comprehending the Human appeal.

"Delay? . . ." he says effortfully. "I . . . I regret. Among other reasons. . . . I am soon dying."

Baram's hope dies, too. Has he waited too long to approach Vovoka?

"Then it is your duty at least to tell me one thing," he says desperately. "Do you know of any plot against the Dameii? You have read our minds—have you read dangers to the Dameii from any here? Have you?"

Vovoka's face has taken on a strange, dreamlike abstraction. *"Avra ki, avra koi,"* he says in no tongue known to Baram.

Then he turns definitively away.

Baram curses himself without seeing clearly how else he might have acted. He goes to Kip. Linnix has done what she could to make him comfortable.

A quick examination shows simple fractures of the right tibia and fibula, which Kip worsened by trying to stand, and an unknown degree of concussion. Normally Baram would take him at once to the infirmary for a full cephalic scan, but now he must stay here and watch for some possible opportunity to help Cory, however unlikely. It will be good to set the leg while Kip's unconscious, too.

With Linnix to help him carry, he goes quickly into the infirmary for his portable scanner and emergency kit. He's opening his safe by its lighted dial when Linnie's hand taps his arm. He looks up to a small shadow slipping through the infirmary door. There's a creak.

Pao! Wait—is there a possibility here?

"Prince, can you hear me?" Baram calls softly.

"No need to shout," says Pao's voice from beside them.

"I need to call on you for something that may be dangerous. You must feel perfectly free to refuse."

"What is it?" says Pao practically.

"Do you think you could slip unobserved down to Hiner and Yule's room and check whether they're sleeping, as Ochter said, or gone, or up and active here? If they're asleep, fine—no danger. If they're gone or awake and up, we're all in bad trouble. That's the danger for you—they may have set a watch or a trap. I wouldn't call on you if there was any way I could do it, and it's not fair to ask a—" Baram stopped as he was about to say "boy," and finished, "a visitor to do our job."

His tact is useless.

"My younger brother is on active duty with our patrol service," Pao tells him coolly. "We consider most grown men ill suited to the best scout work. How do I signal you when I get back?"

"Um . . ." says Baram. From the corner of his eye he can see Linnix' intent stare.

"If everything's all right, I'll say so," Pao answers for him. "Same if they're gone and you're alone. If Ochter—I guess that's who worries you —if he's here, I'll give a chirr, like that lizard thing that was around." He pauses, and a moment later the metallic trill of a night-caller sounds behind them. "A single if they're gone and a double if they're here and active. Got it?"

"One means they're gone and two means they're active here," says Baram to the night.

"Right. . . . Oh, by the way, if those were your Tocharis you put in there, may I have one? I know they're dry."

The lad doesn't miss much; Baram fishes a Tochari out of the open safe and hands it down to the darkness.

"Thank you." The voice is moving away. "Did you notice the main lounge doors are fused locked? Vovoka's gun did that."

A shadow occults the surgery doorway for an instant and is gone.

"Amazing lad." Baram turns up the light to find Linnix grinning. But she sobers quickly. "Doctor Bram, do you really think that those two and *Doctor Ochter* could, could be . . ."

"I don't know, Linnie. . . . Here are the big splints. . . . There's a chance Ochter could be very dangerous. We'd certainly all be unconscious now if things had gone according to his scenario. . . . Or he could be as completely harmless as he seems. In any case I want you to stay well out of his reach until we find out." He shakes her arm gently. "Hear me?"

"Yes. Yes. . . . You mean they—the, the Stars Tears stuff . . . Oh, no—"

"What else? Reach down that RMSO, honey. Now let's get this load out, I'll take those blankets, too."

She reaches for the analgesics. He sees her brows furrow as she turns out the lamp.

"Yule and Hiner," she whispers. "You mean the cold-sleep . . ."

"Could have been a plant. Yes. Let's go."

But he pauses an instant. "I—I didn't mean to frighten you, my dear." What he'd been about to blurt out was, "I love you."

"You didn't, Dad." He can just catch the flash of an impish smile behind her load of bedding.

When they come back to the deck Cory is bending over Kip's head, kissing and caressing the unconscious man. Ser Vovoka stands behind her. As Baram approaches, the tall alien takes her gently by the shoulders and half lifts her away, turns her to face him. She resists only a little.

Bram and Linnix go around them to get to their work on Kip's leg.

"You shall have time for farewells . . . full and private," Vovoka is saying. He seems to regain Human speech again with Cory. "On my honor, I promise." He begins to lead her back to her chair.

But to Baram's dismay, Linnix suddenly is standing in their way.

"Please don't hurt Myr Cory," she pleads. "She's such a *good* person. Whatever she did when she was a child, it was out of loyalty. Please spare her, Ser Vovoka. Please."

Vovoka's weapon hand lifts ominously, but Linnix doesn't yield. Dear brave little fool! Baram moves to interpose himself. Still the alien finds patience to reply:

"Young female, did you not hear what she said to her mate when she asked him to let her go? 'It is both just and kinder'? She spoke truth, for reasons you can never know. Now will you be satisfied with that or must I stop you, too?"

Beside him, Cory nods speechlessly.

Linnix puts a hand over her streaming eyes and lets Baram pull her aside. Vovoka guides Cory to her chair.

When she's seated he says to her, "Look up."

Linnix and Baramji pause in their work with Kip to look up, too.

The great diamond is now filling half the sky. But it's a diamond no longer. Instead they see a great circular rainbow lined with lesser bows, sun dogs of hues and brilliancies no ordinary rainbow ever showed—quite beyond description. Its outer rim is radiant with eerie rivers of color and slow-moving fans of light that brush the horizons.

Any part of the great spectral wonder would have been a jewel, an emblem of fascination. The whole is ungraspable, unbelievable, yet there.

In the very center is an undefined swirl of pearly colors. As they watch, it begins to take on definition. But neither Baram nor Linnix can tell what it is. A head, perhaps a face? It flows and re-forms and flows again, tantalizingly.

A rasping sound comes from Cory: she is having trouble breathing. She lies with upturned face, eyes wide in apparent recognition. Beside her

Vovoka leans against the parapet, staring upward, too, his alien face a mask of sadness.

"The last." Cory gasps for a moment and then goes on. "I was the very last to see it whole and unharmed, glorying in its beauty. The last. . . ." She falls silent, her eyes alternately wide and clenched shut, as if the sight is unbearable, yet resistless. Desolation ravages her once merry face.

Vovoka glances down at her, his strange face showing what they have not seen before, a trace of pity.

"Almost I would spare you if I could," he tells her.

"No." Cory still looks skyward. "Not now . . . now that I know. . . ."

Dreading what is to come, they watch helplessly as he checks his weapon and sets it to a new position, then places it against her head. She smiles faintly, like one who feels the touch of coolness amid burning heat.

Linnix clutches Baram's arm; Cory's strange acquiescence, almost eagerness, has made it hopeless to try to protest again.

"I do not know if this is kinder or more cruel," the alien says. "Know that I mean to be kind. I believe you deserve a few hours of peace and freedom that not I nor any of my race have ever known."

They hear a faint whisper from the gun. Then he withdraws it carefully from her glossy hair.

Cory shows no change but simply sits there, looking attentively from him to the preternatural splendor in the sky.

Baram is almost too dumbfounded to feel joy. *What happened?* Is she—can she be all right? A dozen speculations flash across his mind at once. Vovoka clearly hasn't missed—he appears satisfied, as if he expected no other effect. So it cannot be that some trick brain path allowed the ray—or whatever that thing fires—to cut only the corpus callosum, say. No, the aim had been diagonally down, toward the medulla, Bram recalls. Maximal damage.

Wait, could that "shot" have been a purely ritual "execution," like that business on Kaiters, where people died of symbolic punishments? . . . Maybe the effect comes later, he thinks. . . . A ray of hope touches him— When he can get to her, he can probably prevent *that.*

Now Cory's actually speaking, in a voice they can barely hear.

"Thank you, I think I . . . know a little. I wish I could share with you."

Vovoka smiles in great bitterness and despair, his gaze going back to the Star.

"Your mad captain was quite right, you realize, Myr Cory." He seems to wish to speak a little with the only Human who can understand. "It was a weapon. But self-generated. A seed from space, a germ of suns, who knows? It showed itself first in our clouds. And then one or two of our highest mountains began to . . . change. This was many, many lifetimes ago—ninety, a hundred. We had already a high civilization. This brought beauty such as no one had ever seen or imagined. And in many modes. Even to trees, weeds, rocks . . . like those here."

As he speaks he absently adjusts his weapon to another setting, and holds it loosely by his side. There seems to Bram no possible advantage to be taken here.

Vovoka's voice goes on. "But its wonder fed on the souls of the beholders. With too much exposure to that beauty one becomes strangely incapable of hope . . . and yet haunted by unquenchable, unnameable desire. You alone beyond our race knew something of this. The Federation doctors talked of cell fatigue, but we knew differently.

"And when it had fed full, and was almost through with us, it compelled us to build—what you have seen. Again, over lifetimes. So that it might go forth throughout the Galaxy, feeding . . . reproducing. . . ." He stares up at the Star and then down at the woman.

"Know this: *You have done no wrong.*"

Then his expression changes once more. He gives Cory a brief nod that says more plain than words, "Good-bye," and turns away for the last time. His gaze goes back up to the Star.

It has changed more while he spoke. The forms are breaking up, crystallizing differently, skywide. There is a raining or sifting of impalpable falls and drifts of color, down through the night. All blackness at the horizons has vanished under the silent, sky-filling light-storm. Is the Star upon and around them? Are they actually in it now?

Vovoka glances down briefly at the readouts on the console and nods. Baram hears him draw breath.

Then he throws up both arms as when he first addressed the Star. Now one hand holds a gun.

"We have done your bidding to the end, O Lustrous-Cruel. None remain save only I, who will soon be gone. And your revenge is ours, O Insatiable. Your ambition was too swift, your hatred for those who wounded you too absolute.

"So now you will be again as you were so long ago—a nothing, a spore on the winds of space, whence we drew you to our doom. *Averane!*"

He lets his arms fall slowly.

As the weapon passes his head it speaks again, a brief soft buzz. It is so quiet, and his demeanor so calm, that for an instant the three watchers do not realize that his head is simply gone. His neck ends in a thin gray-and-scarlet mist, dissipating in the air. There is no gush of blood; the whole neck seems to be cleanly cauterized.

For a moment the headless body stands leaning on the parapet, then crumples quietly to the tiles. With a metallic clink the weapon falls from the dead hand and slides out of sight.

XIV

THE NOVA GROWS:
Algotoxin

Stunned silence falls on the deck after the alien's apocalyptic death.

It is so still, under the uncanny radiance of the sky, that Baram, who is finishing Kip's emergency splint, can hear the soft brush of tree branches on the windward side of the hostel, and now and then a faint wind whine which inexplicably troubles him. Linnix, helping from Kip's other side, seems to hear it, too, and frowns.

The stillness brings it home hard to Baram that, of the dozen Humans here, only he and Linnix and Cory are conscious—and Cory may be gravely hurt. She's still sitting where she was when Vovoka fell, but she has turned to watch Baram with Kip. She seems alert, but once or twice Baram catches her looking into nowhere with an expression that reminds him too much of patients to whom he's given the worst of news.

And young Pao—where is his little scout? He should have been back long ago. Has he run into trouble from Yule and Hiner? Has he, Baram, done serious wrong in sending the boy?

Someone should go for him at once. And someone, most urgently, should go down to Yule and Hiner's quarters and settle the crucial issue: Are they locked in drugged slumber, from which it follows that Ochter is indeed the harmless, kindly old body he appears; or was that drugging story a lie and Ochter a dangerous enemy in league with them?

But Cory and Linnix must not be left alone while these three are unaccounted for. And someone should also check the too-long-neglected radiation counters, since this great new flux of radiation has come upon them. *And* Baram should examine Cory at once, not to mention taking a look at the others—

The conflicting urgencies racing through his mind dismay Baram. It's been a long time since the war, he thinks. A long time since a younger Baramji coped with a dozen life-or-death calls at once. Maybe too long since he's had to think of living Human enemies instead of microscopic pathogens. . . . He snaps the last lacing in and suddenly recalls a vital point.

"We're done here, Linnie. Will you go collect that weapon Vovoka dropped? I heard it fall on this side."

"Right, and I'll tend to the decencies." She snatches a blanket off Zannez' screens and goes toward the parapet near Cory, where Ser Xe Vovoka, last of all great Vlyracocha, lies headless in death.

Cory is rising, heading for Baram and Kip. Baram watches her come. She moves quite normally, but with great weariness—understandable enough—and he sees no signs of damage. Nevertheless, his doctor's prescience refuses to quiet; that weapon fired into her brain.

"Cory, my dear, what did he do to you? Let me look—"

"How badly is Kip hurt, Bram?"

"Not badly." He's trying to check her pulse, but she pulls her wrist away.

"I'm fine for now." Her voice strengthens. "Bram dear, stop looking at me as if I'm about to fall dead and tell me how Kip is." She sinks down by Kip's unconscious head. Linnix manages to slip a chair pad under her.

"Kip's fine, too, or will be in a few days." He tells her the details while he studies the glossy brown head, now in full Star-shine. He still can see no trace of injury, or even of disarray, unless it's that slim strand of silver over the left parietal. Surely that's been there some time? Women hide such things. Nothing else—save only that her glow seems dimmed in some way, as if he's seeing her through dust haze or a fine ashen veil. . . . Tiredness? A trick of the light?

"Kip may lunge about and need a restraining hand while he's coming to," Baram concludes. "And we have other urgent problems, Cory my dear—you haven't been exactly, ah, free to—"

"No." She gives a ghost of her old wry chuckle. "Oh, Bram—"

"Wait, Cor. First you should know that while you—a while ago—I seized a chance to send young Pao down to check on Yule and Hiner's room. He's overdue back. I hope I didn't do wrong to let him go; he claimed to be a proficient scout."

"Best you could do." Her gaze is straying back to Kip.

"Also, if Ochter had hoped to render us all unconscious with his wine, Vovoka has done most of his work for him. There's only you and I and Linnix left. And you may recall, Vovoka killed the last alarm cycle. If we still think as we did, I assume you intend to let the next cycle go through? Or do you want to alert Base now?"

Her eyes came back to him with some of their normal authority.

"Nothing . . . significant . . . has changed," she says thoughtfully, "except that we're in a far worse position to handle any violence. We still don't know if we're faced with two sleeping louts and a nice old man, or a deadly criminal and two accomplices who may be attacking, or preparing to attack the Dameii right now. And we can't determine which without placing ourselves and others in possibly fatal danger if the worse case is true. . . .

"Moreover, if the worst case *is* true, and we're heard telling this to Base, it's my feeling that Stars Tears criminals would exploit all here for their hostage value, and probably end with mass killing, before they let themselves be taken. Certainly they would leave no living witnesses. And there's no way of estimating the likelihoods—we have nothing but suspicious coincidences. Therefore it's the course of wisdom to act as if the worst case *is* true until we're certain it's not.

"So—I believe that the only safe course is to wait for the automatic alarm cycle to Base; it's silent. And meanwhile stay well away from Ochter or any vulnerable situation.

"But there is one call I think you can make." She bows her head and slips off the slender chain bearing the plastite-cased microchip that is her sigil of office; her hands are shaking so that it catches on her ear.

"Bram, I'm feeling kind of—spooked. I'd like you to take over officially. It would be normal enough to call and tell them that, and about Vovoka. . . . Will you?"

"Gladly." He sees how great an effort this has been; the weariness is returning on her so heavily that he's alarmed.

"Tell them, until further notice. Green?" She manages to smile.

"As you say, Cor, always." It was an old joke between them.

"Go. . . . Oh, and watch your output index, you'll have to holler to get through this mush."

"Right."

He goes to the console, trying to push his worry for her from the forefront of his mind and consider his Cory-imparted knowledge of the thing's operation. Adequate—he hopes.

He is stepping over and around the sleeping bodies of Zannez and his gallant troupe; Linnie has somehow found time to untangle and dispose them more comfortably. Zannez and the boys are on the near side of the console between him and Cory, and Bridey and Stareem are beyond it by the parapet. He can see no movements of returning life; well, Vovoka had said an hour or more.

When he succeeds in starting the transmitter power-up, several readouts change their spectral glimmering. Baram peers at them, ascertaining as well as he can that no components have passed the red lines Kip had marked. Through his shoe soles comes a faint hum of power, pervading the deck. Deep beneath him the power-cell is silently waking, activating the big transmitter.

The thrumming is so noticeable that he has a moment of panic, thinking that he has in error called up the monstrous energies required for a *c*-skip send. Among the factors necessary actually to perturb the gravitational field is a total chill-down of the sealed 'skip antenna; but when he locates its heat register on the board there is no sign of change. It must be that he's nervously sensitive to the normal transmission process he hasn't worked for so long. . . . And the Star-silence amplifies all.

To calm himself he looks up.

The Star is still in the midphase of comparative quiet. There is no longer a visible Star, but only this dense, dancing, pulsing rain of silver, shot with mesmeric reds, purples, green-blues, which means that the Star-shell, or its midmost layer, is all about them. They're passing through its denser zones. Other shells had showed this phase, only with less brilliant visual effect. Typically, this will be succeeded by a last burst of activity when whatever lies in the innermost zones comes by.

Baram says a silent farewell. The Star as such will never be seen again from Damiem. On the opposite side of the planet, where it's daylight now, the Star-blizzard is contending with the sun. When its twilight comes, there will be a glimpse of the setting lights of the Galaxy from behind the great, expanding wall of the explosion front. And when the turning planet carries the hostel around to night again, they will see only the last shreds of the inmost layer, gaseous wisps over the whole empty sky. The Star will be gone.

Baram suddenly recalls Cory's increasing gaiety over the past weeks. How she must have looked forward to skies forever free of that Star! That Star which, unbelievably, *she* had created, and to which, all unknown, she was so terribly linked. . . . The mysteries of destiny. . . .

Baram's thoughts have strayed only for an instant; now he is jerked back to the present by Linnix, rising from behind the rollbed, holding out empty hands.

"I just can't find it anywhere. Could it have fallen into the trees?"

Baram glances down into the treetops beyond the coping. "I really thought it fell here. If it's down there, we won't find it tonight. Well, neither will anyone else."

The needle is moving at last toward Transmit; only a minim or so more. The brief power-up time has seemed to Baram intolerably long. And he is quietly appalled that they have so far failed to be able to call for help. Is Cory right in her reasoning? She called it, with her usual accuracy, a "feeling" that it might be dangerous to be overheard calling for help. He agrees, in principle—but he has a strong urge to grab up that old-fashioned microphone and simply yell for *Rimshot.*

There's a number code he could use, but he hasn't learned it; maybe he would have done better to take some time from examining Damei uric acid function and learned that—but Cory would brief him if he asked. He's pretty sure that the reason she ignored it is that it's only a Star-Standard code and if these men *are* sophisticated criminals, they'd have made sure to have that, too. . . . His mind is circling unclearly; it's hard to feel sharp, surrounded as he is by flickering Star-light, and quiet sleeping bodies, hard to believe in the possible reality of small Human plottings under the cosmic beauty of this sky—and the light's unremitting pulse beat interferes with coherent thought.

"Linnie," he calls, "I left a pot of kaffy on to warm for us. Could you get it from the surgical stand? It'll do Cor good, too."

"Great thought." She vanishes into the infirmary.

The needle is almost at Transmit.

Just then, the flicker in the air intensifies, and the whole sky suddenly flashes black. Then flicker, white—and again black flash. Baram blinks, hearing himself say, "It'll do Cor good, too."

"Great thought," says a white-clad figure at the infirmary door, and a rush of shadow supervenes.

He frowns and slaps his head to clear the hallucination. There's a name for this, not *déjà vu,* something nasty having to do with synchronic foci in the brain; epileptiform. . . . Oh, no.

"Not *now,* " he groans nonsensically, seeing with dismay how the quiet bodies around him seem to stir and change, becoming shadows rushing movelessly to and fro. Substanceless apparitions—people, chairs, blankets —are vibrating darkly in and out of empty space, like a breaking hologram. Everything flickers, overlaid by a centrifugal whirling that streams across his sight, and his ears fill with rustling sound, a rush of pounding footfalls, collisions, a dreamlike cry. Linnix has vanished.

With peculiar difficulty Baram twists in his seat, to find Kip's body indiscernible under dim transmutations of itself. And Cory—where is Cor?

He turns, seeking her but producing only more unreality—until chaos condenses into clear Star-light on the standing figure of Vovoka by the parapet—Vovoka with head intact, Vovoka alive! He's looking down at a brown-haired figure in the lounger beside him.

Baram stares miserably at the living, solid figures before the flittering lake, which now reflects rainbow arcs, hearing Vovoka say, ". . . cell fatigue. But we knew differently."

And—gods!—understanding comes.

It isn't Baram's eyes or brain at all, it's a so-called time-flurry! He'd been under cover with the Dameii last time; he hasn't experienced one before. . . . Fascinating!

Rocked by relief and excitement, he watches the scene from the past unroll for a second or two. It occurs to him to try Pao's point—to make some mark, to change the past. Is it possible?

He raises his hand to shift Cor's stylus that's lying on the console. His muscles feel distant, tiny, weak; the very air seems to resist him. He recalls Cory saying that one felt "gluey." But he persists, and just as he succeeds in making the stylus roll, there's a weak flash, substance drains from the scene, and all blurs into rushing shadows again.

But it's time-forward now—Vovoka's figure crumples downward, the surging figures of people whirl through their courses and go to ground, and Baram, turning, sees the forms of Kip and Cory emerging into Starlight as he'd last seen them in reality. He sees, too, that Cor has dragged Kip into the protecting shadow of the overhanging eaves.

"Great thought." And the real Linnix disappears through his door.

Baram stares down at the bare console top; there's something he's trying to recall, but it eludes him.

The Transmit light flickers. And still the feared intrusions haven't materialized. Where is Ochter? Surely he can send any short SOS he pleases without being overheard. Should he? Cory has put him in charge.

As he hesitates, fingering the old microphone, a faint sound from the shadows distracts him. He turns to see Cory sitting bowed over, her hands to her face; he can see her shoulders quake. *Cory* weeping?

He can't go to her now even if she wished it, which she doubtless does not. He chokes back a pang of pity—pity and fear; she may know more of her injury than he guesses. The grayness of fatigue still veils her. Even that white streak in her hair, shining in the Star's light, seems broader than before.

A cup of steaming kaffy intrudes on his view—Linnix is standing over him, watching Cory, too. Her wonderful eyes, blue even by this light, turn on him, soft with compassion.

"Drink. I have hers here. Then I'm going to put on more lights to kill this rotten flicker. Green?"

A jewel of a girl, he thinks, thumbing the Send button. Pure zeranaveth. The hum and crackle of power are filling the air.

"Damiem to Base," he says, still thinking of an SOS. But as he identifies the station he remembers Cory's warning about the Star's static and checks the indicator. Sure enough, his words are being lost. He adjusts everything he can think of and repeats his call signal, finding he has almost to shout.

"FedBase Ninety-six, priority override," he repeats loud and clear, watching the led-back indicator. This is going to be work; talking at the top of his lungs does not come naturally to Baram. And partly because of this, partly from loyalty to Cor and concern for her, partly from a dozen wisps of causality, his intent changes.

"Administrator Corrisón Estreèl-Korso has suffered undiagnosed head injuries," he howls, "in an encounter with an alien disguised as a Human tourist in today's landing party. Deputy Kipruget Korso-Estreèl has sustained a broken leg and some cerebral concussion in the same incident."

Linnix' hand flashes into his field of view, pointing. Catching his breath, he looks up to see her with her head cocked and one ear cupped by the other hand. What are those sensitive young ears hearing?

The hand she points with begins to beat time as she stares down the deck toward Ochter's room. Uneven beats—long-short, long-short. . . . No, it isn't the sound he'd dreaded, the stride of two pairs of male feet. It is —of course!—the thud-tap, thud-tap of Ochter's lame footsteps.

Doctor Ochter is limping toward them, well within sound of his bellowed words. The gods had been with him, all right. Assuming Ochter is their enemy, he'd have heard every word of Baram's intended SOS. Whew!

Baram gulps an extra breath and shouts on. "The Deputy is unconscious, but the Administrator is conscious and she has delegated her responsibilities *pro tem* to me, Senior Medical Officer Balthasar Baramji ap Bye. On present evidence the Administrator's injuries must be considered potentially life-threatening, and I hereby direct—"

Thud-tap, thud-tap; very faintly he, too, can hear it now, above the humming of the deck. He listens as well as he can while specifying the equipment and the neurologist he wants *Rimshot* to bring soonest. The footsteps seem to be slowing as they approach.

"The alien responsible, calling himself Ser Xe Vovoka in your landers' list, is now dead by his own hand. Several tourists were stunned by his weapon, which has not yet been recovered; they are now unconscious but are believed to be otherwise unharmed."

Thud-tap, thud-tap. . . . Baram swivels to watch the place where Ochter will emerge into the deck light, suddenly conscious that he makes an ideal target if the man is armed. He searches his memory for ambiguous terms; why, oh, why hadn't he learned that code?

Thud-tap . . . silence. Just beyond the circle of light, Ochter has paused. Under Baram's white crest the scalp crawls slightly.

Suddenly, to his horror, Linnix deliberately walks between him and Ochter and drapes herself casually on the corner of the console. Gods curse this darling girl—if he could reach her, he'd knock her flat.

"Get away!" he hisses. She smiles serenely.

Well, he just must be twice as careful.

"In view of various events and circumstances, some of which have been reported earlier," he says haltingly, "and the condition of the Administrator, I now also direct—" Aha, one of the terms he needs has come back to him! "—that Captain Dayan treat this as a Class F priority. And I further request that he initiate voice contact with us in two standard hours."

Class F stands for Force in an old Rim War code, which Ochter is unlikely to know. Dayan will surely recall it, and it should mean to him that they are in some sort of danger. He puts the message on automatic repeat and signs off.

Thud-tap . . . *Thud-tap* . . . Ochter has resumed his painful march.

The instant the power drains down, Baram realizes he has botched it, several ways. How will Dayan know whether to come at once on the Class F, or delay to fetch equipment and neurologist on the medical priority? It could take a day or so to collect Dr. Schehl. And the two-hour reconfirmation might seem to mean that nothing was to start till then. . . . Well, at the least this should insure that somebody will be in shape to communicate in two hours—no, three, given the time lag. They are so ridiculously helpless. The man limping toward them could take them all if he's armed with a child's rocket starter.

Tap . . . *thud-tap*—

Into the pool of light hobbles a small, old, frail figure wearing a wrinkled sleep tunic and topped by wild tufts of gray hair; Doctor Aristrides Ochter.

His right hand is untidily bandaged.

Baram, like Kip before him, is rudely set back by the gulf between the malevolent, deadly Ochter of their thoughts and this harmless-looking little old man, who seems in constant pain from his leg.

Is the whole fabric of their reasoning insane?

Ochter halts and blinks about with an air of horrified astoundment at the recumbent bodies.

"Oh, my," he exclaims; "I thought I heard signs of trouble, you see, so I . . . But these poor people, are they . . ."

"So far as we know," says Baram, "they are only temporarily uncon-scious—except for Ser Vovoka there, who is dead."

"Dead!" Ochter stares at the ungainly shroud which does not quite conceal Vovoka's feet. "M-may I?"

Baram nods.

The little man limps around the console to the parapet by the alien's body. Only now does he seem to perceive Cory, back in the shadow of the eaves beside Kip. She has lifted her head to watch him. Ochter makes a respectful head bow to her, seeming to understand that she wishes no talk.

She acknowledges his presence silently and returns to her deep, private preoccupation, a statue of grief gazing down at Kip.

Ochter looks at her gravely for a minim or two more, then turns his attention to the corpse at his feet. Diffidently he lifts a corner of the blan-ket where Vovoka's head should be. His jaw drops open as he takes in the condition of the corpse.

"Oh, oh, my *goodness*—" he says, staring down. Then he drops the shroud and collapses feebly into the nearest chair.

Linnix comes over to him, standing close but not too close, Baram is glad to see.

"Would you care for some water, or something more reviving, Doctor?"

He peers up at her through his old-fashioned spectacles, bewildered and grateful. "Oh, thank you, Myr Linnix. Just some water, please. . . . I'm glad you appear well. Doctor Baramji, if you are not too occupied, could you tell me what has happened here?"

"Certainly. Well, let's see—you were at Vovoka's grand unveiling, weren't you?"

Ochter holds up the bandaged hand, smiling joylessly. "I was."

"Of course, sorry, my memory seems to be slipping tonight. Would you like me to take a look, or make you a less bulky bandage? Doing up one's own hand is difficult."

As Baram looks at the clumsy bandage it occurs to him that Ochter can have bound a small weapon, or who knows what, in there. But again, that amputation is probably too painful by now. "Are you getting much pain from it, Doctor? I could help there."

"Oh, no, no," Ochter says stoutly. "I have some topical pain relievers, and I've finally got things comfortable. Why don't we just leave it, unaes-thetic as it is, till morning?"

"As you say." Apparently Baram is not to have a look in those wraps. "Now, let's see. Vovoka claimed that his purpose was revenge upon Myr Cory for an act in her long-ago wartime life. Kip attempted to defend her, tackled Vovoka, and got thrown there; he has some concussion. These five others charged Vovoka to try to help Kip, and he stunned them with that weapon. It's supposed to wear off"—enough caution remains in Baram to make him equivocate—"by morning. Vovoka also did something to Cory with his weapon, we don't know what yet. And then he blew his own head off.

"That leaves Lady P. I'm sorry to say she hasn't yet recovered from the deep stupor you saw, after drinking the Eglantine."

"Oh, dear, Oh, dear. . . ." Ochter muses a moment, shaking his head. "As to the part of my wine in this terrible business, I still cannot think of any explanation other than what we discussed: a students' practical joke. I believe it had nothing to do with you at all. But oh!" he went on, quite fiercely. "If I could only teach them that when they sought to spoil my fun, they actually succeeded in spoiling a happy moment for some charming and innocent young people—to some of whom it seemed to mean much—on far-off Damiem. They'd hear something beside cerebration on informational asymmetry!"

The little man bobs his head vehemently, with surprising fire. Baram chuckles to himself, wholly convinced.

"And I may say," Ochter goes on, "that it was a wonderful stroke of luck we had our young nobleman to warn us. Such an uncontrolled and probably very excessive dose might have done actual harm—or am I wrong, Doctor?"

"No, under certain circumstances and for certain people you could be quite right," Baram admits.

Ochter harrumphs a time or two, a small volcano subsiding, and then asks, "By the way, where is that estimable lad? I'm happy that I don't see him among the fallen."

"No," says Baram. He's feeling entirely foolish in his suspicions, but a sudden resurgence of worry about Pao—really, something has got to be done about finding him!—combines with old habits of duty, and he says, "I believe Pao went up to his tower. I caught him yawning a couple of times despite his interest in the Star. These are long days, and the prince is still a kid."

An outright lie. Baram notices Linnie, who's checking Hanno's pulse with her face away from Ochter, glancing sideways at him or, rather, at his hands. An odd, almost mirthful expression crosses her face. Baram looks down at the loose switch plate he's absently fingering but can see nothing amiss.

Ochter suddenly starts and claps his hand to his head.

"My heavens, I *am* becoming forgetful. Here I've almost forgotten the very thing I was hurrying to pass on to you when I heard you transmitting. If I may ask, you were not sending by *c*-skip, were you?"

"No," says Baram shortly, wondering where this leads.

"Good. Although the vibration alarmed me. Did you not notice an extraordinary amount of throbbing and tension in the air, as though great quantities of power were being used? Or is that the normal performance of your machine?"

"Now that you mention it," Baram says cautiously, "I do recall thinking that there seemed to be an unusually powerful effect. But the transmission was quite normal, insofar as I grasp these things."

"Well then, this may not come amiss. I believe I mentioned that in the confusion in their room, before they became incoherent, Hiner was muttering about something he'd found underwater this afternoon? I really should have relayed this sooner, but so much— Well, as you know, Hiner went diving when we were all at your fairyland village, and he explored around the port leading to your power-cell shaft. The port, you may know, is over a hundred meters down—extraordinary to think a Human can ramble about down there as we would in a meadow, is it not?

"But the serious point is that he seems to have found that some water-dwelling creature has constructed an enormous hard-clay and debris blockage around the shaft vent—not the port, you understand, but the vent which is necessary to all operations. He said it was blocked completely, and that any heavy power usage like a c-skip transmission might blow the cell. He was getting a bit incoherent by then, but he was very clear about the vent being blocked and the explosive possibilities—he kept saying, 'Boom! boom!' with quite infantile enthusiasm. Of course, he may have been fantasizing. You realize I'm no expert at all, but it occurs to me that the blockage of the vent might be why normal use creates so much effect.

"At any event, I thought I'd better tell you at once, when I remembered. Do you know, I was really quite relieved, coming here, when I concluded you weren't powering up for c. . . . That 'boom, boom' quite gripped me." He chuckles. "The idea was that the hostel and everything in or near it would go skyward and come down as splinters. . . . Don't you think it might be a good idea to have a qualified Aquaman take a look at it fairly soon? Our friend Hiner does not quite fill the bill, but he may have given a useful warning. Although I'm sure," he adds politely, "that the unusual vibration and so on would have soon alerted you."

"Needless to say, I agree completely," Baram replies. "And my thanks to you for relaying it." He was thinking hard as he spoke, recalling Linnie's description of how Hiner "gasped and gasped and gasped." Surely a bit of exploration, a simple look-see, wouldn't be so exhausting? On the other hand, if Hiner *himself* had been sealing up that vent, it would be hard work. Some gasping would be in order.

But why should he seal the vent? Pure malevolence? Or part of a long-range plan for completing the job here—destroying the hostel, the other guests, the Guardians, and perhaps even their Damei victims—in such a way that only unidentifiable "splinters" remained?

Here, certainly, is the perfect mechanism for the "killing spree" Cory was afraid the criminals would resort to if driven to desperation. Hiner, Yule, or Ochter could simply turn on the c-skip power-up and have ample time to escape.

And such a blast might cover the fact that they'd survived; at the least it would destroy all who could identify them and knew of the crime. With luck, it might even be possible actually to conceal the fact that any crime had taken place.

Dameii are notably reluctant to talk to Humans; the survivors would just move away, which could be readily blamed on the blast. And the blast itself would be blamed on the presumably convincing-looking animal activities Hiner had simulated. Very neat indeed.

But again—totally hypothetical! Beyond Linnie's account of Hiner's fatigue, there isn't a reason in the worlds why Ochter's account isn't true, and a very helpful act. And Hiner's condition can be blamed on exactly what she'd thought, that he is one of those unfortunates whose gill structures haven't fully matured. The deficiency is sometimes so subtle biochemically that it defies easy test. Certainly Hiner himself would never voluntarily admit it—the "spoiled" Aquas are the most sensitive of all Human defectives.

Another devil-begotten ambiguity! Baram's mind feels torn in two.

To disguise his preoccupation, Baram has risen and is perfunctorily making the rounds of his patients. All are still unresponsive except Zannez; Baram catches a covert glance. Good—an ally. But in what cause? So far, Ochter has done nothing inconsistent with perfect innocence—and nothing inconsistent with secret criminal intent, either.

He concludes with a careful recheck of the Lady Pardalianches's heart action. Warm memories of the morning tickle him as he presses the stethoscope to her perfumed breasts.

"All her signs still suggest a simple soporific," he tells Ochter. "As you see, we're making no special attempt to wake her; such efforts sometimes do more harm than good. Nor have I done a gastric lavage; we've been a shade busy. But if she fails to show REM, and remains unresponsive to strong stimuli, after I've tended to things here I'll give her the full antitoxin treatment. Then we'll know the answer to your concern that some additional poison could have been present."

"Poor lady." The little man has risen too, and is leaning on the golden side of the rollbed. He glances down curiously at the silent sister, the lovely little Lady Paralomena locked in her endless sleep, and shakes his head in silence. Then he lowers himself into a nearby chair.

From the corner of his eye, Baram keeps close watch on Ochter's movements. Persons feigning a lame limb generally slip up. But Ochter's limp and favoring actions are letter-perfect. That bad leg looks miserably genuine, poor man.

Baram returns to the console feeling so emotionally remorseful toward Ochter that it serves to alarm him. Hold on a minim, he tells himself, this isn't rational, either. I'm swinging from hostility to gullibility, from fear to blind acceptance, like a child's toy. But nothing has changed except his own perception of Ochter. Looked at objectively, every response Ochter makes is as consistent with innocence as with deception and guilt. What Baram needs is a really clear-cut test. But he can see no way, nothing that Ochter would say or do only if he has tried to drug them and would not if he hasn't, or vice versa. And if Baram waits too long, and Ochter has evil intentions, too long may be too late.

But again, what can the little man do, alone here? If he has a weapon, he'd have used it by now—if he intended to. And if Yule and Hiner are in it, they're certainly giving no sign—unless Pao's absence *is* a sign? On the other hand, Pao *is* only a very young boy, distractable— Curse the Star's pulsing light! If only he could *think*—

"By the way," Ochter is saying, "whatever happened to that extraordinary weapon of Ser Vovoka's? It seems to have been astoundingly versatile." He looks ruefully at his bandaged hand. "Frankly I never heard of anything like it."

"Nor I," says Baramji, thinking that if the question had come a moment earlier, he would probably have blurted out that they've been looking for it right where Ochter sits.

"I presume you've examined it?" Ochter asks. "I admit I'm curious to look it over, knowing nothing of such things. Still, you might say I have paid a finger for a bare introduction." He smiles, eyes twinkling behind his lenses, a wryly jolly little gnome. "May I?"

"With pleasure, in the morning. The fact is that Vovoka—or rather, his headless body—dropped or flung it over the parapet as he fell. No use even looking down there in the woods till sunup."

Ochter sighs. "So much violence. . . . I confess, I . . ." His voice weakens, he seems to wilt abruptly as though he's been making an effort he can no longer sustain. Perhaps his analgesic has worn off.

He slumps back in the lounger, looking out at the light-shrouded lake and sky. Then his gaze shifts to the shadowed figure of Cory. Linnix is just urging more kaffy on her; Kip is still apparently out cold.

"You believe Myr Cory to have been gravely injured by that desperate being?" Ochter asks. "Yet I see no change beyond an understandable fatigue and grief."

Baram nods. "I know. But Vovoka discharged that thing directly into her head, and then seemed satisfied. *Something* must have happened."

"Hmm. Let's see . . . our nearest Federation Base is, what, approximately a hundred light-minim away. How long will it take your expert to get here, assuming, say, that the Patrol helped him?"

An innocent query—and one of vital concern to the guilty, too. Baram closes off the answer he's been about to make and says that the neurologist will probably not start from Base, but from a med-center in the Hyades complex. "The fellow I want, best man in CNS work, is Mausbridge Schehl. He's notoriously hard to locate. Turns up visiting some patient on an asteroid nobody's heard of. He'll take time to find but there's nobody half so good."

Ochter seems to be about to ask more but sighs again and remains silently gazing out. The world is glorious, enveloped in the Star's iridescent, flickering mists of light. Yet Baram feels an oppressive, imperceptibly mounting tension. Some of Cory's ions, no doubt, he tells himself, checking over the readouts. High but still safe, as well as he can determine.

Ochter stirs. "I do believe I must go back to my bed," he says sadly. "I had hoped to see that the Lady—and all these poor souls—had recovered, and to enjoy more of the Star, but I find—I find . . ." He struggles up, making heavy going of it.

Linnix comes past on her way to the infirmary.

Suddenly the little man's limbs give way. He starts to collapse, catches himself on the chair, slips again, manages to grasp a straight chair, and falls across it, uttering a half-suppressed little cry of pain. His spectacles clatter on the floor.

Linnix is already beside him, helping him right himself in the chair. She retrieves the eyeglasses.

"If I could just sit here a moment before I make another attempt," he gasps, trying to push himself back.

"Of course." She goes behind him, and he gives another cry as she takes him under the armpits and pulls him back and up. "There!"

Belatedly, Baram recalls his earlier warning to her. It doesn't seem to apply now, but nevertheless he calls softly, "Watch it, Linnie!"

They both glance at him. Baram realizes his warning could seem to follow Ochter's cry of pain.

"So embarrassing." Ochter tries to smile. "But . . . could I impose on you to . . . help me undo this? My medicines . . ." He's fumbling at his tunic sash, the hand bandage impeding all.

"Here." She comes around beside him, gently brushes the hands away, and loosens the knot. To do so she must go down on one knee; Baram feels a stab of uneasiness. But Ochter does nothing more than reach his good hand into his tunic pouch and bring out a small vial. Baram recognizes the golden color of Xyaton, a standard quick-acting—and addictive—analgesic. Linnix helps the old man click it open and convey two globes to his mouth.

In a moment he sits up straighter. "Myr Linnix, many thanks. . . . And now I believe you can get me on my way if you will allow me to do as they taught at the clinic, and loop my hands around your shoulder here? These loungers are so low—"

"Certainly."

He slides his good hand under her arm; she leans toward him and he bends his arms so that his hands meet on her shoulder, by her neck. "They tell me the elbow grip is too low, it requires too much strength," he explains to Baram. "Now you rise, my dear rescuer—if I'm not too much of an impediment?"

"Lords, no." She smiles, coming smoothly to her feet with the little man in tow. As he fumblingly releases his grip on the bandaged hand she suddenly starts and gives a tiny yelp.

"Oh, dear, that pin." Ochter quickly massages her deltoid with his good hand. "And I've crushed your collar . . . I *am* sorry."

His tone is subtly different.

"It's nothing." Linnix grins and puts her own hand to her collar, looking a trifle puzzled.

"And now"—Ochter stands straight—"Doctor Baramji, there's—"

At that instant a night-caller chirrs loudly from the eaves right above them. Ochter jumps and peers up and about.

"Just one of our local night fauna," Baram reassures him as the creature jangles again. Two others answer from the trees around the lake. Why is Linnie staring at him so?

Ohhh—gods of death!

And Baram's world splits into horrifying fragments that whirl and reform around Pao's voice: ". . . a double if they're here and active." The call had sounded twice. But was that Pao? It was so real. But a real nightcaller would answer the callers on the shore, and this one stays silent. And that means that—that—Yule, Hiner, Ochter—

It's only a microminim since Baram understood, but it seems an hour. Even his mouth moves with intolerable slowness to say the words, "Linnie! Get over to Cory, quick! She, she's having trouble with Kip."

Slowly, slowly, it seems to him, she slides free of Ochter's hand and heads for Cory. Ochter passively lets her go, looking intently at Baram.

At this instant the extraordinary point occurs to Baram that they have made no plans whatever for action if the worst case is true—all of them must subconsciously have regarded it as too remote, too unlikely. Only the no-alarm principle. Does it still hold? No matter, because his own course of action is plain—to lay hold on Ochter and force him to call off his henchmen.

It would seem that they have given Baram their own hostage, little Ochter—or rather he has put himself in that position. And he so vulnerable—why?

Even as Baram gets up and starts toward the little man, something in Ochter's apparently extreme weakness and defenselessness awakens suspicion. He simply *couldn't* have come among them so totally open to discovery and seizure. He must have some weapon. Or perhaps allies—could Yule and Hiner be on watch in Cory's room ready to pounce out and defend their chief? Surely Ochter is their chief? Yes—but the notion of the others guarding him doesn't make sense.

He must have some personal weapon. . . . Why has the little man come here, anyway?

Baram is almost within arm's length of Ochter now, but Ochter shows no sign of alarm. Nor has he produced any weapon. Indeed, he is standing so peacefully looking up at Baram that Baram finds it impossible to reach out and suddenly do him violence. Is it credible that Ochter actually intends to go on playacting?

"All right," Baram says brusquely. "No more games."

"Oh, I do agree," Ochter replies. "But Baramji, I implore you, before you do anything rash, think! There are three facts you must know if you care at all for Myr Linnix' life."

Baram scarcely hears this.

"I want your precious pair, Yule and Hiner, brought here at once, if you care for your safety."

"Myr Linnix' *life,*" Ochter repeats louder. "If you attack me, she will be thrown into extreme agony and die, Baram. Die! I'm telling you that Myr Linnix' life is now bound by radio to an instrument in my right hand—if the connection is broken, or if I am hurt or killed, she dies."

Baram looks at him in silence, but halts.

"I told you there were facts you need to know. If you're ready to listen, here is fact one: *Algotoxin has been reconstituted.*"

As Baram looks blankly incredulous, Ochter repeats, as if to a child, "Algo-toxin. From *algos,* pain. The poison whose sole function is to cause pain and death. Don't tell me you haven't heard of the forbidden drug, *Doctor?*"

Baram frowns down at him, a sick fear stabbing his gut. "No," he says.

"Oh, yes! You doubt? Watch. Oh, Myr Linnix," Ochter calls over his shoulder to where Linnix stands by Cory and Kip in the dimness under the eaves. "I do apologize for what you are about to experience."

He holds up the bandaged hand.

"You see, Baram, the second fact you need to know is that this hand is maintaining a radio transmission which in turn is holding closed—closed —a very special remote-control, spring-loaded hypodermic needle. The instant my hand relaxes, the needle will open and discharge. Or if the transmission is blocked in any other way, the hypo opens and fires.

"And the third fact you must know is that this hypodermic needle, containing two LD—that is, twice the lethal dose—of Algotoxin, is now implanted in Myr Linnix' pretty neck."

XV

NOVA MAX:
Under Control

"Observe!"

Baram, struck numb in confused, half-unbelieving horror, stares at the uplifted wad of bandaging that is Ochter's wounded hand. He sees a slight shifting of the wrist tendons, and then—

"Aahh! Aaah!" An appalling yell from behind them, as quickly cut off. Baram has not heard that shocking, unmistakable outcry of agony since the dreadful war days.

He whirls, to see Linnix crouched with both hands clutching the side of her neck where Ochter's hands had locked. She's staring at them with eyes so adrenaline-wide that the whites show as rings, and her jaw is rigid with effort not to cry out again. In the instant that Baram can bear to watch her, the torture overrides her control and a pain-driven "Aah-ahh-h!" breaks from between her clenched teeth.

"Stop it! Stop it!" Baram roars, looming over Ochter. He's maddeningly torn between his brute drive to grab and pound the little devil, and his fear of what Ochter can do to Linnie.

The little man steps back nimbly.

"I *have* stopped, Baramji. The Algotoxin lingers. That was the minimum, the absolutely least amount I could release, I promise you. And for heaven's sake, don't frighten me if you care for Myr Linnix!"

He shakes out his monogrammed kerchief and wipes his brow.

"You *must* control yourself, Baramji."

Ochter's voice is strong and clear, he holds himself like a much younger man. The old-pixie twinkle is long gone.

Baram gives a wordless growl and strides back to where Linnix stands, shaking, in the eave shadow. Cory has risen to put her arms around the girl. Baram can't see Linnix' neck clearly, only a gleam of metal under her torn white collar.

Linnix simply stares up at him in silence, her eyes sending love—and something else unreadable, thoughtful and dark.

"Let me look, Cor."

"Do not attempt to touch her, Baramji!" comes Ochter's menacing voice.

"He's right, Bram," Cory says. "I've seen enough to know it's a big spring-loaded hypo, with the spring held compressed by some radio signal, presumably from a transmitter under his bandage. You can't get at the main tube, it's fenced. Maybe with needle-nose wire-cutters and time. . . . But the point is that if the signal is interrupted in any way, the spring snaps open and the poison is ejected." She sighs with the effort to explain clearly.

"He's apparently holding it on transmit: if his hand relaxes, or tires, the hypo shoots. It would also be activated by anything which blocked off the transmission—say, one of those hats. . . ."

Her voice sinks to a whisper. "We could gain control if we could duplicate his signal. But I don't need to tell you that would take time and luck, and probably his cooperation . . . and a slip would be . . . maybe fatal. . . ."

Her voice trembles off. She can't fight anymore against the unnatural, deadly weariness.

"Sit down, Cor," Baram says gently. "Linnie dearest, do you understand I have to leave you, to try to cope with Ochter?"

"Sure." She smiles strangely, takes a breath. "And Bram, dear, do *you* understand that you may have to kill me?"

The grotesque words, so coolly spoken amid the raining glitter of the sky, jolt him inexpressibly. *"What?"*

"Yes, unless there's a miracle. Or would you let me die of this stuff? You haven't had time to think; I have. It's a triage situation. When you think it out—"

"Baramji! Get back here!" Ochter calls.

"No time now," she says. "Just tell me one thing—you *can*, can't you? I can count on it?"

"If . . . if . . . if . . . but—Oh, my darling, my darling girl—"

"Baramji, when I call you, come. Do you need a lesson?"

"Tell me you can," she says implacably. "No if-buts. Cut my throat, or however's best. *Can you?*"

Baram is looking into her blue, blue eyes with their depths of real meaning. He suddenly realizes that he has been too long a man of ifs and buts, too far from any but medical action.

"Yes, I can. . . ." he says slowly. "And I have the means." He touches his pocket scalpel.

"Ah-h-h-h, good. I count—on—OH! AAH-eee—"

Apparently Ochter had found a more minimal dose; this agony is briefer —but to see pain's teeth shaking her as a predator shakes its prey—no. He couldn't let her die so.

"Baramji, that's only a taste. Get back here to the console."

Cory struggles to her feet to hold the girl again. Baram pulls Linnie's hands away from the hypo, kisses them, and goes.

What he finds when he returns to the console makes him stare: Ochter is just freeing himself from a set of harnesses, or hobbles, that had been hidden under his night tunic. Baram had caught a glimpse of it by Ochter's jerkin edge that afternoon and taken it for a brace. Now he sees what it is —the source of Ochter's flawless limp. The little brute's a perfectionist, to endure that.

Ochter straightens up with a sigh of relief. Never taking his eyes off Baram, he kicks off one slipper and picks it up. A pebble clatters out. . . . Baram can only curse himself bitterly: gullible, gulled—a sucking fool.

And now he sees something more—a dulled, varnishlike gloss on the nail and ring finger of Ochter's good hand. The little beast is not as defenseless as he'd looked; that coating carries a so-called Death-Claw, a nearly invisible, surgically sharp point loaded with the poison of one's choice. . . . Sweet.

Meticulously, Ochter dusts off the knee he had fallen on, rewraps the dangling end of his bandage, and puts away his eyeglasses. He gives Baram one of his old impish smiles and says confidentially, "One does look so *helpless* with specs and a bungled bandage. Almost worth the finger, I thought."

Baram's icy blue eyes study him as they would study a purulent chancre.

"What is all this in aid of, Ochter? Why are you torturing Myr Linnix, who helped you when she thought you were in pain?"

Ochter looks Baramji up and down, and sighs. "Surely this is all quite clear to you, Doctor Baramji? Or will be with a little thought, considering which planet we are on? I do not wish to torture Myr Linnix. In fact, as a sensitive man, I deplore the necessity. My, ah, arrangements are simply to ensure that no one attacks *me,* or interferes with my task. And particularly to enlist your help, since you are all so much larger and stronger than I."

"*My* help? Are you insane?"

"No. And you will give it, when you find how little is required."

"Which is what? Talk straight, if you can."

"Nothing! That's the laughable part. I need all these people here to do absolutely nothing at all—oh, perhaps to sleep, peacefully sleep. Just as they—most of them"—he glances slyly at Baram—"are doing now. And you will be my bodyguard—yes, yes—because you are the one who is most deeply concerned for Myr Linnix. You will prevent any misguided souls who have not understood the position from attacking me and thus causing her that hideous agony you saw . . . and death. You see, she can recover from a number of small doses, but at some unknown point the effects cumulate and become irreversible."

During this speech Baram has been very gradually maneuvering himself to within grabbing range of Ochter's hand wrap. But suddenly Ochter steps aside, holding up his good hand.

"Nah-ah! Do *you* want Myr Linnix to die? She really will die, you know, if I forget for an instant to hold tight on the spring switch inside this bandage. And"—he knocks the bandage against the console, producing a hard, hollow rap—"there's a very hard shell around my hand and the switch, so no one can seize it and hold the switch closed by pressing from outside. You're simply not going to outthink me on five-minim notice, Baramji." He smiles cheerily.

While Ochter speaks, Baram has been staring beyond him to where Linnix sits beneath the eaves with Cory and Kip. At Ochter's final words, describing precisely his own plan, a flood of helpless rage shakes him so that he almost bites his tongue in his effort to contain it. For an instant he's blind—and then, as his vision clears, he becomes aware of motion on the Star-lit eaves over Linnix' head.

It materializes into a small dark shape oozing toward the eave edge, near where Pao's night-caller trilled. Bram jerks his eyes away, saying desperately, "But why, Ochter? *Why?* Think what you're risking."

He cares nothing for Ochter's reasons, he wants only to keep his enemy's attention on himself and away from those eaves. From the corner of his eye he sees the boy-sized shadow withdraw uproof again—good.

Ochter is saying, "Baramji, take my advice and stop bothering your head with whys and wherefores. Instead, dwell on something more pertinent, like the characteristics of Algotoxin, for example. It really is a fascinating tale, you know."

"Tell me." Baram scarcely knows what he's saying. Pao has reappeared on the eaves, this time above a drainpipe that runs down behind Zannez' now dark screens.

Oh, no, no, stay up there, Baram implores silently, not daring to look. *Don't try it—oh, gods—*Pao is creeping forward, all too evidently about to try some acrobatic feat of swinging himself out and around and down to the drain. Even if he makes it, he'll be totally exposed till he passes the screens.

"Tell me, I mean it." Baram repeats, forcing his attention back to Ochter. "It's clear you do have some pain-producing material in that hypo —I can think of several that would duplicate such effects—but that it is Algotoxin, I take for a clever story. Algotoxin has been dead for decades. I don't underestimate your abilities, Ochter. Even to have learned of it by name and used the peculiar terror it induces is a considerable feat. But that you have it there, I doubt."

Baram's words end with a choke that he changes to a weak chuckle. Trying to focus only on Ochter, he nevertheless half sees a small cartwheel of flying limbs that dives headfirst around the eaves, ending as a kicking something dangling from the drain. An instant more and it shrinks to a mere blur, a thickening, darkly sliding downpipe to disappear behind the screens.

Ochter sighs. "I pray you don't force me to prove it, Baramji. You would be the saddest man in all the worlds. I daresay you would fairly soon take your own life to be rid of the memory of what you'd seen here. Perhaps if you know how it's come about, you may at least hesitate? There's some need for haste, but it will save time in the end if you believe me."

Baram stares at him in silence. Pao's made it safely down. Now Baram needs to think fast and hard. Let Ochter talk, it may let more people awaken. And if the little horror wants to reveal himself it might be useful.

"As you doubtless know, Baramji, Algotoxin was discovered by a woman looking for a cure for Krater's disease. Algotoxin is useless against Krater's or anything else, but she thought it worth a report. The first person who saw that report forwarded it to Special Branch. When the Federation found out what she had, they acted at once—destroyed all copies and all her notes, excised every conceivable reference to the process that produced it, and took everybody who even vaguely knew of it through Rehab to erase the memory. I may say everyone concerned cooperated zealously. You doubtless learned of it through one of the senior medical watchers the Feds briefed, to see it didn't show up again."

Baram nods slowly, interested despite his appallment. It was indeed a senior chief of pathology who had told him of Algotoxin, so long ago. He can still hear the change in old Doctor Ismay's normally genial voice:

"Balthasar Baramji: You will forget what I am about to tell you. Bury it *absolutely* until such time, which I pray never comes, when it is necessary for you to remember my words. There is a compound called *Algotoxin* . . ."

Now his words come back: "Algotoxin has no beneficial properties whatever. Its sole known effect in Humans is to cause pain. *Algos* means pain. The pain is atrocious, unremitting, and continues unto death."

"Unto death"; the strange formal phrase chilled Baram. And then came the shocker.

"The pain cannot be alleviated in the least by any known means. All have been tried. Even rendering the victim unconscious does not dull the terrible pain. Victims may tear out their own eyeballs, their veins and nerves, or bite the flesh from the bones of their limbs before finally expiring.

"The mechanism of death, and the lethal dose, will never be established. All data come from five accidental victims. Experimentation here would be morally detestable."

But Ochter has said that the hypo on Linnix' neck contains "twice the LD." Has someone experimented?

He pulls himself back to the present, where Ochter is telling him that a solitary researcher, a crazy seeking revenge for his failure to pass med school entrance, had determined to reconstitute Algotoxin. "He set out to read everything recorded on Krater's disease. It took him a decade, Baramji, but he finally came on one overlooked half page; it carried the biochemical leads, and one mention of pain.

"It was enough, Baramji, just barely enough. He rented an infested room on one of the Dark Worlds. He didn't care who gave him the small monies to live and work—which is how certain people came onto it. He had to guess what lines the earlier researcher had followed. It took him another decade—I believe he actually came up with a cure for Krater's and threw it away—but he got it, Baramji. Algotoxin, or as near as makes no difference, lives again."

Ochter's voice and manner are quite different as he tells this; something in this demented tragedy touches his wonder and admiration, almost his love. Baramji realizes they're up against a dangerous animal—the artist of crime. A mad, sadistic artist. Artistlike, he probably wants his cleverness known. Is it possible he'd rather talk about it than execute? Is it the Stars Tears riches that fundamentally attracts him—or pulling off the "impossible" coup? Could this weakness be useful? Certainly the man and his ego require very careful handling.

"Never mind how Algotoxin came to me. It was neither cheap nor easy; in fact, it involved me in some danger. But I deemed it suitable for this task." Ochter smiles proudly.

"A very beautiful composition, Doctor," Baram mimics Ochter's style. "Forgive me if I still have doubts. But a crazed researcher—"

Ochter interrupts him sharply. "It has been tested, Baramji. I insisted on that. Sometimes I actually regret it—as a sensitive man I am still shaken by what I had to witness. But yes, this is Algotoxin. Have no foolish hopes."

Baram's stomach turns at the realization that they *had* experimented. But he has no foolish hopes. Indeed, since he's had a minim to think, he has not much hope of any kind for the lives of either Linnix or himself . . . and little more for the others here.

In the first instant he'd seen clearly that the lives of ten innocent Humans are being held hostage to the pain Ochter can inflict on Linnie, and to his reaction to that pain. Baram, driven by Ochter's threats to Linnix, is to help Ochter inject the other ten with a soporific, after which Ochter can kill them off at his pleasure. And—have no foolish hopes—Baram himself will assuredly be injected the instant his usefulness is over and killed in his turn, while Linnix may well be made to perish horribly through the Algotoxin in her neck.

And Baram cannot, must not, cooperate in this course of action. First, because the attempt to save his own and Linnie's lives by killing ten others is unthinkably immoral. Second, it would be foolish; their own lives would not be spared. And third and worst, his allowing Ochter to protect Yule and Hiner through this blackmail is a breach of his sworn duty as Guardian of the Dameii—and the only Guardian now functional.

But how to prevent Ochter from drugging the others?

The moment Baram resists, Ochter will simply torture Linnie until Baram can no longer endure it—and he has no illusion that he could stand to watch her die so. Ochter will do the same if Baram tries to call Base.

So, either that thing must be gotten out of Linnie's neck, or Ochter must be killed. But how to do that without killing Linnie? Baram is pretty sure he could kill the little man fast, if he is willing to receive a mortal wound from that Death-Claw or some other lethal toy. The prospect of his own death does not, at this point, bother Baram—the point is that Ochter's dead or dying hand would release a doubly lethal dose of Algotoxin into Linnie's neck, and he would not be able to stop her agony. The Algotoxin death is too terrible to contemplate; and he has virtually promised to save her from that; his heart would force it. If only that vile hypo could be cut. . . . At the moment Baram would give his soul for a pair of wire-cutters and a minim's lead on Ochter.

And the other Humans now asleep must have time to awaken and be warned. They hadn't known of Ochter and the two others as their enemies. But if Baram can dispose of Ochter, he feels sure that Zannez and his boys will do their best to stop Hiner and Yule—who may even now be inflicting horror on some Damei prisoner.

Could they all simply ignore Ochter and go straight to capturing his henchmen? No—Ochter can't be left to work his sadistic will on Linnie, and any other helpless body as well. To go past Ochter would mean leaving all these to some horrible death. Ochter must be gotten out of the way first —but how, without killing Linnie?

All depends on getting that hypo out. If he can't, his duty is grim and plain. Linnix had seen it, when she called it "triage." The moment she dies, Ochter's power is all gone. But oh, gods, *is* she doomed? Perhaps, just perhaps, is there some way of releasing that devilish thing without killing his girl?

Baram is gazing absently at Ochter for the instants it takes to race down this mental track, and he becomes suddenly aware that the little man is gazing back somewhat as he had once gazed up at Vovoka. Why—the little butcher is *frightened!* Ochter's calculations tell him he is safe from Baram, but his glands are telling him otherwise—can he perhaps read his death in Baram's eyes? His reaction is to reemphasize his power, and his instincts take him straight to the point.

"By the way, Doctor Baramji," he says with an actor's coolness, "I trust you realize it's useless to think of an ordinary hypo, which can be cut? I will bring Myr Linnix closer so you can see. You will *not* of course attempt to touch her. . . . Myr Linnix!"

Baram goes rigid with suppressed fury at this maggot ordering his girl about.

She comes to them expressionless, only a little pale below her glorious hair. Her eyes pass over Ochter as if he does not exist and lock on Baram's own. Wordless communion—Baram's heart strives to leap to her through his gaze and hold her tight against harm. . . . And yet—his fingers touch the scalpel's steel—he cannot defend her, may instead have to do her dreadful harm. The best he can offer may be a clean death at loving hands. *To kill his girl* . . . How fast she understood this, how sternly she made him know that she accepts it. Even welcomes it, rather than endure Algotoxin or engage in Ochter's foulness. *Oh, my darling, my heart, my brave, brave girl.* . . .

"Observe," snaps Ochter.

Linnix turns so that Baram can see the right side of her neck. Her collar is torn and disordered, letting the tender throat show—will it be there that he must cut?—and Baram is startled by what appears to be a fat, loathsome, many-legged insect clamped to her milky skin.

It's about four centimeters long. Looking more closely, Baram sees a transparent central "belly" holding a bluish fluid; a milliliter, possibly more, he estimates. And dangerously near the carotid artery.

"On certain dark worlds this is known as a 'scorpion,'" Ochter says didactically. "Because it stings even in death. Those protective legs around the central tube are of ultrahard metal, in case you have notions. What Myr Linnix felt as a pinprick was a powerful, fast local anesthetic, to permit entry of the tube.

"But this is no ordinary hypotube, Baram. It is not meant to be pulled out. *Ever.* The shaft ends in long triple barbs which have unfolded themselves in her flesh. . . . And this scorpion has been tested, too, naturally." His grin is pure evil.

"Naturally," Baramji mimics him savagely, his heart sick with dismay. That venomous hypo looks impregnable . . . never to be pulled from living flesh. Baram shudders with rage and despair. But he must not, must not anger Ochter, lest he take it out on Linnie.

Ochter gives him a nasty glance and, resuming his insane urbanity, directs Linnie to return to Cory's area. "Or no, on second thought," he says, "you will sit here in this chaise where Doctor Baramji can see you clearly in case I have need to punish him."

Impassive, Linnix stretches out comfortably in the lounger—and as she does so, to Baram's amazed delight, she sends him a broad, unmistakable wink.

Gallant child, he thinks, trying to smile back with choked throat. She's teaching me courage. . . . *While we live, we live.*

Ochter eyes them sharply, as though they might be working some plot. To the coward, Baram thinks, simple courage is a deeply suspicious mystery.

At this moment a dark glimmering passes briefly through the light-filled air. Linnix' head snaps up, as if to see something looming on her. But nothing is there, only a momentary shadow. Baram himself feels an instant's disorientation and rubs his eyes. Ionization, perhaps. One of the Star's weird effects. He shakes it off. Ochter, too, shudders slightly, looking a trifle disturbed.

Then the little man extracts a small fat roll pack from his tunic pocket. "We will now get to our task," he announces, striding briskly over to 'Lomena's golden bed. The side-rails are down. Ochter lays his pack by the still feet and, working awkwardly with his left hand, unrolls it to reveal an array of tiny medical syrettes, gleaming multicolored in the Star's light. During this he has scarcely taken his eyes from Baram and Linnix. Now he begins humming the old space melody "Sleep," while selecting a pink syrette that Baram recognizes as more Soporin—if it has not been tampered with.

Meanwhile Linnix watches all this alertly, now and then exploring with delicate touch the horrid thing at her neck.

As Ochter rerolls his syrette pack, Linnix finds a chance to whisper to Baram, "Cory says the next Deadman's Alarm cycle should be soon."

Baram has an instant of slightly embarrassed confusion. The fact is, he had forgotten the automatic SOS—because it is irrelevant to Linnix and himself. The response—*Rimshot*—should arrive in time to save the Dameii and all the other Humans, especially anybody who'd gotten into trouble fighting Yule and Hiner. But by no possible chance can it bring help in time for himself and Linnix. Because they must refuse to drug the others: otherwise ten bodies will be lying here helpless at the mercy of these criminals when they discover they're about to be caught by the Patrol. No; his drama, and Linnix', will be over by the time *Rimshot* appears.

Nevertheless he feels the strange sensation of smiling and sees that Linnix looks different, too; at least *something* good is in prospect for most of those in danger, even if it won't help the two of them.

"Baramji! Are you deaf or dreaming? How many reminders does Myr Linnix need?"

"Oh, yes, yes—sorry," says Baram idiotically, and gets up. Just as he rises there's a flicker of light from the board. It's not the Deadman's Alarm, but two different readouts showing peaks above their proper maxima. This means he should switch them over to the large-scale track, to check whether these are true readings or summation effects. He's unpracticed at this.

Meanwhile Ochter is saying, "Ready, Baramji? As I told you, you will come and get down here by"—Ochter peers at the nearest blanketed form —"Myr Stareem. You will turn her blanket back and hold her leg down while I inject the, ah, hip. Your sole task is to make sure she doesn't jar my *right* hand." He holds up the bandaged fist. "Understand?"

Baram understands all right. Sadly, he realizes that he would fight the poor child to keep her from hurting Linnix. And he is aware, too, that by luck or design, Ochter has chosen as his first victim the one person who would be of least help in any physical struggle, the sensitive child whom it would be a kindness to let sleep through whatever lay ahead. A conveniently slippery moral slope down which Ochter proposes that he descend. . . .

"Oh, Bram, no—" says Linnix, just as Ochter snaps ominously:

"Baramji, I am *waiting.*"

"Doctor Ochter," Baram says slowly, unsure of what he can contrive, "it's not that I doubt your word. You have quite convinced me that your meanings are to be believed. But I have spent my life as a doctor of medicine. Before I assist in the wholesale inoculation of unconscious persons, before I can function this way, I do need to know what it is that we're injecting. You have never told me, you know."

Has he chosen right? He watches Ochter's expression go from anger to impatience to self-satisfaction to a type of low-grade irritation resembling a man who has forgotten to complete some trivial task.

"Oh, very well, very well." Ochter sighs. "Put so, I owe it to the gods of medicine. The substance in these syrettes is ambezine hydrate, or Soporin, the same thing you diagnosed in the wine, and the thing I told you the clinic gave me for insomnia." His lip curls scornfully.

"And that you said you gave Yule and Hiner?" Baram is holding out his open hand.

"And that I told you I gave Yule and Hiner," Ochter says straight-faced. "Oh, here." He flips a pink syrette at Baram's hand.

Baram uses as much time as he dares examining the little thing. It does look untampered-with. Why not? Sleep is all that Ochter needs in his victims at this point. Baram has long since deduced that this dreadful crew intend to spend as long as they dare here and thus wish the corpses to be fresh in the scene of the final catastrophe they arrange.

His moment's inattention has lost him Ochter's tolerance.

"My patience ends here, Baramji. Give me that syrette and get down and do as I bid you or the consequences will be severe."

Linnie lets out a tiny gasp. Is she expecting him to cut her throat right now, or what? Baram gives her a pleading look and kneels down by Stareem. Resistance has no point here, and the other sleepers need time.

Gently he turns back the blanket from little Stareem's bare rump and lays a hand on the leg that she might hit Ochter's other hand with. Ochter is deft: the injection goes quicker than Baram had been prepared for and Stareem never stirs. In an instant Ochter is up again and summoning Baramji to the next sleeper's side. It is Bridey, poor little Myr Eleganza, still in her golden finery beneath the blanket.

Linnix is leaning forward, blue eyes alight with reproach.

As Baram rises, he manages to take a natural-seeming look at the console board and utters a grunt of surprise.

"What? Wait, Ochter, something goes on. This is no ploy."

He goes over and looks down at the peaking readouts as though he hasn't seen them before. The board looks somehow different; among other things, a third large blue readout is calling for attention.

"I'll be as quick as I can," Baram says without looking around, and sits down in the console seat to analyze the inputs.

Linnix suddenly speaks up. "I know these old things," she tells Ochter. "We had one on a Swain ship. What they do is to jump to sum, and if the data are dangerous or significant, you can't tell until you break it down

whether it's a true reading. But three at once is rather a lot for a jump."
She gazes up and around as if truly nervous—and by pure luck the sky
cooperates.

A number of odd, beehive-shaped, fuzzy clumps of sparks, which have
been hovering at an indeterminable distance over the lake, suddenly go
into a slow spin and disperse—and those that come toward the deck reveal
themselves to be gigantic. One passes over, or through, the deck, completely swallowing it, and as it does so, flares of cold Elmo's fire play
through the empty chairs and up to the antennae above. The phenomenon
apparently passes through to the front of the hostel, and the garage, and
there is a startling hoot from the jitney's horn.

"Whew!" Linnix is doing a good job of acting like a person who is
scared to death but trying not to show it, and thus rattles everyone; in fact,
Baram is fooled for an instant before he recollects who this is.

She giggles very nervously. "The one on the Swain sh-ship kept sum-
ming so you'd get all the crew's meals for the week if you punched for a
glass of w-water. And once, once—Oh, maybe I better not tell you about
that now. . . ." She giggles again and falls silent, watching Baram work.

And then suddenly she makes another sound—but this is the real Linnix
he hears. In a very odd tone of voice she says, "Doctor Bram, don't you
think it's really all right? Are you sure we need to do all that?"

The change is so abrupt that Baram looks around at her and catches a
wildly warning look—which vanishes as Ochter turns her way. What—? It
doesn't make sense, but he gathers that Linnie wants him to *leave that
board.*

Well, he'd better; she knows more than he about such things. Prepara-
tory to rising, he casts one last look around. A few more peaks, and one
that had been there isn't now, a couple of lights, including a new-looking
red one—rather conspicuous—that triggers a memory of a high little voice
saying, *"the big red one,* what's it telling you?" And—

Oh, gods, gods, gods, gods!

He's been working right around the Deadman's Alarm while it came on.
Drawing Ochter's attention just when it needs time, unmolested time to
work—has his stupidity betrayed them all?

As casually as he can, he gets up, flipping a readout toggle at random,
and steps over to Bridey's side. What does one more sleeper matter, if
injecting her will distract Ochter long enough to get that SOS sent?

"Ready, Ochter?" But, oh, gods, he's overdone it again—Ochter gives
him a puzzled look before opening his syrette case.

"You're . . . satisfied . . . with the readouts, Baramji?"

"Yes," Improvising wildly: "Basically a signal from the drone that the
height of radiation is coming soon. It must be thinning out, ahead."

"Hm'm." Ochter takes out another pink Soporin, looking from Baram to Bridey. "You're ready to help me inject Myr Eleganza, Baramji?"

"As ready as I'll ever be."

And Bridey, on the floor, moves. She clutches the blanket clumsily and mutters "Hno . . . hn-n . . . No!"

Involuntarily, Ochter skips back a step. "Baramji!"

Baram kneels down by the girl, trying to soothe her, trying to release the blanket from her grasp, to expose a shoulder. "Get ready, Ochter."

"N-no!" from Bridey.

"I'll help you, Bridey! Can you hear me?" It's Linnix calling to her from the chaise. In a very clear, cold voice she says, "Ochter, if you try to inject that girl, I shall wrench this scorpion of yours through my veins and arteries and die! Right here and now. And then Baram will kill you. Do you hear me? Do you understand I mean it?"

Both her hands are gripped around the wicked thing on her neck.

"Bravely said, Myr Linnix," says Ochter in a scornful tone. "It's a great pity that there is some pain Human bravery cannot endure. When—"

"When I feel the pain it will be too late," Linnix says coldly. "No one will be able to revoke my act, unless someone may care to shorten my death." She gives a secret little smile—and Baram's back hair prickles in terror. He can do it, he can do what he must—but it will be hard, hard.

"Baramji, I believe we are going to have to tie Myr Linnix' hands down to the chair. I had hoped to spare her indignity—"

"And just how do you propose to get hold of my hands before they wrench your bug?" asks Linnix jeeringly. "The first person who moves toward me will end my life—even you, Doctor Bram."

"But why, Linnie, why now?"

"Simple arithmetic. My life—I have always intended to do this—my life can pay for putting Stareem in jeopardy. But one life can't pay for two."

"Oh, Linnix dear, no," Bridey says. "I don't understand—"

"They *will kill* you, if they can," replies Linnix. "Think. This man, and Yule and Hiner, are after Stars Tears. You will be a witness to the crimes this man intends to commit on the Dameii. You can identify them. There is no chance they would voluntarily let you live—and that's true for everyone here."

"Oh-h-h. . . ."

Ochter rises and paces toward the rollbed.

"Stay in front of me where I can see you," orders Linnix. "And no nearer than three meters."

Obediently, Ochter turns and paces back along the parapet toward the console, taking thoughtful looks at Linnix and Baram. Baram does not at all like his expression. Meanwhile Bridey picks up her blanket and goes, somewhat unsteadily, to sit on Baram's old lounger. She looks as if she might be going to be ill. Linnix simply sits, watchfully gripping the hypo on her neck. Baram tries inconspicuously to interpose himself between Ochter's pacing path and the console. Every minim that passes is in their favor; soon, soon, that distress summons would be sent.

Ochter pauses; he has reached some conclusion.

"Something has changed," he says.

His head turns, methodically checking out everything in their previous field of action. When he comes to the console end of his arc, he lifts his bandaged hand meaningfully and steps past Baram to get a clear view of the board. Bandage held high, he studies the lights and dials. One or two flicker and change as he watches, but not the red light, at which Baram is resolutely not looking.

In the eaves' shadow there's a quite audible murmur from Cory. It sounds like—and is—a blistering self-curse. Unknown to Baram, she is not cursing herself now, but the lighthearted, light-headed Cory of so few hours ago, who without thought doubled the waiting-lapse time on her alarm . . . so she would not be inconvenienced by running to it. How many lives has she menaced by that carefree act? . . . And oh, instead of complaining of the bother, how happily she would set to work to lay in optional triggers, and the capability of canceling that cursed red light! . . . Too late now.

Ochter's beastly, methodical little mind has caught it.

"What's that red light, Baramji?"

A darkness comes over Baram's vision. Even his voice feels faint. "I don't know. Where?"

Ochter thinks a minim. "Switch it off."

"I don't know how," says Baram truthfully. How, how had he been such a fool? Ochter has the paranoiac's acuity; he can smell hope in his victims. Baram has betrayed them all.

The little devil turns to where Cory sits moveless by Kip.

"Myr Cory, the red light which you said you must switch off when the Damei child was here, and which Ser Vovoka called an alarm, is now on. I wish you to come here at once and switch it off."

"She's too ill," Baram protests. "Vovoka's shot—and it's not only that, she has a heart condition. Didn't your snoop tell you she came to the infirmary for another heart scan this afternoon? The mitral valve is under severe stress. Do you know what that means? What good will it be to you if she collapses now?"

"I know what you would have me believe, Baramji," Ochter says nastily. "And I also know that station personnel are required to pass a health clearance every planetary tour. And I know that Myr Cory is just commencing her fifth tour, Baramji. Now—"

"Then perhaps you also know—" Baram cuts in roughly. Time—time is their need: keep the little demon talking.

"Wait, Bram," says Cory's voice from the shadows. "I can do it, Ochter. But there's no use. I disconnected everything but the light while—while Vovoka was here. It was causing me too much trouble."

"Nevertheless, I wish it switched off right now."

"But it's complicated." Cory sighs. "That's why I left it, before. I'll have to get in behind the board. Leave it—it'll just kick on and off harmlessly all night." She understands the deadly game they are playing all right.

"Do *you* wish to hear Myr Linnix scream again?"

"No! Oh, no. Very well." She sighs again. "But I tell you, it's not connected to anything but a timer."

Ochter lifts his bandaged right hand threateningly.

Cory gives a little groan of protest and slowly rises and makes her way to the console. When she comes into the light Baram is shocked at her drawn and sagging face, the dark folds under her creased eyes, her strange stooped, stumping gait. She sits in the console seat he offers, bracing her movements with shaky hands. But when she speaks her voice is strong.

"Sit down there, Bram, and tell me if any of the dials go dead. . . . Oh, gods, what have you men been doing to my board?" She chuckles, in an eerie imitation of her old joking way.

"Myr Cory, I have warned you once."

She grunts and, to Bram's surprise, lays hold of the console with both hands. Click! The outer edge of the board swings away on hinges, revealing a complex of wiring—and a tool cubby, in which lies a fine new pair of needle-nosed wire-cutters. Two pair, in fact: a small one lies alongside.

The gods' blessing on you, Cor!

She has figured out the one tool that might help him, located it, and led him to it. Now it remains only for him to pocket it undetected and find a way to use it before Ochter releases his switch. In the sheer joy of seeing those cutters, of imagining them slicing through that lethal tube, he dismisses the devilish difficulty of the rest—it is so large a psychic leap from impossible to even barely possible at all.

Cory has picked up the small cutters and begun to probe beneath the board where the red light shows.

Ochter watches them intently.

Baram is bending all his attention on a slow movement to conceal his grab for the cutters, when he almost misses his chance: Cory's arm goes right above the cubby as she taps on a dial.

"Watch the reading there, Bram."

"It—it looks a trifle high to me." Bram snakes the cutters into his pocket. Now—now he has a chance to save Linnie!

Cor is saying some time-wasting nonsense about the rise in the readings.

Ochter starts to speak, but she cuts him off. "Ochter, you may not care if you get your brains fried, but those are theta microwaves." She raises her head and stares at him wanly. "These people should all have protective headgear. So should you, although I hate to say so."

For an instant Baram thinks the ruse has worked; Ochter hesitates, chewing his lip. But then, to Baram's dismay, the little man comes behind them and stares down at the board.

"It may surprise you to learn that I can read a simple flux detector," he says acidly. His lips tighten. "You chose ill. Moreover, I see no necessity for these maneuvers with the board."

"I told you I disconnected the alarm wires."

"Ah . . . now I recall. Yes!" He leans swiftly toward the board and his left hand darts down between them to flip an unmarked toggle before he backs away.

The red alarm light goes out.

Ochter's face is tight with fury.

"Return to your place, Myr Cory. I will teach you to try to deceive me!"

Cory rises slowly, painfully, and as she turns she catches Baram's eye and imperceptibly signals negation. Bad—bad; their hope is gone, they haven't managed to delay long enough. No alarm call has gone out.

And their loathsome enemy is meaningfully holding up his bandaged hand.

"No!" shouts Baram. "Ochter, in the name of—Take it out on me, damn you!"

"I am." Ochter wears a twisted, gloating smile. "You shall have something to think of the next time you are tempted to play games."

"Stop! No—here, jab me instead, you must have some more—" Ochter backs away farther, his right fist out.

"It's all ri—" Linnix starts to say, but the words turn to a scream of pain that rips Baram's heart. Both her hands go to her mouth, trying to stifle it—he can see her actually trying to close her own lips. But the pain is too terrible—her feet drum, her body arches, and the scream builds to a horrifying, ululating shriek.

Oblivious to Ochter, Baram springs to her side, is on his knees holding her convulsing body, trying to keep her from harming herself, trying to keep his ear to her twisting rib cage. In her agony she all but flings herself from the chair, rocking them both.

"Stop it, Ochter!" he yells above the screams. "You'll kill her, she'll stop breathing—respiration will quit! No, baby, baby, don't try to pull that out, you'll cut the artery."

He captures her hand that's tearing at the scorpion—a strong girl. But her screaming weakens as she runs short of air. "Breathe, baby, pull in." To Ochter he snarls, "If she dies, you're a dead man, Ochter. Dead! I'll stuff that death-claw down your gullet and tear your head off. You know that?"

Ochter looks a trifle thoughtful. "I have stopped long since," he says testily. "That's merely aftereffect. Come, Baramji, pacify your lady-love and get over here, you have work to do."

Baram growls. Linnix' shallow, airless panting falters, resumes, falters again: in some patients, extreme pain can leave all neural centers dangerously drained. No long-drawn-out death here. He has to get through somehow, restart the engine of her life. "Breathe, my brave girl—breathe! . . . Hold on just a little longer. . . . *Breathe, baby, pull in.*"

A resolve he hasn't consciously formed takes over his tongue. He speaks close to her ear.

"Listen, Linnie, you really are my girl. My d-daughter. I'm the doctor you were looking for. I did it. I *was* on Beneborn, your home—I *was.* I've remembered now."

The breath hesitates again; he hopes it's an effort to listen.

"Linnie, it's true! I was there, on Beneborn. Remember the big gold building over the waterfall? It's come back. Honey, try to hear me—I did it, Linnie. You're mine."

The finality of it is choking him, good-bye, good-bye to dream—but he has to say it. For an instant he forgets the dream is doomed anyway and simply mourns.

"I'm your father, Linnie. You're my girl. My—my child."

It gets through. Pause . . . then two great ragged gulps of air. The screaming is only moaning now.

Slowly, carefully, Baram eases her back in the lounger, whispering, "Think that over, my love, my girl. Now breathe, hear me? Hold on, *breathe.* I'll get you out of this."

As he loosens her arms that have gone around him, Baram gets a clear look at the ghastly hypo in full Star-light. Yes, there's a space between the "legs" into which he could just get the wire-cutters' nose, to clip the central tube. The cutters burn in his pocket, but he daren't try now—her weight is on the pocket and Ochter's eyes are on him. That evil animal would hit her with another shot of poison before Baram could possibly get the cutters in place—and he'd risk losing them, too. He has to wait till Ochter's attention is fixed elsewhere. Thanks to Ochter's cruelty, Linnie's chair is close. . . . Dare he really hope at last?

"Baramji!" Ochter is standing over Bridey now.

"Oh, no," Linnix cries weakly.

Not knowing what to do, Baram goes over and picks up the empty syrette Ochter had dropped, as if to examine it more carefully.

"Give me that, Baramji. Oh, very well, as a doctor I allow you a moment more to satisfy your scruples. You'll find it's sleep pure and simple."

A shudder of darkness passes over Baram's vision as he smells it. Simple Soporin cannot do that.

"What else have you put in this syringe, Ochter?" he challenges, standing over Stareem. "Has it occurred to you, as a doctor—or a Human—I have no right to harm or kill a dozen people to save one?"

Ochter stares oddly, apparently truly taken aback. Baram's vision flashes black again, the Star-light darkens. Dear gods, what had he let happen to little Stareem?

"Ah, the arithmetic of morality," Ochter says vaguely. "Though I fancy another demonstration on Myr Linnix might change the odds. . . ." His voice trails off into peculiar echoes, as a rush of shadowy movement that is not movement sweeps across the deck.

Baram comes to his senses.

The flashing isn't the syrette contents at all, it's the start of another flurry.

And deep, deep—The flashing pastward flicker goes on, long enough for Baram to see strange multiple palimpsests of Ochter, his face in disarray—was this the first time-flurry he'd been caught in? Long enough for him to glance toward the frozen forms of Kip and Cory beneath the eaves and recall that for them this sequence does not exist. Long enough to turn to where Linnix lies in a blur of movement and hear her faint screaming in pain past. Is she frightened of the flurry? Is she again in agony? He must go to her.

"Linnie! Linnie, it's all right." He tries to shout, hearing his own voice fade into weird echoes, *"right-ight-ight-iii."* He exerts all his strength to lean, to lift a foot, to move. Like pushing through glue—and he is succeeding, only weirdly being helped forward and pressed back by the tugs of his own past motions. . . . Is that himself-past ahead there, crouching by Linnix-that-was? He doesn't want to know, wants only to move first this foot, then the other, the separate actions of moving to her. And he—or an aspect of him—does, as in a waking dream, while the scene slows and stabilizes.

At last he's close enough. "Linnie." (*"Linnie-inni-in-n,"* the echo wails.) She, or a past simulacrum of her, looks up at him. Is he a frightening figure, looming through the mad glitter? Or, perhaps, is he invisible? "Linnie! It's me, Bram." (*"Bram-ramm-amm-m-m."*)

"Bram! . . . Oh, Bram-m." She isn't frightened. Her arms open to him, regardless of the dreadful thing riding her neck.

He drops on one knee. Now! He can use the cutters, he can cut her free! *I'm like the Star,* he thinks. *I'm trying to go back and change things.*

His head clears enough to remember the difficulty and delicacy of this task, the frightful danger to her if he fails.

"Hold still, lov-ve. . . ." His hand plunges to his pocket.

But—oh, gods, oh, evil gods!—

No wire-cutters are there!

Nothing—only a damned kerchief. He nearly upsets the chaise, ramming through every pocket, trying not to face the accursed fact: In real past time, at this point in the original sequence *he had not had them!*

The wire-cutters are probably "now" back in the cubby where he had found or will find them. Can he possibly get back for them quickly enough?

"Gods, Linnie, I've failed you. Wait, I'll try—" But as he makes to rise, the scene clouds, the Star-light flickers and speeds up to become a torrential substanceless rush and shuffle of shadows. Only now it is running time-forward again.

He has totally missed his chance.

He can only clasp her tight—yes, she is solid, flesh and warm—and enfold her with all his strength, so that he has to force his arms looser lest he hurt her. He trembles; she is hugging him, too, without heed to the menace at her neck. Wild notions of defying time and space rush through his mind, but they fade before a more rational fear: The pull of reality on this strange, anomalous realm may be dangerous. Attempted defiance by force might cost a physical splitting—or worse, a damaged mind—

"Look out, Linnie. Oh, darling, we must let go."

Their arms drop away slowly; only their eyes hold one another through the eddying time-shadows. She is whispering—a lover's whisper. But the words are *"Father . . . Dad!"* It hurts Baram's heart. Chilled, he lets himself, or whatever aspect of him has violated time, be tugged, jostled by the rush of what is, and is no longer, there.

And just as the whirling flicker begins to slow, with Baram still kneeling by Linnix' low chair, he glances across her legs at the gold-hung rollbed and sees a flash of movement in the drapery below. Ochter had disarranged its drapes, leaving a gap—and through this gap there shows a small boy's figure crouching among the life-support tubes.

Pao!

The lad's head is down, he's scanning the floor; and something also seems to be distracting him. As Baram peers, Pao raises a hand to pluck at his neck and back.

Then the scene blurs—Baram finds himself somehow on his feet, tottering backward—but not before he's seen the thing they'd searched for, that Pao is apparently hunting for now.

In a fold of the bed's floor-length curtain lies Vovoka's weapon.

Any instant now Pao will see it, if he keeps on!

Baram gasps, his wind all but knocked out—the impact of real, unconditional hope after so long is like a blow.

He tries to stoop, to get sight of the boy and signal to him, but he can no longer command his body. Vague nonobjects brush him and vanish under the shimmering Star-light. The rushing time-tumult on the deck is clearing, slowing to solidity. He is now standing by the console, feeling oddly reunified. His head clears back to full present, the reality of his recent actions evaporating in his mind. Only the breathless, perilous sense of joy remains.

". . . might . . . change . . . the odds," Ochter is concluding, like a machine coming up to speed.

Baram is struck by a dizzying disorientation: the half-remembered events of, of—not the *past*, but a no-time; illusory moments that had been unlawfully inserted into the seamless flow of time—events, heartbeats, minim, which had not existed for Cor and Kip, shielded by the eaves. Are they true illusions? Or has Linnix really shared them? If only she and he could talk now!

His hand encounters the wire-cutters in his pocket! How could he imagine they had jumped out—and back in?

Illusion.

But wait—

His kerchief isn't there. The kerchief he'd flung down by Linnix' chaise in no-time! It should be in his pocket.

As he gropes again, his white hair is stirred by a breath of air; it must be backflow from the night wind over the roof. At the same time he notices something moving on the floor near Linnie. He peers . . .

It's his kerchief, now settling. It seems to have been blown about a meter toward him.

On Baram's back the skin crawls, and his ancestral hair follicles come erect. Had he been his own far-off, furred ancestor, that fur would now be standing straight out in horripilation, the threat response to fear. Surely he is seeing the very hand of Reality itself—or rather, Reality's impalpably fine finger—the tip of the force of What Is, and will not be otherwise.

In one or two more such soft gusts, all evidence of his acts during the regression will be gone—unreal, illusory, *gone.* He shivers.

But far more important than his fear: Are Pao and Vovoka's gun really there—*now?* If so, real help is possible. But Baram dares not tempt fate—

or Ochter—again to look. It was such a brief glimpse, in shadow, it could so easily have merely been what he longed to see. Oh, gods of Star-justice, let not this be erased, too!

Meanwhile Ochter has been speaking, commanding Baram to hurry. But the little man seems somewhat subdued at the moment. He, too, has been through the time-flurry; what has he done, felt, attempted? If this was his first, he probably merely endured. Baram recalls his own bewilderment —and he had the benefit of Kip and Cory's talk.

Abruptly there comes a rattle and thud from the main lounge door— someone on the other side, not knowing the lock is fused. It must be Hiner, Yule, or both. On the deck, all who are conscious turn to look—including, Baram is glad to see, Kip. He's now lying propped up, rubbing at his eyes. Good.

But what new disaster is coming onto them now?

Desperately, Baram fingers the scalpel and the cutters in his pouch. Until and unless Pao produces another, these are their only weapons. Linnie should have the scalpel, he thinks, it's more use against an enemy and less temptation to try to cut a hypotube she can neither see nor feel.

As he moves toward her the infirmary door swings wide; whoever it is has given up and found the way. And out comes a figure so unsteady, so besmeared and bedraggled and fouled as to be barely recognizable as Yule.

He heads for Ochter, yammering incoherent complaints.

With him comes a sound.

Bridey and Linnix hear it first—a faint, very high-pitched keening that is almost beyond Baram's hearing. It is alive, it has a frightful heart-tearing quality; unforgettable. Baram has heard it twice before, once from a terribly burned young male, and again from parents whose child had drowned.

It is the sound of a Damei screaming in unbearable agony.

A Damei cannot scream or vocalize like a Human; only *in extremis* is there forced from one this soft, spine-freezing, whispering cry or stridulation that seems to come from everywhere and nowhere at once.

Almost as Baram recognizes it the sound cuts off raggedly as if the agonized one has been gagged. Horrified, Baram is realizing that Hiner and Yule are at their bloody crime, not in the village, but right here near or in the hostel itself.

And that means that the victims must be—he can't finish the thought, can only hear again Linnie crying, "It was children like Nyil they tortured."

And Kip's cheery reply, "That's what we're here for!" The Kip who now lies broken-legged, barely conscious, while the criminals have their way.

Oh, Pao, Baram implores in silence, if you exist—you *must* exist—get that gun to me. . . . Surely the boy has found it by now. But how can he approach Baram? Baram's gaze begins tracing out possible routes, deciding where he himself should stand.

"Mordecai! What's wrong?" demands Ochter as Yule staggers up to the rollbed. "Why aren't you at work?"

"Wrong? Everything's wrong!" Yule wipes his bloody sleeve across his smeared face. "Listen, you said your shot would fix me, it'd all be fun. Well, it isn't fun. Oh, Nat loves it, he thinks he's killing bugs. But it's—yehch, a mess! First we have to wait forever for the bugs to come to, and they're too big to hide; and you said to bring them here, everybody would be out, and then—hey, what goes on here? These types aren't out a-tall, look at him and her and—"

"That does not concern you," Ochter snaps him off. "They're under quite adequate control. But *are you getting the stuff?*"

"Some. But I hate it. You said fun—"

Ochter has looked his henchman over, visibly repelled by his state. But his voice becomes unctuous, soothing.

"Poor lad. Not to worry, Mordy, we really can make it fun. Of course you need a full shot. You see, I only gave you half before, you seemed so, ah, cool. Here, right away—" He selects a syrette. "Let me have your arm. Take that thing off."

Baram can scarcely listen. From his new position he can see the rollbed's floor drape—and a boy's quick hand emerging, feeling straight for the fold where Vovoka's weapon lies. It's real! And Pao is real, and he's about to get it!

Yule is stripping off his wet, stained sports tabard. Heartsick, Baram can recognize the purple of Damei blood and lighter, oily streaks that must be the back exudates, the Stars Tears stuff. Even from here he can catch the faint sweet scent.

"Remember, Mordy," Ochter is saying severely now, "you jumped the gun, with those smokes. I told you I didn't plan on starting with the aliens here, for security's sake. And then nearly smoking them to death! You have only yourself to blame for the wait and all the inconvenience."

"My good coat," Yule mutters. "And that big booger was sick on my shoes. Animals!"

"That's the spirit!" Ochter has captured Yule's muscular arm and smoothly injected him from a red syrette Baram doesn't recognize. "Now, Mordy, you'll feel marvelous in two minutes. Meanwhile, throw that thing away, you'll soon have the credits to buy a new outfit every day. Every hour, if you like. Get rid of that."

Mumbling, Yule flips the tabard onto the floor near Linnix, frowning down at his dirty boots. Under the rollbed, the hand still gropes, maddeningly blind to what's so near.

Hurry, Pao, Baram prays, uneasily trying to look anywhere but at the bed drapes. *Hurry—*

Oh, gods, a dire thought has come to him; should he try to rush Yule now, to give Pao time to find the gun? But it means torture for Linnie—Ochter will use the scorpion on her to stop him. And maybe it isn't necessary—

But it is.

Was.

Too late, he sees Yule suddenly stoop to the floor, saying irritably, "What gives with you anyway, Doc? I crotting well don't think that should be lying around."

Baram's breathing stops.

"What now?" Ochter asks.

"This." Yule straightens up.

Slowly revolving around his fat finger something gleams: Vovoka's gun.

Six, seven pairs of eyes stare in helpless realization at the thing dangling from Yule's hand: the weapon that would have saved them. And saved the Dameii, too.

After the hours of pain, threats, hideous prospects, painfully devised countermeasures that fail, fail—the Deadman's Alarm missed, the wire-cutters unused—and then this sudden unlooked-for miracle of reprieve all but in their hands—Baram is faintly surprised that he can still feel the anguish that invades him as he watches Yule's foul fingers close on the weapon; watches their last hope die.

XVI

STARSTORM:
Baramji Summons the Dead

The stillness of despair grips the watchers on that Starbright deck. Even the pulsing, quivering beauty of the shoals of light around them feels cold; it will soon become their death-light. Against that weapon in their enemies' hands, there is no hope in superior numbers, surprise, courage—no help, no hope at all.

Yule, looking pleased with himself, plays with Vovoka's gun. Ochter looks up from rearranging his syrette pack.

"Give me that."

"I don't see why." Sullenly, Yule toys with the weapon a minim more, but he hands it over.

While Ochter examines it, Baram looks cautiously about. He meets Kip's squinting eyes; something still wrong there, probably Kip's having trouble focusing. But he's grasped the essentials of the situation. Beside him Cory sits with head bowed as if totally drained; she's drawn a Damei veil about herself. Bridey, nearby, is protectively sharing her blanket with the unconscious Stareem. No more the queen of sunlight, her eyes are violet pools of dread.

Zannez, by his two boys, is also sizing up the situation whenever Ochter's gaze isn't on him. Baram sees a coldly alert speculative expression on the bald man's face, which grows more and more grim. Baram guesses he is realizing how that gun can be used to control them all, now that Ochter's control over Baram is attenuating in usefulness. That weapon will let him keep his victims alive but helpless—say, by blowing off hands or feet—without leaving traces to alert an investigator.

Hanny Ek and Snake are also stealing looks around, probably impatient for some leadership. Little Pao, invisible beneath the rollbed, must be on knife-edge. And Linnix, after one appalled stare at Yule, has turned to Baram with eyes blazing suicidal resolution.

But Baram is finally ready. He has settled his questions, or had them settled for him, and he has been taught a lesson—he wastes no more than an instant regretting he hadn't rushed Yule before Yule saw that gun.

The crux of the situation has in fact changed only slightly. Assuming only Ochter keeps that gun while Yule goes back to the lounge, Ochter now has another means of self-defense, and a very lethal one. But he must use his unbandaged left hand to fire it, and he will have to put it down to work a hypo.

And Ochter won't use the gun on them now; too many are awake and would make moving targets. He could easily kill someone by error, he might get into a struggle for the gun, and the small gun can have only a limited charge—it could run dry. Nor would Ochter allow Yule to use it.

No; he will continue with his drugging plan, using threats and indirection as before. Unless he could stun them all with one sweep as Vovoka had?

That question is answered.

"Don't play with this thing," Ochter tells Yule, looking up from his inspection of the weapon. "The settings are marked in an alien script I've never seen. It looks Human but it's definitely not. All we know is that its present point took off Vovoka's head. Now, back to work."

He lays it on the rollbed beside his open syrette pack. Baram's teeth clench; that gun is only centimeters above where Pao's head must be. It might as well be a light-year away.

Very well. As soon as Yule goes back to his devil's work in the bar, and Ochter comes back to his drugging scheme, Baram will take the first chance—maybe while they're bending over someone—to simply grab Ochter and cut his throat. Or break his neck; Baram glances with satisfaction at his own still powerful forearms and hands. That will cost Linnie some pain and undoubtedly get himself, Baram, mortally wounded by that death-claw.

But he's sure he can last long enough to get to Linnix and give her a better death; Ochter wouldn't have loaded that claw with anything instantaneous—it would be too easy to scratch himself.

After that it will be up to the others to take out Hiner and Yule. For that they'll have the gun, unless some impossibly bad luck strikes.

He can't get to Linnie first and—oh, my gods, he thinks, incredulous—and kill—*kill* her—kill *Linnie*—before Ochter can hurt her, because Ochter would get him first with the gun.

So be it—but for an instant Baram can only gasp, soul-stricken at the unbelievable acts and thoughts reality is forcing on him.

As his mind flashes over this grisly route, he sees Yule glance about nervously before saying to Ochter.

"And another thing. Nat wants to know where the crotty hell that ship is at. That *Comet.* So do I. Race is late, he should have showed by now. We want you to call him. Use that thing—" He gestures toward the console. "Their cruiser or whatever could come early; we want Race here."

"And bring the Federation down on our heads in an hour?" Ochter asks bitingly.

Meanwhile Baram is taking it in—they have their getaway ship all laid on, by the gods. Doubtless the ship Pao saw. Their worst hypotheses, all, all true.

Ochter sighs and says wearily, "Oh, Mordy, do use your head—no, on second thought, don't, that's my job. And tell Nat to stop worrying, that's my job, too. Now *Comet* isn't late. She'll be along when we need her. Because Race needs our credits or he'll lose *Comet.* I made sure of that early on."

"So why won't you call him? Just signal *Comet,* it could be any private ship."

Ochter sighs again. "Mordecai Yule, can't you get it into your brain that we're way out on the Rim? There *aren't* any private ships here. or any other kind. One call to *Comet* would tell that FedBase that an uncleared ship is heading to Damiem."

As they talk, Baram watches their distance from the weapon on the bed. Yule strays far enough to kick the blanket half off Stareem, but as Ochter lectures him he forgets her. "All right, all right, Doc," he says sulkily. "But I thought *Comet* was supposed to be an old Patrol boat. Why can't she go FTL?"

"Because all Patrol vessels have their *c*-skip drives spiked before they're sold into private hands." Ochter tells him. "And *Comet*—"

As Ochter talks to Yule, Baram's eye is caught by an oddity behind them. The brilliant gleam of the rollbed's satin coverlet *shifts* very slightly, unnaturally. . . . And not for the first time, either, his eyes recall. Significance suddenly strikes: Under that coverlet little Lady 'Lomena is moving her limbs!

Very minutely, but repeatedly. And—there it comes again, as Ochter is impatiently telling Yule why the *c*-skip can't be replaced in *Comet*. The paralyzed body stirs the Star-lit silken folds. And it seems to come after the speaking of the word *Comet*.

What is he seeing, what—

Memory bursts like a golden bolt of lightning from that golden bed.

Only that morning he'd stood beside it in the marquises' room, his aching loins at last partially eased, listening to the marquise, in fetching seminudity, talk of her twin's terrible accident. How 'Lomena had been battered, jumping a beloved silver horse named—named—yes! Comet. *Comet!* . . . . And how, when Loma was dead to all else, she'd showed signs of protest when some fool had said in her presence that Comet would be killed. Yes!

Can that response be still vestigially there?

Can it be evoked? Strengthened?

Baram's breathing almost chokes; this million-to-one hope hits him bodily so that he has to struggle to remain impassive. The alteration between hope and despair has become physical pain. He dares not think, what if it works? Will young Pao be there, be alert? Will he fumble the chance? Will others interfere? Will—a hundred disastrous sequelae radiate —but Baram won't look at them. Certainly, if this fails, the suicide attack is his only course; neither he nor Linnix can hope to survive a fiasco. . . . Don't think of that now, concentrate on this one incredible chance.

The first essential is to capture Ochter's attention. A wild idea forms and grows as Ochter says:

"Now you feel better, Mordy. I can see it. Think about scooting back to work, think about getting rich-rich-rich!"

Yule squints his eyes.

"Hey, I do feel different." He licks his lips, grins. "Good ol' Doc!" With his bared torso he looks obscenely like an executioner out of history.

"Fine! Back to work you go!" Ochter claps him genially on his back, heads him to the infirmary door. "And good old Doc has some work to finish before I join you." He turns away. "Baramji!"

As the youth shambles off, Baram addresses Ochter in a firm, carefully normal voice.

"Ochter, I'm really surprised you couldn't see the obvious solution to your simple problem. To depend on that lout! That pretty pair of louts, who doubtless intend to kill you as soon as they see their first money."

"Necessity makes strange demands," Ochter says absently, moving toward Bridey as he bites at the wrapper of a syrette.

"What necessity?" asks Baram. "None. None at all. Why didn't you at least check on the easiest and, I may say, the most profitable source?"

Ochter glances at him. "Baramji, I won't tolerate stalling. Does Myr Linnix need a reminder? Get over here."

Baram chuckles quite naturally, hoping that Linnix will stay still. "You don't grasp what I mean? Perhaps it will be plain to you if *you* recall which planet I'm a xenological medic on. Did it never occur to you that a man sitting on a mountain of potential credits might not wish to remain a little back-planet XMD all his life?"

A gasp from Linnix. Baram fixes her with a level stare, wills her not to speak.

"What do you mean, if anything?" Ochter asks crossly.

Smiling, Baram says slow and clear, as if to a child, "Simply that I have accumulated over a liter and a half of the highest quality Stars Tears material, in a *very* private place. And when you kill me, as you so blatantly intend, all knowledge of it will die with me. *And* you can't screw it out of me by torturing Myr Linnix—or myself—because she and I will die quite soon of our own choosing, not yours."

Linnix' eyes widen impossibly as she looks at him; across the deck no one seems to breathe.

"A liter?" Ochter asks tonelessly.

"A liter and a half, of superb quality. I managed to send one milliliter off-planet for test. Superb! And it was obtained, I may add, without any of this messy torturing and illegality and confederates. The Dameii in question cooperated willingly." His tone turns reflective. "But there was, for me, a problem in disposing of it profitably without impairing my ability to obtain more. . . . I thought to wait until I had a dekaliter."

"A d-dekaliter. Baramji, you're bluffing."

"Also," Baram goes on obliviously, "I'm fond of my two co-Guardians here. I'd hoped to find a means of sharing the bounty with them, since it has no evil connotations. If you think I'm bluffing, Ochter, the more fool you. However, I may still have that report on my sample somewhere—though it's not the sort of thing one leaves about."

"You're a lying fool and I should punish you. Get over here at once."

"As you like." Baram makes no move to rise from the console seat. "When you kill me or Myr Linnix the question will become moot."

"Don't worry," Ochter says grimly. "I'll ransack that infirmary of yours, Baramji. If it exists, you probably have it on a top shelf—labeled."

This is so near the truth that Baram has trouble replying coolly. "Do. The place needs a good dust-out. But no, Ochter, I didn't consider the hostel safe enough; power-cells have been known to explode on their own." He has the little man's attention now, time to start. "But if you think I'm bluffing about this, you'll soon be convinced that I know where *Comet* is" —he stresses the name—"and why *Comet* won't get here. FedBase told me what they knew and I haven't had time to pass it on to anybody. Poor *Comet!* . . . Happy waiting."

The tension of the Star in the dazzling air seems to be growing; Baram almost jumps as movement shows on the golden rollbed. Does the syrette case slide just a little? Ochter is too preoccupied to notice.

"That's impossible, Baramji. I heard every word you said to that Base."

"Then you must have noticed my silence at the end," Baram says smoothly. "That was when Poma's all-station alert tape cut in, reciting her actions re *Comet.* I don't usually talk back to tapes."

It all sounds so palpably false; Baram, like many men of integrity, has no idea how fertile and convincing a liar he can be—save for one small trait.

Ochter frowns and asks reluctantly, "Are you telling me your Base was in contact with *Comet?*"

"Your *Comet* contacted Base. Race was lost, you see. It turned out he'd been trying to unspike *Comet's* c-skip drive. That's not illegal because it's impossible. Base just laughed. The result was that he gained some speed and lost half his guidance. He was lucky—*Comet* could have bounced right out of the Galaxy. If you ever ship on *Comet*—which you won't, any time soon—I'd suggest you urge Race to stick to normal speeds. . . . Anyway, they got this call from *Comet* at extreme range. He wanted coordinates, that's his right. Poor *Comet!* For Race's sake, if not your own, you really should try to help save *Comet.* When *Rimshot* comes along with my CNS expert—you did hear that?—they'll pick *Comet* off like a netted goby. But I'll be long dead, of course. Pity."

Here Baram sees he's made a slip—Ochter steps toward the rollbed and his syrette pack just as Loma's legs move again. Will he see it and safeguard the gun? Baram holds his breath . . . and luckily, Ochter doesn't seem to notice; he begins pacing, taking hard looks at Baram, apparently in deep thought.

Baram switches tracks for a moment, to let him get away from the bed.

"It's all a pity. If you hadn't tied up with those two murderous clowns, Race would have made an ideal courier—me working this end and you handling sales. However, I refuse to think about it with those two in the picture."

He can hear gasps and stirrings from around the deck. Linnix has her eyes fastened on him. She seems to be feeling the pain of the barbed hypo; her face is strained and her hands go often to her neck.

"Oh, I intend to get rid of *them* as soon as their work is done," Ochter says abstractedly. "But I don't get you, Baramji. Am I to understand that you have some proposition for me, assuming that any of this is true? Which I doubt."

Baram continues as if he hasn't heard. *"And* I refuse to remain alive if you hurt Linnie anymore. Oh, yes! I can be dead so fast you'll be astonished, Ochter." He rattles the scalpel and cutters in his pocket. "You never figured that, did you?"

Exasperated, the little man strides toward him, away from the rollbed. *All right,* Baram tells himself. *Now or never.*

"Baramji—"

"But that doesn't solve your immediate problem," Baram overrides him. "Where is *Comet?* Are you forgetting *Comet?* Every minim you waste, *Comet*'s going farther astray. Only I or Cory can save her now. Don't you want to save *Comet,* Ochter?"

"What *are* you babbling about, Baramji? Explain yourself this instant, or—"

"Easily!" He grins. "They gave *Comet* the wrong coordinates, you see. I doubt it was intentional—this sector was resurveyed last planetary year." Baram is improvising wildly, speaking past Ochter to the body on the bed. No response is visible now—and it won't be, he tells himself. He's a fool, a fool. Still he gabbles, unable to give up the forlorn hope.

"Poma wasn't in the office; some kid at Base gave *Comet* the old ones. *Comet*'ll be looking for Damiem till her oxy runs out—*Comet* was short there, too, you know. Poor old *Comet!"*

Suddenly, unmistakable motion on the bed. Loma's body heaves, her arms stir; he thinks that even her face changes a trifle. But it's the legs he needs.

Just as he opens his mouth for a last try, out of the infirmary door rushes Yule, a sight of horror with bloody arms and fists raised.

"I heard that! So you're going to 'get rid' of us, you rotten little scut. And *Comet*'s in trouble. Oh, lords—I should have known."

"Be quiet!" Ochter snarls with such authority that Yule actually shuts up, his face working. "Go on, Baram. Can you substantiate any of this? And if by chance it's true, what can you do about it?"

"Remember the strange ship our little prince sighted this evening? Or did you miss that, too? That was your *Comet!* Your silver *Comet."* Baram's voice rises at every repetition of the name: *"Comet,* going by on her course to nowhere. Your first priority is to rescue *Comet.* Save *Comet!* Don't let them shoot at *Comet*—what if *Rimshot* fires on *Comet? Comet* will be killed! Don't let them hurt *Comet, Comet* is your only chance. Help *Comet!* Send the right numbers. And don't let them take *Comet,* either."

As his words grow louder and madder, heads rise and turn toward him across the deck, and Yule and Ochter, staring, take an involuntary backward step, nearer the bed. Still no one notices the silken coverlet wrenched and moving. Linnix cries out, "Bram!" while Ochter and Yule try to shout him down at once. But he can't stop now.

"Save *Comet!*" He yells across twenty years at a girl's dead ears. Still nothing happens. He's a fool. "You can save *Comet!* Get on *Comet,* ride *Comet* away!"

And under the silks little Lady Loma's knees shoot up, while all that is on the coverlet slides and vanishes over the foot and side.

Ochter is closest; he whirls and stoops after his precious syrette case, brings it up in his good hand—and then suddenly leaps over the bed corner, shouting incoherently through the down rails at something or someone invisible on the floor. An instant later he pushes himself back and upright—and, before amazed eyes, abruptly *shortens* where he stands.

His body drops straight down, his chin jolts on the foot of the bed—he falls backward, arms flailing, syrettes flying, to the drape-strewn floor, and begins to scream.

At the same instant, across the deck there is a loud *crack!* and a crashing in the eaves as the main antenna snaps off and collapses into the cable. But Baram has no eyes for such incidental damage. He knows what must happen now.

Leaping from his seat to get to Linnix, he gets only glimpses of that which Ochter's fall reveals.

Standing on the floor where Ochter had been are two Human lower legs and shod feet, the remains of panters dropping down them. Where the knees should be is a mist of reddish smoke.

The grotesque apparitions hold for an instant, so like prosthetics that Baram, trying to get the cutters to Linnix' neck, is slow to realize that they are the lower halves of Ochter's real legs. Then, amid rising screams, they topple one after the other onto Ochter's thrashing, almost legless body. His knees have simply disappeared.

When Baram next glances up, Ochter's free, Death-Clawed hand has vanished, leaving a waving wrist-stump; now the bandaged hand puffs out of existence, too—and with it the switch restraining the deadly hypo in Linnix' neck. There's no blood. Ochter's screams change to wilder cries as he shakes his handless wrists before his face.

Yule crouches paralyzed beside the bed, staring down stupidly at the wreckage of his employer. And behind him, Baram—his ears filled with Linnix' shrieks, his hands fighting hers—glimpses something like a rising wave of silk topped by a girl's blind head. Loma struggles up, reaching for the gods know what, and is falling over the edge, making a hoarse roaring noise.

As her long hair swings onto him, Yule looks up, gives a bellow of fright, and bolts for the infirmary door. Behind him Loma falls, to hang head-down over the bedside, her naked back unrecognizable under a welter of broken tubes, scars, wires, hoses spurting ichor and air—her life-in-death support, now ruptured forever.

As Baram struggles with Linnix he's marginally aware of young Pao darting from under the torn gold drapery to take steady aim at Yule, who's just reaching the infirmary door. With a last yell, Yule goes down, a smoking head-sized hole suddenly between his shoulders.

Then Linnix' heart-stopping shrieks and writhings of pain drive all else from Baram's mind. She's in full-body convulsions now, her knees jerking up to her chest, then straightening rigidly as she arches backward in the flimsy chaise. But she's breathing. Hyperventilating, in fact—possible Cheyne-Stokes coming on. Baram has to straddle her to hold her shoulders and neck, and tear away the top of her uniform to get at the ghastly scorpion hypo. Its belly is not quite empty, Baram sees. He strives to force the point of his wire-cutters underneath and keep her hands away. Perhaps the hypo mechanism failed, perhaps Ochter wasn't able fully to relax his grip. But he'd said it contained "twice the lethal dose." Far more than half has gone into her.

Baram's mind wraps Linnix in the cold quiet that comes on him when a patient dies.

Still he fights to sever the scorpion's tube—until the tremendous paroxysm topples their chaise and sends Linnix screaming and sprawling away. Before he can crawl to her she gets both hands on the scorpion and wrenches it outward with all her might. Only a change in the timbre of her shrieks tells of the new agony that those barbs must have caused.

"Let go! Linnie, let go!" he shouts in her ear, working to open her fists. And then she lets go, but a bright red pulsing jet of blood bursts up between her fingers, sluicing everywhere. He knows what that means— she's cut into or severed her carotid artery. The filthy tabard is across her neck, and the scorpion lies half-out, revealing two of its sharp hooks.

He tries to get his fingers into the wound, but one hook catches the tabard cloth as she writhes and before he can free her, her shrieking dies down, her body goes limp. The sky around them gives a black flash. The blood gout is dying away.

As he finally gets a fingertip onto the torn arterial membranes, deep in blood, he's astounded to see her eyes come open. She looks up at him quite peacefully, almost as if she would smile—as though some secret sweet relief has eased her. He has seen death come thus. His fingers find the murdering barb, push it from the vessel. But there is almost no pulse—one weak beat more . . . another . . . none. The sky flickers.

Baram retains still enough sense of duty to lift his head and call strongly: "Zannez!"

"Yo?" comes the reply. People are on their feet.

"Take over, will you? Can you get Hiner?"

"Will do." It's Snake Smith's voice.

"And pull your people under cover, quick."

On that, Baram, sometime Guardian of the Dameii, lets his eyes and heart go back to his dying girl. She seems beyond pain; he gathers her to him under the darkening sky. And shortly she dies so, in his trembling, blood-soaked arms.

XVII

THE GRIDWORLD
WAY

Zannez jumps up at Ochter's first screams, very glad of the chance to move. The deck is a bedlam of screams and shrieks. He edges around the console for a clear view, trying to grasp the fate that has befallen Ochter, and what it is that Baram has done.

When Pao emerges firing Vovoka's weapon, Zannez dodges back and bumps into Hanno and Snake coming the other way. Bridey is just beyond, wearing a blanket and hovering protectively over Stareem on the floor.

They all stare, breath held, as Yule dies.

"I think that thing is running dry." Snake whispers. "The hole didn't go all the way through."

Zannez shudders, but he thinks Snake's right. He's also very conscious of the rising tension in the air, the alien energies of the Star around them. It feels as if it's mounting to some peak. Like a sensi-effect special running wild, he thinks; but this is no Human made effect. For the first time he is really nervous about radiation. They should be back under the eaves, he thinks: get the girls.

At that moment Baram, struggling with Linnex under the strobing sky, calls to him, and he and Snake reply.

"I think Hiner's in the bar," Snake says then to Zannez. "With his—with the Dameii. We can take him."

"I want Bridey and Star under shelter first," Zannez tells them. "Doc says take cover. Things are going funny again. One of those was enough."

"One of what?" Hanno asks. Zannez remembers that they were both unconscious during the earlier time-eddies.

"Never mind—just move! Can you take Star?"

Bridey is sobbing when they reach her. "She's d-dead!" She clings to Zannez' chest. The screeching is dying down.

"*Star?*" Zannez drops to his knees, to feel Stareem's peacefully breathing flanks. She's curled in sleep like a silvery kitten.

"No. That girl-officer, that Linnix—I saw her die-ie—" Bridey's words are starting to echo in a way Zannez doesn't like. He looks toward Baram, bent over the white limpness of Linnix, but it's becoming hard to see.

Hanno stoops to get Stareem's arms and sling her over his back, as he's done a hundred times on camera. But now he staggers—everything is acting like high-gee. The air flashes darkly.

"Help him, Snako. Bridey, grab my arm. We don't—repeat, don't—become separated. Hear-ear-r?" Again the echo. "Hurry-y! Push hard."

He heads them for the closest point of sheltering eaves. All over the deck, shadows are beginning to glide and jitter, and a ghostly chorus of past screams murmurs in their ears. This one is coming on slower, Zannez thinks. Maybe it's big. They push, plow forward.

Just then he remembers Pao. Gods—the kid! Superboy. "I forgot the prince," he can only whisper.

Snake points effortlessly ahead, and Zannez makes out the small shape of Pao; he seems to be going to their right, where Cory and Kip are. Longer that way.

"Nobody much alive back there-ere," Hanno pants. "How 'bout Doc?"

Zannez grunts again. If Doc wants to be with his dead girl, or die with her, that's his business. And Lady P.? Tough. She did it to herself. They can do no more than they're doing. Everything is becoming indistinct, each footstep forward is a fight.

The effort to traverse eight meters of level deck takes all their strength. Twice they circle shadow chairs, only to strike into something solid they can't quite see. The rushing, whirling effect is starting, but slowly, clumsily, thank the gods. Are they struggling upstream against time itself? Zannez doesn't want to think about it. It's warped time, anyway—one of the Star's crazy effects. . . . The ghost-sounds are getting louder. Push.

Just as the retrograde rush hits them hard, they reach the real darkness of the overhang and stumble, half-fall under it—

—and are suddenly in clear, silent air in a stable world.

Bewildered, gasping and panting, they stare back at the deck they fought their dark way across. It is brightly Star-lit, calm and empty.

Baram and Linnix are gone. There's scant trace of all the violence, save for Loma's tragic little body hanging over her deathbed rail and, on the floor, a mutilated caricature of Ochter. Beyond the rollbed, a drift of sparkling violet veiling from a turned-away chaise marks where the Lady Pardalianches has slept safely through it all—or has not. Vovoka's body is only a still mound of blanket by the far parapet. Zannez remembers there's one more body—Yule's, out of sight somewhere along the wall by the infirmary door. But the whirling chaos of shadows, the echoes, all are gone. It's like striking a show set. The glittering Star-rain seems to have diminished a trifle, too.

"I feel funny," Hanno says, shifting Stareem around to carry her now easily over one shoulder: sleeping, she burrows her nose into his neck. "Like part of me is still out there."

"Hold my hand," says Snake, not joking.

"I know, I felt it," Zannez tells him. "Hold on, it goes away. Time to move, kids. Hiner's back there in the lounge doing terrible things to some poor wing-people. Doc laid it on us to stop him." It's like setting up a fast live show. He feels great, his team okay and a job to do. There'll be no suicide charges, either. All his people are coming out of this alive. I'll remember all my life, he thinks: for a few minutes I was in charge of defending a planet.

"This is the front of the Korsos' room," Snake says. "There's a door leading through to the lounge in there."

"Goodo. But we check in with the Korsos first. I think something bad happened to the boss lady while we were out, and Kippo's broke himself a leg. They have to know what goes down."

"I'll park Star with them," Hanny says.

"Do that."

They squeeze close to the wall to pass a place where the eave thatch is battered in. A big tangle of broken antennae is hanging over the edge.

"Hey, look, we may be out of contact," Snake says.

"Pao's gun did that," Zannez says. "Firing up at Ochter. See the big chunk missing?"

"Thank the gods he was pointing up."

They go along in the shadow in front of the lounge, toward where Kip and Cory sit beyond the big doors. As they pass they can hear faint sounds from within.

"I thought that was leaves," Bridey says brokenly. "It's—it's wings. Feathers."

"Hurry."

"Do we rush him?" Snake muses. "We have four ways in from the sides:

Korsos' room, infirmary, arcade doors. What if he goes out the front? Do we want him out or in? In."

"What weapons has he?" Hanny asks practically. Little Prince Pao, hurrying to meet them, overhears.

"A nasty harpoon thing," Pao answers. "Like a crossbow. It was disguised as underwater defense. It shoots a barbed bolt at almost bullet speed." His manner is sober, befitting one who has just killed. "One suspects they may be poisoned."

"Sweetheart," Zannez comments. "Hey Prince, well done! And thanks from us all." The others chorus appreciation.

"Thank you," the lad says gravely. "I was fortunate the weapon fell into my hands. After my unforgivable blunder that left you all unarmed."

"Blunder? What blunder? Oh, you mean the antennae?"

"No; that was unavoidable." Pao breaks off as they reach Cory and Kip. Cory has veiled herself in a Damei fabric; what they can see of her looks . . . different. But her voice is gracious and nearly the same.

"Myr Zannez—and your people. Is the little girl all right? Baram said she was merely drugged asleep."

"We believe so, Myr Cory, ma'am." Zannez bows, followed by the others. Hanny ends his bow by dumping Stareem into a nearby chaise, then straightens her out solicitously. "Pass me your blanket, Bride."

"Well . . . here." Bridey fetches another from the nearby line of screening.

"And Myr Kip?" Zannez is asking.

"Oh . . . I'll do," Kip forces a grin. "But I'm fairly useless. My eyes won't focus at all; Doc says it'll wear off. But how in the name—" He jerks his hand to point toward the lounge wall behind him. "Every minim he may be—of all times for me to—"

"The doctor asked me to attend to Hiner," Zannez says rather formally. "We think we can. With your permission we'll go right ahead. The, ah, Gridworld way." He grins ferociously. The Star's light reflecting from his bald head and red suit gives him the look of an antique demon.

"You can? . . ."

"I'll need someone to open doors. How about you, Prince? Can you open a door hushy-quiet?"

"I think so." The boy is definitely changed, Zannez sees. It's this unknown "blunder," more than the killings, at a guess. Proud little bastard. No time for that now.

"We need an idea exactly how he's set up. If he has the wing-people there, he's probably in the center space, between the stairs and the bar. But—"

"That's correct," says Pao. "I had a look in, from the roof. It's . . .

quite abominable." Behind his formal words, the boy's upset. "He has the t-two adults tied to the bar, bent over so he can get their backs. He's in front of them by the stairs with Nyil, with the little girl. He's cutting her—cutting at her wings. And then he runs behind them and scrapes. It's . . . vile . . ."

"Easy, kid."

"You and your people face a terrible sight, Myr Zannez," Cory says. "I regret that the prince had to."

Kip grunts evilly but says only, "Weapons? Due to my—" and subsides as Cory grips his shoulder with a shawled hand.

"And Vovoka's gun is dry," the prince reports.

Snake nods.

Hanno and Bridey are exchanging murmurs.

"I saw a box," Bridey says. "Maybe there's more. I'll ask." She asks Kip and Cory her question.

"That's it," Kip replies. "No others."

"Means you two get across, what, at least ten paces bare-ass open," Zannez comments. "Hey, maybe Doc has some. Myr Cory, may we check the infirmary for more? We won't disturb—"

"Ask Baram, he's in there," Kip tells them. "He must have finished his clamps by now." They all looked puzzledly at him; Kip amplifies: "Linnix' neck. She needed stitches. Lords of death, that little devil."

"But, but she's—" Bridey starts to protest when a small hand comes up and clamps over her lips. It's Pao.

"I think one must be careful what one says," he explains as he takes his hand away. "While one is on this planet."

"Oh—" Bridey begins, and then just repeats, "oh."

"Forget it," Hanno tells Kip. "The box is enough."

"Okay, script session—one minim." Zannez beckons them around him. "You remember *Kiddy Cannibals,* three seasons back? And *The Corpse Fuckers?*"

They do.

"Keep remembering. Now: places. Pao starts with Snake and me at the Korsos' door and then scoots like a rocket around to the infirmary for Hanny and Bee. And—"

He speaks on fast, giving precise directions. He feels exhilarated, confident. He hasn't used all his abilities for so long! This is living as he'd never known it on Gridworld—yet they're working Gridworld skills.

"What I really need is some of those flashy gold drapes," Snake says as they brake up. "Only I'm goosey about trying to go back out there."

"No trouble," Pao tells him. "See?" He trots out of the shadow and back to them. "It's just the present, of course. The flurry's always in the past. You can only get in a time-flurry if you're there when it starts; I figured it all out." A trace of his old Superboy manner has revived.

"Goodo!" Snake hurries out to the rollbed and starts ripping drapes.

"I'm glad somebody has it all figured out," says Bridey. She and Hanno disappear into the infirmary.

"And what I need is *that.*" Zannez strides out to Ochter's body. "Myr Cory, maybe you better not look." Before he picks up Ochter he rearranges his own red suit, flips up the collar, and works his face.

Then, "Green, go! Pao!" he shouts, bounding with sudden energy toward the Korsos' room, Ochter held stiffly before him like a grotesque doll. He's done the actor's magic of face and body change, he looks frighteningly like an ancient picture of the Lord of Evil carrying the damned to Hell.

With Pao rushing ahead and Snake running behind, trailing golden stuff, they disappear through the Korsos' door.

Hanno and Bridey hurry into the infirmary, passing Baram by the operating table where Linnix lies.

"Excuse us, Doc, no time. We're going after Hiner." Hanno starts stripping off the robe and Bridey drops her blanket.

But her head snaps around as she sees Baram helping Linnix sit up and pin her torn white tunic together. Linnix smiles at her. Dumbfounded, remembering Pao's warning, Bridey only waves back.

Then, as Pao runs into the room, Baram picks up Zannez' hand camera and, to Bridey's and Hanno's astoundment, starts awkwardly taking a run of Linnix, with side takes at themselves.

But there's no time for more; they can hear Zannez yelling from the lounge and Pao is silently opening the door between infirmary and bar.

Naked, black leading white, they stoop low and move stealthily out into a scene of horror and peril.

Looking past them, Baram and Pao can see Nathaniel Hiner at bay above his victims, bare to the waist, his great red membranous gills standing out in desperate rage, from ears to chest in a blood-gorged ruff, while beyond him and taking all his attention, there sallies and gyrates and howls a demon of vengeance and terror. Blood and torn plumage are strewn about, and great fanning wings, crudely tied and pinioned, almost cover the bar, toward which the naked boy and girl swiftly and silently go.

Young Pao eases the door closed after them, leaving a crack to watch through. Behind him, Baram has laid aside the camera and is leading Linnix out to the deck to join Cory and Kip.

This gives Pao an idea. He turns briefly from the door.

When he comes back to peer, a screaming blood-red monster is dancing across the lounge, making skittering, howling dashes at Hiner. Zannez has burst into the bar leaping, whirling, zigzagging, and dangling Ochter's mutilated body with amazing strength, while from his throat pours such a barrage of whoops, snarls, roars, terrifying peals of devil laughter as Pao had never imagined an unamplified Human throat could make.

"Here's your boss, Nat Hiner! See your little bossy?" Zannez cackles with mad laughter, shaking Ochter's stump legs. "Say hello to your friend Nat, Ari Ochter! Hello, Natty-boy, hello!" He makes Ochter's handless arm wave cruelly.

Ochter isn't quite dead, Pao sees—he squirms in Zannez' grasp, crying weakly, adding to the horrible effect.

"You didn't know they have gods here, Hiner!" Zannez shrieks, amid inchoate yelpings. "See what they did to your pal? And Yule—Mordy Yule's in li-i-ttul pieces. Ha-ha-*hah!*" Zannez screeches, dances from side to side, forward and back, no part of him still an instant.

Hiner, momentarily paralyzed, crouches knife in hand above a tragic tangle of plumage, blood, small limbs, wires and rope, at which Pao cannot look. Then, with a peculiar neighing sound, Hiner flings the knife in the general direction of Zannez and grabs up his spring bow. He aims it one-handed at his tormenter while his other hand tries to stuff a bloodied flask inside his tunic, his wild ruff of gills in the way. Crack! Clang! A bolt shatters vitrex above Zannez' head and another hits the staircase beyond him.

At this moment something like a spinning golden comet hurls itself into the lounge behind Zannez, giving out ear-splitting hoots and yowls.

Hiner fires another bolt that goes into Zannez' tunic, and breaks at a run for the main front doors.

But the gold-streaming thing reaches them first, circles to head him off from escape. Amid a riot of cartwheels, somersaults, leaps, and hand-walks, Pao finally makes out that it's Snake, his body almost invisible behind whirling gold drapes gripped in hands, teeth, and feet—a show that would tax a professional acrobat, which he is. But he and Zannez are performing for their lives now.

In another minim Hiner will realize they're harmless, but he's given no time. Zannez edges closer. As Hiner turns back, Zannez powerfully flings the wretched Ochter straight at him and dodges away, yelling falsetto, "They're coming for you, Natty-boy, gonna get you-oo-oo! Ha-ha-ha-ha-hee-hee-woo-oo-oo!" Snake joins in the uproar.

"Nat! Nat! Help me!" Ochter cries through the din, slipping down Hiner's body, clasping his stub-ended arms around one of Hiner's legs.

"Keep off me! G-get away, get away!" Hiner breaks free, kicking brutally, and suddenly sees Hanno and Bridey ducking behind the tied-down Dameii. He sends two more bolts at them; they clatter into the bar mirror.

Meanwhile Zannez has snatched up the skinning knife Hiner threw and is advancing in lunges, fencing fashion. Hiner fires another bolt which just misses Zannez' head, and then, to Pao's anguish, stoops and grabs up a tiny body from the tangle on the floor and holds it before him as a shield.

It's Nyil: one of her little gold wings droops brokenly, and there is only a terrible gash on her back where the other should be.

Clasping her across his chest, Hiner takes aim at Zannez with his free arm, snatching looks around the child's body.

For a second Pao's breath catches, while something pale whips up and down behind the center of the bar.

And suddenly a metal shaft is sprouting out of the socket of Hiner's aiming eye. He drops the child and, screaming, claps both hands to his face. Another knife flies into his open mouth, and another tears through his gills into his chest.

Bridey and Hanno have gained the open knife box by the stove.

Hiner staggers backward, turns, under a hail of knives. Knife handles march down his belly and sides, the impacts seeming to jolt him upright. Behind the bar, dark and light arms rise and fall together. Zannez and Snake fall silent. Then Hiner pitches forward and sprawls, away from Nyil.

And it is over.

Really over at last.

Hanno vaults the bar and begins the task of gently releasing Wyrra and Juiyn, while Zannez, roaring for Doctor Baram, converges with Snake above the heart-breaking form of Nyil.

But Bridey's in a killing rage. Her naked young body mounted on the bar, her white arms flashing like avenging lightning, she pours her steely missiles into Hiner and Ochter, making their bodies quiver and convulse.

"Turn her off! Turn her off!" Zannez shouts hoarsely.

"Okay, okay, sweetie." Hanny Ek cautiously reaches up to her. "Bee? Bridey! It's over now." He gets a hand on her throwing arm. "We have to leave enough of them to identify, honey. Sweets? It's over, you did it, Bridey-pie, you did it."

Slowly she comes out of it and lets him help her down from the bar, seeming fully to see the Dameii for the first time.

"But look what they've *done,*" she wails, her eyes flooding with tears of rage.

Hanno eases the rest of the knives away from her. "They're dead now, honey, we killed them dead-meat. You did just great, Bee, you never touched a feather."

"Oh, you Bridey-o!" Snake dances up to her. "If you were a man, I'd marry you!"

"Oh-h-h—" In reaction, she melts weeping onto Snake's chest; then pulls away to throw up into the bar sink.

Doctor Baram is bending over Nyil, his face haggard. "She's alive . . . barely." Cory, at the doorway, watches through her veil, impassive.

"How did you like the Gridworld way?" Zannez can't help asking the world in general. His arms and legs hurt, he has a bolt cut on his ribs, he's stiffening up all over, and his voice is almost gone, but he feels wonderful. He's done the job and his people are all okay.

"Fantastic. I'm shaking," Baram says. "But now I have to work fast with the Dameii." He has passed his wire-cutters to Hanno, and the two Dameii adults are slumping to the floor, so nearly unconscious that they seem only dimly aware that they are free. So far as can be seen, apart from their flayed backs, neither is physically hurt.

"Put this salve on them." Baram hands it over. "And tell your boys that most of those so-called feathers have nerves in them, go very easy. Let the Dameii move however they seem to want to." He says a few words in careful Damei, but Wyrra and Juiyn do not respond. "I'll take over Nyil. Oh, gods. . . ." as he feels more of the savaged little body. Then a desperate idea comes to him.

"Prince?"

The boy is beside them, emotions contending on his face.

"Can you take on one more small mission? Go out on the deck, and at the very first sign of a time-flurry—you know, that dark-flash effect—at the very first suspicion, dash into the surgery and call me. And better be wrong than miss one."

"Right." The prince salutes and hastens out.

"Oh, lords of pity . . . Myr Zannez, listen, if your people can stand it, would you get them to search through this mess for, for body parts? For fingers, Nyil's, the little girl's fingers especially. Toes. The adults', too." He clenches his jaw painfully. "Any bit of flesh. And any of the longer plumes that look to have had a blood supply, bring them to me quick. We'll move all this into the surgery. . . . Dameii heal amazingly. I've sewn on a hand that'd been off half a day without refrigeration, and it's functional. . . ."

He gathers Nyil up in his arms, the severed wing in his hand, holding her facedown to spare her back. Zannez helps him through the infirmary door. To his surprise, when Baram lays her prone on the padded table, her neck lengthens and bends far back, and her small chin comes out naturally to point straight forward where a Human forehead would be. An adaptation to the wings, he thinks, choking down the sight; she looks so dreadfully like a brutally plucked, half-butchered little bird—who only hours ago had been all compact of life and fun.

"If you could help the other two in here," Baram says over his shoulder. "And bring Kip to translate for you—tell him I said to tow him on a blanket. Right?"

"Right." Zannez starts for the bar. He no longer feels exuberant. The helpless, sick rage that rose in him at the sight of Nyil, the aching pity for Wyrra and Juiyn, the shame that it is Humans who have done such irreparable vileness, will, he fears, live with him in nightmare to the end of his life.

XVIII

STARFIRE
PASSING

As Zannez leaves the infirmary, Prince Pao dashes in from the deck.

"It's starting! I'm certain it's a real one! Can I help?"

Baram brushes by the boy, carrying Nyil in his arms. He is a lifelong atheist, but at that moment he's praying with such silent fierceness that he barely hears Pao. *Oh, gods—God of Asclepious, god of Galen, of Pasteur, let this work! This one last time, oh, gods make it work—*

Aloud he says hurriedly, his eyes on the Star's light, on the flickering sky outside, "Yes. Get Wyrra and Juiyn out here. But—" he realizes he hasn't yet decided whether Nyil's parents should go through it: would they help? The memory of Linnie's screams decides him. Nyil would have to go back through torture, and terror; better they not see.

"But make them stay here, under the eaves," he concludes as he reaches the shadow edge, Pao running alongside. "I think I'll be out very soon in real time." It crosses his mind that this extraordinary wave of time-flurries is what lay in the Star-shell's last and inmost zone; it must be a great concentration of the Star's special energies, its "yearning" to be back, back before *Deneb*. The other shells had shown nothing like it.

"Right." Pao starts off at a run, but the boy in him can't resist spinning around at the door to say, "Mind you don't meet yourself coming back!"

He disappears.

In fact it's good advice, Baram thinks, veering sharp left as he carries Nyil toward the brightest pool of Star-light. He must remember to take the other tack coming back . . . coming back, with what in his arms? The same heart-searing burden, or a miracle?

Don't hope, he warns himself. The peak of the Star's energies is passing. The air still feels charged, but not with quite the violent intensity with which it worked the miracle of Linnie.

Then the Star's retrograde time-pull was in flood. Swiftly it had borne Linnie back from death itself, through agony, to the near past, when the fatal artery was uncut, and blood filled her beating heart, and she lived again. She lived!

But he knew that if the time-eddy ran its course forward again with her, she would die again, and forever. He had to carry her alive from the time-flow's power, literally wrench her from the past to the present that existed so close at hand, in the shadow protected from the Star. So close—yet so agonizingly far in effort. It had taken all his strength only to move her, to lift and pull and tug her forward. He had ended crawling, just as the time-rush changed, dragging her beneath him with her wrists held around his neck, as he had once dragged the war-wounded under fire—and sick with terror that he had failed, that this was too gross a defiance of Time's power —until they fell across the shadow threshold and he could be sure she lived. Yes, she lived again—Linnie lived!

Yet even as he'd exulted, Ochter's damned triple barb had tangled itself in her hair, and he'd barely caught it starting to drag across her throat.

The memory of that kerchief blowing after the earlier eddy came back and scared him witless. Would this evil hook work its way from the ends of space, to reassert death's reality by killing her again?

He'd slammed it into his safe and frantically set about making this reality—the reality of Linnix alive—real. He made her speak to Kip and Cory, hand them objects, move chairs—anything to build the living Linnix into other's memories, to make her mark on *this* present.

It was then that he'd thought to make a camera record of her (shuddering with fear lest it turn out blank) and intermix her with scenes of *this* present. . . . It was then, too, that he'd understood the price this miracle had exacted; but he'd counted it as nothing, then.

And now he must hope that this last time-flurry will carry Nyil back a greater distance yet, to the moments before these unspeakable mutilations had begun—and that he has the strength to bring her out, to contest for her against Time itself once more, before the backflow spends its force and returns her to this grievous present again.

If he succeeds—will something be left behind? Don't think of it. You don't fight Reality unwounded. He'd been crazy enough to fight for Linnie's life. Now he's demanding another miracle.

So be it, he thinks, carefully spreading the barely living little body to Star-light. There's no other way. No Human skill can mend the dreadfulness that has been done to Nyil—that abomination, Hiner, not only slashed, but shredded, crushed the child's delicate wings, hands, arms. Baram can't stand thinking of what must have gone on: not clean cuts, but a progressive ruin, holding for a time the desperate hope of repair. Oh, that they'd been able to act more swiftly—and he can't help adding, Oh, that he had the living Hiner in his hands! This time-flurry is his only desperate last recourse.

Courage, he tells himself; we have the aid of the Star.

Holding Nyil steadily to the dark-flashing sky, he sets his mind to believe. *Back—take us back!*

But the Star's influence is weakening. The active principle, whatever extra-Galactic entity gives it strange powers, is passing Damiem. He can see how slowly this time-flurry comes on; slow, so slow that only now is the familiar uncanniness beginning, the unmoving motion, the clutter of displaced objects, ghost-people.

Back, he wills. *Carry her back!* And then to his dismay the tiny body in his arms begins to writhe and struggle, and her all-but-ultrasonic wail pierces his ears. Oh, gods, she *is* back—in Hiner's grasp. Will it carry farther, take her back to wholeness? *Back, restore her,* he prays to the universe. Summoning all the Dameii tongue he has, he croons to her, "It's all over, Nyil my dear, you'll soon be better. You're free, Wyrra and Juiyn are free. The bad Humans are gone. Hold on, soon you'll be better—"

It seems to help a little; amid her pain she gives him one clear look.

But her legs and wing-remnants are making a curious drumming, vibrating movement; he recognizes it as the Damei response to great physical or mental pain. It crosses his mind that it must have been the great drumming wings of Wyrra or Juiyn that the little showgirls took for the sounds of sweeping. But now in Nyil he fears it may impede the miracle he hopes for.

There's a site between the wings where pressure sometimes quiets the reflex. On Nyil it is bloody meat, but he lays his fingers down hard, and the quivering eases. And as he holds her thus he feels something—*something* —brush his fingers where nothing was before.

Oh, gods of mercy—can it be her lost wing, coming back? Are they receding to a time when she is whole?

He peers down but can see nothing clearly through the dark-flickering air. Or is there what might be a transparent projection of *two* pale golden little wings, that spread and still, as he presses the reflex point? . . . Not solid substance yet, but *there?*

And now under his fingers there is a growing sensation of normal flesh, even downy skin. Other wounds he can see are healing, too; the pitiful stumps that were her hands have shadow fingers now.

Will it continue? Or will the Star's fading energies collapse too soon and let the flow rush forward again to anguish and ruin? *Go on, go on, go on,* he prays, as if one tiny Human will could aid the Star.

And wholeness *is* coming, solidifying—the wings fan once, and a perceptible flow of air touches his face. But is the healing real enough? Dare he take her out now?

He's half-mad with indecision: To stop too soon, or to wait too long—either may risk losing all. His eyes, ears, his very skin, are feeling for the first sign of the retrograde flow. He's oblivious to any weirdness around him, even to what might be his shadow self with Linnix, over there—he can spare no instant's attention from the ambient air.

Then he remembers: It will take time, getting out. Almost without willing it he begins to move. Or tries to move—the difficulty appalls him. They have gone deep, deep. All his being focuses on the extreme effort to carry her out. He is climbing beyond exhaustion, carrying a load too heavy to bear. For a time he despairs of making it. But a fierce joy gives him strength—the little form in his arms is whole, *two* gleaming wings shine up at him, and once she twists to send him, unbelievably, a smile.

Afterward he can recall little of the struggle to get out; the traverse of those few meters of deck drain him even of reserves he didn't know he had. The two things he remembers are that smile, and changing Nyil's position, as he nears the shadow, so he can pass her to her parents. He's learned how to do this—to stand her feet on one palm at breast height, with his other hand supporting her narrow front, her wings over his shoulder. The joy of her restored life thrills through her, it's like holding living lightening.

As she sights Wyrra and Juiyn through the flashing murk of the shadow's edge, her wings buffet his head, and just as they're reaching safety, she takes off with a violent beat and *flies* the last steps into her father's arms.

Baram, seeing her safe, lets himself fall to his knees. As he's done once before, he crawls feebly from the past into the sudden silence and clarity of the present beneath the eaves. He becomes vaguely aware of a cluster of Human legs around the three Dameii . . . and someone has gotten Kip into a rollchair.

But as he is trying to haul himself upright, he sees that all is not yet well.

Nyil is leaning across her father's shoulder to embrace her mother's head. Suddenly her eyes close and she sags, limp.

Baram is so weak that he must cling to a chair back to get one hand to her breast, while Wyrra cradles her face upward, in his arms. The strong, running quiver of the central ganglion, the Damei equivalent of a heart-beat, is gone.

Baram has learned to restart it as he would a Human heart, but with a sharp, heavy double squeeze. At his first try the vibration resumes, and Nyil lives again.

Only there is a kind of darkness on her face, Baram thinks. It vanishes when she smiles, but between smiles and loving murmurs to her parents, there comes a look he's never seen before.

He steps back to greet Kip where he sits watching, with Cory standing, still veiled, behind.

"They're saying good-bye," Kip tells him quietly. "Bram, what is it? Didn't the time-thing work?"

"It worked," Baram says grimly. "But . . ." He doesn't know how to phrase it without sounding crazy. Nyil has gotten back her wings, her body: what has she left behind? Her life?

"But there's a price," Cory finishes for him, in a grave voice.

"It took too much out of her—is that it?" Kip demands.

At that moment Baram sees her collapse again and steps forward to Wyrra. But when his hand reaches her chest, he gets a strong feeling of protest from both parents, He works the necessary compression as gently as he can. Too gently: he has to repeat the starting before her body takes over.

"No, no," says Wyrra in Galactic. Juiyn, looking wild, bursts out with a spate of Damei that Baram can't possibly follow.

"Don't they understand?" Baram asks Kip. "Don't they know I'm doing this to keep her alive?"

"They understand," Kip tells him. He ripples off a question to Wyrra in Damei, and both Nyil's parents reply at once, with Nyil herself joining in, until she sinks back exhausted.

Before Kip can begin translating, Nyil turns her face to Baram and crooks her fingers—her fingers!—at him, beckoning him near. He bends over her in Wyrra's arms.

And just as he does so, she takes two weak breaths, and he sees her quivering chest fall still. Baram brings one hand up to steady her back so he can seize the sternum area. She gives a plaintive little cry from almost airless lungs, and Wyrra's free hand plucks at Baram's. But the Damei's light touch can't break into the doctor's absorption; Baram's fingers squeeze in sharply, twice. Nyil breathes—and the life-throb is there.

When he's satisfied that function has been restored, Baram faces Wyrra. "Life," he says in his clumsy Damei. "Her life . . . not death, not dying." He mimics the hand squeeze. "Needed for life."

Wyrra gives the slow side tilt of his head that is the Damei "No," and speaks in his own poor Galactic. "Pain," he says. "Too much pain. Have bad dream, say."

Baram's first thought, that Wyrra means that the restarting is too painful, changes when he hears that "dream." Is it that the child has simply been through too much and can endure no more? Helplessly confused, Baram can only repeat, "Life. Not dying," to Wyrra's unreadable negation.

Baram turns back to Kip. "What is it? What's wrong? Don't they believe she'll live?"

But Nyil beckons him to her again and speaks first.

"You save—you *have* saved me," she says carefully, faint but clear, and pauses to smile bewitchingly up at him. "You have saved me, terafore, no, *there*fore"—she brings out with unmistakable pride—"now I can die good; no right; well."

"But you don't have to die, my dear!" Baram explodes. "Now you can live!"

She tilts her head. No.

"No, I am to die. But well; it is all right now. I fly! Before you have saved me, it was no good." Her voice trembles. "Very, v-very bad."

"Yes." He understands that, at least. And evidently to these people not to die maimed, tortured, *wingless* is very important.

"But I *can't* let you die, my dear. We may have to do this"—he makes the squeezing motion—"a few times more, but you are ready to live now. Don't you want to live? Your parents—Wyrra, Juiyn, they want you to live."

The little head tilts, sways for emphasis. She sighs. "No, no. To understand diff-i-cult. I know you good, Doctor Baram." Again the heart-melting smile, this time with, incredibly, a tinge of mischievous mimicry. "Good-bye, my dear."

Her gaze goes from him to her parents, she says a word or two in Damei —and he sees the movement of her chest weaken and cease.

As his hands come up to restart the beat, a rough grasp fastens on his right wrist and jerks it away. It's Juiyn, towering over him with wings aloft. She makes the sharp sound that means emphatic "No" in Damei, holding his arm with almost Human strength.

Helplessly, he lets her pull him away.

Nyil's eyes have closed momentarily in a grimace of pain. Now they open wide. She looks at the faces that surround her, her gaze calm, clear, smiling, with only a scarcely perceptible shadow of what might be fear. Then her eyes go to Juiyn and Wyrra, and close.

She is whole, winged, untormented: she looks like a child in peaceful sleep. But a child who does not breathe again.

No one speaks. In silence the two tall Dameii, beautiful even in their ravaged state, turn away with their burden. They pace out of the circle of Human light, into the silvery mists on the deck beyond.

Just at the edge of visibility Baram sees Wyrra pass their daughter's body to Juiyn, and they turn to the parapet. Baram understands. Their horror of passing closer to those end rooms is so great that it has overcome Wyrra's reluctance to expose his defect of flight. A moment later comes the beat of his bad wing as they take off.

Baram, too, can't bear to think what must have gone on in and around those rooms. He'll have to, soon enough; tomorrow, the investigation doubtless will begin. . . . Afterward, those rooms—perhaps the whole hostel—will be simply destroyed. Erased, obliterated. . . . A pity, maybe, but there's no other thinkable way.

He's frowning absently at the spot where the Dameii vanished. Now he becomes aware of Linnie quietly holding his arm and pressing it against her warm side, as if to comfort them both. He looks down into her cerulean eyes. Some expression is coming back, he sees, a change from the vacant stare that so frightened him.

"I remember, I knew the little—the young one," she says softly.

He nods, smiles down at her. "Yes."

Then he looks up and deliberately meets the eyes that surround them. It's time. Linnie spoke quietly, but not so quietly that all did not hear.

Zannez is standing closest, his arms around the shoulders of Hanno and Bridey at his sides, his face carefully blank. Hanno looks frankly more and more curious, as the oddness of Linnix' remark sinks in; Bridey's violet eyes are open wide. Snake, quicker than Hanno, is examining the floor.

Even Kip, sitting in the medical rollchair, has paused in working at his eyes and is squinting at Baram. Behind him Cory leans against the wall; her face unreadable behind the veil; he can see that her hair beneath the cloth is now snow white. Baram's heart skips a beat as his gaze passes over her, but he has Linnix' problem to attend first. The boy Pao is sitting cross-legged nearby, beside Stareem. His head is up, studying Linnix. Only little Stareem, curled in sleep on Kip's vacated blanket pad, is peacefully oblivious to it all.

"Linnie, my dear," Baram says, "all these people are your friends, and we must tell them that you've had a loss—a lapse of memory."

She nods. Her response is childlike, docile, but light-years away from the drooling blankness he first saw. That was when he faced the terrible possibility that he'd brought her body out alive—without a mind.

"Call it traumatic amnesia," he tells the others. "We don't know yet if it's permanent or temporary, nor whether it's very extensive or localized and spotty. We simply don't know. Just don't be surprised if she doesn't recall your name." He smiles, then sobers. "There'll be plenty of time for introductions later if they're needed. Right now we have more urgent matters to attend to.

"Bridey, if I may I'll leave Linnie with you. And can you also stand by Myr Cory and Kip in case they need anything? I should see about the marquise."

"Oh, gods." Bridey moves to Linnix' side. "Poor Lady P.! I forgot all about her! And—Oh!" She puts her hand to her mouth, glancing meaningfully toward the rollbed. "Well, yes sir, Doctor B. I'll stand by here, if Myr Linnix will stay with me. Oh, I'm Bridey. Hello."

"Hello," Linnix responds interestedly. "I'm L-Linnix, I think."

"And Myr Zannez," Baram goes on. "Do you suppose you and your boys could do one last dirty job? We seem to have a surplus of—" He gestures toward the blanketed heaps that were once Yule and Vovoka, and the rollbed, where he'd pushed Loma's corpse back onto her pillows. "Or have Snake and Hanny had enough?"

Zannez squeezes Hanny's shoulder. "You—and Bridey, too—remember what we said about props? Just keep telling yourself they're props—it's true. And you've seen a million worse ones, kiddies. Hold the thought—props."

"Vovoka's can go in his room," Baram says, "and those three animals can go in Ochter's. Be careful not to disturb anything at that end; Base will need to see it all. And the rollbed with poor little Loma can go in my surgery. Perhaps you'll do that first."

Zannez and his three get the rollbed moving, and Baram goes around them to confront whatever has happened to the Lady.

His first glance shows her not only alive but coming awake. She's tossing restlessly in the lounger, muttering, "Where's Loma? Loma!" with closed eyes—a charming sight even in disarray.

Now to tell her that Loma is dead, and her lifework gone. Baram gropes in his pocket for more of the blue tranquilizer pills and goes for some water.

Five minim later he's wishing he had one of Ochter's sedative syrettes. It has been decades since he coped with open, raving hysterics in a Human. At his first word, she rushes screaming after the rollbed into the lab and, amid vituperative denials and calls to Loma, attempts to climb into it. Despite her femininity, she's as strong as a wild animal.

Baram calls Zannez and his youngsters from their work, and among them all they manage to get the poor marquise into her room and into bed, and loaded up with calmants. But she will not relax until the rollbed with its still cargo is pushed into her room.

"That's the best we can do for now," Baram says. "I'll get the body into a coffin and work with her sister, as well as I can, when we've coped with the living. I think there's a Lord Protector of Rainbow's End I can contact to meet her at Central, if we ever get to that."

As he speaks he's conscious of a blended sound coming from somewhere and everywhere.

Partly it is a soft, high-pitched keening. That would be Dameii, singing or chanting in the trees around Nyil's home. He's encountered the death-song ceremony before.

But there's another sound underneath, a bass so low-pitched as to be more of a shudder than a sound. He knows it—but he's distracted by seeing Linnix abruptly straighten up and brush at her uniform, seeming for the first time to notice the rips and bloody smears on her breast. Of course.

The rumbling bass grows louder as he speaks till it drowns his words. A new light has sprung up in the Star-hazed sky, over the roof of the hostel. It's a ship's exhaust flare.

Somebody is coming in to land.

Baram's first thought is that it's *Rimshot*'s pinnace—but why would Dayan have come so soon, without their SOS or his requested callback? And he couldn't have picked up a neurological expert this fast. Besides, it doesn't sound like the pinnace, or like a Moom ship's lander. It sounds like a larger Patrol vessel capable of touchdown.

Which is exactly what *Comet* is supposed to be.

And *Comet*—wait!

Baram's story to Ochter, about *Comet*'s being lost and Race contacting FedBase, was made up of whole cheese. But he'd told it with so much effort and conviction that he's ended by half believing it himself. In fact he knows nothing whatever about *Comet,* and there is no mortal reason why this can't be Captain Race landing his ship to pick up his duly chartered passengers.

His lavishly chartered passengers.

How will he take the news that his passengers are dead, his promised payment gone glimmering—and he himself has landed on an Interdict planet and will be detained the moment FedBase learns of it?

All Baram knows about Race is that he's an adventurer who doesn't mind taking risks and is determined to get the credits to keep his ship.

These thoughts flash through Baram's mind as all activity stops to listen. They are followed by another.

An unarmed spaceship still has offensive capabilities: if its low-altitude guidance is good—as an ex-Patrol escort's would be—its exhaust and auxiliary thrust rockets can be used as flying torches to wreak havoc on the ground.

And Race has been told that his three passengers expected to get very rich here.

What are the chances that he's put one and one and one together and come up with Stars Tears? Or at least some gem find? Very good. And he has a threat by which to extract some or all of his payment from the station. He's already in violation; why should he care about further charges?

Oh, gods. Baram feels suddenly tired, tired and old. He's spent the night faced with an endless array of frightful threats and pains and dilemmas and assaults, and thought it at last over. But here's one more. For the first time, his internal feelings match his white hair.

He looks up at the strange ship; its trail seems to waver a bit, as though the pilot is looking the place over. And it is definitely not *Rimshot*'s pinnace.

When he looks down, Zannez' sharp eyes are on him.

"More trouble?"

Baram beckons him over by Cory and Kip and explains the situation. Cory listens but says only, "That ship will have a transmitter . . . not c-skip, but better than—" She gestures at the wreck of the antennae.

Kip is reviving fast, though his eyes still squint. "If we can get at his caller. Race won't be eager to let us use it to report him in," he says gloomily, and then bursts out, "Amesha Spentas! Of all the accursed—I still haven't recharged the Tocharis. . . . Cor, you've got a stupid, blind, leg-broke Deputy, one overworked medico, and friend Zannez here—and two boys and a girl armed with kitchen knives!"

She lays a veil-covered hand on his shoulder.

Pao has been listening quietly from his seat on the floor. "Myr Kip, I have one of your Tocharis charging; it should be about full. I thought it might be useful. . . . You did tell me to, you know."

"Oh, my gods. Get it—no, we'll pick it up in the garage."

"Superboy," says Zannez.

"I'm the surprise factor." Pao grins at Zannez.

"Well, well, well!" Baram is purely astonished at good news.

Kip struggles to his feet in his excitement, frowning hard.

"And if we tape the LED indicators on the other two, they'll look functional." He grins. "So we give the charged gun to the best shot—that's between you and Zannez, Bram. Or one of the boys? The aim is to get

Race and his crew under control, either in the ship or on-planet, in case he has ideas, while we use his caller. How does that sound, Cor?"

"Green. . . . But of course," Cory adds tiredly, "he may be quite peaceful."

"And we aim to see he stays that way. Let's see: How many crew would he be apt to carry for a charter of three? We can probably assume he isn't paying any more wages than he has to."

"Look," Zannez says, "numbers aren't everything. How about we bring along a girl? Bridey'd have the best chance of being invited in."

"With or without her cutlery?" Baram asks. He, too, feels a lot better.

Bridey touches her APC robe pockets and smiles.

"Best we put her in that gold thing of Pao's," Zannez says. "You can stick the knife up your sleeve; I taught you."

Snake gives a leer. "That outfit would get her into a Special Branch vault."

"Time to go!" Kip points upward. Insanely, everyone's grinning.

The unknown ship is coming in fast. Its thunder suddenly increases to a horizon-shaking scream as the ground retros cut in, then fade.

"Gods, doesn't it ever get light around here?" Zannez is trying to think. "Look, we need some tunics or something that looks like travel."

"I'll get ours," says Hanno.

"And I can get yours, Kippo." Cory moves toward their room, walking tall and fast.

"And we need—my gods, I almost missed—some dummy duffels. Snako —can you quick make up some from ours?"

"Done." Snake lopes off.

Baram has retrieved his own medical tunic at a trot and crosses through the lounge to help Cor.

In a couple of minim the group is reassembled, looking surprisingly different.

"Time to move it," says Kip. "My eyes are still no good, but I can't hurt anybody with a dry gun. Stick me in back, will you?"

Pao has been watching excitedly.

"You are the king of the castle now, Prince," Kip says. "We haven't left you much in the way of troops. You'll be green?"

"Go!" Pao tells him.

"We'll try to get word back," Baram says.

Bridey quietly kisses Cory as the others pick up their "bags."

"You really look like voyagers," Cory says, suppressing a cough.

"We are," Zannez says, grinning, as they exit. "That we for sure are!"

XIX

ON
THE RAMP

The jitney bearing Zannez, Snake, Hanno, Bridey, and Kip, with Baram driving, arrives at the field just as the strange ship flicks on its floodlights. In the glare on her side Zannez sees a salad of scripts, topped by *COMET II.*

"Stop ahead," says Kip. "If we are where I think we are, just turn the car a little crossways and we can block the road. We don't want them roaring out past us."

Baram obeys. The ship has a Space-type drive, but her landing rockets ignite the brush. She is also closer to the road than the Moom ship's usual spot.

As the fires burn out, Zannez looks up and sees the huge white wings of a Damei settling in the branches above them. He nudges Baram to look up.

"Kip! One of the elders is here."

"No time." Kip calls out something in Damei. The wings fold and seemingly vanish.

That Damei's staying really close to fire, Zannez thinks. Curious? Or maybe he has something important to say.

But what's in front of them is more important. The fire has sunk to embers now. He hears ship locks clank. Suddenly a landing ramp is angling down.

"I thought I heard the cargo latch let go, too," Kip says. "Let's stay right where we are, Bram."

A short, slight, erect figure appears at the port, with something in his hand. Captain Race? As the officer moves forward, a beefy-looking crewman comes out behind him and trots down the ramp.

"One," says Zannez. Kip is squinting hard.

There's a polite attention chime, and a nasal voice from a loud-hailer says, "This is the private spaceship *Comet Two*, landing to pick up a charter of three passengers for Federation Central. Ready now to board." After a pause, the voice adds, "Baggage will be hand-stowed, please. Pass your things to the crewman here."

"Now what? I—" Baram starts to say.

But to Zannez' amazement Kip has seemingly gone crazy. He's reached over and is hugging Hanno, Snake, and Bridey, and trying to hug him, too, and making weird whinnying noises.

"That voice," he chokes. "Oh, that accent—if only Cor was here!"

It's a minim before he calms enough to say, "Chums, I don't know how or why, but that isn't any Captain Race. It's Captain Saul Scooter Dayan of the Federation Patrol cruiser *Rimshot*—our friend! Bang on that hooter, Bram!"

"Friends?" Zannez explodes. He leans over Baram and starts tapping out the Federation anthem on the hooter.

"He must have taken over *Comet* somehow, and he's here to booby-trap Ochter and company. Oh, we have to tell Cor!"

"Oh-h-h, coloss!" Bridey sighs, once more resplendent in her Queen of Fire lace robe.

"Let's go!"

Everyone hangs on as they lurch out to the ship over the smoking sod. The familiar Horsehead accents from the port are repeating, sounding a trifle puzzled and peremptory.

"Hurry!" Kip urges from the back. "The tires'll hold; they have to."

Boom! Bffoom! Two tires blow as they near the ship. Baram careens to the ramp base on the rims.

"Saul! Saul! Scooter—it's us!" Kip bellows.

Cautiously, Captain Dayan comes halfway down the ramp, looking them over.

"Myr Kip, and Doctor Baramji, is it? I'm glad to see you seem well. But I must hold back until we establish certain facts and formalities, especially that you are what you appear to be. And who are your friends?"

"Oh, stow the formalities, Scooter! We've been fighting boogers all the long night—they've done awful things—and we've done a few—" But he falls silent. Even on far Damiem they've heard of Black World SC—techniques of simulation and control.

The hefty crewman has been joined by a sergeant carrying electronic gear.

"Retinal scanner there," says Baram aside. "I'll get him to check out your eyes, Kip."

"Green, Saul, Green," Kip concedes to the captain. "But listen, send a signal to Cory that you're here. She's not well and we've been fairly spooked. Oh, wait—the antenna's down; you'll have to send someone."

"Can't you get some of your flying friends to go?" Dayan's already testing Kip, Zannez thinks.

"No way, you know that, Scooter. And I tell you, terrible things have gone on."

"Very well," Dayan says grudgingly. "But it's against principle."

"If you'll step over here, Myr Korso," says the sergeant.

"I can't step, but I can hop if your pal there will help me."

As the crewman boosts Kip out, the cargo hatch flips down and three space marines in full battle dress emerge, tugging man-lifts. They mount and whistle off through the treetops toward the hostel.

The examinations are thorough but quick; soon Kip and Baram are up on the ramp, where the huggings and back thumpings recommence, and their story comes out in disconnected chunks.

"Gods, are we glad to see you!" Kip repeats. "But how in the name of All did you get here, in this?" He whacks *Comet*'s port. "Where's Captain Whatsisname, Race?"

"At Base."

Zannez, still at the ramp base, can see that Dayan is keeping one eye on the proceedings below as he goes on.

"Race took one look at your planet—you should see Damiem from space. He figured everybody was fried. So he went over to Base to find out what's what. Exec heard he was heading for Damiem, and I reckon Race is still explaining hisself. Meanwhile we decided to have *Comet* flown out to rendezvous with *Rimshot*, and some of the boys and I transshipped into her and came on here to look over these charter types."

"Beautiful."

At the ramp foot, Zannez is impressed by the sergeant's ingenious methods of countering any attempted audio surveillance, or control by hostage. Nice authentic touch for the documentary, he thinks—and thinks also to ask, "By any chance is this classified?"

"Yes sir," says the sergeant, not smiling. "And not by chance. We're getting to that."

And shortly Zannez finds himself being sworn, by his loyalty to the Federation, to keep it all to himself. Oh, well, he can see the point.

When it comes to the two boys' turn to be checked out, Hanno is found to be incapable of speech above a hoarse whisper.

"What's the matter with him?" Zannez asks Snake.

"He's never seen a real live Space Patrolman up close before," Snake replies. "That's the problem I was going to tell you. It was bad enough when we were with Service people. But now the Patrol is here. He really *wants* it, you know? It hurts."

Zannez remembers: *"The Patrol doesn't take animals."* That was because of the porn. Damn. . . . But he's distracted by the increasingly unpleasant sensation in his left side, where Hiner's bolt hit.

"You, Myr-in-the-red suit," a woman's voice rings out from the ramp. Zannez looks up to see a big, rangy woman in medic's whites, standing by Doc Baram. "Do you always carry your left arm like that?"

"Uh. Well, ma'am, no, I don't—it doesn't feel—"

"I'm Siri Lipsius, *Rimshot*'s battle medic." She's striding down the ramp, giving Zannez a grin from a knobby, friendly-looking face. "I see your suit has taken a hit on that side. Were you in it?"

"Zannez is the name, ma'am. Oh, yes, I was."

She grabs his rubbery left arm and does something to the palm that he can't feel.

Snake speaks up. "Remember, Zannie, Pao said he thought those bolts could be poisoned."

"I'm getting my kit."

Doctor Siri lopes back up the ramp, passing Baram hastening down. He, too, takes up the arm, frowning.

"I've been very remiss, I fear," he says ruefully. "Good thing Siri saw you. You couldn't be in better hands; she's my idea of a top battle surgeon."

Doctor Siri returns and Zannez' rib cut is soon diagnosed, detoxified, and taped. The consensus is that he's had a narrow escape. The bolts apparently carried a neurotoxin of the Parat type, which could have stopped heart action if it'd hit head-on or near a major blood vessel.

"Don't forget he was shooting at Hanno and me, too," mutters Bridey as the examiner packs up. "Brrr!"

"A very beautiful young lady," observes Dayan from the ramp. "Do I understand that she killed one of your raiders by throwing knives?"

"That she did!" Kip chuckles. "Listen, time to head back to Cor. What time are you on?"

"Midmorning."

As he speaks a whistle sounds, and two large space marines issue from the port behind him, stretching and stamping their legs. Above them, the darkness is just graying toward dawn, behind the last drizzle of Star-shine. *Comet*'s floodlights suddenly look yellow.

"You've fed? How's about your men come over to the station for evening chow?"

"You may want to rethink that." Dayan grins, and steps back as several more marines emerge from the cramped six-passenger spaces of *Comet*. And more still, as everyone moves aside, until a full squad is unfolding tents and gear from the cargo hatch onto the field's cleared edge.

"Whew. You came prepared, Scooter. Let's see, with the crewmen . . . say, twenty-two? I think we—I—can make that, we have rations ahead for some characters who won't be eating. Ah—there's your car, let's go. But take it easy with that engine. We'll have to leave the jitney."

Rimshot's command car is rolling out of the cargo hatch, its hydride-fueled motor puffing out water vapor. They all start down the ramp.

Dayan waves the girl driver to the back and gets in to drive. "I fear you'll have to wait for the next trip, Myr Zannez."

"No problem, sir." Zannez finds his Gridworld kids have closed in around him, reluctant to be separated. So is he.

Dayan gives them a sharp look and a smile. An odd little moment of empathy warms Zannez; the captain understands how it is when people have been through things together.

As they get Kip in, Zannez hears him ask, "Where exactly is *Rimshot?*"

"Looking for Doc's neurologist in the Hyades," Dayan tells him.

"Neurologist? Hey, Bram, listen, I'm green. My eyes just tracked in. I don't need anybody."

"Good," says Baram. "No, not you. I want Cory looked at by an expert. *And* by you, Siri."

"You can fix her up, Bram. Can't you? I figured you just needed a few minim without some godlost emergency cutting up."

"I can try."

Kip subsides, apparently satisfied. But Baram's tone chills Zannez. He listens closely as the two medics exchange a word before they get in.

"Don't forget, I'm only a battle hand," Siri tells Baram.

"Exactly what we need. The Administrator—that's Cory—had an alien energy hand weapon discharged point-blank into the parietal arch. There were no immediate signs of damage, but later—well, you'll see for yourself, Siri. You've forgotten more about alien artillery than I'll ever learn."

Then they're in. With Dayan driving, their car lurches sedately away and disappears into the dawn mists on the rocky station road.

Left alone on the ramp, Zannez leads his people over to the parked jitney, which is awaiting tires from *Rimshot*'s supplies. He feels naked without his cameras, but also easier for it in a way. Only, what shots he's missing . . . or is he? He looks around; the magic ship that bore friends —it would show up like any small space vessel sitting on a far-planet field before sunrise—he's seen a thousand such shots. And the Patrolmen who look like angels to him, not to mention to Hanno—could be any of a million routine shots. *Our Brave Space-Fighters* . . . He's losing his objectivity.

"Everything all right here, sir?" It's the squad leader with the interrogation sergeant, come alongside.

"Super. You'll never know how good you look to us."

"Glad to hear it."

Over their heads Zannez can see other large marines sauntering casually toward them and catches a good many covert glances in the direction of the golden flame that is Bridey. She is looking unusually demure.

Zannez has been in more situations like this than he wants to remember; he hopes the Code is as firm as it's said to be. From long habit, he starts a distraction.

"Am I allowed to tell you what happened?" he asks the squad leader.

"We'd admire to hear." That Horsehead twang, they must practice it.

"Well. The ringleader, see, was a little old fellow called Doctor Ochter, posing as a regular tourist. So kindly-acting, with a bad limp—faked—that nobody could believe he was a cold-blooded sadist. Oh, he was sweet.

"He had these two accomplices who did the actual dirty work on the Dameii—you all know about the Stars Tears thing, right?"

"Yes, sir," in a grave tone. "You mean they really . . ."

"Yes. They jumped one family before we could stop them. The wing-people who live by the hostel, they have—they *had* a little girl." The memory of little Nyil comes back sharply; Zannez pauses. This isn't just a Grid-show plot. Nyil was real, and she's gone.

"But, I should say, the butcher-boys got here uncleared by faking an error in the ship's sleep doses, so they had to be let off here—and their bags were full of bad stuff disguised as water-world gear."

"Grunions Rising." The sergeant nods.

"Right. And—" Zannez goes on tracing out the complicated events of the evening, the gift of poisoned Eglantine, Vovoka's devastating irruption, and Ochter's fallback plan of control by hostage; the loss and final recapture of the gun—though exactly what Baram did to make Loma move, Zannez still doesn't know—and Pao's destruction of Ochter and Yule.

"Wait till you see Superboy." Zannez grins. "But the last, best act was these kids—my kids here. They went in after Hiner, unarmed, and Snake and I distracted him while Hanno and Bridey got to the knife box, and whew!—you should have seen those meat choppers fly!"

"It was Hanno, really," Bridey says. "He never misses. And it was hard, the man held the little girl up to cover him."

Hanno has again lost his voice, and his normal blue-black face is turning a startling plum-purple shade. The Spacers look at the youngster curiously. Several of them are part Black.

"Knife throwing," the sergeant muses. "I tried it once. I was no good."

Zannez swallows. "As a matter of fact, Ek here has been trying to enlist in the Space Force. To be a Patrolman, like you Myrrin. They won't take him because of his job. But gods, people have to eat."

"Flat feet, eh?" the squad leader says sympathetically.

"No. He's fine physically. They turned him down because he works for me. Some of my shows—well, I don't know how to say it, they're somewhat low class."

"And they won't take him for *that?*"

"Right. It seems unfair." And what am I *doing* to myself? thinks Zannez. "Sna—Smith, here, was too discouraged to try."

"I've seen your Commune show," the squad leader said. "Last time we went near the grid, Lee and I watched," he told the sergeant. "It's not bad, it shows how the civvies live."

"Well," Zannez says, "but we do other stuff, too. We have to. Stuff you wouldn't see out here, thank the gods."

"Oh." The big squad leader stops himself staring.

The sergeant, more worldly-wise, grunts. "Still, if the boy's serious—"

"He is."

"Then he or you should speak to Captain Dayan. Out here on the Rim things are a little different. Any isolated Patrol unit can accept field enlistments, subject to evaluation. And that could be done at FedBase. Would you like me to have a word with the captain?"

"Oh, my-oh-my. That'd be tremendous. Hey, thanks!" Now he's done it. Godlost fool. Glory.

Hanno has his face under effortful control, but his eyes give him away. He ducks his head at the two Spacers. The sergeant nods back, a slight smile on his jaws. Those eyes, Zannez thinks. You wouldn't think black eyes could do all that, he should remember to use it. . . . When, fool? If this doesn't work out, he'll have one heartbroken boy on his hands. And what about Snake? Oh, gods. . . .

"Here comes your ride. Need help with that baggage?"

Bridey has jumped out and is hauling out stuffed duffels.

"Oh, no, thanks." She smiles at last; the sergeant backs into his friend. "They're just props." She tosses one up. "Fakes!"

"Nice meeting you." Zannez stops himself from reminding the sergeant not to forget; this isn't Gridworld. The sergeant doesn't look as if he forgot much.

The command car is driven by a hearty young Patrolwoman, Ralli. She and Bridey look at each other with obvious eagerness; Zannez can see about a tonne of temporarily suppressed questions each side.

Hanno gets in, radiating obliviously.

Snake sits quietly beside him, refraining from certain slyness with Hanno that the presence of a strange woman normally provokes him to.

"Snako, did I do right to hint about you? Do you want to decide this on your own? Or shall I . . ."

Snake smiles, a lopsided version of his sinister look. " 'Whither thou goeth . . .' "

"Huh?"

"Maybe it's 'goest' . . . old saying. Anyway, I will go, too . . . I've nothing for or against the Patrol. Even if I had . . ." He sighs, then breaks out a real grin. "Somebody's got to see our boy gets fed."

XX

TO
THE SUNRISE

Baram, who has gone ahead with Dayan, Kip, and Siri, is very anxious to get back to the hostel.

They've left Cory alone with a young lad, two unconscious women, and an amnesic girl. More than that, Baram is sure that Kip has no idea how severely stricken Cory may be. Kip wasn't able to see her clearly, beyond the whitening of her hair. Baram himself doesn't know precisely what's wrong, but he's seen enough of Cor to be very fearful. That gun in Vovoka's hand had not misfired, whatever she's told Kip.

Behind his fear for Cory lies a deeper, visceral fear for Linnix, that Baram can't shake. Superstitious idiot, he calls himself. Yet, after the early time-flurry, when he'd displaced that piece of cloth, that kerchief, it had come blowing back to its original position on gusts contrary to the steady *V'yrre* breeze.

No. Wonderful as it is to have Saul Dayan and his men here instead of an angry, unpredictable Captain Race, Baram cannot be easy about Linnie's life—not until that beastly triple-barbed hypo now in his safe is somehow destroyed, made incapable of getting back to Linnie and killing her again. He has an idea about that.

They arrive at the hostel just as the first rays of *Yrrei* come towering up from the east. The sky is still quietly spectacular. Cut by the western horizon, the passing Star-front shows as a great contracting lens of multicolored light, fading up to the pale green zenith, that is embroidered with pearly filaments and tendrils of light. And there is a sense of change, of leaving, passing away, as the Star-light almost perceptibly withdraws.

As Baram looks, a disquiet touches him. *Is* something leaving? Something quite other than Nyil's life or Linnix' memory. Has something Starborne been here that will soon be forever gone away?

His attention comes swiftly back to Damiem Hostel.

There's a quick view of Wyrra and Juiyn's treehouse as they enter the drive. It looks crowded. Several pairs of big wings are fanning from the porch, and Damei faces turn to the car. There seems to be a meeting going on.

As they pass the garage he glimpses two of Dayan's battle-clad marines checking it out. The third stands guard by the main doors.

As soon as the car comes to a halt, the driver's side snaps open apparently of its own volition, revealing little Pao holding a handsome salute.

"Meet our Commanding Officer, Liaison, Logistics, and Intelligence," Kip announces, laughing. "Prince Pao, meet Captain Saul Dayan."

Baram, watching, has seen the boy's face tighten at Kip's ebullience and gives thanks to the gods that Kip is too far to hug him or tousle his hair. A prince is a prince. But Dayan has spotted it, too, and gravely returns the salute as he gets out.

"Nicely judged, young man. The door, of course, I mean."

Pao's face melts into a smile. Baram's mystified.

"What?" ask Kip and Siri together.

"Tell them," says Dayan as they're helping Kip out.

Baram, taking medical license to push ahead, hears Pao say, "You exit a closed vehicle in inverse order of rank, as a usual thing. But I felt this was an operational situation where the commanding officer would wish to be first on the ground."

"Inverse *what?*"

"Don't sneer at protocol, Kipper. Our young friend's royal life will be full of it. All right, Ralli, back you go for the grid-show people. . . . Oh, great gods, what an unholy mess!"

Behind him, Dayan has seen the lounge.

The infirmary door cuts them off. Baram is just going through his quarters to the deck, when he sees Linnix in the shadows smiling at him.

She's too damn close to that safe where Ochter's scorpion is.

"Hello! Look—I know how this works!" And her hand goes to the knob, turning. There's a click. Gods! By pure chance she's hit the first mag point. With the sureness of sleepwalker she starts to spin it back. It all happens so fast that Baram, panicky, can do nothing but grab her arm and yank her away.

"Get out! Gods damn it! Get away from that, my dear—my dear Linnie, forgive me. I'll explain later—just for now, never, never go near that thing. Hear?" He shakes the arm, shakes her in his fright.

"Come." He's scared her. "It's all right, it's all right, dear. Come out with me." Oh, gods, if he'd been a minim later . . .

He pulls her with him out to the deck.

For an instant he thinks it's deserted, then sees Stareem on Kip's pad, holding her head over a basin. Beside her in the shadow is the shawled figure he knows is Cory.

"Hello, Bram—is Kip all right? Dayan sent word." The voice is Cor's and not Cor's. . . . He's heard such changes before.

"Hello, my dear—yes, everyone's fine. Kip's vision seems to be all cleared up."

She makes a strange little sound. "Then my small . . . stolen time . . . is over."

"What, Cor?"

"You'll see in a minim. Bram, can you do something for this poor girl's headache?"

Stareem peers up at him pleadingly. Of course, that Soporin leaves unpleasant effects.

"A minim. Linnie dear, stay out here."

He goes in for his kit. As he's getting it he hears Kip's voice from the deck outside.

"Hallo—hallo! Where's Cor?"

"This is Cor," the hollow voice replies. "Kip . . . my dear love . . . you might as well see it now."

Baram comes back out with a capsule and a drink for Stareem just as Cory is clumsily loosing the shawl. (Cory with fumbling hands?) It drops and she leans forward into the dawn light.

She is an old, white-haired woman, with lined and sagging face; her legs are veined and wrinkled, the knobby knees cruelly exposed by Cory's shorts.

"You—you're not Cor! Cory!" Kip tries to shout but his voice breaks.

"I *am* Cory, my dear. I . . . was. Vovoka didn't misfire—I let you believe that for a while. . . ." She draws a panting breath. "What it is, I'm . . . aging very fast . . . as well as I can estimate . . . a year or two per hour now. . . . He said I'd have time to say good-bye. . . . That means, Kip, that . . . some time tomorrow . . . I'll be dead of old age."

"Bram!"

It's a cry from Kip's heart, but Baram isn't hopeful. He goes to her, just as Siri comes out to join them.

But Cory waves them off, feeble but firm.

"Please," she gasps. "I know what's happening to me . . . quite well enough, Bram dear. Or do you . . . think you can reverse old age?"

Siri speaks up.

"I've heard two reports of effects like this, Myr Cory. Basically it's destruction of glandular function by selective resonance, at the atomic level. In one case mainly the pituitary was affected, and yes, we could reverse the effects by replacement therapy."

"That's it," Kip cries. "Do it! Get the stuff! Scooter, can we use your caller?"

"And the other case?" Cory's asking quietly.

"In the other, whole glandular systems were knocked out, and we couldn't help much. Now we need a blood sample from you, then we won't bother you anymore for a while. I can get the medication by emergency 'skip."

"Get it," Kip orders.

"All right." Cory makes the croak, or cackle, again. "But I don't think that alien . . . V-Vovoka"—she struggles for the name—"would have failed."

"Don't be gloomy, Cor. We'll have you out of this," Kip says heartily, not looking at her.

"Thank fortune you're here, Siri," says Baram. "I can take the sample, while you go signal Base."

Dayan has been standing to one side, quietly watching. Now as they hear the car come back, he nods to Siri. She follows him. Baram can hear Zannez admonishing his troupe as they enter the lounge.

"Wait, kids." The cameraman shows himself and bows briefly to Cory. "We'll be in our quarters if needed." He disappears, a tactful man.

"I'd like to go to my room, too, now, Bram," Cory says. "You can take the blood there. Kip . . . my dear, if you don't want to . . . look at me . . . or be with me . . . I truly understand."

"It's only for a while," Kip says. "I know my girl is there waiting."

"She . . . is," and Cory's old-woman chin quivers, the easy tears of age brim her sagged eyes. She veils herself, and Kip helps her rise. His touch is halting, as if he were forcing himself to touch something icy.

As Cory reveils herself Baram catches a glimpse of a familiar beauty-spot mole on her nape, and for one flash the young, vital Cory of yesterday is there. Next instant she's lost in the white-haired scarecrow figure of Cory-now. He finds himself close to tears.

"Oh wait." Baram remembers the sigil. "Cory, you should have this back."

"Give it to my . . . Deputy." She's trying hard to hold herself tall and walk well. "Tell . . . Dayan to notify Base, with Siri's opinion . . . *both* her opinions."

When the medical doings are over, Baram corners Pao and asks him a question. Then he goes to Dayan, who has made his first inspection of the dead.

"Sir, I am about to destroy some evidence. Or I should say, I intend to attempt to. The automatic hypo, that demonic so-called scorpion that Ochter put in Myr Linnix' neck. I think you should look at it first."

"Oh? And why are you going to destroy it, Baram?" Dayan's walking with him toward the lab. They pass Prince Pao.

"That's what I feel I can't explain to you fully until much more time has passed and we're safely off this planet. I think it's only safe now to say that the thing nearly ended her life once before, and there seems to be an affinity—an unnatural affinity between it and Linnie, that suggests to me that more than simple physical effects exist here. Such things are possible. You may call me farfetched, or impose any penalty you please, but the point is that I intend to disperse that thing down to its constituent atoms, right now, if possible."

Dayan considers. He respects Baram, but he's never seen him in this light. "Linnie?" Evidently more is at stake here than normal concern for Human life.

Baram pushes the lab door closed—it sticks, where he's been meaning to plane it—and goes to the safe.

"This is the thing." He puts it on the lab sink. "I'm going to call in young Pao. He thinks there's just enough charge left in that weapon of Vovoka's to destroy a small object at close range."

The scorpion, fully revealed, is even more hideous with its vicious triple barbs besmeared with blood and ichor.

"Nasty piece of work. . . . No, I don't believe the investigators will miss it."

"Oh, I didn't tell you, I photographed it. Do you agree there's no point in looking for fingerprints or other body traces?"

"Agreed."

Baram opens up and calls the prince in: they position the thing on an expendable box, before the dense metal splash-board.

"All set. I'll turn it so the barbs at least will go— Oh, damn!"

The door is pushing open.

"Excuse me," says Linnix. "I know you don't want me to come in here, but Myr Cory sent me—"

"Get out!" Baram yells, rushing at her. "I don't care if the gods themselves sent you—get away!" There's a tiny clink.

In his haste to get her out, Baram doesn't notice that the scorpion has caught in his sleeve. When it appears on the ground by the door he almost screams.

Linnix, frightened, is pulling the door to. Baram bangs it shut and sighs relief—and then sees that the scorpion is gone. Somehow his foot or the door must have knocked it away. He looks around the floor.

Nothing.

It takes him a horrified minim to realize that he must have knocked it *outside* with Linnix when he banged the door.

Oh, no—no—*no.*

"Linnie! Linnie!" he yells, wrestling with the sticky door.

She's about two meters away, stooping curiously over the wicked thing. Her hand going down—

"No! No, darling! No!" Baram can only throw himself bodily on the hook. Linnix stumbles backward in alarm as his arms and body knock her away.

And the worst pain he's ever felt tears through him from the barbs in his chest. "Aaiiee! Ah—" He rolls and kicks in agony; dimly through the pain he is startled to find he can't draw breath.

A moment—or a year—later he has a temporary, precarious control. Someone is bending over him. The pain is unrelenting.

"Go," he gasps, "go into my—lab cooler—bottle, top shelf—labeled—aah-aah! Oh, forgive me—label—"

"Yes, bottle in cooler top shelf. Don't you want morphine?" It's Siri.

"No! No morphine. Al-alg—" He can't say it. "Bottle, label WYRRA. W-Y-R-R-A. Try, fast. *Please*— Aaii-oh—"

An eternity later the bottle is swimming before his eyes. He's afraid he's been yelling and groaning shamelessly. How did Linnie stand it? . . . Bottle, WYRRA, a blur of dates.

"Yes! Pour on pad—apply—don't waste," he gets out between screams. Another eternity . . .

. . . And then the most blessed ease he's ever felt, the truest, purest no-pain, spreads through him. A sweet familiar smell fills his nose.

He closes his jaw, blinks, finds Siri has bared his chest and is holding gauze to it. He can't help smiling, beaming. Beautiful Siri. Beautiful world.

He looks around at quite a lot of people, all beautiful. Dayan is somewhere.

"I'm going to surprise you," he tells Siri and Dayan. "Two surprises.

The stuff—on the barb—is Algotoxin. Algo-toxin," he repeats as Ochter had. "It's been remade on a Black World."

"Algot—" Siri breaks off, obviously remembering. "Oh, *no.*"

"Yes. And you know the pain can't be stopped. But it *was* stopped." He still feels wonderful but awfully weak.

"I saw it happen once before. Linnie—" He finds her sitting on the floor on his other side, holding his hand. "Linnie had a bad dose of that pain. Twice the lethal dose, almost. But she—you, darling, you rolled on that tabard Yule had been wearing when he scraped the Dameii's backs. It had that sweet smell. It was their nectar, the secretions of their back glands. And it stopped your pain, Linnie. . . . *It stopped the pain of Algotoxin.* Do you understand what that means? Siri?"

"Yes," she says, very gravely.

"Dayan, maybe you can't. She'll tell you. . . .

"I collected the nectar during medical procedures . . . where there was pain. Wyrra and others let me sop their backs. We hoped, if we could get enough to analyze and synthesize, it would stop the Stars Tears horror forever. . . .

"As to the Algotoxin . . . I was going to experiment . . . I guess I *did* experiment. Very messily. Sorry, all." He's about to go to sleep but remembers he can't and struggles against Siri to sit up.

"I've got to destroy that thing! What did you do with it?" He stares wildly around, holding Linnix by the arm.

"Rest easy, Baramji." It's Dayan's voice. "The thing is destroyed. The lad and I carried out your plan; the whole thing is in vapor, gone. It can't do any more damage."

As Barem lets himself slip off, his next to last thought is that many decades from now, a frozen hunk of painfully regathered molecules might come blasting down from space through some planet's atmosphere, to intersect with Linnix. No help for that . . . best they could do.

His last thought is that Linnie's eyes look different. Better. Vaguely, as he drifts off, he hears her say, "Doctor Bram, I think—I think I've . . . ."

An hour later, he is awake and in Cory's room, with Kip and Dayan, at her request. The morning light is clear gold green. Prince Pao comes as far as the door; when Cory hears his voice she asks him to come in, too. She's on the bed, fully dressed and shawled. Only the silver of her hair can be seen clearly through the gauzy stuff.

"This is intended as business, not an emotional orgy," she says clearly, and chuckles in nearly her old way. "Bram, thanks for the stim-shot. It helps. . . . I think I got the weepy stage over last night. One comes through, you know. Now I need to dispose of a couple of decisions . . . that you'll have to make otherwise."

Kip stirs, says vigorously, "Cut it out, Cor. Rest now, for the gods' sake."

"Let me speak, Kip dearest. Please . . . I know you believe this is reversible—but if it's not, I don't want to leave loose ends."

Kip grunts, folds his arms, and looks away.

"The matter of Vovoka. We spoke, you know," she tells Kip's stony face, "after you were knocked out. I believe he was a fine, honorable being, and the very last of a great race. In his tragic end, he tried to be kind. His body mustn't be—Saul, Captain Dayan, I leave it to you to see that his body is laid away with honor. Unless we find other instructions in his effects, I suggest Damiem's moon, where he will be nearest the place his world was. And please—this is a strong wish—don't use a short coffin because of his, his condition. I believe that Myr Zannez must have images of him as he truly was. Put it to him to provide good ones for the burial place. Will you undertake this, too, Saul?"

"I will. And we'll put his effects with him. . . . Last of his race—it's a terrible thought. You've met a being from history."

"Yes," she says. "People who hear of the Star may visit his tomb."

"Now, me. . . . Yes, Kip, please. Even if you think it's all nonsense. I'd like my body to be—do we have the resources to stick me up there on this moon, too? I'd love to think I was in sight of the world of the happiest years I've ever had. Oh, Kip, please. My dear, what will you do with me, if I'm right—or if I die of the treatment? Or if I stub my toe dancing for joy and bash my head in? I guess they'll put that chore up to you, too, Saul. What do you say?"

"I say yes, will do. If necessary. . . . Near or far from Vovoka? After all, he may be your murderer, Cory."

"Near. Funny, I don't feel murdered. I feel it was just the end of what I started at fourteen. It *is* odd," she says reflectively. "I've had such a busy life; if you ask me—yesterday—I'd been Administrator here, and Deputy on Herrick's, and had an expedition to Hundanaro Vortex and all the rest. Years and years of exciting work. But to anybody on the worlds who ever thinks of me, I'll always be only the cabin girl on *Deneb* who pulled the trigger that killed the Star. It's possible . . . to do something in your childhood that changes and dominates your whole life. Prince?" Her head turns restlessly, then she sees Pao.

He's obviously sleepy, but he straightens and nods gravely. "Yes, Myr Cory."

"If you wish any words of aged wisdom, I'd say, everything you do in your youth, everything that happens, *counts.*

"One last thing." She's tiring, Bram sees. The shot he's given her is wearing out. He hopes he hasn't put too much of a strain on the damaged adrenergic system. But a person is a mind, too, and Cory had demanded it.

"Zannez. . . . There's a reward for warnings, information about Stars Tears raids. No one but me knows that it should go to Zannez. Yes. He warned me clearly. I was too busy to do more than listen, but he was right. His data were purely subjective, he simply perceived them as criminal types who came here deliberately, and knew the Tears were here . . . but he has a history of such perceptions and I . . . should have listened. Will you, Kip or Saul, raise the question of the reward and see it goes to Zannez? I think he can use it. . . . And my failure to heed him could have cost their lives."

"Right," Kip says briskly. "Old Zannez will appreciate that. His team is breaking up."

"Now . . . if I *am* irrevocably aging, I want everybody to carry out their normal lives around me just as you would . . . if I were aging slower. No . . . long faces and tiptoeing and whispering . . . right? And I want you to serve the Ice Flowers tonight. I'd like some. . . .

"And finally—Kip, it's about you. If you ever wonder what . . . Cory would have wanted—" She makes an effort, her voice clears. "Remember Cory would want you to be happy. Really happy. That's not just sentimental. Kip, you're one of those people who should be happy in order to be you. . . . You function best, you're most valuable then. Bram, Saul, never let him make himself miserable because of me. Hear, Kip?"

As Kip squirms uneasily she manages a little laugh. "Darling, you're a booby trap for any woman with eyes—the temptation to make you happy is irresistible." She tries to laugh again but ends in a fit of feeble coughing.

"We've got it, Cor," Baram says. "Time to rest now."

"Overtime!" says Kip. "If you want me happier, stop this and rest till the drugs come."

"Right. I'm finished. . . . Thank you, all." She lets herself sink back. Baram, touching her hand to say good-bye, hears her whisper, "I wonder . . . is it possible? . . . No."

She means there's no hope. Despite himself, Baram agrees.

He and Dayan and Pao go out; Siri passes them going in. She's taking charge until Baram can get some rest. Nobody on Damiem has had any true sleep that night—except Stareem, who can be heard, leaning on the parapet in the morning sunlight, singing and strumming her little zither. *"We have made it, we have made it to the sunrise."*

Pao goes to her.

It's a beautiful Damiem morning, framed in the unreal rim of Star-light. Kip comes out after them, unspeaking, until he lifts his head sharply and makes a faint sound in his throat. Baram looks, and sees a young, brown-haired trooper, arms loaded, looking for an instant like Cor . . . Cory-that-was. What's left of Cory now is in there behind them, on her bed. . . . Hard to believe. Kip doesn't believe it yet, Baram fears. The gods send he's right.

Half an hour later, Baram has dragged a lounger into Linnix' small room. He's so exhausted he doesn't feel sleepy. Nor, seemingly, does Linnix; her eyes have a wide, unseeing abstraction he doesn't like, as if she looked upon private dread.

And that's just what must be happening, he thinks. She's told him she was remembering. At first it seemed to be a good experience, coming to herself, but now the darker side of the past could be coming through.

Her silence, her air of aloneness, bothers him. This must be what her life was like—solitary, stoic endurance of whatever hurt. That can't go on. But how to break through? Is she withdrawing from him now as a stranger—she, who'd been so childlike and confiding when her memory was gone?

Or is it deeper, more chilling—the difficulty of pulling her whole self from a reality that killed her, to this reality of life? Despite himself, he shudders a little. He has actually fought Death bare-handed, has reshaped reality itself to bring her here. And he'd accepted the scorpion's pain to keep her; that counts as nothing, but it gives him an idea.

"Linnie, it strikes me we have something in common that no one else has. Not that it's very nice. Excepting whatever poor devils Ochter and company experimented on, you and I are the first Humans in generations to know what Algotoxin feels like. Of course, you got it worse than I, but I got the idea. My dear, I knew it was terrible—but believe it or not, I'm glad now I've shared it."

"Oh, *no*, Bram—"

"Yes. You know my one thought was, How did Linnie stand this?"

"I didn't," she says. "I was awful."

"You saw *me*. Remember how I yelled? That's another reason I'm glad. You're a proud girl, you might get some insane idea you were cowardly. I don't normally holler, either."

She's looking at him, really at him now.

"And to be at the mercy of that monster . . ." he reflects. "Gods!"

She gulps. "I—I kept telling myself he wasn't Human—it was like being attacked by a crazy alien, or a w-wild animal—" Her voice breaks, her hands cover her face.

"Ohh, I wanted to die—the *shame*—"

"Linnie, Linnie darling, look at me." He's out of the lounger on his knees beside her, gently pulling down her hands. "You did it—now it's all over, it's all right—"

"No!" And the flood breaks; for the second time she's weeping in his arms. But this is a different weeping; raw, uncontainable. "But I pulled it out, I did, didn't I? I pulled it out?" The sobs stop as she looks at him anxiously for confirmation.

"You certainly did, my dear. You frightened me out of my skin." He smiles tentatively. "I knew you didn't have that red hair for nothing."

Answering small smile. He's so pleased he fails to see the danger.

"F-funny," she says. "You really can't remember pain. I can remember what I *did*—yelling and k-kicking around—but I can't remember the *feeling*. Can you?"

"No. And that's good. Let it lie."

"I . . . I just fainted, didn't I?"

Too late, he sees where this is leading.

"Yes. You fainted. A momentary syncope due to hypertension and general trauma. Anybody would have. And now I suggest we let this topic go, my dear."

"Yes . . . I just remembered how great it felt when the pain stopped, and the sweet smell." She sniffs. "And trying to fight you or something when you said, 'Move.' And bumping—being bumped along. My tail's sore." She laughs, and he thinks it's all right, but then she frowns.

"Bram, we were in—there was a time-flurry going on, wasn't there?"

"I don't recall," he gets out, sick with dread. "Linnie, I want you to think of something else, right now. Think—think of being an officer again. I'm serious, darling."

But she mutters, "I think there was, a time-flurry, I mean. Something . . . queer. I wonder—"

"Stop it, Linnie!" he shouts. Gods, is she going to talk herself dead, the damned redheaded little fool darling? "Linnix! Stop it, do what I tell you, right now this instant. What—" He forces his voice down. "What was the name of the last world you stopped at? Tell me."

"We didn't stop." She's stubborn: her gaze is inward again, he can't get through.

"Linnie, I know it's hard to stop yourself thinking, but if you're an officer, you have to have the self-discipline to do it. Can you? I tell you, it's necessary, and I can't tell you why. Later you'll understand. Right now, *if you value our lives,* you'll turn your mind away from—from what you were saying. And keep it turned away until I tell you it's safe. Hear me? Hear me, Linnie darling?"

She looks at him opaquely.

The terror of the threat—it's as if some personal enemy keeps trying to return and kill her, using now her very mind. This isn't Linnie alone, he thinks. The force of that other reality is pressing on her, pressing her to know herself dead. And die again, for good, in his arms. He trembles, fighting away from the thought of how she had lain thus before. Maybe the very act of holding her is too much like, is dangerous. He makes himself let her go and sits back. Yes. Better.

"I'll help you. What was the name of the Moom captain on your last ship?"

"There wasn't any."

"No captain? Honey, how can that be?"

Very reluctantly, she amplifies. "The loser, I think has to be captain."

"Loser? What loser? *Tell* me, Linnie." He would have listened to her recite timetables if it would keep her mind off that terrible quarter hour.

He takes her through what she knows of the Moom Life-Game: it comes out in stiff sentences that only gradually relax. When the topic seems exhausted he realizes that he and she are, too—in fact, they're both stunned silly with fatigue. He hitches the lounger over and rests an arm on the pillow beside her flaming head, tentatively smiles down. Suddenly she grins up at him, the old Linnix again. He's inexpressibly warmed.

"Oh, Doctor Bram, I'm such a—I *know* you've done so much, and I . . . I . . . I think I love you."

Is this gratitude? Or Daddy? He's too tired for tact. "What about your father, all that searching?"

"Strange . . ." She smiles pensively. Somehow they've moved so he's more or less beside her on the bed.

"What's strange, darling girl?"

"I remember all that, I really do—Beneborn, the Sperm-ovarium, Lintz-Holstead . . . Were you really on Beneborn, or did I dream that?"

He takes a breath. How much hangs on this? But he's too tired to think; the truth wins.

"No."

She squints at him, then reaches for both his hands. "Say again?"

"What? Oh. No, I never was, I'm sure."

She nods, letting his hands go. "Oh, Bram, when you said all those things, and I thought you meant them—and then I saw your fingers!"

"My fingers . . . what about them?"

"Crossed."

"Oh . . . oh, gods, if Ochter—"

"But he didn't." Her eyelids are drooping.

"You were saying . . . about Lintz-Holstead . . ."

"Like a story," she says sleepily. "As if it . . . happened to somebody else."

The force with which he exclaims, "Oh, darling, darling!" wakes her briefly. "Then you'll come . . . with me . . . r'search," he concludes, and just catches himself falling asleep on her neck.

As he struggles up, her breathing changes; she's asleep, too. He collapses into the lounger and knows nothing more.

An unknown time later a nightmare of paraplegia wakes him. Linnix is sleeping peacefully. But one of his legs is numb and his old shoulder wounds hurt. The lounger has developed strange lumps and horrid angles; he's cramped all over.

Kaffy, he thinks. A nice cup of hot kaffy. He'll go make it.

But when he gets up he stands gazing down at the girl in bed. His girl now. His Linnie, sleeping hard. She sleeps attractively, rosy and warm amid that wonderful hair. The bandage on her neck is untouched.

He's pretty sure, now, that he'll have many nights and days to look at her so. And to shepherd her through: she mustn't be left alone for a while. His long leave is overdue, he can go tomorrow. But where? There's his research to do, the Damei nectar and its miraculous neutralizing effect on Algotoxin pain. Maybe one of the Hyades schools will give him lab space. But it's sensitive; he'll have to take a lot of security precautions. The Hyades rumor mill works overtime. Not ideal. He rubs his stiff shoulder, pondering effortlessly.

Kaffy.

He stoops and touches his lips to her sweet, sleep-scented mouth and stumbles out into Damiem's noon light. Thankful that no one is about, he makes it to his red-cross door.

The infirmary smells alive—that's right, Siri was working here. He dreads what she's found. But that's for later.

As he's brewing up the kaffy, he imagines Linnix in the musty but splendid bridal robes of his House, becoming the Aphra Bye. When he takes her back to Broken Moon, on one of his rare, brief visits. He has told her a little of his home world.

On Broken Moon, he is no longer Doctor Baramji, XMD, but *the* ap of Bye, fifth Balthasar, ninth Baramji, and nominal owner of the vast estates of the Clan Bye.

Like all of Broken Moon, Bye is rich only in tradition and gorgeously rugged scenery, relieved by occasional glens in which half-civilized clansmen raise Terran-hybrid sheep. Its chief exports, aside from a special wool, are rugged young people who want to do something other than sit in unheated castles adjudicating the squabbles of the yeomanry and planning the endless tourneys, jousts, and games that have more or less replaced the clan wars. Luckily he has a blood cousin who is content to occupy the Seat of Bye while Baram works in the Galaxy. But his few visits home are occasion for endless ceremonies of fealty. Linnie can take it—and she'll make a resplendent Aphra. . . . He smiles, thinking of red hair.

The kaffy is ready—but a vague sense of trouble from the marquise's room is making itself felt. Oh, no. . . . But he'd better check. Groggily he sets the kaffy down after one sip and goes through the connecting door.

The bed is empty, open and cold to the touch. A trail of lacy bedding shows where the Lady has staggered away. It leads toward the golden crib in the corner, with its cold freight . . . gods.

He goes to it.

What he feared is there. Lying beside Loma's body, her finger in her mouth, is the Lady Pardalianches.

"Marquise! Lady, Lady—Pardie!"

Despite the massive load of tranquilizers in her system, she blinks at his call.

" 'Oma," she mumbles around her finger, essaying to smile. " 'Oma . . ." and something that sounds like "at last." There's a rictus smile on dead Loma's face, too—the sight is grisly.

Baram looks closer: the Lady's pupils are unevenly dilated. Real trouble here. On impulse he bends to inspect the controls on those golden caps.

What he sees makes him curse himself for negligence again. He should have torn that cap off the corpse, and off the Lady as well.

Somehow she has managed to turn the power way up. And has lain there "receiving" from a dead, disintegrating brain, for who knows how long.

Receiving death through that cap.

Clumsy with fatigue, he slams the controls off, and as gently as he can, over the Lady's agitated flailing, he finds the cap deep in her hair and pulls it from her scalp. She lolls back on his hands during the process, still sucking her finger, and is asleep before he gets it free.

What to do? He can't leave them thus, living and dead, and no one seems to be stirring. Is there no end to this? He goes out the arcade door and into the lounge.

Two of Dayan's men are cleaning up, and Dayan himself is working on his report at a side table.

Baram explains his problem.

"There's a fridge compartment in *Comet,*" Dayan tells him, "and we have body bags here. Jordan can transport the dead woman to the ship right now. You can leave the other poor creature where she is; I'll ask Siri to get clean bedding on her. And you go back to sleep, Baram."

"My fault, my fault," Baram mutters.

"Shut up and go to sleep and forget it," Saul Dayan says. "You're clean pizzled out of your mind."

The comfortable drawl has its effect on Baram. Maybe he is a little irrational. As he's told so many students, nobody can do everything for everybody, everywhere, all the time.

He picks up his kaffy and takes himself back to the lounger in Linnie's room. Pity that bed isn't wider.

He thinks of his own bed, and of the fact that the scorpion is destroyed. Be rational, he tells himself. She's sleeping like a rock. He lets his mouth brush Linnie's cheek and turns to go back and sleep in his own place.

But as he goes out he glances toward Ochter's room, only one door away. Unspeakable little devil, Ochter; his hellish fate doesn't melt Baram's loathing. That scorpion hostage act must have been his fallback plan, in case the drugged wine didn't work. . . . But one hostage wouldn't have been enough to control them all, if Vovoka hadn't stunned them. Ochter must have planned on capturing the group. How? No telling how. But perhaps, just perhaps—are there *more* scorpions in his luggage? . . . It's so near, so close . . . and people will be opening those bags.

Without noticing it, Baram has turned and is gathering up a pad, a blanket, pillows, with numb hands.

Be rational: too much is at stake.

Back in Linnix' room he lets down the back of the lounger and lays the padding. Really quite a decent cot. He kisses Linnie's brow again, collapses onto the lounger, and gratefully lets go of consciousness.

Two hours later, while the Damiem people are sleeping, the parcel of hormones shrieks into upper-atmosphere orbit and is remote-landed from *Comet.*

And an hour after that, Siri, completing the analysis of Cory's blood samples in Baram's little lab, realizes that any attempt at therapy is useless. Vovoka's weapon was sophisticated, lethal; whole glandular complexes are missing from his victim's system, and there's other damage she can't define.

Cory's little speech was necessary after all. She may see Damiem's sun rise tomorrow, but she will never see it set.

XXI

STAR'S
SONG

When Damiem's long afternoon sends up blue-and-gold reflections from the lake, Saul Dayan, in the hostel's cool, newly cleaned lounge, finishes his report. It's in written form; he doesn't trust what the vocoder printout makes of his accent. And he likes the stable feel of a document in hand.

He's been conscious of a gentle presence in the room. Now he looks up and sees that the little silver-haired girl he's come to know as Stareem is leaning on the bar, watching him. Ah, yes, she's the one who was unconscious through it all. Even prettier than her knife-throwing friend, too.

He smiles. "Hello."

"Please, sir . . ." She has a gentle, clear voice. "If I'm not bothering you . . . I wonder if you could tell me—I mean, I slept through the whole thing. Only I had bad dreams." She shivers a little. "First that alien stunned us and then Doctor B. had to drug me. They explained that—but I still don't really understand. What were those men trying to do to us? I mean, why didn't that Ochter person kill us all right then while he had the chance, if he was going to? I mean, I'm not sorry he didn't, but I don't *understand.*"

"Well . . ." Dayan respects the appeal for clarity. Somewhere under the extravagant looks is a Human mind. "The answer is a mite gruesome, Myr Stareem."

"That's all right." The chilling Gridworld maturity behind the child's face.

"H'mm. Well, he planned to blow the place up, you see. Going to over-load the power-cell down below. Seems Hiner had done demolition study, too—we ran onto manuals on power-cells in among those music tapes. That way Ochter hoped to get away clean; he hoped the blast would make such a mess-up that a few bodies wouldn't be missed. Probably would've worked, because there'd only be one absent. Ochter said he figured to cool off his little helpers after they finished the job for him."

"I see—but I still don't see—"

"Why he didn't do you in right then? Well, he knew there'd be an investigation. And it would look pee-culiar if folk's flesh was found to be full of poison, and dead for a day or so too long."

"He was keeping us fresh." She nods, satisfied, and then shudders de-spite herself. "Oh, my—and Doctor Baram and the others saved us all while I just slept."

"Best thing you could have done," says Dayan gruffly.

While they're talking, the small figure of Prince Pao comes down the stairs, rubbing his eyes. He bows to Dayan and advances to Stareem, takes her hand, and kisses it lightly, to Dayan's amusement. Kip has told him of the boy's devotion to Stareem. Fine smile the lad has, he thinks, catching the scent of what's doubtless very expensive cologne. Pao's three-plumed gold cap is tucked under his arm. Quite the little dandy.

"My dear, I'm sorry I left you alone so long."

"No problem. Want some juice?" She goes to the bar cooler.

"It's good practice for her," Pao says confidentially to Dayan. "She doesn't get much solitude. On Pavo I shan't be with her as much as I'd like."

This sounds serious, on the part of the future monarch of Pavo. "You plan to take her away from, ah, Gridworld?"

"Yes. I believe it's time now—thanks, Myr Star." He drains the glass at a gulp.

"I'll get more. And how about saniches? I see some that look like cheese."

"Goody-o!" Pao plunks himself down at the table beside Dayan, sud-denly a boy eager for food. "Yes," he tells Dayan. "She's had adequate experience now. On Pavo it's customary for young ladies to have full sex training before the happiness of love and marriage. Young men, too, of course. And Star needs to go to school for a proper education. Including music— Oh, that looks fine," he breaks off, opening the huge sanich Star has put before him. Between bites he explains to Dayan, "Myr Star's untutored things are quite lovely, but one really can't stay untutored on Pavo long—we discussed all that, Myr Star."

"Yes," she says gravely. "I'd love it." She bows her head, thinking, then suddenly bursts out at Pao, "Do you *really* mean it? I mean, joking's fine, but I— And Zanny says—" Her huge eyes are like a wild thing's, wondering whom to trust.

The boy gives Dayan a man's look—or a mother's—as if to say, "Isn't she a gem?" He takes her hand.

"Did you think I was joking, my Star? I assure you I'm not. And with all respect to Myr Zannez, as regards Pavo or me he doesn't understand much. I suggest you listen to *me*, from here on. I am really, really serious."

"Ohhh." The eyes melt, brim. Then she ducks her head and says very low, "You won't be when you know my real name. It's awful. It's— Sharon. Or Sharone."

"Oh, I know all that," Pao says airily, Superboy again. "It's Sharon Roebuck, to be precise. When our Special Information Branch saw I was interested in this APC person, they looked into you. Very thoroughly. They were able to trace Star's mother," he tells Dayan. "On Pavo we feel it's essential to observe how a young lady's mother ages. More often than not, it gives advance notice of what the young lady will become. Of course, it's not infallible"—he digs into his sanich—"but Star should age very acceptably, given better care."

Star's hands are at her throat.

"But my mother's dead. They always told me she'd died."

Pao swallows hurriedly. "I forgot, my dear. Of course, this is a shock." With surprising gentleness he says, "Myr Roebuck is indeed dead now. I'm sorry, my Star. She was in very difficult circumstances, which I was able to improve without her knowledge. We think she was unaware that she was breeding babies for a flesh mart. Your father we don't know for sure: it's been narrowed to three possibilities, all—"

"Babies?" Star interrupts. "You mean I have brothers and sisters? Oh—"

"None living, my dear. Oh, I am sorry—I didn't mean to drop it on you this way." He looks in appeal at Dayan, who's engrossed by the little drama. "She'd have to know sometime, and she has friends here."

Dayan nods agreement. "Right."

The lad's fluency and seriousness have so diverted him that he can't believe he's not dealing with a much older person. But Pao looks in all respects like a normal, healthy lad of ten or twelve, who will be shooting up taller soon. And the voice in which he speaks his grown-up words hasn't changed yet.

"Myr Roebuck lived, ah, near the spaceport," Pao continues after another bite.

Dayan nods. That's by custom defined as the worst area on most planets.

"And two of the children perished from the effects of the fuel dump. Then, there was a tragic crash—not on the regular lines," he clarifies to Dayan.

But Star gets it. "Oh. A *Black World!*" she cries.

"I'm afraid so." Pao puts his sanich down carefully to reach up and pat Star's shoulder. "Be brave, my dear. I know you will. This doesn't affect anything." He smiles winningly and waits for her answering smile before taking up the sanich. "Look at it this way, my Star . . . as the SI Branch said, those tragedies preserved them from miserable lives." A pause for bites. "Your own life was only saved by your promise of beauty and a series of incredibly lucky accidents."

Zannez has come quietly in from the arcade stretching and rubbing his arms; he overhears the last. He nods at Dayan, then nods again because what Pao said is so true: he recalls that Gridworld night, and the thing on a rope.

"Morning, all—or is it evening? Gods, I'm stiff. Getting old. Where does that juice come from, Star?"

"I'll get," she says. "More saniches, Prince Pao?"

"Yes, please. And you don't have to use my title, Myr Star, except on formal occasions, of course."

Dayan and Zannez find themselves looking at each other blankly. Zannez rolls up his eyes.

"Just what is your status with respect to these young people, Myr Zannez?" Dayan asks thoughtfully.

"Contractual. Contractual employer." Zannez puts a foot up on a chair to rub his leg. " 'Scuse me."

"Contracts with their parents or guardians, I reckon?"

"No. With them."

"And he's great to us," calls Star from the cooler. "He's not like the others. We love Zannie."

"They seem a mite young to be self-employed," Dayan persists. "How old is that little girl?"

"Thirteen, going on fourteen." Zannez pauses in his rubbing and looks at the floor as he says, "On Gridworld kids of five can sign valid contracts."

"Valid? You mean to say, a court would enforce it?"

"All the courts. . . . A few are starting to require the employer to show the kid continues in good health, or is getting treatment for whatever."

Dayan digests this a minim and then says mildly, "Seems like the Federation might blacklist your Gridworld one day."

Zannez laughs, not merrily. "Oh, they can't. That's been tried. Their people demand our product."

Prince Pao is consuming his second lot of saniches. Now he licks his fingers judiciously, saying, "Naturally, I intend to purchase Myr Star's contract from you, Myr Z., if you will."

"Why not? Oh, lords, I'm a softy. The team is bust. I'm letting Snake and Hanno go to the Patrol."

"I reckon you don't have a choice there," says Dayan dryly. "Enlistments if accepted take precedence over civil contracts. But I'm real glad the parting's friendly."

"Oh, sure it is . . . but I'll never see another team like that again."

Dayan remembers Cory's requests. "I'm not sure you'll need to, Myr Cameraman. Anybody tell you yet about the reward?"

"The reward? What reward for what? Nobody's even seen the doc—the documentary."

Dayan laughs. "This isn't for any picture show. It's for something you said to Myr Cory. You best talk with her." He bethinks himself. "When you go to, ah, say your farewells."

There was a short silence.

"Yeah," says Zannez. "Thanks, Captain. . . . So! You young ones are all set. Wait a minim. I'm as close as Star has to a father, so I better ask you what you plan to do with her on Pavo, Prince? She'd best stay with me rather than be abandoned on a strange planet."

"Oh, no danger of that. I respect your interest, Myr Zannez"—Pao selects a sausage sanich—"and you will receive formal documents, plus a periodic report, if you wish. I plan to appoint Myr Star Royal Concubine A. That's a constitutionally protected position—all the royal concubines and consorts are. I have a copy of our Constitution, if you'd like—"

"Great—but not now," Zannez rubs his neck.

"You'll receive one, of course. Later on, she will move to the position of Senior Hostess, Hostess A, that is, on the informal side. She'd think up things and find talented people . . . we do an awful lot of royal entertaining," he groans, suddenly boyish. "Part of the diplomacy." He pounces on a ripe *lopin* fruit.

Zannez frowns. "Informal, eh? . . . I get it." He takes a *lopin*. "What's 'consorts'?"

"Well, if Myr Star proves to have other talents and passes the exams, I'd love to have her as Royal Consort One. Otherwise I have to choose be-

tween Alwyn and Jo's Paradise—two of our client worlds—they both
have, uh, marriageable daughters." He sighs. "I have to see a lot of
whoever's Consort Number One, you see. And she gets a try at bearing the
heir. Later on, she becomes Senior Hostess Number One on the *formal*
side." He sighs again. "The statuses—A, B, or One, Two, Three, whatever
—are for life. It's all planned and programmed, it's part of our diplomatic
work. . . . It isn't as though we were having fun," he says wistfully. To
console himself, he selects another *lopin* fruit.

"Hm'm," says Zannez. "Hm'm! . . . Well, how does that sound to you,
Star? I'm not selling you off against your will, Star baby."

"He's told me a little about it before," she says, wide-eyed. "I thought
he was joking. It sounds coloss."

"Never, my Star," says Pao. "And by the way, that's a word we want
out."

"What? 'Coloss'?"

"Yes. Horrible."

"I've a lot to learn," she says humbly.

"Yes. But you'll make it. I've observed you learning acts."

"You were *watching* me," she says wonderingly.

"I wonder what else is in that cooler," says Zannez. "Will you join me,
Prince?"

Pao needs no urging. But as they're uncovering dishes of spiced *bicklets*
he sighs heavily again.

"Anything wrong?"

"As soon as Doctor Baram awakes I must apologize."

"What for? Oh—the 'blunder.' Want to tell us?"

"Why not?" The boy seems genuinely depressed. "Dreadful. . . . Captain Dayan, it was my fault Myr Linnix was trapped by that despicable
man. If only I'd been on time. . . ."

"What'd you do," Zannez asks, "stop to pee?"

"Much worse. When I went down to Yule and Hiner's room, on the
roof, I stupidly blundered right into one of the nets they must have used on
the Dameii. Unforgivable. I've been trained on them and Myr Kip actually
mentioned nets. And I trod right in." He makes a disgusted noise and
fiercely bites a *bicklet.* "I still have pieces of it on me."

"Nets. You mean those sticky, stick-tights? They're illegal."

"That's right. You're acquainted with them?"

"We used one in a show one time; we had to cut three people loose.
Almost choked to death. . . . They cost, too."

"They must have jerked. That tightens them."

"It cursed well does. . . . How'd you ever get loose?"

"I have been trained, you know. This thing was on the eaves; Yule or

Hiner must've fired it and missed. I could have spotted it if I'd sighted along at foot level, as is correct. But I was *sloppy.*" He's really angry at himself, Dayan sees. It occurs to him that the lad could become quite a little tyrant if Star doesn't take whatever lessons she'll be given seriously.

"*Overconfidence,*" Pao is saying grimly. "There I was in midstep, with one leg up—it took me nearly ten minim to get that foot down—and another half hour to get at my knife. You have to move slowly—slowly—slowly—slowly—and all the time I knew I must hurry. It was horrible. The only thing I can say is," he tells Dayan, "I didn't tighten it once."

Dayan nods. "Good."

"Even when you get your knife you have to know how to cut," he explains to Zannez. "Whew! I've certainly learned a lesson, but at what terrible price to Myr Linnix and Doctor Baram—and the little Damei child."

"It could happen to anybody," says Zannez. But Pao ignores him. Pao doesn't identify with "anybody," Dayan sees.

"Unforgivable," Pao says again, and chews for a minim in silence. "I must make my confession to Doctor Baram and Myr Linnix. But how can I make it up to them?" He's suddenly an appealing boy again.

Dayan is listening interestedly to the future royalty of Pavo reproaching itself while consuming a monstrous meal. The appetite is certainly that of a boy. Could it be that General Federation educational standards are a trifle low?

"I know!" says Pao, swallowing briskly. "It won't be adequate, but it's something." He pursues a last *bicklet* methodically. "The doctor should really get some leave after this. And I believe Myr Linnix will go with him, don't you?"

"Looks that way," says Zannez. "I don't see her taking up as a Log Officer again right now."

"Yes, that's what I thought. So I could invite them both to Pavo. I have to return, you know." He grimaces. "They can just relax and rest—or maybe he has some research to do." He takes his plate neatly to the bar, then opens the cooler for another look. "He could use our facilities. I'm told they're quite good." He brings a dish of sweet dessert to the table.

"I bet they are." Zannez stretches, extends his legs, and rubs his lower back. "Never again. Hey, Prince, how did you like our act?"

"I was most impressed." Suddenly he chucks his maturity. "Beautiful! As Star would say, coloss! Oh, how I wish I could do that. Especially—" He sketches a no-hands spin in the air with his spoon. "Can you do that?"

"No more. I could once, that's what you learn when you're too broke to afford a double. I taught Snake."

"You did?" Pao thinks a minim. "Could you teach me?"

"Yes, I'm pretty sure. But Prince, it's not too safe. You can take some spills."

"No matter. A modicum of real danger is thought essential to royal education. And skis and horses bore me. I'm entitled to choose." He draws himself up, grinning. "Myr Zannez, I hereby invite you to Pavo for a tour as Royal Tutor in Advanced Gymnastics—all expenses paid. How about it?"

Zannez, eyebrows high, mumbles something about his contract and then about Bridey. Pao waves his spoon airily.

"Can all be arranged. I'll signal from Central. And Myr Bridey can come with you, of course. She'll be company for Myr Stareem—after classes. And Pavo can have the first showing of your Damiem documentary— Why, wait, you can also act as consultant to our holodocumentary staff! They're good, but just a bit *dull.*"

Stareem is beaming. "I love Bride; I hated to think I was leaving her forever."

Dayan, highly amused by the fairy-tale turn of events, says reflectively, "I'd really admire to have seen that act you finished Hiner with."

"Oh, but you shall!" the little prince exclaims. "I almost forgot. It's on your hand camera, Myr Zannez. At least, I hope it is," he amends worriedly. "I've only had one lesson. I don't know how good a job I did. I just started shooting as soon as my two charges went in."

"What?" Zannez is purely astounded.

Pao repeats.

"Listen, am I still asleep and dreaming?" Quite seriously, Zannez pinches himself twice and shakes his head. "Reward, job offer—and now this. Wait—Prince, did you take the lens cover off?"

"Naturally." It's Superboy again.

"Whew! Then you got it. . . . Gods—the greatest act we ever did in my life, and I thought it was all gone bye-bye. And you say—oh, man—" He jumps up, visibly checking himself from mauling Pao. "This I've got to see! Camera, camera, where are you? Bye, all."

He bolts for the infirmary, Pao puts down his bowl and follows at a run.

Dayan reckons the boy has forgotten all about Royal Concubine A, but at the red-crossed door Pao checks to say, "Oh, good-bye, sir. Till later, Myr Star!"

He kisses his hand to her and then tears after Zannez, a boy again.

There's a silence in the lounge; Dayan turns his gaze on the charming girl-child beside him.

"Well, little lady, and how will you like it on Pavo, with your life all mapped out?"

"Oh, col—no, uh, very much, sir." She nods seriously. "Well, you see, sir, I think my life on Gridworld was all mapped out, too. Only it *was* all *down* . . . and maybe not very long, either. . . . And on Pavo I think they like you to learn a lot. Like, keep on learning. Oh, I'd love that. I love to understand. I was in a—a *library* once. There's so much to learn, you'd never run out. I guess you know all that, sir."

"By no means," he says guiltily. "Tell me, Myr Stareem—or should I call you Sharon now?"

"Oh, no, please! Sharon is—is gone. Never was."

"I reckon that's so. Well, then, Myr Star, tell me honestly: Is your prince really a young boy? The age he looks? Do you know how old he really is?"

"Yes, sir." She smiles dazzlingly. "He's just turned eleven. He told me his birthday the day we met. He's two years younger than me. But I don't think that matters so much. Do you, sir? Especially since he says I'll age all right?"

"No," agrees Dayan gravely. "I reckon two years won't matter. But it's hard to believe that boy isn't a lot older than he looks."

"You mean, because he's so grown-up? People say 'mature,' but it sounds so dismal." She cocks her head, studying him. "You mean you really, really, don't believe it?"

Dayan grunts. "Should I?"

"I think so, yes." She nods. "I saw some papers—from Pavo—something's s'posed to happen when he's twelve. 'Man's estate.' That's why he has to go home. Zannie asked him about it, too; that's when he showed the papers. Why he's so mature—ugh—is because of what they do to children on Pavo. 'Specially to children—wait . . ." She looks up, remembering hard, a darling sight. "Destined for great responsibilities. Yes. That's what he is, right? So some ancient philosopher, Miles or Mills, I forget the name —I have to start learning and remembering now, don't I?"

"You do, little lady. What about this ancient man?"

"He said, Keep the child away from other children. Don't waste his best early years learning how to be a child. Because he'll just have to unlearn it, see? So they put him with grown-ups right from the start. Bright grown-ups, the best. Even his mother wasn't allowed to talk baby-talk to him."

"You mean Pao never had any playmates? Pretty rough on the kid."

"Oh, no. Adults play with him. Zannie's playing with him right now, isn't he? Partly because he's a prince, but mostly because he's—what's the word I need, sir?"

"H'm. Word for Pao? Well, 'mannerly' is a word we used around the Horsehead."

" 'Mannerly'—that's nice. He is." She sighs. "And I have to learn to be mannerly, too. I wouldn't ever want him to be *ashamed* of me. Do you think I can, sir?"

"I do."

"I hope so. . . ." She sighs again, pensively. "In a way, they did that to us, to me, too. We're always with grown-ups. But they don't teach us anything but a little acting and mostly sex—but not really that."

"How do you mean?" Dayan asks incautiously. He's mesmerized by this delicate, fresh-looking little Human, raised in a life he conceives of as inhabited only by loathsome subhumanity.

"Well, you know, I've never— Oh!" She puts a hand to her lips. "Zannie told us not ever to talk to space people, we'd offend them. I don't want to offend you, sir, Captain Dayan."

"You can't offend me, Myr Star. Since I asked the question I have only myself to blame. What were you going to say you 'never'?"

"Well, let's see . . . I don't know your word for it, but is it all right if I say I've never done—oh, you know—never with anybody I *liked?* Except Hanno and Bridey and Snake, but they don't count."

Dayan is transfixed. There's some shouting outside he should check on; it will have to wait a minim. But out of a hundred questions he can't phrase, all that comes to his lips is, "Why don't they count?"

"Because it's just their job, you know. Like me. And Hanno and Snake are really *for* each other. I've never been for anybody," she says wistfully. "But Pao says that's all right, it's training. He has to get his training, too," she says. "It's even more important for boys. And then he'll be for me. He says that being *for* somebody grows, it doesn't come all at once like the stories. I'm really looking forward to being with him. Captain Dayan, do you think really possibly, we could be *for* each other? At least for a while?"

It's a serious question. The shouting outside is louder, too. He must go. He rises to leave and takes her small hand.

"I think there's a real good chance, Myr Star, and I most certainly hope so, for you."

She has heard the shouting, too, and understands. Oh, lords, Dayan thinks, heading out, something's happened to Valkyr, the crewman who's making up cheap utility coffins.

He shows his teeth in a brief grin. One thing there's no doubt about is those dead-boxes: they're *for* Yule, Hiner, and Ochter.

Patrolman-Tech First-Class Valkyr, out behind the station workshop, curses the portable plastic-formant rig. The ratsass thing is made for midgets, which Valkyr is not. It's late afternoon and he's finishing the last of the five coffins the captain says they need. All vacuum-seal. That station must be full of corpses. If he only had his proper shop on *Rimshot,* they'd all be long done.

Still, this is a pretty little planet; everything safe for Humans and the locals are supposed to be worth seeing, but shy. Most of the dead are said to be Black Worlders who came all this way to kidnap some for a nasty job. That's why the bodies have to be preserved, for the Crime Section.

Whatever, as soon as he's finished this last dead-box, he's going to take a swim in that fine lake down there. And then go see what's to be seen before chow time. Chow's to be at the station, too. Nice change . . . Valkyr appreciates fresh food.

He steals a glance at the glittering lake behind him—and the inadequate holder on the hot plastic tilts. Some plastic goes on the ground, setting up fast.

Valkyr snaps out of his reverie and takes one step for his tongs. His foot goes onto the plastic puddle and skids, smoking.

Off-balance, he slides into the rig.

Next second a scream tears out of his throat as the hot plastic hits his pants, sticks, and burns through. No help for it; he goes down in a yelling frenzy of spilled plastic and the stink of burning flesh.

"Doc! Doctor Siri!" Another Patrolman runs up shouting and gets the rig off him, but he can do little with the stuff sticking to Valkyr's body, face, and arms.

Siri gets there fast, as usual. She grabs up the can of solvent and gets his vital parts clear before the can runs dry. Her impartial curses at the solvent, the rig, and Valkyr blue the air comfortably.

"Ice! Tally, you scoot back with the first double handful of ice you can get your paws on. Bing, you search out every godlost piece of ice they've got. Including frozen food. Run!"

Even more comforting is her needleload of painkiller. Presently Valkyr feels green and go. But he is not; he's lost a lot of skin, and he needs *Rimshot*'s tissue bank. Help will come, but during the hours ahead his life will depend on skilled nursing.

Dayan is watching.

"I'll have to take him up myself, Saul. How soon can *Rimshot* get here?"

"Under an hour after I signal." He's already in the command car.

"Meanwhile I'll get some fluids into him and get a wet-bunk made up on that trailer of theirs. Can your car tow it to the field?"

"It can."

"Right, then. And I'll have to stay with him at least until we know the first grafts have taken. This'll change some plans. . . . All right, Rango and Maur, see he doesn't move. Hold his hands quiet. Rip, Jorge, come and help me carry." She heads for Baram's infirmary.

This will indeed change plans, Dayan thinks as he bumps along the spaceport road. Siri had been going to stay behind with Kip and Cory, until Cor either improved or died. That would permit Baram to take off with his redhead he's so nervy about; the gods know the Doc has enough leave coming.

But now Kip would be left alone with—whatever. Cannot do. . . . Too bad; looks like Baram stays on. . . . "Move it, Ralli," Dayan says, "a few bumps won't break me." Ralli grins happily and corners on two. Dayan hangs on, thinking, It's a pity there's no one to take Baram's place.

In the rearview mirror he notices a surprising number of the winged folk taking off from the station grove, in the evening light.

A great, faintly quivering rim of Star-light is brightening eerily all around the horizon, as the sky light fades above.

XXII

GREEN,
GO

Dawn is brightening to daylight over the landing field of the small planet called Damiem. Two fiery sparks move in the pale sky, one receding, the other descending. Above the horizon there glimmers a fading ring of opalescent light that no sun ever cast; it has a just perceptible pulse or flicker in it.

At the edge of the field stands a ground-jitney, attached to a freight trailer. Six Human civilians and a Space Patrol officer wait in the jitney. On the trailer is strapped a modest pile of luggage and a long, plain official Patrol coffin.

In the car's front seat sits a very old, frail woman. The driver beside her is a handsome man in early midlife who might be her grandson. Behind them is a man with white hair and startling blue eyes, holding the hand of the red-haired girl beside him, whose eyes are the same turquoise blue. Her other hand rests protectively on the shoulder of the old lady in front. Behind these sits the Patrol captain; beside him sit two youths, one ebony black, the other tan with oddly slanted eyes. Their hands lie close but not touching.

"See, the . . . new moon," says Cory Korso, gazing east through clouded eyes. "Tomorrow . . ."

Kip, in the seat beside her, presses her hand briefly and clenches his jaw.

Then his face resumes its look of dismayed bewilderment, as of one who has returned home to find his house gone and his friends strangers.

Captain Dayan clears his throat and addresses his young seat mates. "I assume you two don't need passenger accommodations? I'm bedding you down with the crew."

"Oh, yes, right, sir," they say together. Then Hanno bethinks himself. "Sir, are the eats the same?"

Dayan chuckles. "Better."

"We'll be up to see you, Myr Linnix," Snake says, "if they let us."

"That can be arranged," says Dayan. "Just don't either of you mistake this for duty."

"Oh, no, sir. No."

All fall silent again in their separate preoccupations.

They are awaiting *Rimshot*'s descending pinnace, which will take off with Captain Dayan, and Hanny, Snake, and Linnix, all bound for FedBase. But without Baram.

Wearily, Cory speaks. "Bram . . . it isn't fair, making you stay. . . . If it's for me, please go . . . Siri will be . . . back so soon, Kip dear."

"I know," Kip says. "Bram—you know how I feel. Go. Your girl needs you worse than we do."

Baram smiles and shakes his head no. His face is drawn and worried.

It had been a nasty blow to him when they found that Siri was held up on *Rimshot* by a badly burned crewman and couldn't be expected down for several days. If Baram went with Linnix now, it would mean leaving Cory and Kip alone to face what lay ahead—with Kip as sole Guardian. That couldn't be.

So Linnix is headed for Base hospital alone, to await Baram. Siri of course will be what help she can without full knowledge. Baram has warned Linnix and warned Siri to keep Linnix from talking of the scorpion episode. But Linnix must then wait alone in Base, until someone comes to relieve Baram. And she is so vulnerable, so exposed to the first well-meaning idiot who wants the story. Baram can hope that being off this planet will lessen the menace, but his heart rebels. He terribly fears her danger—not only of physical harm or death, but that some essential part of herself could be pulled away to that not-quite-extinguished *other* reality. Suppose, when he finally gets to her, he finds her as she'd first been, a mindless body?

Brooding, he's vaguely conscious that Kip and Dayan are remarking on the presence of several Dameii in the high streamer-trees overhead. Presently old Quiyst floats down to them, sending up a cloud of the mobile tree leaves. Kip greets him, and the old Damei speaks volubly, pointing at Dayan.

"He wants to talk to you, Saul," Kip reports. "He's not too clear, but he knows you're chief honcho over us." Dayan is in fact on the Damiem Reparations Council.

"Talk away, if you interpret."

"It seems they're waiting for two more of their people before they begin."

"Not to wait too long."

"Right. . . . He says it's *franivye*—superimportant. Gods, I can't see what it could be; we've apologized till we're hoarse, we've offered reparations, plus keeping all tourists off, plus destroying the hostel. The gods know we've lost all kinds of face."

But Dayan's gaze has turned up to the other, receding light, now almost lost in daylight. It's the exhaust flare of *Comet*, leaving for Federation Central under a Patrol scratch crew. It will pause at a staging asteroid near Base to exchange Dayan's men for Race and his crew. Race is being released on his own recognizance, to deliver himself and his ship to Central's Far Planets Branch, which supervises Damiem; they will impose his penalties if any.

But Race is less unhappy now. Since Moom ships will not board Human passengers without a Logistics Officer to supervise cold-sleep, FedBase is paying Race a reasonable fee to carry the five live Humans and four coffins bound for Central. Up there behind those fires go Zannez, Bridey, Stareem, Pao, and the poor marquise, still mute and smiling in her twin's rollbed. Prince Pao and his Star will change at Central for Pavo, along with Zannez and Bridey—it's felt that Zannez' contract and documentary copyright negotiations will go better if he's not in Gridworld's grip. And the two marquises, living and dead, will be put into the waiting hands of the Lord Protector of Rainbow's End, while the three criminals' remains go to Special Branch.

The parting has been emotional: as always, in this great Galaxy, friends, once parted, too rarely meet again. Beyond *Comet*'s flare are doubtless a few moist eyes. Down here, Snake and Hanno look up from time to time unsmiling. "You don't get many like old Zannie," Snake says. Hanno nods. "And if we ever see Superboy again, I guess it'll be Your Royal Majesty." They sigh.

Dayan watches until *Comet* is seemingly beyond sight, then continues to gaze. Shortly he's rewarded by a brief flash as *Comet*, under Dayan's pilot, changes to space drive. Dayan nods and transfers his gaze to the descending pinnace.

At this moment the jitney's transceiver bursts into life. Amid whistles and squawks, a coded message is coming through from *Rimshot*, in orbit high above. Dayan bends to hold an ear to the speaker.

"Say again?"

The screeches repeat.

When Dayan answers, his normally soft twang changes to a bellow so penetrating that his companions wince. To their surprise, Kip and Baram make out "sixteen-sixty"—return to ship—and another code group too.

"What's up, Saul?"

There's a sky-lightening flare of flame from the pinnace.

Dayan grins a broad 'I-have-a-secret' grin. "New passenger."

"Not Siri?" asks Baram.

"Nope." The grin broadens. "How'd you folks like a little surprise? Want to guess who's come dropping by to stay awhile?"

Blank looks.

"What would you say to your old pal Pace Norbert, first Guardian of Damiem?"

"*What?* But he's—"

"Yes. But it seems the good soul heard there was trouble and bundled himself into a one-seater freight pod and came all the way here to help you out. He's just docking with my ship."

"No!" Kip is beaming; even Cory is trying to smile.

"Do you think Norbert could stand in for the Doc here, till we get Siri back?" Dayan asks. "I understand he's qualified as an MD since you've seen him last."

"Yes, he was into medicine," Kip remembers. "Pace Norbert! I can't believe!"

"Wonderful," whispers Cory. She means, wonderful for Baram; she alone understands why he needs to stay close to Linnix: to keep her alive. Cory, too, had clearly seen her die.

Baram and Linnix are looking from Dayan to Kip to Cory. Baram has never met the former Guardian, was unaware of their friendship. Does this mean . . . ?

It does. Kip and Cory are delighted with Pace Norbert's company as a substitute for Baram's. Indeed, the prospect of a new face, an old friend, in place of the poor worried doctor cheers Kip mightily.

"You see those man-lifts over there the crew left for us to bring up?" Dayan asks Baram. "Can you navigate one?"

"I have done. Why?" Baram is so happy and relieved he's forgotten all else.

"Green. I'll help you get started. Then back you go to the station and pack everything you can in ten minim. Go!"

After a couple of hair-raising tries with the man-lift, Baram finds the knack again and sails away at a very conservative altitude above the road. Linnix turns to look after him with eyes like blue stars.

Overhead, the light of the pinnace has visibly reversed direction and is dwindling upward and northward toward *Rimshot*'s orbit.

Dayan walks back to the jitney to find a cloud of Damei wings fanning out overhead. The missing must have arrived, and the Dameii are ready to parley.

"Hallo, there's Black Golya, from Far Village," says Kip. His face clouds; Golya has been a troublemaker. "And there's Juiyn! Weird." He switches to Damei and greets the group.

Old Quiyst speaks briefly, making a sweeping gesture at Dayan.

"They have something they want you to record and act on, Saul."

"I can only lay it before the Council. But naturally, any reasonable requests will be honored."

Quiyst ducks back, and another Damei from the Far Village group, whom Kip knows only as Yrion Red, comes forward along the branches. With wings formally leveled, Yrion delivers himself of quite a long address in Damei, punctuated by the Galactic words, "He-ar me!"

Kip tries a running translation.

"They no longer wish—wish *us?* I could understand that—No, wait, he means they no longer wish Guardianship as it is today. But they still want protection on call—that's you, Saul—and they want more instruction in Galactic, and medical help, and—wait, something— Great Apherion— wait—"

He asks two questions in Damei.

When the answers come, Dayan thinks he hears the words, "Sta-ree Te-Yas."

"Well! Well! Well! Well! In the name of Holy All! The thing they want, Saul, beside protection, teachers, et cetera, is a kind of commercial consul! It seems—it seems they plan to manufacture and export Stars Tears themselves! Yes! And they want a chemist to show them ways of distilling it from the raw nectar. . . . Great Apherion in flames! *They want to make money!* I've been explaining the financial facts of life to Wyrra, and it seems he told it to Juiyn, who got her Far Village family all hotted up, and— Oh, whew! They even think people should pay to *see* them!"

"What use do they have for Galactic credits?" asks Dayan practically.

Kip asks the question. He receives a voluble reply from Yrion Red; and others join in. Kip starts to say something in reply or objection, but the dialogue is cut off by old Quiyst:

"Talk finish."

"Well!" says Kip. "Primarily they want a water system. Seems they're tired of lugging water. Gods—we were going to make them one, when we found a silent pump—but I guess we've been a little slow. They never *looked* unhappy. . . . And they want other things. They want to live like us. Yrion says we have a book of things—that'd be the *Federation Supply Catalog,* I think. Anyway, they want one. Oh, my, my, my!"

Cory coughs, trying to say something. Finally she gets it out, in a hoarse wheeze: "How . . . how do they plan to . . . to get the nectar?"

"Right. Good point." He questions Yrion. Again there's a voluble response, cut short by Quiyst.

"Well? Are they setting up to torture each other?" Dayan asks.

Kip frowns. "I don't think so. Yrion was saying something to the effect that they know good ways, although I don't know whether he means good-and-efficient, or good-as-opposed-to-bad. But old Quiyst just said it was none of my business. . . . Great purple gods!"

"Looks like your pets are growing up," says Dayan dryly.

"But what about it, Saul? Can they do this? Oh, I forgot—they want to *use* the hostel; we're not to destroy it. So much for sensitivity. . . . So what do you say?"

"Speaking unofficially, my flash reaction is that their plan is within the Terms of Human Restitution—provided their methods of, ah, extractions are humane. We don't want them massacring each other. . . . Do they know about this painkiller business of Baram's?"

"I don't see how. But here comes Doc."

They watch as Baram parks the man-lift with a mild flourish, leaving his duffel on it, and walks over to them. He bears a quilt-wrapped package.

The light of the pinnace has reappeared again, descending as before—but now bearing Pace Norbert to the rescue. It's coming fast, already they can hear it.

"This doesn't leave me." Baram laces the package carefully into the shoulder-hung travel medkit under his cloak. "It's the Damei nectar I intend to work with."

Kip and Dayan fill him in on the new developments. Above them the Dameii are leaving as the pinnace's sound grows louder.

When they ask Baram what the Dameii know of the nectar's analgesic properties, he hesitates.

"Of course I haven't had occasion to tell them," he says. "But you'll note that the nectar changes character when the donor is in pain. It may be that it's part of their natural pain-control system, and they could well know that. In any event, after this new revelation I just wouldn't be too sure what they don't know. We—you—may be in for some surprises."

Last of the Dameii to leave is old Quiyst. He holds his ground long enough to ask a question.

"He wants to know whether you have heard and will act," Kip tells Dayan.

"Tell him I hear, and I will carry their desires to the Council. And the

Council will, I'm sure, take action—but probably not as rapidly as they wish."

Quiyst, who knows some Galactic, disappears before Kip finishes translating: the sky roar from the pinnace has grown shattering.

As the big g-blockers cut in, the decibels rise still more. Only Cory can hear Kip's exclamations to the world in general—broken phrases of wonderment and amaze, half-uttered plaints about their own projected hydraulic system, astonishment at the Dameii's knowledge of the *Federation Supply Catalog*, astoundment that they should wish to change their immemorial way of life, dire predictions of their disappointment, bewildered curses of dismay. And amid it all, Cory hears distinctly, "D'you know, they even *looked* different to me! Oh, they're beautiful. But I never really believed they were evolved from, from *insects* before. Maybe that's how that devil Hiner saw them, that's why he could . . . Oh, my goodness, it'll all change—"

She understands too well what all this means—beneath his excitement is heart-hurt, the pain of rejection. And beneath that again lies something only she knows, waiting to come . . . the thing Vovoka spoke of.

And she won't be . . . here to help him through that, to share it.

She longs to comfort him, to open her arms to him as she used—was it only yesterday? But she's locked in this shattered scarecrow body that he fears and hates. Perhaps she could stroke his hand or his knee? But she has no strength, she'd topple sideways. It's not hour by hour she's going now, she thinks: it's minim by minim.

And she *must* have strength, to help Kip, to greet Pace; and there are instructions to give.

"Bram . . . Bram . . ." she whispers hoarsely.

By chance Bram has leaned forward between them, thinking Kip wanted to be heard. His ear is near her cheek; to turn those few centimeters takes all her power.

"Bram—Bram . . . listen!" she mumbles hoarsely. "Oh, please!"

Ah, he hears! "Yes, Cor?"

"Stim-shot. Now. Quick. You . . . have?"

He's dismayed. "Yes, but Cory dear, remember! *Try* to remember what I warned you of—the risk—"

She closes her eyes, tries perilously to shake her head no. *"Stim-shot now . . . urgen' . . . Order, Bram."* She gets that out clearly. "After . . . no matter."

He gives her a deep look from those unearthly azure eyes.

"Very . . . well."

To her impatience his hands in the medkit seem so slow. Slow enough that she remembers something. After he plunges the needle in her unfeeling triceps she says: "Bram . . . try to hear me."

"I'm listening, Cor."

"Bram—'nother order. . . . Do not . . . no matter what . . . you'n Linnix . . . must not . . ."

"Must not what?"

Oh, lords, didn't she say it? "Not turn back," she gasps. "If I . . . trouble . . . not turn back, not look. . . . She . . . mustn't see." Her voice is suddenly clear—but an instant later she feels a front tooth give and puts up a hand. Please, fate, for Kip's sake, don't let me go toothless.

"You, Linnie, do not . . . turn back. . . ." she says muffledly. "Order. . . . No matter what. . . . Repeat please . . . Bram dear."

He sighs. "Yes. You order Linnix and me not to turn back—from boarding I presume."

Cory nods. "N-not . . . come back."

"Or if we are boarded, we must not come back out . . . all this regardless of—of whatever may be happening behind us, with you— Oh, Cory, my dear—my dear, do you know? Do you?" he asks incoherently, meaning simply, love.

He captures her shaking, gnarled old hands and kisses them tenderly, pushing heedless against Kip, who is absorbed in the pinnace landing. Neither Baram nor Cory notices when the uproar from the pinnace dies. As it grounds a brief flare of burning brush crackles out around it, then subsides.

Baram sinks back to his seat and meets Linnie's understanding smile. After a pause she says, "That man-lift ride must have been exciting. I've always wanted to try."

"I'm glad you didn't see some of the gyrations I cut. Look, the ramp is down. I've never met this Norbert, but I bless his name." He squeezes her hand. Never to be separated again, if he can help it.

Cory, waiting for the stim-shot to take effect, peers toward the pinnace. A slender man's figure appears on the ramp. Kip is waving joyfully, starting the jitney.

"Green we run up there now?" he remembers to ask Dayan.

"Go." The new set of tires from *Rimshot* are flameproof.

But the short run to the ramp jolts Cory almost to blackout. Her strong legs that used to brace her are no longer there. Just as she crumples down she feels steady hands slide beneath her armpits, pulling her back to safety. That nice red-haired girl behind her, Linnix. Cory manages to pat her hand.

But how fast everyone moves! Baram and Linnix are already out and going up the ramp; she has a confused memory of good-byes. And here's

Pace at the car, in a barrage of rapid-fire talk with Kip. Has she greeted him? "Hello . . . Pace dear," she says painfully—and just then her heart changes rhythm and the stim-shot comes to her aid. Her voice clears and strengthens. "You came all that way in a freight pod? Lords!"

"It wasn't too bad." He's trying not to look at her—and the odd thing is, how old he's grown himself!

She retrieves her shawl from where it fell, covers herself. "It's pretty bad, Pace, isn't it? And it's going to get worse before the end. The one thing is, it's natural. It's what you'd see at the end of our lives. Just think of it as a kind of time-warp, a preview. . . . Now Pace dear, I have to tell you something in confidence . . . but I can't hobble far—" She casts a pleading look around.

"I'll get the bags," says Kip, sliding out.

Dayan says abruptly, "We've got to get Vovoka's coffin aboard," and heads for the pinnace, followed by the boys.

Pace climbs into Kip's vacated seat.

Cory thinks a minim. "Pace, were you told that an alien did this to me?"

"Yes, but why, Cory, why?"

"Because he was the last Vlyracochan—the last member of the race of the Murdered Star—and his mission was to kill the last surviving crewman from *Deneb,* the ship that did it. . . . Pace, I was that person . . . I was young, and war-crazy. When the regular gunners refused to do it, I was the criminal fool who fired the fatal missile at Vlyracocha. . . . They sent me to Rehab for memory erasure, but it came back as soon as Vovoka, the Vlyracochan, spoke."

"Oh, dear lords of space, Cory, to take revenge on a child—"

"Pace, it wasn't quite like that, but we can't waste time. I've had a stim-shot specially to tell you something. Please listen, Pace."

"Right."

"Before he died . . . the alien told me something that changed the whole picture. He said that in their antiquity, when they already had a high culture, an invisible entity, a space-borne *something,* quite likely from outside the Galaxy, somehow impinged on Vlyracocha. There was no doubt of its presence; its effect took the form of a great and growing beauty in all things; in Vovoka's words, 'Beauty such as no one had ever seen or imagined . . . even the trees, weeds, rocks . . . like those here.'

"And after generations of exposure to this beauty, the people of Vlyracocha began to weaken and die. They had no doubt as to the cause."

For an instant she gasps for air, her hand on her withered breast.

"Cory dear, you shouldn't be exhausting yourself like this," Pace says. "Rest, lie back a minim."

"I'm aging—correction, I'm dying—every minim, Pace. Don't you understand? No rests. It's now or never. Please, listen, there's a point.

"The form of the disease seems to have been a terrible loss of the ability to hope, a boundless despair—coupled with what Vovoka called 'an unquenchable, unnameable desire,' a yearning, I think. As if the entity had fed on the souls of the beholders. And then . . . he said . . . 'When it had fed full, it compelled us to build'—the thing *Deneb* destroyed. It was a gigantic work of art, with all the culture and history of their race, and powered so that it might, I quote, 'go forth through the Galaxy, feeding and reproducing.' It housed the entity, you see. Vovoka seemed both to reverence it and to hate it bitterly. . . .

"At the end he told me I had done no wrong in blowing it to atoms. . . . And he addressed it, saying, 'Now you will be again what you were—a nothing on the winds of space, whence we drew you to our doom.' His tone, his words are graven on my mind."

Pace is silent an instant, shaking his head. "An evil marvel beyond easy grasp. . . . I've heard of nothing like it in the Galaxy. . . . Was that what you wished to tell me, Cory?"

"The—the prelude only. . . ." She's tiring. "Understand, Pace, it *was* blown to atoms. Its particles were mingled with those of the Star. If it was still alive . . . or latent, it rode in the great . . . explosion-fronts that passed us here." She breathes for a minim, speaks more strongly.

"But did they all pass? Did some remain, or adhere? Or were we judged unsuitable, if such a dispersed entity can by said to judge? I don't know.

"All I know is that the one being, the Vlyracochan who had experienced it, who knew it, said two things very pointedly. The first I've told you, that the entity gave beauty to 'trees, weeds, rocks *like those here.*' The second—He was a very silent being, but he took occasion to tell me that Damiem has '*a peculiarly flattering light,*' . . . and Kip says he added something like, '*Don't feel too secure.*'

"You know for yourself how lovely all things are here. The Dameii—if one isn't careful, one can feel an almost sickly infatuation with them, Pace. . . . Incidentally . . . do the Dameii feel it, too? Remember, find out that. . . .

"What's convincing is that no . . . no mention of the beauty of the planet or the people is found in the very old writings. . . . Of course I haven't examined them all, and they were the work of unimaginative men —soldiers, criminals, engineers. But still . . . See, that would be before the first Star-fronts came . . . before Damiem . . . began to live in the explosion's ambience."

She pants again, jerking up a hand to stop Pace's protests.

"The Star has passed now, Pace. I don't know whether something of it

. . . some traces of glamour or magic . . . still remain, or will . . . and I don't know if that's good or bad. I fear . . . fear; it's headed into the Galaxy. Will it infect other planets in . . . its path? Terrible. . . . But point is, Kip immersed himself in Damiem's Star-beauty . . . I, too. I, too. We lived in an enchanted garden, Pace . . . all aglow. So—" She is shaken by rattling coughs, she looks deathly, but somehow energy is still there.

"When the Star has all passed . . . everything may seem cold, dry. Shabby—a bleaker . . . ordinary landscape . . . perhaps . . . Even the Dameii will be . . . more like big insects. But the point"—again the dreadful coughing—"point is, *Kip* . . . may be a very sick man . . . on your hands." She takes a ragged breath, struggles to sit straighter.

"Pace, maybe psychologically a dying man. . . . *Get him off this planet.* . . . Can't order, only beg. Get him away."

Pace says slowly, "The loss of illusion, eh? But that's reality, Cor. We all—"

"Reality—" She tries to laugh, jeeringly, coughing, shakily holding up one feeble, crabbed, vein-encrusted hand that's like a little clutch of deformed twigs.

"*That's* reality, Pace. . . . Yesterday that . . . was a h-hand. . . . People . . . say, 'Be realistic.' As though reality needs encouragement. . . . Tell you, Pace . . . *reality doesn't need friends.*"

The almost-laugh catches, turns into frightening coughs.

Pace gives a bark of laughter, marvelling.

"Ah, you're Cory—you're Cor to the bit—" He stops himself.

"Bit . . . bitter end?" she gasps, or maybe she's trying to laugh. "Strange thing . . . it isn't bitter, Pace. . . . If . . . I could only—tell you—"

But it's all gone now, all really gone, forever. Her eyes hold his for a desperate minim, and then she collapses back in the seat, a shrunken, feebly choking, dying old woman. It's an instant before he realizes the coughs are rasping: "Don't call . . . Baram. . . . Order, Pace. . . . Do not . . . call Bram."

Her eyes close, her breathing is noisy.

Pace puts his ear to her chest and hears the dreadful price of that stimshot. Kip and Saul Dayan are nearby; he calls them over.

"She doesn't want Doctor Baram called," he tells them. "Get him and his girl into the ship. Saul, can you spare the time to drive us back to the station? That way Kip and I can hold her from each side."

"No problem." Dayan strides up the ramp and slams the port closed behind Baram and Linnix. "Put that last man-lift on the trailer," he calls to the crewmen who are loading them. "I'll use it coming back."

Kip and Pace are crowding in on either side of Cory now, to leave driving room for Dayan. The front seat will just hold four, and the tight fit will help. As they settle, Cory, with enormous effort, turns her head enough to see up.

She sees the flowering tree branches arching overhead, against an opalescent sky. The flowers show as lapis-blue plumes, downy lilac puffs—and between them is her last view of the crescent moon, fading into sunrise.

It's all still beautiful, as well as she can judge. But the horizon is still ringed in Star-light; the Star-front has not completely passed from Damiem.

Her movement has caused a small commotion. Such looks, such long faces! She'd asked them not to do that, before she was even sure. If only I could tell them how I feel inside, she thinks. So light and free, all duties done. . . . *And at last I know it all; my whole life is my own.* . . . All known. Like a child on a high hill, like a first plane ride—I can see it all from horizon to horizon, and think it all over. There are patterns, where I didn't know patterns were. . . .

Like overfondness. Overfond of Kip, overfond of Captain Jeager. I suspected his gunners were right, but Jeager's lonely mad heroics wrung my heart. . . . Same about Yule and Hiner: I knew I should get them off the planet, but Kip's smile—that dear smile—melted my wits. . . . And little Ochter, I couldn't see past that mask of pathos. . . . Unfit for command I was, really. . . . But it doesn't matter now. . . .

The eyes watching her are amazed at the smile that spreads the deep wrinkles of her face. Next instant her hands are up, fumbling at her mouth. Curse the teeth, she tries to say, pushing at the shrunken roots. Talking's over. . . . But that doesn't matter, either.

She's gotten everything said. . . . Baram will be all right with his girl, and she's warned Pace. Kip . . . He'll be unhappy, but Pace will get him away, and he'll wait in some new station with his wonderful looks and his sweet nature and his red neckerchief, and another woman will come.

Even that funny brave cameraman and his young ones will be all right, and the little prince. The only one who isn't is that poor marquise—but who knows what the very mad, very rich, really want?

A happy ending to the tale of the great Star, really—except for tragic little Nyil. But even she said it wasn't so bad, because she flew . . . flew to her death. I can understand that, somehow. . . .

And me . . . funny, I'd forgotten myself. I suppose they count this as tragic. Oh, if I only could tell them—all they see is this rotting body; they don't see I'm perched in it like a bird in an old tree. When the tree goes I'll only float away. Maybe, when it crumbles, could I just fly away, free? Flying to death, like Nyil?

No. That's nonsense.

I must have made more sounds; they're all saying things. ". . . her own bed."

Do as you wish, my dears.

Starting the car, now. Starting—oh, good lords, the jolting! Hands everywhere—they're trying to hold me together, with their fine young strength. No use, I fear. But it's not so bad . . . not too bad. . . . Oh, pain. Not much . . . only I can't breathe . . . *pain* . . . can't—GODS, GIVE ME AIR—

What happened? What're they doing? Car's stopped. Pace—I think it's Pace—is squeezing, pounding on me.

Oh, please, it hurts—

"I think we have a problem." She hears that. No, dears. *You* have a problem. I don't. Oh, if I could only tell them. . . .

Problem is, I'm alive. Technically, I guess.

But they don't dare start the car.

And life goes on. . . . How strenuous the living are. I think it's Saul Dayan, driving . . . and the ship waits.

But such a beautiful sunrise—so comfortable, so radiant and limitless! I wish they had time to enjoy. . . . When you're dying you have time. And you don't need help to die. No arrangements. You can just do it, all alone. Right the first time. . . .

Won't be long—but I was given back my life just right, just in time. In time to be whole. . . . I wonder if that Rehab's really so good? I lived all my life *muffled*. Until now. . . . I guess something has to be done . . . for people where unbearably bad things happened. But . . . it's amputation. Until now I was an amputee.

They're still debating their "problem." Hello! One of my little friends.

Perched on the windscreen beside some leaves is a furry, bird-sized, brightly colored arachnoid, a sort of flying spider. They're usually nocturnal. Its color is peach and green, with bright vermilion knee joints, and it has a comically surprised expression in its large, stalked eyes. Cory's vision is dimming, but she can just make out that one of its eyes is bent toward her. . . . She wishes now she'd ignored the regs and tried to tame one . . . but that was never her style.

"Thank you, Saul," she whispers to herself. His delay has gained her this last sight.

But delays must come to an end; she knows that.

She feels a new jostling. What? Oh, it's Pace, putting his ear to her heart again. She tries to hold her breath so he can hear, is suddenly conscious of the hoarse racket she's been making. Wheeze-in, wheeze-out; wheeze-in, wheeze-crackle-out; wheeze—

Pace looks closely into her face; she tries to look back, hoping he will see some trace of a spark deep in the ruined eyes. Maybe he does. He pulls back to let Kip come closer. But Kip doesn't know what to do, finally brushes his lips against her wattled cheek.

You didn't have to do that, darling, she wants to say, but can only cough feebly . . . in, out; in, out; in, out . . .

"If you shake her up, that heart will stop," Pace says. Her ears still work, after a fashion.

She must speak, must. No matter about teeth now. Must. Mouth, *move*. . . .

But not enough breath. Must try again.

Try. Try, for the gods' sake. . . . Tremendous effort—

"She's trying to say something," Pace says. "Yes, Cor, dear. What?"

Again the groaning whisper is achieved; she's panting in total exhaustion.

Kip utters a wholly incomprehensible sound. He understood, she thinks, but he can't make himself say it.

Studying her face, Pace says carefully, "I thought it . . . sounded like 'Green, go.' "

Yes, the spark in the old eyes tries to say.

Kip chokes. He's not overly imaginative, but the memory-picture of a brown-haired girl putting a bunch of bright yellow flowers on their breakfast table suddenly devastates him.

There's a silence. Air rasping laboriously through an aged throat; out . . . in . . . out . . . in . . . out . . . in . . . out . . . in . . .

Green, go?

Dayan breaks the silence. "Right."

Carefully, he starts the motor, engages the drive. The car moves off, not smoothly despite his care, on the rock-strewn road under Damiem's empty sky.

APPENDIX:

Cast of Characters and Glossary of Terms, Titles, Places, and Things

Damiem—The planet.
Dameii—The people of Damiem, plural.
Damei—One of the people; or adjective, as in "Damei music."

1. The three Human residents of Damiem, all co-Guardians of the Dameii:

Corrisón Estreèl-Korso (Cory or Cor): Chief Federation Administrator of Damiem and mate of Kip.
Kipruget Korso-Estreèl (Kip): Deputy Administrator of Damiem and Liaison to the Dameii; mate of Cory. (Mated couples take each other's surnames as hyphenated last names for the duration of the Mateship. This facilitates computerized records. Although Kip and Cory are overdue to redeclare, they keep the forms as evidence of intent.)
Balthasar Baramji ap Bye (Baram or Bram): Xenological MD, doctor to the Dameii. Bye is Baramji's vast feudal estate on Broken Moon; "ap" is a hereditary landowning title. At home he is the ap of Bye, but abroad he is simply a senior doctor with a xenological specialty.

2. The tourists, Human and otherwise, listed in order of appearance from the ship:

Zannez (Beorne—last name never used; Zannie): Subdirector and cameraman for four of the 35 stars of the popular interstellar soft-porn grid-show, *The Absolutely Perfect Commune.*

Stareem Fada (Star): Her stage name. One of the four *APC* actors here.

Hannibal Ek (Hanny or Hanno): His real name. Another of the four actors.

Snake Smith (occasionally Snako): His permanent but not real name. The third of the four actors, and a professional acrobat.

Bridey McBannion (Bee): Her real name—she refuses to use the stage name, *Eleganza*. The fourth of the four actors. A knife-thrower.

Prince-Prince Pao (Pao, Prince, or Superboy): The heir to the royal throne of the planet Pavo. His actual first name is "Prince."

Ser Xe Vovoka (Vovoka, but not to his face; "Ser" is an honorary title): A light-sculptor.

Doctor Aristrides Ochter (Ari, occasionally): A retired professor of neocybernetics-E.

Lady Marquise Pardalianches (Pardie or Lady P.): Of the nobility of Rainbow's End.

Lady Marquise Paralomena ('Lomena or Loma): Lady P.'s twin sister, paralyzed.

Mordecai Yule (Mordy): A student of water-worlds, bound for the next planet, Grunions Rising, and at Damiem by error.

Doctor Nathaniel Hiner (Nat): An Aquaman, also bound for Grunions Rising and wakened at Damiem by error; a representative of the Aquapeople's Association doing a survey of water-worlds to update the old *Aquatica Galactica*. Aquapeople are the successful products of a long-ago genetic effort to achieve a true-breeding gilled human, able to live underwater or in air.

Linnix (Linnie—no other name): Logistics Officer tending to Humans on the Moom ship.

3. Other Humans (Humans are but one of many races in—and out of—the Federation, like Dameii or Moom; hence Human is a proper noun and is always capitalized):

Captain Saul Dayan (Scooter): Captain of the battle cruiser *Rimshot*.

Doctor Siri Lipsius (Siri): Battle surgeon of *Rimshot*.

Valkyr: Technician First Class of *Rimshot*.

Jordan Tally, Bing, Rango, Maur, Rip Jorge: Patrolmen from *Rimshot*.

Ralli: Captain Dayan's command car driver.

Poma (never seen): Chief of Communications at nearby FedBase.

Captain Race (never seen): Captain/owner of a charter ship, *Comet II*.

Pace Norbert (Pace): Former Guardian of the Dameii prior to the Korsos. Now an MD.

Kenter, Janny, Pete, Saro (mentioned only): Wartime colleagues of Kip.

Captain Tom Jeager (mentioned only): Mad wartime commander of battleship *Deneb*.

4. Dameii:

Quiyst: A Damei elder, spokesman for Near Village.

Wyrra: ⎱ (m) The Damei couple who live adjacent to the station.
Juiyn: ⎰ (f)

Nyil: Their young female child.

Feanya: Second Damei elder, friend of Quiyst.

Zhymel: Damei elder from Near Village, part of group inspecting Humans.

Black Golya: Dynamic-type Damei from Far Village.

Yrion Red: Ditto.

5. The Moom (barely glimpsed and heard): A large, pachydermatous, slow-living, virtually immortal race of aliens who run most Federation interstellar shipping.

6. The Swain (mentioned only): Another race of ship-faring aliens.

7. Ships:

The Moom ship (no name given): A more-or-less regular Federation passenger and freight ship on the Rim-and-back run.

Rimshot: A Federation space Patrol warship assigned to guard Damiem.

pinnace (no name): A small craft berthed in *Rimshot,* for landing capability. *(Rimshot* cannot land.)

shuttle (no name): A small landing craft berthed in the Moom ship, which likewise has no landing capability.

Comet II: A passenger/freight charter ship precariously owned and operated by Captain Race.

Golan: A former official ship, mentioned only.

8. Places:

The Rim: That part of the rim of the Milky Way Galaxy that terminates one arc of the perimeter of Federation space.

FedBase: Short term for Federation Base, the nearest to Damiem being about 100 light-minim away.

Grunions Rising: The nearest planet to Damiem. It lies in the direction of the Rim and is the end of the Rim shipline. A water-world.

Rainbow's End: A wealthy planet, home of the Marquises.

Vlyracocha: The name of the Murdered Star. The planet, along with its sun and an artificial satellite, was destroyed at the end of the Last War, and formed the nova-front now passing Damiem.

Gridworld: The interstellar Hollywood planet, originator of all shows for transmission over the Grid, a *c*-skip (FTL) communications network linking star systems and other Human and alien habitations. Technically under
Federation law, but in dubious compliance, internally.

Broken Moon: A romantic, backward, feudal world; Doctor Baram's birthplace.

Beneborn: A biologically high-tech world, mad about eugenics, where Linnix was born.

Pavo: A small but important world, a royal principality, where Prince Pao will rule.

Alwyn and *Jo's Paradise:* Two planetary neighbors of Pavo, dependent on it as the financial, economic, diplomatic center (mentioned only).

Rehab: A quasimedical center for compassionate and other rehabilitation of Humans and others deeply traumatized as victims—sometimes perpetrators—of violence and crime. Mem/E is the Memory-Erasure section.

9. Glossary of some Damei and other unfamiliar terms:

Yrrei: Damiem's sun, a GO-type star.

V'yrre: A wind that blows WNW during the Damiem season of the Star events.

Avray: A large (50 cm diameter) plum-colored arachnoid or tarantuloid animal of Damiem. Like all Damei fauna, including the Dameii, it has an extra pair of limbs as compared with its Terran homolog, making ten in all. Though harmless, shy, and rare, it is hated and feared by the Dameii as an ill omen.

Tochari, Daguerre: Two Last War hand weapons, nonballistic.

c-skip: Faster-than-light-speed *(c)* transmission, by inducing temporary perturbations in reciprocal gravity-field configurations. Requires super-cooling of transmitting nuclei.

Myr, Myrrin: Myr serves for Mr., Mrs., Ms., or Miss and is often prefixed affectionately or jokingly to a person's first name or nickname. Myrrin is the plural, corresponding to "Ladies and Gentlemen."

"gods," "lords,": As ejaculations, these are always in the plural and lowercase; this convention, now automatic, was a part of the treaty which, it is hoped, ended forever all religious factional strife. Only when a god is named, which is only done jocularly, using a mythical entity, is the exclamation singular. All this has of course no effect on private personal prayer.

"The All": The only singular entity that may be secularly referred to, all religions having given their assent to it.

Saniches, Morpleases (and native-tongue edibles): Food items.

Algotoxin: Is, so far, by the mercy of Fate, a fiction.

Zeranaveth: A carbonaceous gemstone similar to colored diamonds, but more beautiful. Found only on a few planets such as Rainbow's End and the Hallelujah system.

THE STAR PASSES

DAMIEM

moon

SUN

Nova front
expanding and dissipating

to center of Galaxy